# RONAN

## ZIVA PAYVAN BOOK 3

## EJ FISCH

Transcendence
Publishing

RONAN

First edition: September 2015

If you would like to use material from the book, prior written permission must be obtained by contacting the publisher at transcendence.publishing@gmail.com.

The Transcendence Publishing name, imprint, and logo are trademarks of Transcendence Publishing.

ISBN-13: 978-0692443248
ISBN-10: 069244324x

# THE
# ZIVA PAYVAN
## SERIES

*A full dramatis personae and glossary of series terms*

*can be found at*

**www.ejfisch.com/glossary**

# RONAN

# · 1 ·
# WAREHOUSE DISTRICT
## NIIO SPACEPORT

T he sudden cloud of smoke was certainly unexpected. The only reasonable reaction was to shield her face and duck away. It was already pitch dark inside the warehouse, but the billowing black cloud rendered her night optics completely useless. She tore the headgear off and stumbled back the way she had come, coughing and sputtering. The thought occurred to her that retreating was the *last* thing she should have done just as rough hands seized her by the arms and dragged her to the floor.

If this was a trap—and that seemed to be the case—she'd fallen directly into it. Her first instinct was to yell, to shout out her location. She only got about half a sentence off before a gloved hand clamped down over her mouth and her earpiece was ripped away. As far as she could tell, there were three assailants: one restraining her legs, one pinning her shoulders down and covering her mouth, and a third holding her left arm and fiddling with her sleeve.

She wasn't sure where her rifle was—it had been torn from her hands just before she'd hit the floor. She continued to make as much noise as possible with the hand over her mouth and even went so far as to bite down on the fingers. Before her teeth broke skin, however, she felt a powerful pinch followed by a stinging sensation just below her left elbow. The last thing she remembered was hearing a hushed voice ordering someone to carry her away.

Then the darkness swallowed her whole.

# · 2 ·

# REHABILITATION CENTER
## HAPHEZIAN GRAND ARMY BASE, NA

rom the surface of Na, the world of Haphez—though a mere twenty thousand kilometers distant—was hardly more than a gray arc stretching across the moon's pale-yellow sky. It looked almost white today thanks to the sunlight beating down on the silver buildings that made up Na's sprawling military base. The light bounced off the flat surfaces and created a blinding glow that reached all the way to the moon's horizon. Ships of all shapes and sizes appeared out of the haze, transporting supplies and soldiers to and from the mother planet. One vessel in particular, a brand-new shuttle bearing the Royal Officer's insignia, touched down in a grassy training area near the center of the compound.

A pane of thick glass reinforced with electrified wire separated Ziva Payvan from the view outside. Being in this room always made her feel like a prisoner, and in a sense, she was exactly that. 'In custody' was the technical term, though she'd had free rein of the entire rehab facility nearly every day for the duration of her stay. Today, however, was different. Going anywhere or doing anything was out of the question, lest she get into trouble somehow. She couldn't fathom what could possibly go wrong—all the more reason to stay put and not find out. She wasn't known for being so overly cautious. It made her entirely uncomfortable, in fact. But today, unless she actually *wanted* to be a prisoner, each and every rule had to be followed. She needed to have a clean slate.

She drummed her fingers against the glass, watching as several well-dressed figures emerged from the shuttle and entered the nearest building. They were there for her, of course, and she was ready for them. She'd even opted out of breakfast in favor of remaining in her room to prepare, both mentally and physically. She'd done her best to make herself as presentable as possible, despite the fact that the rehab center's simple white inpatient garments weren't much to look at. Not a single strand of her black and red-streaked hair was out of place. It had been a long time since she'd felt the need to make so much fuss about her appearance.

Ziva sighed. "It's time," she said, partially to herself and partially to whoever had just come up to stand in the doorway behind her.

It was Doctor Anson Baez, just as she'd expected. He maintained a respectful distance, looking sharp in his formal military uniform that almost seemed incomplete without the white lab coat he constantly wore over it. He was flanked by two armed soldiers, one of whom held a pair of handcuffs. *That* she hadn't expected.

"You've got to be kidding me," she said, warily eyeing the cuffs.

"It's just a formality," Baez replied as the MP approached and gently fitted the bracelets over her wrists. It was the same thing he'd told her when she'd awakened in the HSP med center chained to her bed. "This will all be over soon enough. I don't think it will hurt any of us to follow protocol for a couple more hours. We've come this far— wouldn't want to drop the ball now, would we?"

Ziva stole another look out the window. Her homeworld had all but disappeared in the bright haze. "No, we wouldn't," she muttered.

Baez placed a hand on her shoulder. "Hang in there just a little longer. Has anyone explained to you how this is going to work?"

She shook her head.

"This will be a little different than your average post-grace-period hearing. It'll be more of a public interrogation than anything. If everything runs smoothly and you go with the flow, there's no reason why you shouldn't be walking out of here this afternoon. They'll question you about what took place on Chaiavis just to make sure your story lines up with the evidence, then that evidence will be presented to the public and the magistrates will announce their decision. I'll be there to represent you."

She lifted an eyebrow. "So you're my surgeon, my rehab specialist, *and* my lawyer?"

Baez laughed. "I'm not quite that talented," he said. "A public defender has been assigned to you just to keep the magistrates on track. I'm prepared to give my professional testimony regarding your injuries and recovery just in case you need a boost."

"You think I'll need one?" Everyone at the Na Facility had been optimistic about her hearing since she'd still been bedridden. But regardless of their encouraging words, Ziva was dreading the idea of going before the magistrates. She'd killed Nejdra Venn, a fellow HSP agent—a *superior*—in cold blood. It hadn't been self-defense, and it hadn't been a sanctioned hit. It had been murder for the sake of toying with someone, something she had not done in a long time. Venn had of course been guilty, but there was no concrete evidence that actually *proved* she'd been involved in the planned genocide of the residents of Argall. At least Ziva was no longer being held responsible for assassinating the former Royal Officer, Ikaro Tachi. Even so, the false evidence brought up against her on that front had been convincing, and for a while, everyone had believed wholeheartedly that she had committed the murder. All the more reason to dread going before judges sent by the current Royal Officer.

Baez gave her the impression he could sense her apprehension. "I think everything will be just fine."

That didn't answer her question. She wondered if he'd already been made privy to the magistrates' verdict. Because of the nature of her alleged crimes, she had been denied most of the privileges the facility's patients usually received. She may have been free to move about the compound, but for ten weeks, all information about the investigation had been withheld from her—in case she really was guilty, of course—and she hadn't been allowed to contact anyone back home on Haphez. It was quite possible that everyone knew her fate but her. The idea brought her minimal comfort.

She sighed. "Let's get this over with, then."

The two MPs positioned themselves on either side of her, sending her apologetic glances as they took hold of her arms. They led her out the door, keeping her about half a pace in front of them. Baez took the lead.

If everything went according to plan, this was one of the last times she would walk this hallway. All the rooms in this corridor belonged to patients who, like her, had been granted full autonomy in their final days of recovery. This was the third room she'd been in since being admitted to the rehab facility, having been moved to a different wing for each stage of treatment. She was currently the only HSP agent there, but she'd gone through the ten-week session with a few Grand Army soldiers who'd been injured in an explosion around the same time she'd been shot. They stood in the doorways of their own rooms now, watching in respectful silence as she moved down the hallway.

The rehab center was currently at less than half capacity. Admission was a rare enough privilege that there were only fifty rooms available in the first place. The doctor-to-patient ratio certainly made for an efficient recovery process, though Ziva had often wished she could be more anonymous. With a job that usually required her to be invisible, it was hard to get used to everyone knowing who she was. For eight of the ten weeks she'd been there, she'd had a supervisor hovering over her, checking her vitals constantly, monitoring her workout sessions. It hadn't been so bad at first, back when it hurt to move and she'd needed caura treatments every day. But the stronger she got, the more irritating it had been to always have someone breathing down her neck. It was good that it had been Baez the majority of the time. She liked him well enough, and he'd been more willing to let her bend the rules a bit.

The MPs marched her out the door of the rehab center and across the grass to the building where the shuttle had touched down. Armed guards from the Royal Offices eyed her warily from the boarding ramp as she passed the ship, but there was hardly time to worry about them as she arrived at her destination. The massive doors of the GA's court slid open before she could even draw a breath. This was it; she held her head high and straightened her shoulders as best she could, pushing her feelings to the back of her mind. She wasn't quite sure *what* she felt, but one thing was for sure—right now, it needed to be nothing.

The courtroom was tiny compared to the big public courts on Haphez, but the layout was exactly the same. A center aisle divided the room into two halves, one for the defense and one for the prosecution. It appeared all the people seated in the observation area were base officials or reps from the Royal House. At the front of the room, six desks were set up on risers, two on each of the three levels. Anyone sitting in the top row would have to be careful not to hit their head on the ceiling.

The escort guided Ziva to the defendant's area on the left. A long platform bordered by a metal railing stretched the length of the room; she climbed a couple of steps and walked the remaining distance on her own, elevated nearly a meter above the two MPs as they moved along on either side. She didn't dare look around—it would only showcase her apprehension. She tried to search the little crowd with her peripherals, looking for signs of her team or any other familiar faces. Maybe the communication rule still applied and they hadn't been allowed to come, though it seemed unlikely.

She took her place at the front of the platform, feeling small with those risers looming in front of her, and watched as Baez slid into a seat at a table just below her. He leaned over and said something inaudible to the man beside him, presumably her public defender. The man's thin white hair was streaked with blue, and deep creases etched his face. He sat there reading over a data pad without even acknowledging her. She already didn't like him.

A door hissed open somewhere behind the risers and desks, and a man's voice rang out: "All rise!"

There was a dull shuffling throughout the room as everyone got to their feet. Ziva watched as the six magistrates emerged from their private chambers and made their way around to the front. Nobody made a sound while they slowly filed into their seats. Unsure where to look, she resorted to meeting each of their gazes individually as they passed, challenging them a bit. She sighed and folded her hands in front of her. *Don't feel.*

Everyone remained completely silent until the magistrates were seated. The Grand Magistrate, denoted by his seat in the front row and the yellow sash over his shoulder, lifted his hands and motioned for all the onlookers to take their seats as well. Elevated above everyone else, Ziva stuck out like a sore thumb as she remained standing.

The Grand Magistrate, the only one of the six who would speak during the hearing, cleared his throat. "I am calling the case of the People versus Ziva Payvan. Is the defense ready?"

Such formal proceedings seemed strange considering there was no official prosecution. The fact that there wasn't one confirmed that her fate had already been decided. After all, they'd had over two months to examine the evidence. Everyone already knew what happened on Chaiavis—they just needed multiple witnesses to hear her testimony. But she wasn't entirely sure what this 'evidence' they'd found consisted of, and not knowing whether her word would back it up made her nervous. "*Go with the flow*," Baez had said. What exactly did that mean?

"Ready, Your Honors," the public defender replied.

"And is your client ready?"

"Ready," Ziva said before the man could respond.

"Lieutenant Payvan, after an examination of the evidence brought forward, this court holds you responsible for the unjustified murder of a fellow HSP agent, Captain Nejdra Venn. How do you plead?"

The wheels spun in her head for a moment. She thought she could sense Baez looking back at her, but she didn't dare break eye contact with the magistrate. "Guilty, Your Honor. I killed Captain Venn."

"The forensic examination of the projectile that killed her was inconclusive, but we do know the bullet was partially composed of bariine. A rifle was recovered from the ship aboard which you returned to Haphez after the shooting. What can you tell me about this weapon?"

On cue, a soldier appeared pushing a small platform hovering on repulsors. On it sat a battered projectile rifle, which Ziva recognized immediately.

"This is the gun I used to kill Venn," she said, drawing murmurs from the observers behind her.

The judge shook his head and examined the rifle. "This weapon is not of Haphezian origin."

"No, sir," she replied. "All of my weapons were confiscated by the agency when I was taken into custody. This is a Korberon rifle I purchased and modified while on Chaiavis."

"Further investigation revealed you took the shot from nearly a kilometer away. You're saying you were able to make a successful headshot from that distance with an antique rifle?"

She fought away a smirk. "I'm good at what I do."

The magistrate eyed her thoughtfully from behind the hologram projected on the visor he wore. "Lieutenant, you and your team specialize in, shall we say...*permanently neutralizing* threats. Is that correct?"

"Correct."

"Records would indicate that you are indeed very good at what you do. Would you say the agency considers your ability to kill your greatest asset?"

Ziva tilted her head, wondering why her defender hadn't spoken up. "I'm not sure how that's relevant to the—"

"Yes or no, please."

She answered without hesitation: "Yes."

Once again, a dull buzz rose up throughout the room. The people didn't seem to be against her, but neither were they on her side. If anything, their attention was focused on the Grand Magistrate, waiting to see how he'd react to her words.

The man watched her silently for several seconds. "Would you please explain to the court your reason for killing Captain Venn?"

"I won't call it self-defense because I was not in immediate danger," she replied with a sigh. "Diago Dasaro framed me for Ikaro Tachi's assassination and employed Captains Venn and Hoxie to assist him."

"Yes," the judge said. "Findings submitted by Royal Guard Supervisory Special Agent Luko Zona reinforce that claim." A holographic screen came alive across the room, displaying the very information Ziva had once read on Kade Shevin's computer—information that proved Dasaro was behind the mass murder of the citizens of Argall.

"Dasaro framed me for Tachi's assassination in order to shift the attention away from himself," Ziva said, gesturing toward the hologram. "When the captains lost track of me, the three of them went to

Chaiavis to search for more leads. They killed a Haphezian native, Bosco Jagger."

To her surprise and relief, Bosco's information appeared on the screen. "Jagger was indeed murdered in his own shop on Chaiavis," the magistrate confirmed. "Ballistic fingerprinting verified that the projectiles which killed him came from Dasaro's weapon, the same weapon he shot you with, Lieutenant."

In that instant, Ziva found herself lying on the landing pad in Argall, bleeding out as Dasaro loomed over her. Her bound hands curled into fists as fire surged through her nerves, and for a moment, she had to fight to remain calm.

"When I found out Dasaro was on Chaiavis, I wanted to confront him," she continued, struggling for a moment to remember where she had left off. "But I knew he would kill me the first chance he got, so I opted to maintain my distance. When I read the notes Zona had compiled, it was clear Dasaro had already tried to eliminate me once in the past, and I was ready to kill him outright. But when the time came, I realized there was still information I could learn from him, and killing him would have compromised that." That wasn't entirely accurate, but she could think of no other way to justify her actions. "Instead, I turned my sights on Captain Venn. It was a split-second decision."

"You're saying you killed Venn in cold blood." It was a statement rather than a question.

"I sent Dasaro a message," Ziva replied firmly, "one he received loud and clear. I showed him who was in control, and he panicked and led us to back Argall." That was a flat-out lie. They would have returned home to investigate Argall regardless of Dasaro's actions. She stood quietly for a moment, wondering if they would catch the deviation. "But yes, you could say I killed Nejdra in cold blood."

Once more, a soft murmuring rippled through the crowd. The Grand Magistrate stared her down through his visor; she met his gaze, unfazed. As far as anyone knew, her story matched up perfectly with the evidence on display. But these questions were random, the interrogation process unstructured. She was answering as best she could, but her answers didn't seem to be leading up to anything definitive. They were putting on a show, making her squirm because they could. *Don't feel*, she reminded herself again. *Don't show them anything.*

She saw the two magistrates in the top row whispering to one another and sent them a hot glare. She could feel every set of eyes in the room boring into her back and wondered why nobody spoke. Everything she'd just said was old news to the magistrates and Royal House, so no deliberation should be necessary. She hoped a couple of snarky responses hadn't somehow affected their decision.

"Thank you, Lieutenant," the Grand Magistrate finally said. "That will be all."

A tingle of panic coursed over her skin and her eyes widened. *That's it?*

"Bring in the witness, please."

*Witness?* Ziva stood there, frozen, attempting to contemplate all possible definitions for the word. Someone who could reinforce Dasaro's guilt? Someone who had seen her shoot Nejdra? Or worse, someone who had seen Dasaro shoot her in Argall and had subsequently witnessed her use her Nostia to kill him? The panic became more than a tingle.

The courtroom's massive doors slid open once again. She whirled, wincing against the light streaming in from outside. Three silhouettes appeared and entered the building, two MPs from the base escorting a prisoner in the same manner as she'd been escorted. They made it several strides into the room before she could see the person's face clearly.

Even then, it still took her a split second to recognize the man. Judging by his unkempt hair and scraggly beard, Kyron Hoxie had already been incarcerated for some time. Last she knew, he'd been there on Chaiavis with Nejdra and Dasaro, but he hadn't been in Argall to her knowledge. Had he defected from Dasaro's team and been captured by HSP later? It was unlikely—the amount of time that elapsed between Chaiavis and Argall would have been more than enough for him to disappear. She watched him walk up the center aisle of the room, meeting his gaze from behind furrowed eyebrows. The look in his eyes and the way he held his shoulders spoke volumes. He'd turned himself in.

Part of her was relieved to see him alive; when he'd disappeared after Nejdra's death, some had blamed her. On the other hand, he could very well be testifying *against* her. Perhaps this was all part of a scheme Dasaro had concocted to take her down even in the event that he was killed. She certainly wouldn't put it past him. She clenched her hands so tight her knuckles turned white. *Breathe. Focus. What's the matter with you?*

*"I think everything will be just fine."* Ziva shifted her attention away from Hoxie and down to Baez just in time to see him wink at her. This is what he'd meant when he said everything would be okay? Why couldn't he have just told her the former captain would be testifying? Why put her through this?

She couldn't remember the last time she'd taken anyone to court. Her jobs more often resulted in death than arrest, even when the objective wasn't necessarily to kill. But after thinking for a moment, she realized why the situation was playing out like it was. Depending on the offense, charged criminals were no longer allowed to know who the witnesses in their trials were—or even if there *were* witnesses—in order to prevent them from collaborating or changing their stories. It was a relatively new law, implemented about halfway through her career at HSP. It was effective too, considering she'd had no idea Hoxie would be there.

All the noise in the room became a dull, mangled buzz in Ziva's ears as she watched the guards position Hoxie on the small platform directly in front of the magistrates. She felt her skin crawl for reasons she couldn't explain. Part of it was confusion as to why he was there, and part of it was the idea that he'd had a hand in everything that had happened to her, good or bad.

"What I have to say is very simple," Hoxie said after the Grand Magistrate had asked him a few basic questions. He pivoted on the platform to face Ziva directly, and she was glad. It was clear that Baez and the judges already knew his story, so there was no point in pretending they didn't. Besides, she felt like she deserved a nice, long explanation.

"Ziva Payvan is innocent," he said. "It was Nejdra Venn who broke into the palace and killed Ikaro Tachi that night at the gala. I was responsible for recreating Lieutenant Payvan's fingerprints and DNA signature, and Captain Venn planted the items in Tachi's room after murdering him. The purpose of the frame-up was to shift the attention away from Captain Dasaro and his plan to harvest all the niobi crystals in Argall. The idea was that authorities would be too busy chasing her to worry about what he was doing."

Short of Nejdra herself killing Tachi, this was all information Ziva had deduced before they'd even gone to Argall. Baez had told her that her involvement in the assassination had already been waived anyway. She waited for Hoxie to continue, hoping he'd give her some information she actually wanted—and *needed*—to hear.

He droned on a while longer, explaining how he had been chosen to participate in Dasaro's scheme due to his connection to Sergeant Loric during his time in the military. He and Venn had both been promised a share of the crystals harvested from Argall as payment, but he had opted out when Dasaro gave the order to murder all the mining town's residents. He'd dropped off the grid for several days before returning to Haphez and surrendering himself to HSP.

*Get on with it*, Ziva thought, refusing to break eye contact with him. *Get me out of here.*

Finally, Hoxie turned back to the magistrates. "Your Honors, under the capital punishment laws put into place by the Haphezian crown, Captains Dasaro and Venn would have been put to death as punishment for their crimes. Lieutenant Payvan was responsible for killing both of them, although it was deemed self-defense in Dasaro's case." He shot a reassuring glance over his shoulder. "Despite the circumstances surrounding Venn's death, would it not be appropriate to assume that she would have been executed by a Cleaner anyway and that her murder was, in that respect, acceptable?"

The room was dead silent for several long seconds as everyone mulled the idea over. The Grand Magistrate stared straight ahead, reading the holographic text scrolling across his visor. Just when the silence had become nearly unbearable, he cleared his throat.

"You've got an excellent point, Captain, one that was taken into consideration as we deliberated a verdict."

Ziva tensed. At least they were acknowledging the fact that her fate had been predetermined—these games were just wasting everyone's time. But despite the way Hoxie had just tilted the odds in her favor, she couldn't bring herself to feel relieved just yet.

"Lieutenant Payvan, after examining the evidence and taking the witness's statements into account, this court has elected to drop the charges against you. But make no mistake—this ruling does not by *any* means condone your actions. You may be the executioner, but leave the judge and jury parts up to us. Understand?"

She dipped her head. "Yes, sir."

"As such, you are being placed on disciplinary probation for the duration of one year. You will resume your duties at HSP in a normal fashion, but your actions will be under continuous review by a probation agent from the Royal Offices. Any breach of protocol will result in your immediate termination from the agency and incarceration in the Haphor Facility."

The boom of the Grand Magistrate's gavel hitting the desk sent a jolt through Ziva's body and echoed through her head, drowning out the shuffling as everyone rose and began to leave. She stood there on the platform, still cuffed, staring straight ahead as her mind struggled to process everything. *One year...probation agent...immediate termination... incarceration....*

"I told you it would be okay."

Eyes wide and brows knit, she turned and found Baez smiling up at her. "Why didn't you just tell me?" she said. *Why didn't you* warn *me?*

"Go get yourself packed. I'll meet you in the training center with your discharge information."

One of the MPs reached up and touched her arm before she could ask further questions. "This way, ma'am."

She turned and made her way back down the long platform, watching as the two soldiers who had escorted Hoxie in took hold of the man's arms and began to lead him out of the room. His green eyes shifted toward her, and she slowed.

"I'm sorry for everything," he said as the MPs shoved him forward. "I'm glad you were able to stop Dasaro. And...I'm glad you're okay."

Ziva stepped down from the platform and was cut off as one of the soldiers moved cautiously between her and Hoxie. "Why'd you do it?" she called as they hauled him out the door. She hesitated, recalling the way she'd asked the same thing of Aroska Tarbic when he'd gotten the director to pardon her life after she'd saved him at Dakiti.

Hoxie turned back toward her, forcing his escorts to slow down. "After I parted ways with Dasaro, I hid like a coward and did nothing to stop him. Add that to the fact that you could have just as easily killed *me* that day at the embassy and…it seemed like the right thing to do."

One of the GA's armored cars swooped down in front of them, and he was hustled into it before he could say more. "I'm sorry!" he called again just before the car door slammed shut.

Then he was gone.

# · 3 ·

## REHABILITATION CENTER
### HAPHEZIAN GRAND ARMY BASE, NA

With a jingle of chains and a soft click, the shackles fell away from Ziva's wrists. She gave the MP a terse nod; he dipped his head in return and hurried away down the hall, leaving her alone in her little room. She turned and looked over the space, letting her gaze settle on the clothes and boots that had been set out on her bunk. Baez had thought of everything.

Unsure what exactly she was supposed to be doing, she took up the clothes and went into the room's tiny lavatory, quickly changing out of her inpatient scrubs. She pulled the clean tank top over her head, pausing a moment to examine the scar running along the lower left side of her breastbone. The caura treatment she'd been subjected to had done its work. The scar had been reduced to a thin line, with only a small mass of excess tissue at the exact place Dasaro's bullet had entered her body.

She folded the scrubs and returned to the main compartment, where she found Baez waiting at the door with a data pad.

"You didn't trust me?" he said with a twinkle in his eye.

"Why didn't you just tell me?" She felt compelled to ask again even though she guessed he legally couldn't have.

Baez smiled and waved a device past her head before letting it hover over her heart for a moment. "And spoil the surprise? Where's the fun in that?" He entered the readings from the device into the data pad. "Vitals look good. You're in better shape than you were when you came in here."

"Isn't that the point?"

"I mean you're in better shape than you were even at HSP. This is the best physical condition you've been in since spec ops training."

Ziva lifted an eyebrow. She did feel good, more rejuvenated and energetic than she'd been in a long time. Despite the accelerated healing process, lying immobile in a hospital bed for several days had set her back, and the first few days of rehab had focused on regaining simple mobility. The last weeks of the session had been brutal and exhausting, but they weren't kidding when they said the Na Facility could restore patients to one hundred ten percent functionality.

"I suppose this is goodbye, Lieutenant," Baez said. "It's been a pleasure."

She shrugged and looked around the room again. "So that's it?"

"That's it," the doctor replied. "Once you make it back to Haphez, you'll be Director Arion's problem again." He handed her the data pad. "Just show this at the transport hub and you'll be on the next ship out of here."

As eager as she was to get away, it seemed like everything was happening too fast. "Thank you for everything," she said, returning the handshake Baez offered.

"A rep from the base will meet you downstairs to sign you out," he said. "I'll be in my office if there's anything else you need before you leave."

He turned and strode out, leaving her alone again. With no personal effects to speak of, she had nothing to pack—anything she'd used during the course of her stay was a temporary provision from the facility. The only thing that really belonged to her now was the data pad. She looked down at it, studying her stats for a moment. As good as it felt to be done with rehab and the trial, the thought of going home to face a new kind of confinement in the form of her probation officer made her hesitate before rushing out the door. It was far from the first time she'd been placed on disciplinary probation, but never before had it been for longer than a week or two, and never before had anyone been holding her leash so tightly. Breaking rules didn't bring her any great pleasure, but sometimes it was the best and only way to accomplish a task. It was something Emeri and the rest of HSP had learned to deal with over the years, but likely something the Royal Officer was not going to tolerate.

Sighing, she wandered into the hall and headed for the stairs just as she had less than an hour prior, sans the armed escort. Up until this point, the prospect of going home had excited her, but now the thought had lost some of its charm. She wasn't happy with the way HSP had handled things after Tachi's assassination. While it was true that Haphezian culture followed more of a guilty-until-proven-innocent model than most other civilizations, the agency had taken one look at Dasaro's fabricated evidence and had immediately believed his side of the story. Maybe they'd been right in doing so; he was the trusted veteran agent, after all. Regardless, the fact that everyone had been so quick to turn against her still bothered her. She'd always been led to believe she was one of HSP's most prized assets, a tool they couldn't afford to lose, but now she was doubtful. The organization she'd devoted her life to had been willing to throw her away like a piece of trash without bothering to hear her out, and that meant she'd somehow become less valuable to them. Worse, it meant she was expendable.

She was no stranger to the concept of expendability. It was something every one of HSP's operators knew they might have to deal with someday. If a spec ops agent—or, galaxy forbid, an entire *team*—was captured on a mission, it was no secret that the agency would deny all involvement with the operation as a means of protecting itself. If the agent or team managed to return home, it was considered a victory. If not, well...that was too bad, but it came with the territory. This was one of the reasons the director had refused to send in reinforcements when Ziva's team infiltrated Dakiti.

But the situation she faced now was different. This was a matter of trust, of knowing the agency would have her back in everyday circumstances. Being abandoned in the field was one thing, something she could deal with. But being abandoned within HSP's walls was another matter entirely, and she wasn't sure if she wanted to risk letting it happen again.

These were all things she'd contemplated during the countless hours she'd spent using the exercise equipment and staring out the window during the past ten weeks. Part of her had considered not returning to HSP; as much as she'd come to care for her teammates over the years, she'd always felt she worked best on her own, responsible for no one but herself and free of any outside interference. The measure of autonomy the director had granted her was one of the only reasons she'd ever functioned as well as she had in the agency setting. Skeet and Zinni mercifully understood that, and they enjoyed the freedom as much as she did. They would lose most of their independence with a probation officer hovering around, and if that was the case, Ziva wasn't even sure if she wanted to go back.

On top of all that, her face had been plastered across every news screen planetwide following her arrest and escape. Half the Fringe probably knew who she was these days, which rendered any effort the agency had made to keep her identity a secret over the years completely futile. Not only was she uncomfortable with the idea of losing the privacy and anonymity she'd spent the past nine years basking in, but recognition from someone with unfriendly intentions could endanger a mission, even her life. The thought made her shiver.

She paused halfway down the hallway and leaned against the wall, eyes closed. The thought of leaving the agency almost made her sick—she'd been relatively happy there for so long. For a moment, she wondered what she might do for work if she did decide to call it quits. Surely there'd be plenty of contract jobs throughout the Fringe Systems that wouldn't be much different than what she and her team did during their independent service term each year.

*Her team.* Her thoughts drifted to Skeet and Zinni, and then to Aroska. She'd sent word directly to Emeri authorizing Tarbic to join the Alpha squad during her time on Na, so they would still have the mandatory three members. Skeet was a good leader, maybe even better than her, and certainly better with people. He would carry the team well in her absence. She wondered how Marshay and Ryon might feel if she up and disappeared, and she was momentarily bothered that it was even something she was concerned about. They didn't know the details of what her work consisted of, but they knew enough to realize there was always a chance she wouldn't return from a mission. Her leaving would be no different. They had her house, and they had her money. They would be fine.

Ziva let a growl escape her throat and heaved another sigh before continuing down the hall. On the other hand, running off when she was supposed to be reporting to her probation officer would probably get her in worse trouble than she was already in, even if she was only gone for a little while. If she left, it would have to be permanently, and she would spend the next several years constantly looking over her shoulder. That was almost worse than just staying on her leash at HSP, she decided. Besides, her ship and weapons had all been impounded by the agency, and unless she wanted to dip into her off-world accounts to purchase new gear while on the run, she'd have to return home for at least a little while to reclaim everything. And maybe sucking it up and pushing through a year of disciplinary probation wouldn't be so bad. She'd managed to behave herself for the past two months, after all.

She shoved all her thoughts to the back of her mind as she reached the training room and angled toward a man in military dress blues who stood near the front door. He looked vaguely familiar, and the flicker of recognition that flashed across his eyes when he saw her told her she should know him from somewhere. He offered his hand as she approached.

"Lieutenant, it's good to see you well. You probably don't remember me."

Her mind made the connection when she heard him speak. "Colonel Sheen," she said, shaking his hand. "I tend to remember anyone who has pointed a gun at me."

Kevyn Sheen's smile made him seem like an entirely different man than the pissed off soldier she'd met in the sublevels of Dakiti. "I don't blame you. And it's just *Major* now, thanks to the court-martial that followed that whole fiasco on Sardonis."

She lifted an eyebrow. The two weeks of disciplinary leave she and her team had been subjected to as punishment for defying orders seemed mild in comparison. "I'm sorry."

"Don't be. We got the bastards, didn't we? I'd have gone to Dakiti even if it meant scrubbing lavatory floors for the rest of my career. The fact that my men and I didn't get outright discharged has to tell you we did something right."

"I suppose that's true," she replied with a smirk. "I'm not sure how things would have turned out if you hadn't shown up when you did."

"All part of the job, ma'am. Let's see what we've got here." He took her data pad from her and looked it over for a moment, nodding approvingly as he read. He produced a stylus from his pocket and scribbled his electronic signature onto the pad. "You were clinically dead three different times in the medical transport after you were shot, and now look at you. You're a tough lady, Lieutenant. HSP is lucky to have you."

"That they are," Ziva muttered, not bothering to suppress the nasty edge in her response.

Sheen took one last look at the data pad and chuckled again before handing it back. "And I'm probably not the first person to tell you this today, but *bhen ghetan*. All the best on your birthday."

Her eyes grew wide. With all the other thoughts that had consumed her mind all morning, she'd nearly forgotten. Oddly enough, it had been the first thing she'd thought of upon awakening; depending on the outcome of the approaching hearing, it would either be one of her best birthdays or one of her worst.

"Actually, you are the first," she said, stiffening a bit. "It's not something I like to call attention to."

"My apologies, then. May I walk you to the transport hub?"

She would have preferred to walk alone and take more time to consider her options, but she nodded anyway. Sheen's words had struck a chord in her and she'd already made the decision to at least return home for a little while. It would be easier to think in her hollow under the sarmi tree than the busy base spaceport.

"So, twenty-nine," Sheen said as the two of them started off across the compound. "You've still got a long career ahead of you. How long have you been at HSP?"

"Almost ten years—been in ops for a little over eight," Ziva answered, omitting the part about being one of the agency's contract assassins for nearly as long. "My team reached Alpha status two years ago."

"They start you that early in ops?"

"Considering half of us are dead or retired before we're forty, they don't have much choice. It's no different than joining the military at eighteen."

"I suppose you're right," Sheen said. "You people in ops get the job done, and that's what matters."

She kept her gaze focused directly ahead, watching the ships coming and going from the base's little spaceport. When the time came to leave the facility—assuming the trial ended positively—she'd pictured herself being escorted home by HSP or getting picked up by her squad. The thought of riding into Noro aboard a military transport full of sweaty GA recruits was less than appealing, but adapting to unappealing circumstances was no new concept.

She had just opened her mouth to ask Sheen about his court-martial when the man's communicator crackled to life. "Major, are you seeing this?" a voice hollered over the open transmission.

It was then that Ziva noticed the whine of an approaching aircraft, not from the transport hub ahead but from behind them. All the base personnel in the vicinity stopped what they were doing and turned their attention to the sky. She swiveled to get a look for herself, immediately fixing her sights on the small ship descending toward them with a plume of jet-black smoke billowing from its rear end. She studied its trajectory for a moment, calculating that they had approximately five seconds to get clear before it crashed into the building they were standing beside.

"Get back!" someone yelled as she grabbed Sheen's arm and began to run.

They made it across the walkway and managed to duck behind a low decorative wall just as the ship reached the earth. The impact sent tremors rolling through the ground and brought a hail of broken glass and debris raining down around them. Ziva threw her hands up to shield her face, feeling the sting of burning material as it met her skin. She held perfectly still and listened, risking a peek up over the wall as soon as most of the dust had settled.

The nose of the craft had penetrated the building's walls, and judging by what she could see of the tail through the billowing smoke, it was one of the GA's own fighters. She worked her way to her feet, eyes to the sky as she searched for any sign of where the ship had come from and what had caused the crash. The air was completely clear, and based on the chatter flooding the nearby soldiers' comm units, even the spaceport traffic was being directed out of the area.

She stepped out from her hiding place, ignoring Sheen's warnings about subsequent explosions. "Affirmative—it came down against the northwest corner of Mess Hall Three," she heard him saying into his communicator. "Do we have any idea where it came from?"

Sirens wailed within the building and military personnel poured out the front door, coughing and sputtering and looking wildly about. Ziva grabbed one man by the shoulders and helped him steady himself against the wall, narrowly avoiding a pair of base firecars that came swooping onto the scene. The emergency response crews leaped into action, working to augment the mess hall's gaseous fire suppression system that had been rendered nearly useless by the gaping hole in the wall.

She could hear the voice of whoever Sheen was on comm with shouting through the device. "But you said the clearance codes checked out," the major responded. "What do you mean *MIA*?"

Ziva found she was only half-listening as she began to cautiously move toward the wreck. The fire crews had blanketed the downed ship in a thick layer of blue foam, successfully smothering the worst of the fire. Emergency responders closed in ahead of her, but even through the crowd and remaining wisps of smoke, she could see that the fighter's cockpit was empty.

A loud *bang* echoed through the air just as her mind made the connection that something was very wrong. A large projectile shot up out of the cockpit, shattering what was left of the glass, and sailed into the air above the mess hall. Everyone in the vicinity froze and watched as the object reached its apex and burst into perhaps a dozen smaller pieces. A low hiss reached Ziva's ears as the chunks rained down on the crowd, and she saw that each had begun to release a thin cloud of greenish-gray smoke.

"Gas!" someone screamed.

For once, she was glad to be stuck on Na at the base rather than dealing with a crowd of civilians in the city. The soldiers around her—for the most part, anyway—responded in an orderly fashion, throwing jackets over the gas canisters and moving about with minimal scrambling and jostling. She sucked in one last breath and held it, but she knew it was too late; everyone in the area had been exposed the moment the main projectile broke apart.

She pivoted and began to run back toward the rehab center with Sheen hot on her heels. The gas had an odd smell to it, but so far, it didn't seem to be having any adverse effects—she felt no dizziness or faintness, had no trouble breathing. Her eyes smarted a bit, but whether it was a result of the gas or the fire, she wasn't sure.

"That ship is one of ours," Sheen called to her, his voice muffled by the hand clamped over his nose and mouth. He removed it when they had made it a suitable distance from the crash site, breathing hard. "We need to establish a quarantine zone!" he hollered into his comm. "Make sure nobody from ground zero makes it out of the area. We have no idea if this stuff is contagious."

Ziva released the breath she'd been holding and looked back at the scene behind them. The people were nothing more than shapes rushing about through the haze of smoke and gas. She could hear Sheen still on comm, reporting what he was seeing to whoever was on the other end of the transmission. Aircars from the base swarmed to the site, hovering at a safe altitude and barking instructions over their loudspeakers.

As she took it all in, she couldn't help but scoff. "All the best on my birthday," she muttered.

# · 4 ·

# UNDISCLOSED LOCATION
## NIIO SPACEPORT

T he sound of the portable comm grid coming to life startled Skeet Duvo out of his thoughts. His long legs already dangled over the edge of the stiff little bunk he lay on, so he worked his way into a sitting position and planted his feet on the floor, standing bolt upright when he saw that the indicator light on the comm console blinked red.

He made it across the darkened room in two strides and hovered over the console for a moment, wide-eyed. A red message light meant only one thing: a transmission straight from Emeri Arion's office at the Haphezian Special Police's Noro Headquarters. And that in itself meant only one thing: bad news.

Skeet ran a hand through his spiky orange hair and drew in a deep breath before accepting the transmission. "Duvo, Alpha 40318," he said in response to the prompt preceding the message. A series of tones and static followed, odd for a call coming directly from Emeri. But instead of the director's gruff voice, he found himself listening to the eerie feminine voice of HSP's virtual intelligence.

"General distress. Agency-wide emergency protocols in effect. All agents currently dispatched to the field are ordered to cease communications immediately. Operate under Condition Black until further notice. Warning: for security purposes, do not attempt to establish contact with HSP or any affiliates during this time."

*Condition Black.* The team had conducted a mission under Condition

Black once, Skeet recalled, but mainly for training purposes. They'd been allowed no contact with the agency, no contact with any other ops teams, no contact with anyone on Haphez, for that matter. Although it seemed like they were being hung out to dry, the protocol was in fact designed to protect agents. If the agency was somehow compromised, anyone in the field could remain anonymous and, theoretically, work independently to counter whatever force threatened Headquarters. If Condition Black was in effect now, it could only mean—

"Does the user have any queries before this transmission terminates?"

Skeet drummed his fingers on the console. "What's the status of Noro Headquarters?"

"One moment...Noro Headquarters remains under Code Red lockdown following an attack on the Grand Army's Na Base. Casualties have been reported."

He felt his pulse spike at the mention of Na. "Nature of the attack?"

"Base officials have initially categorized the attack as type: chemical. No other information is available at this time."

"Find person: Ziva Payvan."

"Accessing personnel database...searching. Alert—status of person 'Ziva Payvan' not found. Please try again."

"*Sheyss*," he muttered, ruffling up his hair again. "No more questions. End transmission."

"Ending transmission. Warning: Condition Black protocols in effect. Please cease all communications immediately." The VI repeated itself twice more before the call went dead.

Skeet swore again and immediately began packing the communications equipment into its compact carrying cases. Everything in the room had been set up in a manner that allowed it to be torn down and stowed in a matter of minutes. Even on his own, he got the job done in no time. He held his pistol up to check the plasma charge, bristling a bit when the door of the room slid open. A quick glance revealed that the intruder was only Aroska Tarbic, and Skeet slid his finger away from where it had subconsciously come to rest above the weapon's trigger guard.

If the former field ops lieutenant was surprised to see the room empty and their supplies packed, he concealed it well. "Can I assume this is about the emergency code I just received from Headquarters?" he asked, holding up his own comm.

Skeet nodded and gave Aroska a quick rundown of what he knew, which, he regretted, wasn't much. "Sounds like the agency is secure for now. I'm sure they'll be on board with the investigation on Na."

Aroska was quiet for a moment as he checked his own pistol and slid his field pack over his shoulders. "Ziva's status?"

"Unknown," Skeet answered. "There...were casualties. But I'm sure she's fine. That base covers most of the moon—what are the chances she was even in the vicinity of the attack?" He forced a good-natured snort, trying to ignore the knot that had formed in his throat.

"We can't worry about that now," Aroska said, brow wrinkled as if it pained him to speak the words. He held up the data pad he'd been carrying when he entered the room. "We may have a lead, and you know as well as I do that we're running short on time." He offered the pad when Skeet reached for it. "Emissions signatures from a ship matching our target were picked up by a science team on Bectin. They said it was headed farther out into the Fringe, toward Aubin or Plaunus."

Skeet handed the data pad back and gathered up some of the cases he'd packed. "Then what are we waiting for? Let's get moving."

# · 5 ·

## QUARANTINE ZONE

### HAPHEZIAN GRAND ARMY BASE, NA

Ziva sat motionless as the syringe impaled her arm and looked on in silence as the barrel slowly filled with her blood. The medical bot removed the needle and replaced it with a caura pad, which she continued to press down on as she rose from the chair. She watched as the bot pivoted and discarded the needle before sealing the vial with a cap and placing it gingerly in the padded case containing everyone else's blood samples.

She was one of the last people to have their blood drawn. The other soldiers from the crash site had already filed through the line and now loitered on the other side of the quarantine zone that had been set up in one of the base's med centers. Everyone who had been within a certain radius of ground zero had been rounded up along with those who had escaped the mess hall. Combined, there were ninety-two people currently being held under observation. Every one of them had been stripped, hosed down, dried off, and sent through a decontamination chamber, after which they'd all been asked to give blood samples for further analysis.

Nearly four hours had passed since the attack—that's what everyone was calling it. The gas canisters and downed ship had been whisked away to secure areas; the former were now in the hands of some of the GA's chemical warfare specialists, and the latter had undergone its own decontamination procedure before being moved to a garage to have its internal computer salvaged. Ziva hadn't heard any news on that front, but the scientists had already discovered that the gas had a chemical structure similar to known nerve agents. They hadn't been able to identify it, though, and so far, no one from ground zero had exhibited symptoms of being exposed to a nerve agent of any kind. No abnormal pupil contraction, no loss of motor control, no convulsions. Still, they'd all been told to remain in the quarantine zone until everyone had given blood. The blood samples were meant to determine who had been exposed to the greatest extent, and, thus, who should be watched most closely in the coming hours.

Ziva moved forward to allow the last few people in line their turn with the medical bot. She caught sight of Sheen standing just outside the door of the room they were all being held in, communicator pressed to his ear. He'd been one of the first to have his blood drawn and had been on comm ever since. He beckoned when he saw she was watching him.

"Lieutenant," he said, nodding her way as he ended his call. He glanced around and took a few steps farther down the hallway.

"Have you learned anything?" she asked, instinctively lowering her voice.

"Five from the mess hall are dead, all ground marines. Eight others are injured, including pilots from the airborne division and a fleet commander."

"And what of the fighter?"

"It entered Na airspace approximately two minutes before the crash. Air traffic control was treating it like any other GA ship, at least until they realized the tail number matched that of a fighter reported missing in action out on the edge of Fringe Space several years back. It was one of several ships presumed lost in a skirmish near Forus."

Ziva took a moment to mull the information over. "Do you think someone captured it back then and reprogrammed it to fly here and release the gas at the base?"

"Considering there was no pilot, that's what we're wondering," Sheen answered. "It has been confirmed that the autopilot system was active. But these fighters aren't equipped with FTL drives. It would have needed a carrier to bring it here, just like it needed one to get to

Forus in the first place. We've checked and rechecked the traffic patterns in this quadrant, but with the number of ships coming and going from Noro Spaceport, it's difficult to draw any conclusions."

"I need to *get* to Noro."

"I know, and we're letting you go. All air traffic to and from the base has been shut down, but HSP is teaming up with us to take care of running the blood tests, so we're sending a single shuttle planetside with the samples. Your director requested that you return to Noro aboard that ship. The agency headquarters has been on lockdown since the attack, but they've been told to expect you, and someone will grant you proper clearance when you arrive."

Ziva nodded. "When do I leave?"

"As soon as all the samples are packed," Sheen said, peering past her into the larger room. "Are you still feeling okay?"

"Fine. You?"

He nodded and held up his communicator, transferring a code he'd received to the data pad she still carried. "Here's your clearance to board the shuttle. I've got to go set up briefing sessions and give an eyewitness testimony at a press conference. Someone's got to tell the rest of these people what's going on. Take care of yourself, Lieutenant."

"You, too," she replied with a dip of her head.

She watched him go then wasted no time in returning to the large room, where the crowd was finally beginning to disperse as the quarantine was lifted. A couple of MPs had taken over the medical bot's position and were sealing the padded cases containing the vials of blood. She showed them her data pad then picked up one of the cases, following them out to the shuttle that had touched down just outside the med center. They stowed the cases and strapped into their seats, and without further ado, the shuttle lifted into the air.

Through the craft's tiny viewports, Ziva could see the anti-aircraft guns come to life throughout the base and begin tracking them as they ascended. Pairs of GA fighters fell into position on either side of the shuttle, though she wasn't sure how much good they would do against whatever enemy ship was big enough to have brought the old fighter into Haphezian airspace. If anything, a fighter escort was only calling attention to the fact that the shuttle contained valuable cargo.

To her relief, the journey remained uneventful. A trio of aircars from HSP came to meet them as they descended into the sky above Noro; the presence of the police vehicles kept the surrounding traffic at bay, and the procession followed a clear path down to the agency headquarters. A large group of agents waited on one of the landing pads jutting from the side of the campus's tallest building. The moment the military vessels touched down, personnel from HSP's forensics and disease divisions were climbing aboard the shuttle, gathering up the blood samples and hustling them away to the labs.

Ziva waited for the chaos to ebb before stepping out of the ship. It was the first time she'd set foot on the HSP campus since being arrested for Officer Tachi's assassination, and it somehow felt surreal, especially after all the things she'd been considering earlier that morning. She started across the landing pad toward the door, wondering how she was going to get into the ops wing if no one had given her clearance yet. As she walked, she couldn't help but notice the woman standing just inside the doorway, watching her intently with pale yellow eyes as she approached. She was tall, only a few centimeters shorter than Ziva, but thin and wiry. Her thick black hair was woven into a braid that wrapped around the back of her head and cascaded over one shoulder, and she wore a sharp business suit and heels. As Ziva drew nearer, she could make out the Royal Officer's insignia on the screen of the data pad the woman carried.

"*Sheyss*," she muttered.

"Ziva Payvan," the woman said, taking several stiff steps toward her. "Agent Aura Stannist, Disciplinary and Personnel Control Specialist from the Royal Offices." She extended her hand.

Ziva crossed her arms, ignoring the handshake offer. She wondered how much time had been spent sitting around trying to come up with such a creative title for a probation officer.

"Director Arion warned me about you," the woman sighed, returning her hand to her side. Her face remained deadpan, her eyes scrutinizing every aspect of Ziva's appearance and posture. "We can do this the hard way if you want, but I'll warn you now: I will not tolerate any *sheyss* from you. You should know that on the authority of the Royal Officer, I virtually have control of this campus for the duration of my stay. That means I can make your life a living hell if I want to. But if you do your job right, I get to file clean reports and you don't have to go to prison. We both go home happy."

As much as Ziva despised the situation, she had to admire this Aura Stannist's tenacity. "I won't let you stop me from doing my job," she said, continuing to move in the direction she'd been headed.

"I'm not here to stop you," Aura retorted, effortlessly matching Ziva's long strides despite the shoes she wore. "I'm here to watch you. Like I said, if you do your job *right*, we won't have a problem."

"So, what, are you going to follow me around everywhere I go?"

"Do I need to?"

Ziva shot a hot glare over her shoulder.

The probation officer quickened her pace and cut her off. "Here's the deal. You maintain a clean slate, and I back off and give you some space. You cause trouble, and I'll be riding your ass for the rest of your probation period."

"Are you always such a *shouka*?"

The expression on Aura's face still hadn't changed. "I'm just fighting fire with fire, Payvan."

Ziva heaved a sigh. "Fine. I need to get moving."

"Your spec ops clearance has been reactivated," Aura said, passing her an access key. "This will get you into the ops wings. Director Arion also instructed me to send you to his office forthwith."

Without another word, Ziva snatched the key from her and kept walking. "I have an office on the spec ops squad floor!" she heard Aura call after her. "I'd like to see you there as soon as you're finished with the director!"

Ziva ignored her but could feel the woman's cold gaze boring into her back. She quickened her pace a bit, muttering under her breath. *Fighting fire with fire,* she thought. At least the Royal Officer—it occurred to her that she didn't even know the new guy's name—hadn't sent some spineless rodent to babysit her. Judging by the way Aura Stannist carried herself, the woman had spent at least a little time in the military or even at HSP. Despite her thin build, she was obviously strong; the desk job hadn't softened her at all, physically or mentally.

*Maintain a clean slate.* If she could stay out of trouble for the first couple of months, the probation officer might ease up and she'd be able to resume her old habit of bending the rules. She wasn't one to misbehave out of spite, but at the moment, she wanted nothing more than to toy with Agent Stannist, in much the same way as she had toyed with Dasaro by shooting Nejdra on Chaiavis. Leaving the agency was out of the question now, too. A formal resignation might do the trick, but getting up and running off while this woman was watching her would be nigh on impossible.

"Ziva!"

The sound of the man's voice shattered her train of thought. She whirled, almost annoyed that someone would dare interrupt her brooding, but she relaxed immediately when she saw who had called to her. Adin Woro jogged down the hallway after her, gray eyes bright but face hardened by worry.

"You made it. When we heard about Na, we feared the worst."

"Adin," Ziva greeted, nodding in his direction. The fact that he seemed to be taking so much interest in her arrival set her on edge. They'd collaborated on a couple of missions in the past but they'd never been close, and Ziva made a point of avoiding anyone outside the spec ops division as it was. "Where is everybody? I thought Skeet and Zinni would be around when they heard I was coming."

The shadow that fell over Adin's face made her bristle. "Nobody told you?" he said quietly, taking a step closer to her.

"Told me what?"

He shook his head. "You need to go talk to the director."

Ziva closed the distance between them, looking him directly in the eye. "Told me what?" she repeated. "Where's my team?"

"Look, if nobody's explained anything to you, I shouldn't—"

All the anger Ziva had felt throughout the morning—at the magistrates, at Hoxie, at the gas attack, at Aura Stannist—came flooding back. She let her data pad slip from her fingers and seized Adin by the shoulders, pushing him back against the wall and taking up fistfuls of his jacket. "What *happened*?"

"Take it easy, Ziva," he said. His voice remained low and even, and he maintained eye contact despite the passersby who had stopped to see what was wrong. Although Ziva had never known him that well, she'd always admired his ability to keep his cool regardless of the situation. "There's not much I can tell you because I don't *know* that much. You'll need to talk to Emeri if you want details, but...there was an accident."

She released him immediately and took a step back, fighting away the sickening wave that coursed through her stomach. "What does that even mean?" she snarled, hoping she hadn't sounded quite as desperate as she felt.

"Short version? Zinni has been taken and I lost contact with Skeet and Aroska earlier this morning."

"Taken? When?"

Adin swallowed hard. "Four weeks ago."

Ziva stood with a gaping mouth as the word 'weeks' echoed through her mind. Hours she could live with, maybe even days. But weeks? "*Huhren shouka souhn,*" she swore, spinning on her heel and taking off as fast as she could down the corridor. She tore through the employee canteen and up the stairs, pausing just long enough to swipe her access key and grant herself entry to the spec ops wing. She slipped into the first open elevator she found, pacing back and forth across the car for the duration of the painfully slow ride. When the doors opened onto Director Emeri Arion's private floor, she stormed across the room and slammed her fist against the call button outside his office door... then again, and again.

There was a soft click as the director disengaged the locking mechanism from the inside—apparently he'd gotten tired of people barging into his office uninvited. The door slid open and she strode in, immediately fixing her gaze on the man standing in front of the massive picture window across the room.

"*Four weeks?*" she shouted.

Emeri sighed and moved over to his desk. "This is exactly why I told Stannist to send you up here immediately," he muttered, running a hand through his graying hair and disturbing the impeccably combed turquoise stripes.

"Why the hell didn't anyone tell me?"

"Ziva, I need you to calm down and listen to me." He passed her a data pad, and she suddenly realized she'd left her other one on the floor in the hallway. "We've compiled all the information we have on the situation. You can look over it more thoroughly when we're done here."

"I said *why* didn't you tell me? You think some damn communication rule trumps *this*?"

"Payvan, please!" Emeri closed his eyes, pinching the bridge of his nose between his thumb and forefinger. When he spoke again, his voice was quiet but carried a commanding tone that compelled her to listen. "I can assure you the communication limitations had nothing to do with it. We chose not to inform you because you were barely halfway through your rehab session at the time, and we didn't want to risk you trying to return to the planet before you were healthy enough to do so. The Royal House wouldn't hear of it anyway, not before your hearing had taken place."

"That is the biggest load of *sheyss* I've ever heard," Ziva said. She'd been tempted to leave the base several times throughout the last few weeks of rehab, not necessarily with the intention of avoiding her trial, but just to get a taste of freedom again. She'd refrained, of course. Despite the brutal training sessions, the short break from the insanity of ops had been enjoyable, and the thought of the Royal Officer's people chasing her down seemed rather unappealing after her bout with Dasaro. Now it appeared the one time she'd chosen to settle down and follow the rules, everything had gone to hell.

For a moment, Emeri didn't seem convinced that keeping her in the dark had been the best move, but he composed himself and cleared his throat. "What do you know about an entity called Ronan?"

The question caught her off guard. She found herself sitting in Kat Reilly's shop on Chaiavis, listening to the young woman talk about the mysterious disease that had killed her friend Corey. "I...barely anything," she replied, giving him an abbreviated version of the same story Kat had told her before returning to Argall. Nobody knew for sure what Ronan was, only that it had been responsible for Corey's death and would have killed Kat too if she hadn't sacrificed herself in the mining town. "She gave me some information she wanted me to look into after she had passed."

Emeri waved his hand over his own data pad, sending whatever he'd been looking at to the device Ziva held. "*This* wouldn't happen to be that information, would it?"

She'd never had time to take an in-depth look at the pad Kat had given her, but a quick glance at the screen revealed that this was indeed the young woman's data, copied word for word but now marked with an HSP case logo. Ziva opened her mouth to ask how the agency had gotten the original data pad, considering it had been locked in the hidden strongbox in her bedroom, but her mind made the connection before she could say anything. She saw herself lying in her hospital bed with Aroska hovering over her.

"*Where's my kytara?*"

"*I found it on Bosco's ship on the way back here. I'll put it away for you.*"

Of course. As of this moment, he was the only other person in the galaxy who knew the location of her strongbox. "Damn you, Tarbic," she muttered.

"Tarbic brought this information to our attention shortly after returning from Argall," the director said, shooting her an unimpressed glance. "He said he found it in your backpack after you were shot."

Ziva forced her facial expression to remain unchanged. Despite the fact that Emeri knew of her Nosti abilities, she was thankful Aroska had left her kytara—and the strongbox, for that matter—out of the picture.

"After meeting Ms. Reilly in person and witnessing what took place in Argall, Tarbic insisted we open an investigation," Emeri continued. "We delegated the case to Adin Woro's field ops team until we had enough information to act on. There was a lead on the other side of the Fringe, and they found evidence of Ronan's presence on Niio..."

# · 6 ·

## 4 WEEKS AGO
## WAREHOUSE DISTRICT
### NIIO SPACEPORT

A roska Tarbic stepped into the tiny room and swept his gaze across the space, lowering his rifle a bit when he saw it was empty…just like most of the other identical rooms he'd already looked in. The corridor he'd been assigned to stretched farther than he could see with his night optics, and the walls were lined with hundreds of storage rooms roughly three by three meters. Most contained nothing but dust and rodent feces. He'd found the occasional empty box, and one room had housed a pair of strung-out Elsara whose beady eyes had glowed as he viewed them through his headgear. But the rest were empty, with nothing to see but cold, windowless gray walls.

Despite thus far finding nothing of interest, he continued to proceed with caution. He moved forward slowly while following a heel-toe pattern, treading so lightly he could barely hear his own foot-steps. This warehouse complex was massive, and Ronan's men were somewhere in it. Danger could literally be waiting around any corner.

He still wasn't entirely sure if Ronan was a person or an organization; maybe it was both. Whatever it was, it had numerous soldiers at its disposal. The ones they'd been tracking through the Niiosian spaceport appeared to be human, though it had been difficult to tell for sure since their faces had been covered by sleek helmets. None of them were overly tall—roughly Zinni's height—but even with the light armor they wore, it was clear they were well-built. Nobody else on the spaceport moon had given them a second glance; they fit right in with the merchants, smugglers, mercenaries, and thousands of other people traveling to and from all corners of the galaxy.

Aroska continued down the hallway and found the next five rooms to be, yet again, empty. This was of course the closest anyone had ever gotten to Ronan's people, other than Kat Reilly herself. He had no idea if they were simply using this warehouse as a storage space or if it was a prison and lab like the building Kat had found on Chaiavis. The information she'd accumulated on her data pad had been so thorough. She'd interviewed her friend about his time in captivity and had documented all the stages of his horrible symptoms right up until his death. She'd kept detailed records of her own struggles with this mysterious disease Ronan had given her and had written out a lengthy description of her findings in the warehouse she'd searched. Aroska imagined it wasn't much different from the one in which he stood now, and after reading everything Kat had compiled, he was confident he would recognize evidence of Ronan's presence if he saw it.

He still found himself wishing she would have shared her story with the entire group before they'd returned to Argall. If her theory about the seizures was correct, it had been too late to save her anyway, but it bothered him that she'd chosen to confide only in Ziva after they'd all become a team.

Oh, Ziva. She'd kill him when she found out he'd taken the data pad and syringe from the strongbox while putting her kytara away. For a moment, he'd debated over whether to take the items at all, but as soon as he'd realized they belonged to Kat, he'd decided investigating further was the best way to honor the young woman after she'd sacrificed herself to save all of them. Several weeks had gone by before they'd understood the full magnitude of the situation, and now here they were finally closing in on some answers.

Aroska paused a moment and glanced back the way he had come. "Anyone having any luck?" he said into his earpiece.

"Everything's still quiet," came Skeet's voice.

"Looks like the area ahead of me is opening up a bit," Zinni replied. She hesitated a moment. "Nothing's registering on infrared, but I've got some containers I want to check out. Stand by."

Aroska was beginning to wonder if they were even looking in the right building when he came to a storage unit whose door was shut. Every unit was equipped with a sturdy metal door that unfolded and sealed the opening, but all the others had been open. A locked door likely meant the room actually contained something important, and he was greatly curious as to what that might be.

The door control was crusty and obsolete, probably dating back to the original establishment of the warehouse complex. A bit of fiddling with the wiring behind the control board was all it took to disengage the lock. Aroska lifted the door, wincing at the abrasive metallic scraping sound it made, and repeated the process of stepping inside and sweeping his eyes from corner to corner. The room itself was identical to all the others, but the carefully stacked pyramid of shipping crates it contained was new.

He approached slowly, studying the ground for any form of booby trap before looking over the stack in the same manner. None of the crates were marked with any sort of identifying logo, but it appeared they had all originated from the same place and held the same goods.

"I've got some shipping containers here," he said quietly, receiving affirmative responses from both Skeet and Zinni. He carefully reached out and flipped one of the lids open. Inside, he found rows upon rows of packaged parcels, each of which contained a fine yellow powder. He lifted a package and gave it a quick sniff—zanix, a narcotic popular among the Fringe Systems, unless he was mistaken. While it was the most interesting thing he'd found so far, it didn't appear to have anything to do with Ronan. With an exasperated sigh, he dropped the package back into the container and returned to the hallway.

"Just drugs," he announced. "Smugglers probably stashed them here."

"Keep moving," Skeet said quietly. "They've got to be in here somewhere."

Rather than respond, Zinni swore and began to cough. "You okay?" Aroska asked, picturing the intelligence officer disturbing some built-up dust. There was no shortage of the stuff in the building.

When she didn't respond, he stopped. "Zinni?"

The sound of her scream immediately set him in motion again. He opened his mouth to ask for an explanation, but Skeet's commanding voice dominated the comm channel: "Zinni! Status report!"

Her response was garbled. "Got smoke...third quarter." All that followed were muffled noises.

Aroska continued moving and glanced down at the tiny view-screen strapped to his wrist, noting that he was also three quarters of the way through the route he'd been assigned to. Though she was two long corridors over, Zinni was somewhere directly across from him.

The only sound he could hear over the comm now was Skeet's heavy breathing as he too hurried through the darkness. Zinni had gone completely silent, prompting Aroska to quicken his pace. He finally came to a connecting hallway and ducked down it, sprinting toward the areas Skeet and Zinni had been searching.

Unsure if there was any point in being stealthy anymore, he tore off his night optics and activated the spotlight mounted on his rifle. The beam cut through the blackness, and he caught sight of Skeet rounding a corner up ahead. He had also shed his headgear and was now guided by the beam of his own spotlight. Aroska hurried to catch up and the two of them ran together for another minute or so before stumbling into a space that appeared to be the open area Zinni had described.

After taking one look at Skeet, Aroska could tell he was trying hard to not just call out Zinni's name. "She has to be nearby," he whispered, sweat glistening on his forehead.

Aroska nodded and they pressed on together, he shining the beam of his light as far down the corridor as he could and Skeet playing his about on the walls and floor. A cloud of what appeared to be smoke drifted out of one of the rooms ahead, and their lights reflected off something shiny on the ground as they neared.

It was Zinni's night optics.

Skeet bent down to examine the headgear while Aroska cautiously peered into the room from which the smoke had originated. The dissipating cloud swirled around him as he moved in and recovered a small circular device that had adhered itself to the floor: a smoke grenade. He turned to show Skeet just as the other man approached him with a small object of his own.

"Her earpiece," he said. "Someone took her."

"Come on," Aroska replied, "they can't have gotten far."

They took off down the corridor as fast as their legs would carry them.

## · 7 ·

# HSP HEADQUARTERS
## NORO, HAPHEZ

Ziva sat—she didn't even remember sitting down—in one of the chairs opposite Emeri's desk, massaging her eyes as she attempted to wrap her head around everything she'd just been told. She should have known better than to leave Kat's items in a place anyone, even one person, knew about. Then again, she hadn't planned on being shot in Argall and never envisioned anyone but herself putting her kytara away. Still, taking something she'd obviously made a point of hiding had been a bold move on Aroska's part. It wasn't the first time she'd been overcome with the desire to skin him alive.

"There would have been a small syringe with that data pad," she finally said. "What became of it?"

"It was sent to forensics along with a copy of the data," the director answered. "Based on the chemical composition of the residue found in its barrel, and taking the documented symptoms into consideration, it appears it was designed to affect the nervous system. But the substance still hasn't been identified."

"Sounds like the gas on Na," Ziva mused, wondering briefly if there was any connection. "Adin said he lost contact with Skeet and Aroska this morning."

"I implemented Condition Black protocols for all field-bound agents after the attack. They've been ordered to cease all communications, to become invisible. Lieutenant Woro's clearance level doesn't make him privy to that information."

"Isn't that something he should know if he's overseeing the case? He probably thinks they're dead."

"Ziva, you know as well as I do that that protocol is meant to protect our agents at all costs, even from the agency itself. We've had our fair share of dirty agents throughout this past year. I'd think you of all people would opt to err on the side of caution in this situation."

He was right after all, and she responded with a simple nod.

"I want you out there, Ziva," Emeri continued. "We need you to go connect with your team and find Officer Vax. We're considering this an act of war against the agency, and we've already got most of the spec ops teams on the hunt for any signs of Ronan. But you heard Kat Reilly's story in person—you know how a run-in with Ronan affected her. You may have been out of commission for the past ten weeks, but you still just might be the best suited for this investigation."

"If my team has gone dark, how the hell am I supposed to find them?"

"Finding people who don't want to be found is what you do best. After Vax was taken, Tarbic and Duvo set up a temporary base of operations on Niio while they searched the moon and nearby systems. That's where they were when we sent out the distress call this morning. If they're smart, they're probably long gone by now, but you know how they operate. I have the utmost confidence in your ability to track them down."

Ziva bowed her head and had to force herself to say what she was thinking, something she normally had no trouble with. "Is there any sense in even searching for Zinni at this point? Four weeks is a long time."

Emeri gave her a slight nod of understanding. "I know. As of right now, we're still operating under the pretense that she's alive, based on what we know about Ms. Reilly's life expectancy after she was captured. And even if it's too late for Officer Vax, galaxy forbid, I feel it is imperative that we continue the search for Ronan. Whatever it is, it needs to be stopped."

"What about this Aura Stannist woman? She's not going to let me just walk out."

"Leave her to me. I'll stall her and take any flak from the Royal House until you return."

An odd tingle slithered up Ziva's spine and she lifted her gaze to meet Emeri's. This was the man who usually denied any involvement with her operations so he could *avoid* trouble from the Royal House.

"Why?" she said quietly. "Why are you doing this?"

"Because, even though you sometimes make my job a thousand times harder than it needs to be, I've never doubted your abilities for a second. I may not agree with the way you handle some things—a lot of things—but you get the job done, and I want you to know I've got your back. And I want to atone for *not* having your back sooner when you were in trouble with Dasaro."

Ziva thought back to the things she had been considering all morning. It brought her some comfort to know he'd at least realized he was essentially throwing away his best weapon, but at the same time, it made her even more angry that he'd felt that way and had still been willing to ship her off to the Haphor Facility without question. She appreciated the apology nonetheless and acknowledged it with a terse nod.

Emeri cleared his throat. "When your team was dispatched to the field, we thought it best that they travel in a vessel not directly affiliated with the agency, so they took the *Intrepid*. We'll provide you with an unregistered ship you can use to go after them. A variety of weaponry and equipment was also recovered from your home after Tachi's murder, but the items are available for immediate pick-up down in evidence."

Ziva rose, excited by the prospect of being able to handle something other than an antique rifle she'd had to modify on the fly. "Thank you," she said, a bitter edge to her voice.

"I'll have your ship left in the east landing zone—you should be able to avoid Agent Stannist that way. And Ziva, one more thing."

She paused and turned back toward him, having been on her way to the door.

"With Dasaro, Venn, and Hoxie—three ranking officers—all out of the picture, that left us with a significant gap in the chain of command. There was some shuffling and testing of personnel while you were gone, and we've managed to fill Venn and Hoxie's positions, but you were next in line to take Dasaro's place. Duvo was named the Alpha team's acting lieutenant in your absence, and he will now retain that title. Officer Vax requested that she maintain her status as intelligence officer, and since Tarbic hasn't received the specialized training required for the position, we agreed. He was vetted thoroughly and then bumped to sergeant. While not a direct member of the team, you will continue to oversee their operations and carry out assignments on your own, *Captain* Payvan."

Ziva stood perfectly still as the gears turned in her head. She once again found herself thinking back to her previous debate over whether she should leave the agency. *Not a direct member of the team,* she mused. Surprisingly, the thought saddened her a bit, but it also meant that measures had been put in place to ensure her team's stability even in her absence. Then her thoughts drifted to Zinni. Leaving now was completely out of the question. As much as she disliked relying on others and being relied on, she knew Skeet and Aroska needed her now more than ever.

"Just like that?" she said with an incredulous shrug.

"The others went through a bit more official processing," Emeri answered. "Even though you were gone, your credentials have been updated in all the agency's systems." He lifted an eyebrow. "I doubted you'd want any kind of formal promotion ceremony anyway."

"You're right, I wouldn't." Ziva continued moving slowly toward the office door.

"Dasaro's old office is at your disposal when you're ready. For now, get out there and do what you do. And remember, you'll be operating under Condition Black as well."

She dipped her head. "Sir."

"Good luck, Captain."

The new title continued to echo through Ziva's head as she went downstairs and took a shuttle across the HSP campus to the landing area Emeri had mentioned. While she was by no means complaining, she'd never had any overwhelming desire to be promoted to a unit captain. She liked the idea of taking charge, but, just as she'd been pondering earlier, she wasn't a particularly good leader. Most people only followed her because they knew she could get the job done, even if she wasn't very congenial. That, she decided, was their problem, though, and she would simply continue to—as Emeri put it—do what she did best.

She arrived at the landing zone and found the ship waiting for her. It was similar in make to the *Intrepid*, fast and stealthy, but about a decade newer with far fewer scratches and dents. She piloted the craft over to the evidence lockup, where a team of techs had packed up all her belongings per the director's orders. Most of the items were from the formerly-hidden weapon safe in her hall closet—guns, ammunition, explosives, and other ordnance. Her personal computers and communications equipment were included as well, and with the help of the techs, she had everything loaded onto the ship in a matter of minutes.

Then she was off. Just to be on the safe side, she double-checked the nav computer to make sure tracking had been disabled. She doubted it would take Aura long to realize she was gone, and she knew Emeri would do everything in his power to make sure the Royal House didn't send anyone after her, but she liked the idea of being invisible all the same. She soared into the midst of Noro's afternoon traffic, catching a glimpse of her own house far below as she flew out over the Tranyi River. Na was visible through the front viewport as she broke out of the planet's atmosphere, and part of her couldn't believe she'd been a prisoner there that very morning. But the thought was not a lingering one. She directed the ship past the military moon and out into open space, and after a few careful calculations, the vessel lurched forward at FTL speed.

# · 8 ·
# Unknown Location
## Fringe Space

She was reasonably sure her eyes were open, yet she could not see anything. She blinked a few times just to be sure—still nothing. From what she could tell, she was slumped against a wall, her neck and shoulders bent at an awkward angle. There was a certain closeness in the air that told her she was in a small room, though there was no way of telling *how* small. The room didn't have a noticeable scent; she guessed she had been there a while and had simply grown accustomed to it. The darkness seemed familiar, but whether she knew it from sleep or consciousness, she had no idea.

*What do you know?*

It was a question she vaguely remembered asking herself before, so maybe she had been awake at some point after all.

*My name is Zinnarana Vax*, she told herself as she pressed her palms to the floor and tried to heave herself into a more upright position. *I am an intelligence officer in the special operations division of the Haphezian Special Police.* Her arms felt like lead, and it took what seemed like all her strength to move her body. Fire pulsed through her neck and back as she was finally able to straighten. *I can feel pain. That's a start.*

Zinni fidgeted a bit as she settled into the new position. She lifted a shaky hand, almost startled when she felt her own fingers brush against her face. She slowly began a systematic exploration of her head, finding her eyes, nose, lips, ears, and even taking the time to run her fingers through her hair. Nothing seemed out of the ordinary—she found no blood or fluids, and she felt no further pain aside from a dull pounding in her skull.

It felt like she was moving in slow motion as she lowered her hands and repeated the examination process on her neck, chest, arms, and abdomen. *I have some bruising on my left side,* she thought, pressing down on a sore spot below her rib cage. *Feels like blunt force trauma.* She couldn't imagine that she could have inflicted such an injury on herself. Either she had left this room at some point, or someone else had come in.

For the first time, she noticed the subtle changes in the tilt of the floor she sat on. She wasn't sure if the space she was in was actually moving or if it was just her mind playing tricks on her, but she added the sensation to the ever-growing list of things she was aware of.

She sat still for a while, focusing on the darkness once more. For a moment, it seemed heavier than normal, almost as if she had passed out again, but everything looked exactly the same. Other than a low vibration that seemed to be coming from within the walls around her, her ears weren't registering any sounds. The silence combined with the blackness left her with no concept of time, and she had no idea how long she sat there staring before beginning the self-exam again.

*What do you know?*

She heard the low metallic groan just before the sliver of red light pierced the darkness. *Red hues are less intense,* she told herself. Nonetheless, the light seemed blinding in comparison to the void around her and she squeezed her eyes shut, overcome with a sudden bout of nausea. The groaning continued and the light became brighter, even through her closed eyelids. *A door is opening.*

She commanded herself to open her eyes, to determine the location of the door, to see who or what might be approaching, but the light burned and intensified her headache. She settled with listening, smelling, feeling. A hand took hold of her arm, a device beeped somewhere near her head, and she heard muffled voices that echoed as if they were far away.

*My name is Zinnarana Vax. I'm still alive.*

# · 9 ·

# APARTMENT COMPLEX

## ZYLKA, AUBIN

T he force field enveloping Aubin's capital city shimmered in the sunlight, casting odd dancing shadows on the ground that reminded Taran Reddic of rippling water. After three weeks of using the desert planet as a base, he had finally begun to grow accustomed to it, but it was still enough to make him dizzy if he spent too long looking at it. He blinked several times and wiped away the drops of sweat gathering on his brow. The force field did a good job of blocking out the sun's harmful rays, but it did virtually nothing to quash the intense heat that continuously beat down on Aubin's sandy surface.

He crossed the dusty courtyard in the center of the old apartment complex his people had called home for the past three weeks. It was large enough to sustain them comfortably for an extended period of time, but small enough that they attracted little attention and could easily pack up and move at a moment's notice. There were twenty of them total, all members of the Durutian Special Forces under his command. Less than half the group was currently present in the complex—at this time of day, most of them would be out combing the streets of Zylka, looking for any evidence of their target.

He entered the first door he came to and reveled a moment in the coolness of the room. The lights were currently powered off, but the space was still well-lit thanks to the glow from several mobile computer terminals and comm grids. He made his way across the room, taking a second to glance at the readings displayed on each monitor he passed. The information they showed wasn't unpleasant, but neither was it what he wanted to see.

Taran cursed under his breath and heaved a sigh. "Anything?"

The woman standing at the terminal on the far side of the room turned and shook her head, the cybernetic implants in her eyes glowing a soft silver in the semi-darkness. Her features had been hardened by focus, but her face softened as she watched him. "Nothing," she said quietly. "Still no contact."

Taran's throat tightened, though whether it was from sadness or anger, he wasn't sure. It had been close to fifty hours since they'd received any word from his sister Devani, one of several government representatives from their homeworld. Though Duruta was an independent Fringe world, the Galactic Federation kept a large portion of the planet's mercenary population—including military—on retainer, using them to patrol the surrounding Fringe systems for signs of the Resistance. Taran's unit in particular had been commissioned to seek out pockets of Resistance in the Fringe and drive them back toward the Core worlds where the Federation's powers-that-be could inflict due punishment. As part of this arrangement, the Durutians dispatched representatives to some of their neighboring Fringe worlds—Midore, Haphez, Cobi, Sardonis, even Chaiavis—every few months to scout for Resistance activity under the pretense of a friendly political visit.

That was the situation they found themselves in now. A Durutian patrol had recently gone missing, captured by Resistance fighters during a scouting mission, and Taran had volunteered himself and the other members of his Special Tasks Unit to track them down. But after a three-week wild goose chase around the Fringe, they'd had no luck. The Durutian government had deployed its representatives in hopes of gaining some extra intel, and they'd gotten reports from all but one. Last anyone had heard, Devani Reddic had landed at the Noro Spaceport on Haphez and was due to speak with the director of the Haphezian Special Police. The thought made Taran shudder. He'd had his own run-in with an HSP operative during a solo mission a couple years back, and the memory drew his attention to his cybernetic left arm, a replacement for the one that had been blown off by a high-caliber projectile sniper rifle. The Haphezians were ruthless, and if Devani was on their planet and unresponsive, well...the implications were unpleasant.

"I think we have our answer then, Mae," he sighed.

The woman tilted her head. "What do you mean?"

"The Delta Patrol was lost just outside the Noro system. Devani is on Haphez, and I know she'd respond if she could. This could be our hidden Resistance hub."

Mae strode forward and placed a warning hand on his arm. "Taran, we can't jump to conclusions here. We don't know the circumstances."

"Do you have a better explanation?"

She hesitated. "No, but think about it. Haphez has always been independent, just like us. I've heard they imprison or even kill any Res members found there, just to keep the Feds off their backs. Why would they be allied with the Resistance now, after all this time?"

He pulled out a nearby chair and slumped into it, bringing his elbows to rest on his knees. "The Resistance has always tried to recruit Haphezians to their cause. Haphez may not have any quarrel with the Feds, but I know damn well that those people want to avoid Federation control at any cost. Their military would be a huge asset to whichever side they're on—maybe the Res leaders finally managed to talk them into joining forces."

Mae said nothing, but the shock of red curls on her head bounced as she nodded. "We'll just keep trying," she murmured, moving to the back of the chair and placing her hands on Taran's shoulders. She began massaging, methodically working out the knots that had formed after several days of tension. "Like you said, the Haphezian military isn't to be trifled with. Wouldn't want to start a fight over nothing now, would we?"

He understood she was only being cautious, and her ability to remain levelheaded and think situations through never ceased to impress him. He reached up and placed one of his hands over hers, interlocking their fingers and pulling her down far enough that he could plant a light kiss on her cheek. She leaned over his shoulder and responded with one of her own, this one on his lips. He sighed when she finally pulled away, wishing he didn't have to return to reality.

"Let me see that dossier again."

Mae straightened and moved around to face him, hands resting on her slender hips. "You've looked at it a dozen times today. What good is it going to do to keep staring at it?"

"It helps me focus. Reminds me who the real enemy is."

"Fine," she sighed, moving back to the terminal she'd been working at. Her hands flew over the holographic controls until a series of profiles appeared on the terminal's viewscreen. The Feds had provided their group with all the information they had about the current leaders of the Resistance, hoping it could help them keep better tabs on any Res groups moving through the Fringe. But despite the Federation's superior size, the Resistance had always proved to be a formidable foe, foiling plans and detecting Fed spies before they could gather much useful information. The dossiers were helpful, but their details were vague, particularly those for the person presumed to be overseeing the entire Resistance. Taran watched the screen until Mae reached the final profile in the list. The sight of it made another lump form in his throat. This was the person responsible for the capture and, if Federation intel was any indication, most likely the *death* of the Durutian scout team. And, if Taran's gut was correct, this was the person indirectly responsible for the capture and…. He paused before his mind could go any farther—he didn't even want to think about what could be happening to Devani at this very moment.

He was almost relieved when the door of the room slid open, disrupting his train of thought. He stood and turned, squinting against the light and blast of hot air that rushed in from outside.

"Sergeant Reddic, Corporal Nasser," sputtered the young soldier who entered. Taran could see his silvery ocular implants adjusting to the room's dim lighting as he stopped dead in his tracks and gave them a rigid salute.

The time for formalities was so far gone that Taran found it odd to hear anyone address him by his title, much less salute him. The

Durutian army had spent so much time working for other organizations over the last several generations that formal military procedure had almost become a thing of the past. He'd grown accustomed—during the past few weeks, especially—to interacting with his soldiers on a more personal level, even going so far as to be on a first-name basis with most of them. Right now, they were all partners trying to get the job done so they could rescue their comrades and get paid. But apparently old-fashioned respect was still taught during training; many of the younger soldiers still clung to tradition. This man was a prime example.

Mae and Taran both offered half-hearted salutes in return and motioned for him to move inside and shut the door. "What's the problem, Cowen?" Mae asked, folding her arms across her chest.

"You said to report in if there was any suspicious activity at the port," the soldier replied. "Two of our people posing as port police inspected a ship that touched down just an hour ago. The internal computer shows the vessel is of Haphezian origin, though the exterior has undergone extensive modification. According to the flight logs, it was last docked on Niio. One of our recon teams reported possible Resistance activity on Niio, didn't they?"

"That's correct," Taran replied.

"What do we know about the passengers?" Mae said.

"They do appear to be Haphezian, ma'am," Cowen answered, swallowing hard and shooting a glance at Taran that seemed almost apologetic. "There were only two men, but our scouts at the port said they were heavily armed, and their cargo included an assortment of high-powered communications equipment." He swallowed again. "I know Representative Redd—well, your sister, sir. I know she's on Haphez right now. I figured you'd want to know about this."

Taran's mind raced, leaving him speechless. He directed his gaze toward the floor, trying to come up with all possible explanations for the arrival of the Haphezians. He knew Mae was right about jumping to conclusions, but anger, fear, and desperation were beginning to take root, and he couldn't help but feel his instincts were right.

"Thank you, Cowen," Mae said, snapping Taran out of his trance.

"We'll look into it." Her voice was quiet but carried a commanding tone that told the young soldier the conversation was over.

He bowed his head and rushed out, letting another wave of scorching air rush into the room. All was silent for several long seconds as both Taran and Mae contemplated the new developments.

Her sigh finally broke the silence. "Maybe you were right," she said. Her face was once again hardened by the focus and determination that made her one of the best soldiers the Durutian military had to offer. "Maybe this does answer our question. What do you think they want?"

"Good question," Taran muttered, grasping the back of the chair he'd been sitting in. "They could just be scouting out our squad. It's probably no secret we're here—three weeks is a long time to stay in one place. Or they could be probing. There could be an entire unit on its way here to wipe us out. Or...it could still be a simple coincidence."

"Orders?"

He shifted his gaze to meet hers. "We'll start by scouting right back. I want more information about these guys. Where's their base of operations? What kind of weapons are we dealing with? Who are they communicating with? I'd like to go down to the port and get a personal look at this ship they arrived in. I want them to know that *we* know they're here."

Mae nodded. "I'll call everyone home for a briefing."

Taran's eyes followed her as she moved back to the main console where the Resistance dossiers were still displayed. "The moment they do anything hostile, we'll retaliate in kind. Let their people lose contact with them the same way we've lost contact with Devani." He directed his attention to the dossier that remained on the screen, eyes fixed on the leader's name, the name that had been plaguing him since the disappearance of the Delta Patrol.

TAV RONAN.

"And if they can't lead us to Ronan, someone else will."

# · 10 ·
## DOCKS
### NIIO SPACEPORT

Ziva had never been a fan of Niio. The place was even more of a cesspit than downtown Noro and the entertainment districts on Chaiavis. Like Chaiavis, it served as a major transportation hub for the Fringe worlds on this side of the galaxy, but a person had come to the wrong place if they were looking for political asylum. There were no foreign embassies, no formal governing bodies. Who was in charge depended on which gang's territory you landed in. She made her way down the boarding ramp of the little HSP ship—called the *Zenith*, as she had discovered—with a distasteful eye on the surrounding docks. Niio's filth, crime, and debauchery weren't restricted to certain areas; they were prevalent across the entire moon. Carrying out a mission here meant being twice as cautious, keeping one eye on the target and one eye on the general surrounding environment. She'd had to set some would-be muggers straight on a couple of different occasions.

Even during the nighttime hours, the moon's sky remained a soft orange thanks to the gas giant it orbited. The planet itself was Niio—the little moon had no formal name and had come to be known simply as Niio Spaceport due to the transportation center it boasted. But if you said you were going to Niio, chances were you meant the moon, and chances were you weren't planning on staying long. For every person who landed at the port, someone else left. Not many people had the misfortune of calling the place their permanent residence.

Ziva turned her attention back to the *Zenith's* boarding ramp as it shut, confident the ship's security system would deter any potential thieves and alert her if there was trouble. She carried only a backpack, not planning on staying long enough to need any additional supplies. Skirting around a small shuttle delivering cargo to a nearby dock, she angled toward the public transportation terminal, one of the only respectable areas she'd ever come across while visiting the moon. She scanned the docking pass HSP had provided and marveled for a moment at the impressive flight log they'd fabricated for her ship. As far as Port Control knew, the *Zenith* was part of a small courier fleet for a company based on Aubin—good, considering she was familiar with the desert planet after spending numerous independent service terms working there.

She continued walking and found herself on the main concourse, lost in the sea of travelers ranging anywhere from jaded smugglers to wanna-be pirates to nervous civilians. A massive locker room lay down the corridor to her right, so she slipped inside and began navigating through the rows upon rows of secure storage lockers. It took a good three minutes to find the one she sought, a medium-sized space just outside the nearest security cam's field of view. She glanced around and, seeing no one, pressed her thumb to the print pad and lowered her eye to the optical scanner.

The locking mechanism released and the locker door swung open, revealing a deep space occupied by several large stacks of credits, two pistols, a pair of spare plasma cells, and a temporary false identity that would at least allow her to make it off the moon in an emergency. Skeet and Zinni had similar lockers somewhere in the room, though she had no idea where they were or what specifically they contained. HSP required its operatives to keep an emergency cache somewhere in the galaxy, but these here on Niio had been mandated by Ziva herself. She had other stashes elsewhere, and she suspected her teammates did, too.

Taking another look around, she slid her backpack from her shoulders and removed another pistol, submachine gun, disassembled rifle, and a variety of grenades that had once belonged in her home's weapons cache. She had every intention of restocking that closet, but in the event that she did end up leaving the agency, she preferred to have ready access to her supplies from wherever she was in the galaxy.

Just to be on the safe side, she took one of the stacks of credits and dumped it into the depleted backpack before shutting the locker door and sealing it with another thumbprint and retina scan. Finding people, particularly people who were just as good at disappearing as she was, often meant relying on outside resources. And those resources never came cheap.

She made her way out of the locker room and back out to the docks, sweeping her gaze around until it settled on a burly human man about her height who stood and watched as several containers were unloaded from a nearby ship. The tattoo visible above the collar of his jacket told her he was someone who could help. She made a show of advancing toward him, successfully attracting his attention. He kept a wary eye on her as she approached, patting the telltale bulge under his jacket that could only be a concealed sidearm. She opened her own jacket in response, allowing him to catch a glimpse of the pistol that dangled in her shoulder holster, and continued toward him without breaking stride.

The man stiffened as she drew nearer, clearly unnerved by her display of audacity, and plucked his communicator from his belt. He began speaking in hushed tones, and with all the surrounding noise, it was impossible for her to hear the specifics of the conversation.

"That's right," she called in Standard, keeping her arms at her sides but her palms open where he could see them. "Call your boss. Tell him I need to talk to him."

She stood motionless until he finished talking, maintaining a distance of a couple of meters. The man kept his eyes glued to her as he spoke, scrutinizing every inch of her, assessing the threat level she posed. He ended his transmission with an unimpressed grunt and turned, motioning for her to follow. "This way."

The two of them made their way through the crowd to the far side of the platform, where another man similar in appearance waited beside an idling aircar. Ziva sensed movement in her peripherals and found two more men who had moved from the shadows to flank her. The one she'd approached opened the door and waved her into the back seat before he and the pilot climbed into the front.

She sighed and settled in as the car lifted from the platform and glided out of the port, soaring high above the tops of the towering buildings. Like Chaiavis, many of Niio's structures were built upward due to the fact that most of the moon's habitable space was already occupied. The layout of the city was random at best; a person always had to be on the lookout for cables, bridges, and the odd landing pad protruding from the side of a building. The thug piloting the car clearly knew how to handle the vehicle and maneuver through the surrounding airspace, as did the majority of these world-weary types who called Niio home.

The aircar angled down into a sharp dive, making Ziva tighten her grip on her safety harness. They swooped down to a darkened street and came to an abrupt stop in front of an old restaurant that appeared to be the only occupied establishment on the block. There were several other vehicles parked outside, and a variety of well-muscled men in dark clothing loitered in the shadows around the entrance.

The car's back door slid open and the man in the passenger seat turned his head, shooting her a glare out of the corner of his eye. "You know the drill."

Ziva eased out of the car and strode toward the building without so much as a look back, once again keeping her arms relaxed but her hands visible. The door opened before she even reached it—someone had obviously gotten the memo that she'd arrived—and warm air drifted out, countering the chill of the dark street. She stepped inside and took a look around, not the least bit surprised to find that nothing had changed since her last visit. The walls were dark, covered by a layer of what was no doubt synthetic wood paneling, and the lights were dim. But she'd always thought the place had a sort of unorthodox charm, with the catchy music, the smell of homemade food, and the quiet murmur of voices. Under different circumstances, it might have been a place she'd go to relax.

The sudden silence her presence triggered was a harsh reminder that this was no time to be thinking of such things. All eyes in the restaurant fell on her, then shifted to the massive man who approached from the back of the establishment. She knew him only as Cole, and quite frankly, she didn't care if it was his first name or last name. He bore a striking resemblance to Diago Dasaro, easily ten centimeters taller than her and *emilan*...or whatever the humans called it. Like all the other men, he also bore a detailed tattoo on the right side of his neck, marking him as not only a member of the group but as someone of high status within it. She had to give him credit—his stature and temperament made him an excellent enforcer.

Cole let out a coarse laugh and clapped his hands as he drew nearer. "Look what we have here!" he said, shaking his head. "Miss me, baby?"

"Cole," Ziva muttered, relinquishing her backpack to a man who had come up behind her. She spread her arms and Cole removed her concealed pistol, handing it off to the man who held her backpack before patting her down for further weapons and bugs—a process he enjoyed far too much for her taste.

"You'll lose a hand if you're not careful," she warned.

He offered a sly grin as he stepped back and looked her up and down, satisfied in more ways than one. "Let's not get harsh, now."

"*Go froucht tsuse.*"

He only looked perplexed for a split second before laughing again. "Don't let me keep you," he said, waving her toward the back of the building. "Tobias is waiting."

Ziva made her way toward the far corner of the restaurant with the thugs hot on her heels. She found the large table exactly as she remembered it, surrounded by several sofas upon which three men were lounging. Two of them promptly vacated their places, and the third motioned for her to take a seat as he sipped at the drink he held.

"Tobias," she greeted, settling into place on the sofa across from him and dismissing the waitress who offered her a tray of food.

Tobias Niio—no doubt some distant relation to the family who'd first discovered the gas planet and colonized the moon—set his glass down on the table and smiled, studying her through squinting eyes. "Ziva Payvan. Please, make yourself comfortable. Cole, return our guest's weapon. I trust she's smart enough to not use it here."

A challenge. A warning. Ziva nodded and took her pistol from

Cole's outstretched hand, sliding it back into its holster.

"I must admit I was shocked when my man contacted me and told me you were at the port. What a surprise to see you here again. To what do I owe the pleasure of this visit?"

The man had never struck her as mob boss material. He was short and stocky, only about Zinni's height, with a balding head and an odd, square jaw. He wore a pair of ancient spectacles that were probably just a fashion statement considering all the modern technological options for correcting poor vision. They were no doubt a collector's item that had cost him a small fortune. Ziva guessed it was just one of many ways for him to showcase his dominance. Despite his docile outward demeanor, Tobias was not to be trifled with. Even the other gangs who roamed Niio's streets kept their distance or pledged their full loyalty. Everyone on the Fringe knew better than to cross the Niiosian Mob.

"I'm looking for someone," she said, "and I think you can help me."

"Looking for someone," he echoed. "I thought finding people was what you did for a living, Agent Payvan. Where's your team? Why not ask them for help?"

"That's who I'm looking for," Ziva answered, bristling a bit in response to the emphasis he'd put on the word 'agent.' Tobias knew that she, Skeet, and Zinni were HSP, but that was as far as it went. Still, he'd always liked to call them by some sort of title, usually in a tone that alluded to the fact that he knew some secret about them. He didn't, of course, and he knew that *they* knew that, but it was unnerving all the same. It was no doubt one more way for him to demonstrate that he had absolute control over any given situation.

"They arrived here a little over four weeks ago," she continued. "Two of them left two or three days ago aboard a modified H-15 *Infiltrator*-class runner. I need to know where they went."

"Ah, yes. I thought I recognized one of your men at the docks. That orange hair is hard to forget." He chuckled. "Why should I be able to tell you where that ship went?"

"Because I know you keep track of every vessel that comes and goes from this port," she responded, deadpan, "regardless of its affiliation."

"Of course, of course," Tobias laughed, reaching for his glass and taking another drink. "I'm afraid you know me too well. But tell me, assuming I did know how to find your lost ship, what would I get in return? What are you offering me?"

Ziva threw a glance at the man holding her backpack. He appeared puzzled for a moment but opened the bag with a cautious hand, revealing the credits inside.

"Fifty grand," she said.

That prompted a bout of hearty laughter from the men surrounding her. She sat motionless with folded arms, forcing her facial expression to remain unchanged.

"I'm not entirely sure whether to be amused or offended, Agent Payvan," Tobias said, mimicking her posture and countenance. "Do you really think a man like me could be swayed so easily by petty cash?"

"No," she answered without hesitation. "That's why I'd like to offer you my services as well. I have what you might call a...*unique* skill set."

"You're a killer," Tobias said before she could elaborate further. "News travelled fast when you were on the run after Ikaro Tachi's assassination. Special operations, is it?"

Ziva tried not to grimace. This was exactly the problem she'd been mulling over at the rehab center. Half the galaxy probably knew who she was by now, knew who she worked for, could pick her face out of a crowd. It would make functioning as a covert operative rather tricky.

"I never did peg you for an ordinary field agent. The way you carry yourself, the apathy in your eyes...dangerous people recognize these things in other dangerous people." Tobias stopped and watched her for a moment, then laughed again. "And don't worry—I know your precious organization doesn't like to talk much about who or what the special operations division consists of. I like you, Agent Payvan, and I have no reason to reveal your secret. Unless you give me one, of course."

Another subtle warning. Ziva smirked. "Wouldn't dream of it."

"Excellent. Now, let me see if I have this straight. You want to offer me your services—"

This time, it was her turn to cut him off. "I will carry out a hit for you. Maybe you want to maintain a low profile, don't want anyone to know you sanctioned it. Or maybe you don't trust any of your apes here to get the job done." She paused and took a look around, reveling in the looks of contempt all the thugs gave her. "You name the time and place, and I'll be there—within reason, of course. I'm a busy woman, you know."

Tobias had yet to stop smiling, but it was a cold, forced smile that told her he was silently weighing the benefits and potential consequences of her offer. "All right, Agent Payvan, I think you've got yourself a deal. And you know what? Go ahead and keep your money. The prospect of having an HSP agent in my pocket, even temporarily, is rather irresistible."

Ziva remained silent, refraining from specifying that she most likely wouldn't be employed by HSP anymore by the time she paid her debt, but she decided he didn't need to know that. The thought of owing anyone anything was almost unbearable, but at the moment, striking a deal like this seemed like the most efficient way to move forward. The galaxy only knew what kind of trouble Skeet and Aroska had gotten themselves into, and if Zinni had already been gone for four weeks, well...time was of the essence.

"So. Tell me what you'd like to know about your friends."

She gave him a quick rundown of the situation, describing the data they'd obtained from Kat but keeping the details to a minimum. The Alpha team had come to Niio to investigate a warehouse similar to the one Kat found on Chaiavis, and while there, Zinni had been taken. Skeet and Aroska had set up a temporary headquarters on the moon as they'd searched for clues, but they'd gone dark two days earlier when the agency implemented Condition Black. As she spoke, she studied Tobias's face and saw, to her surprise, what appeared to be genuine interest.

"Yes, we heard about that incident at your base," he said. His furrowed brow spawned a series of lines that crisscrossed all the way up his forehead. "Very unfortunate, indeed."

"You wouldn't happen to know who was behind it."

"I'm afraid not, but I think I have some information that might interest you." He snapped his fingers and held out his hand, receiving a data pad from one of the men standing nearby.

"Your team arrived a little over four weeks ago, just like you said. And, like you said, I know about everything that goes on in my city. They settled into one of the flophouses near the docks and ventured into the warehouse district after a couple of days. Then these interesting individuals showed up just a few hours after your friends."

Ziva took the data pad when he offered it and examined the photos on the display. They were stills taken from various surveillance feeds around the port, all depicting the same armor-clad figures. Their faces were all obscured by helmets, but everything about their outward appearance was identical, telling her they were from some sort of organized group.

"Who are they?" she asked, sliding the data pad back across the table.

"Couldn't tell you," Tobias said with a disappointed wag of his head. "And normally I wouldn't give a sewer rat's ass who they were, but they killed three of my men. They left in a real hurry after they took your friend. But see here?" He leaned forward and pushed the data pad back toward her, zooming in on one of the photos. "That armor is Durutian. I've had a few of them in my ranks before, even hired a couple as hitmen, so I'd recognize it anywhere."

The wheels spun in Ziva's head as she stared at the photo again. It was obvious that these were Ronan's soldiers, but with so little information regarding what Ronan even was, that still didn't really answer the question of who they were. The vast majority of Durutians were mercenaries, hiring themselves out to fight, kill, and sometimes just do odd work for whoever was willing to pay. Hailing from a barren, rocky planet, their primary export was their own people, or, more accurately, whatever specialized service each person provided. It made sense that they'd be working for or with Ronan if the mysterious entity was as powerful as it seemed to be.

"And my team?" she finally said.

"After your agent was captured, they came and went from the port several times—they were no doubt out searching nearby systems for her. Like you guessed, they packed up and hauled out of here a couple of days ago. Don't know if they found a new lead or just thought it was time to move on. According to my man at Port Control, they set an FTL course for the southwest quadrant, the same direction those Durutians went four weeks ago."

"There's not much out there," Ziva mused.

Tobias produced a second data pad and manipulated it for a moment, comparing a map of the nearby Fringe Space to the route the *Intrepid* had supposedly taken. "Charted settlements include Bectin, Plaunus, and Aubin. I've heard Aubin has a respectable little spaceport these days."

Ziva nodded. Skeet would be just as familiar with Aubin as she was thanks to all their independent service terms. If they'd been headed that direction, they'd most likely stopped there to regroup and look for signs of Ronan's ship, just as they'd done here on Niio. And even if they weren't there, that's what she planned on doing.

She stood up, drawing tense reactions from Tobias's thugs. "Well then, I suppose I should be on my way."

Tobias gave her another ominous smile. "A pleasure doing business with you, as always. For what it's worth, I hope you find your friend, Little Blue. I always liked her. So feisty."

"Shall I save a slice of Ronan for you when we find it?"

"Oh, would you?" A sparkle of delight danced in his eyes, but it was immediately replaced by some cold quality that could only be what made him the most dangerous man on this side of the Fringe. He grinned. "Anyone who spills my family's blood will pay dearly for it. Be sure to give me a call when it's time."

"I will."

"In the meantime, there's a car waiting outside to take you back to the port. And regarding your offer—I'll be in touch."

# · 11 ·
# RESIDENTIAL SECTOR
## ZYLKA, AUBIN

Aroska brushed the tattered curtain aside just far enough to see out the window. As usual, Aubin's scorching afternoon sun beat down on the city's clay and brick structures, giving everything a distinct yellow glow that always made him squint after being accustomed to the dim lighting indoors. He almost wished the city could have been built in one of the jungles on the other side of the planet, but so much of the flora was toxic that living there was nearly impossible. Besides, he was pretty sure he preferred this dry heat and direct sunlight—however intense—to the heavy humidity of the jungle.

His eyes flitted about, taking in every person and creature moving through the dusty streets below. He still hadn't grown accustomed to the faint rippling effect produced by the force field above them; he kept seeing it out of the corner of his eye and being startled by the unidentified movement. Even now, the undulating shadows made it seem like there were extra people moving around, and his mind had to work twice as hard to process what was real and what was simply a product of the force field.

They'd been there a total of two days after the two-day journey from Niio. Their first priority had been to investigate the reports they'd received from the science team on Bectin, but by the time they'd arrived, Ronan's ship and Zinni had been long gone. It was Skeet who had suggested they set up a new base there on Aubin, hoping a change of scenery might help. Thus far, they'd found no signs of their original quarry, but it seemed they'd still found something—or more accurately, *someone*—of interest, and that same someone had also managed to find *them*.

"Damn it," Aroska muttered as his gaze finally fell upon a dark figure lingering in the entryway of the building diagonal from them.

"Still out there?" Skeet asked from his place at the tiny dining table across the room. He sat motionless, staring at their collection of portable computer equipment with a deep crease cutting across his forehead.

Aroska grunted an affirmative. "Just the one guy, but I'm sure there are more."

What unnerved him the most was that there was no way to tell *how many* more. These soldiers—some men, some women—had begun to appear almost immediately after the *Intrepid* landed two days earlier. Some were dressed in what appeared to be mismatched uniform attire, and some wore the same armor as the men they'd spotted roaming the spaceport on Niio. But unlike the figures from the spaceport, none of these people had their faces covered by helmets. Based on the eerie silvery color of all their eyes and the various implants protruding from their faces and heads, they were Durutians. While technically human, the race had been known to make use of extensive cybernetic modifications that gave its members many of the same abilities Haphezians possessed naturally. Despite no longer having a formal military or organized fleet, the Durutians were still a force to be reckoned with and were the only civilization the Haphezians had ever come close to considering 'equal.'

"You really think these guys are working for Ronan?" he said. He'd meant to keep the thought to himself, but the words escaped his mouth before he could stop them.

"Would I put it past them?" Skeet replied. "No, I wouldn't. Whatever Ronan is, there are chemicals and scientific research involved, which means there's probably a lot of money in it. Do I know for sure if these people are working for Ronan? Again, no. That's something we need to find out, but right now, we can't exactly go waltzing out into the street."

He was right. The Durutians had been on their tail since they'd arrived. They'd settled into a small hotel initially so as not to compromise the apartment Skeet and the rest of the team had always used during their independent service terms. They'd already packed up and moved once after discovering they were being followed; now they were holed up in a different lodge, and it seemed Durutian scouts had found them once again. Aroska couldn't imagine that the cyborgs were actually that good at finding people. They probably had spies and contacts throughout the city. According to one of Skeet's local sources, they'd been there for about three weeks, long enough to establish themselves. This could very well be the group that had taken Zinni.

"You think that apartment complex down the street is their main base of operations?" Skeet asked, still staring absentmindedly at the computer.

"They certainly seem to be most concentrated in that area," Aroska answered, eyes still glued to the man outside. The Durutians weren't the only ones who had been doing some recon. He had spent much of the previous afternoon studying the little compound the 'borgs were calling home. He'd watched them interact with one another and made note of any changes in shifts. There were at least fifteen of them, probably a few more considering some of them were out patrolling the city at all times. Either way, he and Skeet were severely outnumbered, and they'd been forced to keep their distance, not wanting to risk one or both of them getting caught.

As he stood there watching, his mind once again drifted to Ziva, something it hadn't stopped doing since they'd received news of the attack on Na four days earlier. After a bit of calculating, he realized it had happened right around the time of—if not the *day* of—her hearing. Assuming she was still alive, and assuming the attack hadn't stalled the trial, he wondered what the verdict had been. He'd volunteered to testify in her favor, but the Royal House wouldn't have it, saying he'd be too biased. When Kyron Hoxie had shown up at Headquarters and offered to tell his side of the story, Aroska hadn't known what to think. The former captain's testimony could help solidify the idea that Dasaro was dirty, but it could also reinforce the fact that Ziva had killed Nejdra in cold blood. There was no way of knowing how the magistrates would respond to that.

In the event that the trial had ended positively and she'd avoided the attack, he wondered where she was and what she was doing at this very moment. Surely she'd gone to the director and learned of their predicament. He again found himself dreading the confrontation that would ensue the next time they encountered one another. All of this was his fault, after all; if he'd left Kat's data pad and syringe in the strongbox, the team would never have gone to Niio and Zinni would never have been captured.

He scoffed and shook his head. *And Ronan would still be running rampant somewhere out in the galaxy. At least now we're closing in on some answers.*

He finally turned away from the window, not terribly concerned about what the Durutian scout was doing. So far, the 'borgs had done nothing but sneak around and spy, no doubt reporting everything they saw to someone higher up in the chain of command. They didn't seem to be trying very hard to keep their presence a secret—it was almost as if they wanted him and Skeet to see them, hoping a glimpse of their superior firepower would deter them from approaching the base. He had a hunch they might be holding Zinni there. Even though there was no sign of the ship that had taken her, this could easily be some sort of drop site.

"I think we should go in tonight," he said. "Maybe see if we can get a little closer under the cover of darkness."

The room was silent for several seconds before Skeet made any move to respond. "Fine," he sighed, running a hand through his hair. "We can't stay cooped up in here forever."

Operating under Condition Black was disconcerting at a time like this. Even if they *could* call in support, it would take at least four days for any backup to reach Aubin. Going in alone was the only way they were ever going to get any answers, but it was also the most dangerous option. With the Durutians scrutinizing them so carefully, the chances of them getting captured or killed were through the roof, and it would take the galaxy only knew how long for anyone to notice their disappearance. Aroska sighed and reminded himself that this was the reality of special ops.

"This will still be strictly recon," Skeet continued, rising and moving to the window to get a look for himself. "There's nothing I want more than to take these guys down, but there's no sense in getting ourselves blown away if we can help it." The bright light from outside reflected off his orange eyes, giving them an even more fiery quality than usual. Aroska could tell that he too was considering the consequences of going through with this mission but also knew this was the only way to save Zinni...assuming she was still alive.

"We have those jet suits in the ship," he put in. "We could fly over and use infrared to get a bird's eye view of the compound. It'd be stealthier than a larger vehicle."

"With the way these guys are watching us, there'd be no way to get the suits back here from the port without being seen," Skeet said, shaking his head as he stared at the man outside. "We could wait until dark, but by then we won't be able to afford to waste the extra time. Every minute will count. We go in on foot."

The next several hours were spent pacing around the tiny hotel room, reviewing the notes they'd compiled on the Durutian compound, and drawing up a plan for approach. Skeet had studied their nighttime arrangements the previous evening as Aroska moved all their supplies from one hideout to the other. Unlike during the daytime hours, all their soldiers remained in the apartment complex at night, though there were at least three of them standing watch at all times. Assuming their patrol patterns remained the same—which was likely if the group had indeed been on the planet for an extended period—it would be possible for the two of them to get close enough to see in through a few windows. After a bit of reluctant consideration, it was decided that they would split up, enabling one of them to theoretically escape should the other be captured. They would be armed, but lethal force was only to be used in the direst of circumstances.

The two of them set out two hours after nightfall; with Zylka's long days and short nights, there wasn't a moment to lose. They left their room illuminated so it might appear occupied to anyone lurking in the street. If their previous observations were any indication, none of the Durutians should be spying at this hour, but they treaded carefully regardless, not wishing to take any chances. They went their separate ways the moment they hit the street, with Skeet circling around toward the far side of the apartment complex and Aroska heading down the street toward the observation post he'd used the day before.

"Comm check."

Aroska reached up to touch his earpiece. "I hear you."

"Let me know when you're in position."

He turned down the first side street he came to, opting to approach his post from the rear. There weren't many people out at this time of night, making it easier for him to spot any suspicious activity but also for anyone suspicious to spot him. He checked all reflective surfaces he passed and paused periodically in the entryways of any shops that were still open, studying his surroundings and searching for anything that had changed since he passed. Nothing seemed out of the ordinary, and somehow that unnerved him.

Sighing, he ducked down the next alley he found and wove back and forth between buildings for several minutes, keeping his eyes and ears open. It wasn't long before he reached a rusty set of steps he recognized from the previous day. He ascended on light feet, wincing as the metal nevertheless squealed under his weight. The stairs took him to a small landing area on the roof of the building, a loading zone for the business below. He jogged across to the far side, stepping onto the lift that lowered cargo into the store. With a small roof over his head and a protective railing on three sides, he was well concealed and invisible to anyone passing by in the street. The buildings across the way were shorter, giving him a nearly unobstructed view of the apartment complex where the Durutians were holed up.

Skeet's voice crackled in his ear. "All set. Where are you?"

"Just got settled in," Aroska replied. He lifted his spotting scope to his eye and zoomed in on the Durutians' compound, sweeping the area with the scope's night optics. As far as he'd been able to tell during his previous investigating, the entire complex was occupied by their group. There were three buildings, each with five units, situated in a

U-shape around a dusty courtyard. A small landing pad lay on the far side, closing off the circle.

From his vantage point, he could see one of the sentries pacing back and forth along the front of Building Three. A second man stood on the landing pad among the various groundcars parked there. Several of the apartments had lights on, but the courtyard was dark. Still, with cybernetics embedded in their eyes that could automatically adjust to a variety of lighting levels and color spectrums, Aroska imagined the sentries could see their surroundings perfectly. Haphezians could see well in the dark, but night optics still helped. *All* the Durutians had those optical implants, giving their eyes that eerie metallic quality and allowing them to operate in the dark better than any other civilized race.

"I've got two of the sentries," Aroska said, "one in the landing area and one in front of the easternmost building."

"I see the one on the landing pad," Skeet replied after several seconds. "There's another circling Building One."

"You said it looked like they only use three sentries at any given time, right?"

"As far as I could tell last night. You move up and see what you can learn about Building Two. I'll circle around and see if there's anything interesting on the back side of Building Three."

"Got it." Aroska remained in his place for another couple of minutes, watching for variations in the movements of the two visible sentries. Seeing none, he crossed back over to the stairs and made his way down into the alley, slinking along the exterior wall of the building until he reached the front. He paused in the shadows and swept his gaze back and forth, looking for any new details the lower vantage point presented. He'd be totally exposed as he crossed the street, and he sincerely hoped all the Durutians were in the compound and that he and Skeet hadn't missed something. He pictured himself being picked off by a sniper hidden on one of the nearby rooftops, or, if not picked off, at least spotted. To his relief, he made it across unscathed. It didn't guarantee he was in the clear, but it was a start.

With only two buildings between him and the outer edge of the apartment complex, he moved more carefully than ever. He shifted his attention between what was ahead of him and what was below him, watching for security devices, traps, and anything that might make excess noise if stepped on. There were no unusual sounds or smells, though various noises could still be heard in the direction of the busier part of town near the spaceport. Usually, he was glad to have such exceptional senses, as it allowed him to move undetected while *he* detected the enemy. But the Durutians were no ordinary enemy—with their cybernetics, they had just as good a chance of hearing him as he did of hearing them.

Another minute of creeping brought him within sight of Building Two. He crouched down behind the cooling unit of the nearest house, watching for movement with bated breath. All the building's units were dark except the one in the center, and based on the bluish-green hue of the light pouring from the window, whatever illuminated the space was electronic. He wound up the muscles in his legs, ready to close the distance between himself and the window, but the sound of shuffling feet stopped him dead in his tracks.

His hand settled on his holster, but he refrained from drawing his weapon just yet. The sound had come from his right, farther down the alley and away from the compound. He rose and moved across to the adjacent house, risking a peek around the corner. The fact that the area was clear brought him little comfort.

Preoccupied by the unexplained noises, it took him a moment to catch the whiff of body odor—likely human—somewhere behind him. The sound of hurried footsteps and the hum of a stun baton reached his ears just as he drew his pistol and began to turn.

"You'll want to drop that," a female voice said as something was jabbed into the small of his back.

Aroska straightened and started to whirl, but a sudden electric current shot through his body, turning his legs to liquid. He collapsed to his knees with a groan and held up his hands, watching as two armed men appeared from the direction of the noise he'd originally heard. One of them relieved him of the pistol while the other searched him for further weapons.

"We've got one of them," said the woman behind him as she reached around and tore out his earpiece, keeping the stun baton pressed into his back as she did so. "The hotel room is empty. The other one is around here somewhere."

She hit him with the baton once again and he fell forward onto his stomach, his nerves on fire. The two men in front of him were hardly more than shadows as they reached down, picked him up by the arms, and began to drag him toward the apartment complex. The soft silver glow of their eyes seemed to linger in his vision even as his mind began to go blank.

## · 12 ·
## APARTMENT COMPLEX
### ZYLKA, AUBIN

"Who are they?"

"I don't know. They're not talking."

The whole compound had come alive the moment the Haphezian spies were apprehended. They'd been spotted leaving their hotel by one of the locals Taran had commissioned as an informant, and thus he had ordered the formation of two extra three-man teams to covertly patrol the perimeter of the complex. Both Haphezian agents had gotten closer than he'd anticipated, but in the end, numbers had not been on their side.

He'd had every intention of killing them outright if they ever came near the apartments, but he'd ordered that they be taken alive when it became apparent they were only performing reconnaissance. He was already running low on patience and doubted either of the men would talk, but the prospect of potentially gaining some new intel on Ronan had left him feeling merciful...at least temporarily.

"Did you hear back from your squad at the hotel?"

Mae nodded. "These guys are HSP—that's all we know. All that communications equipment they brought was present in the room, but it was powered down and the call logs were empty. Chances are they erased them before they left tonight. They were in possession of data regarding Ronan, but it's all encrypted. It might take a couple of days to break into it."

Taran sighed and rubbed his eyes. He had, by some miracle,

actually been asleep when they'd received news of the Haphezians' movements. Mae stood as alert and ready as ever with her red curls bundled into a thick ponytail. She'd personally been responsible for the capture of one of the agents, the tall yellow one. He'd been ready to put up a fight but was luckily no match for a good old-fashioned stun baton. The big orange one had managed to take a swing but had still gone down after a couple of hits from a baton. In all honesty, Taran was glad. Both men were at least a head taller than any of his soldiers and could no doubt best all of them in hand-to-hand combat. They were currently being kept in separate apartments, thoroughly restrained and neutralized by a chemical that paralyzed their limbs but left them awake and coherent.

"I want to see them," he sighed. "Let's have them moved into the same room."

Mae shrugged and led him to the door, relaying orders to the current guards via comm. They crossed the courtyard, which was now fully illuminated and bustling with nervous members of their squad, and came to a stop in front of Building Three. The door to one of the units opened and two of their men appeared, dragging Yellow along with his legs scraping on the ground behind him. Taran followed them into the room and watched as they seated him in a fresh chair beside his partner.

Both men were slumped awkwardly in their seats, unable to support themselves with their arms or legs, but they watched him with intent stares as he took up a stance in front of them and crossed his arms. Orange had a split lip thanks to the brief struggle he'd put up before falling captive, but his hardened features told Taran he barely noticed it. The man's fiery hair stuck out in all directions, and he had at least four piercings in each ear plus another in one nostril. He certainly didn't *look* like an operator, but the cold focus in his eyes gave Taran the impression this was not the first time he'd been captured and interrogated...and that he was indifferent about it.

He shifted his attention to Yellow. This man also demonstrated a cool collectedness that could only be a product of thorough training. But rather than stare straight ahead, he put his eyes to work, taking in every detail of every face and object in the room. This was a man who could take one look at his environment and remember everything he'd seen. Both of these agents were operatives—Taran could tell that much just by looking at them—but they were very different types. If his theory was correct about them being in league with the Resistance, he wondered what Ronan had hoped to accomplish by sending them here.

He considered kneeling but decided he'd rather not have them looking down on him. "I don't suppose either of you wants to just tell me who you are and who you're working for."

As expected, there was no response. Both men were watching him now, and unless he was mistaken, they almost looked amused that he would even say such a thing. In all reality, there wasn't much point in questioning them. These were people who would readily choose death over betraying their comrades, so part of him considered just executing them now and saving himself some time. Even if they did end up giving him useful information, he still had every intention of killing them outright. How had he put it? *Let their people lose contact with them the same way we've lost contact with Devani.*

"They're cowards, Taran," Mae said behind him. Her tone told him the words were directed more toward the Haphezians than him.

Once again, neither man had any visible reaction to the jab, but Taran couldn't help but notice the way Yellow's attention shifted to Mae as she spoke. He watched her through slightly narrowed eyes, no doubt unhappy that she'd managed to best him in the alley.

"*Shouka*," he muttered.

It took a second for the translator in Taran's cochlear implant to do its work, and when it did, he was unable to stop himself from stepping forward and laying a hard left hook across the man's jaw. "Bastard!" he shouted, their faces centimeters apart. "Who do you work for?"

Mae's hands closed around his arms in an instant, pulling him to the door. "That's not going to help," she said, her voice firm. One of the soldiers stepped aside and opened the door, and the two of them stumbled out into the courtyard.

"I know, I know, and I'm sorry." Taran crouched down, biting his lower lip to keep from shouting, and stared into the dirt. "I'm sorry," he whispered again, "but they have Devani. We have to stop them. We have to stop *Ronan*."

"I know we do," Mae said, squatting down in front of him and touching her forehead to his. She placed her hands on either side of his head and tilted it upward, forcing him to look her in the eye. "But like you said, if these men can't lead us to Ronan, someone else will. Maybe it's time to start fresh."

The anger welling up inside him finally began to overtake the weariness and fear. Taran stood up, staring at the apartment door for a moment before turning his attention to the sky and the air around him. A warm wind blew across the desert from the east; there was an ominous quality about it, and his implants told him the air pressure had increased. A storm was coming.

*Let their people lose contact with them.* "What's the weather forecast for today?" he asked, lost in thought.

Mae consulted her wrist-mounted data unit. "Satellites are tracking the formation of a sandstorm about two hundred klicks out," she announced, eyebrows furrowed. "Based on predicted wind currents, it's supposed to shift this way. It's expected to reach the city by zero seven hundred."

Taran gave her a terse nod of approval and checked the time. Beckoning for her to follow, he went back to the apartment door and moved inside, pleased by the sight of the split skin and trickle of blood his metal arm had left on Yellow's cheek. "Give them two more hours," he said, glancing to each of his men in turn before focusing on the Haphezians. "If they haven't given us anything by then, take them out to the desert and execute them. The sand will bury their bodies—there's no sense in making a mess here."

He couldn't be sure, but he thought he saw flickers of fear flash through the agents' eyes. They had every right to be afraid. Even if they weren't sedated, they were still alone and outnumbered; trying to fight back would be futile and would only expedite their deaths.

They had no way to call for help, and even if they did, it wouldn't get there in time.

Taran turned, satisfied by their reactions, and faced Mae. She said nothing, but the look on her face told him she was glad he'd decided to take action. "You're right. Maybe we need to start fresh." Setting a timer on his wrist unit, he gave the Haphezian agents one more once-over before striding from the room. "Your time starts now."

# · 13 ·
# City Center
## Zylka, Aubin

It was the wee hours of the morning by the time the *Zenith* touched down in Zylka. Ziva opted to avoid the spaceport entirely and brought the little ship to rest on the landing pad behind the team's apartment. There didn't seem to be any sign of the *Intrepid*. Part of her worried that Skeet and Aroska hadn't come here after all, in which case she had no idea where they were. Or maybe they were just out on a scouting run like the ones Tobias had mentioned.

The apartment was dark when she entered, and as the lighting panels slowly powered up, she was surprised to find everything exactly as they'd left it the last time they'd been there. A fine layer of dust had settled over the furniture, as was the norm when no one had set foot in the place for several months.

She sighed and returned to the ship to gather some things before settling in. The sky was just starting to turn gray on the horizon—it would be dawn in less than an hour. At its high latitude, Zylka only saw between five and six hours of darkness at this time of year, and with no mountains or forests to block out the sun, the scorching days seemed extra long. She wasn't sure if she wanted to know what the climate was like closer to the equator.

The force field above her was invisible in the darkness, but it was always there, activated even when the sun's rays weren't beating down on the city. Passing through it to enter the city reminded her of entering a planet's atmosphere, but on a smaller scale. Any space-worthy ships with proper heat shielding could come through unscathed, but smaller vessels and vehicles were forced to use one of several portals on the outskirts of town.

Ziva picked up her backpack—the credits still sat heavy in the bottom of it—and filled it with a variety of weaponry nearly identical to the stash she'd left in her locker on Niio. Feeling almost giddy, she opened one of the other storage containers and removed the long case that housed her favorite projectile rifle. It sat disassembled at the moment, encased in protective gel. She'd developed the custom design close to three years earlier; it included various parts she could mix and match, enabling her to switch back and forth between common projectiles and her signature superheated bariine rounds. This was the first time she'd had this particular gun in the field since…well, since before Dakiti, and the idea of getting to wield her baby again after dealing with that *sheyssen* Korberon rifle she'd acquired on Chaiavis was refreshing. She ran her fingers over the stock and down the barrel, then drew in a sharp breath and paused.

This was the gun she'd killed Soren Tarbic with.

A quiet growl escaped her throat, and she slammed the case shut. There was work to be done. She slung her backpack over one shoulder and the rifle case over the other and exited the ship once more, ensuring it was properly secured. Rather than take the stairs up to the apartment, she moved instead toward the garage door below. She was pleasantly surprised to find the groundcar the team had invested in during their last service term still parked there. They'd lost the last one to thieves, one of the drawbacks of having to leave the apartment unattended for the majority of the year. She placed the rifle and backpack in the car's cargo space and found their collection of goggles and head wraps that protected them from the sun when they were outside the safety of the force field. She picked Zinni's up and held it to her nose—even after sitting in the dusty garage for months, the intelligence officer's scent still lingered in the material.

"I'm coming for you, Zin," she said aloud. "And if it's too late, you can be damn sure I'll take Ronan down for you."

The thought sent a new wave of motivation through her, and she climbed into the car instead of returning to the apartment above. There was no doubt someone up and about who could help her; the majority of Zylka's inhabitants went to bed while it was still daylight and rose when it was still dark to avoid the heat. She pulled the vehicle out of the garage and secured the door behind her, then sped off toward the spaceport.

Compared to the massive Haphezian cities she was used to, Zylka was miniscule, but it was still one of the largest settlements in this part of the Fringe, second only to Niio. Despite the relatively short distance from the apartment, it still took a good twenty minutes of weaving back and forth through the narrow streets to reach the port. People were beginning to emerge from their homes and set out for early morning work, accounting for larger crowds and more time waiting for traffic. Aubin's primary export was glass—no surprise considering the abundance of sand—and like mining in Argall, many of Zylka's citizens were involved with the glass-making industry in one way or another. It was no wonder they liked to get early starts; Ziva couldn't imagine trying to work out in the desert during the heat of the day.

She brought the car to a stop in front of a block of shops near the edge of the port. Their windows were all still dark, but smoke rose from a pair of pipes jutting from the roof of the café a few doors down.

After fishing a few credits out of her backpack, Ziva approached the little restaurant with her hand resting on her sidearm. She didn't anticipate trouble, but people in these parts could be unpredictable. She paused for a moment outside the front door and listened, picking up the sounds of footsteps and machinery inside. The smell of cooking meat wafted out, and she kicked herself when she realized her mouth was watering.

She pounded her fist against the door several times and waited. The footsteps stopped. "We're not open yet!" a tired voice shouted in accented Standard.

*Exactly*, she thought, knocking again. The man inside cursed and let out an exasperated sigh, and she heard the footsteps resume. She stepped to one side and curled her fingers around her pistol's grip.

The door of the café slid open, and the speaker turned on a light.

"I *said* we're not—" The man's voice trailed off when he caught sight of her, and his eyes widened. "You. What are you doing here?"

"Nice to see you too, Ray," Ziva muttered, arching an eyebrow. "I hope you're not planning on making me stand out here all morning."

The man shook his head and stepped back, opening the door wider to allow her entry. "You've only been gone, what, four, five months? Why are you back already?"

"Oh," Ziva said, tilting her head and feigning disappointment. "You mean you haven't missed me?"

Ray made no move to respond. He stood there wiping his clammy palms on his apron while sweat gathered on his brow, shifting his attention between her and the kitchen.

"I'm not here for work this time," she explained, following him deeper into the café as he returned to what he'd been doing. "You could say I'm here for personal reasons."

"Then that must mean you don't actually need me for anything," he said with a nervous chuckle, throwing her a glance to see whether she was laughing at his attempted joke. He looked back down at the grill in front of him when he saw she wasn't.

Ziva smirked and took a moment to study him as she took a seat on one of the tall stools at the serving counter. He was small even for a human, a far cry from the burly men Tobias employed. In all the years she'd known him, he hadn't gained a single kilo in fat or muscle. She wasn't entirely sure how he could be so scrawny and stay alive. His hooked, pointy nose seemed far too large, and his receding hairline only served to make his face look even more disproportionate. He was a pitiful, unattractive little creature, someone who was easily manipulated—and the exact sort of person she enjoyed manipulating.

She remained silent just long enough to make him squirm. "I need you to give me a little information," she said, watching as he used a pair of tongs to remove several slabs of meat from the grill, probably flanks from one of the various species of lizard native to the desert. He began to chop the blackened meat into cubes—she kept a wary eye on the knife as he did so—and methodically slid each chunk onto a row of skewers.

"Why do you do this to me?" he muttered.

"Look, Ray. Our arrangement is still the same. You give me information I want when I want it, and I don't tell anyone this place is a front for zanix trafficking. It's as simple as that."

He stopped cutting and glared at her for a moment, his thin lips pressed into a straight line. "I'm still not sure if I want to know how you figured that out."

"Relax. If you think I care about a bunch of two-bit drug smugglers, you're wrong." She paused, recalling what Tobias had said about her spec ops status. "I have no reason to reveal your secret unless you give me one."

She pulled out her data pad with one hand and the stack of credits with the other, slapping them down on the counter side by side. "You of course remember my sergeant," she said, pointing to the images of Skeet and Aroska displayed on the pad's screen. *Lieutenant...Skeet's a lieutenant now.* "Have you seen him or this guy around?"

The sight of the credits seemed to bolster Ray's spirits a bit. "What is this, some kind of vacation spot for you people?" he quipped, picking up the stack and counting through it. "Yeah, Skeet was in here a couple days ago, asking about a group of Durutians and something called Ronan."

Ziva's pulse spiked. "What did you tell him?"

"I told him I'd never heard of Ronan and I didn't know what the hell he was talking about. But there's been a squad of Durutian soldiers camped out here in the city for the past three weeks or so."

"Three weeks? Did they come from Niio?"

"Beats me," Ray answered as he continued skewering the cubes of meat. "They've been holed up in an apartment complex on the other side of the port." He stopped to enter an approximate address into the pad. "They come out and prowl around the city during the day, but they mostly keep to themselves. A couple of them came in here to eat once. Everyone knows they're here, but they leave us alone, so we leave them alone."

"See? That wasn't so hard." Ziva was on her feet and tucking the data pad back into her pocket before he'd even finished talking. She turned to leave but paused for one last second, dropping another credit onto the counter. "Give me one of those," she said, reaching across and snatching up one of the kebabs before Ray could protest. She bit into one of the juicy chunks of meat as she jogged out the door and leaped into the car. If Skeet and Aroska were in the city but not at the team's apartment, she had a hunch she'd find them tailing the Durutians.

She entered the address into the car's navigation system and took off toward her destination as fast as traffic would allow. If this was the same team of Durutians who had taken Zinni, she wasn't sure why Skeet and Aroska would have waited until only a few days ago to come after them. Maybe they'd discovered a clue during a scouting run that had led them here and reunited them with the group, or maybe this was a different group entirely. Regardless of which was true, her team was severely outnumbered, and with Condition Black in place, they had no way of calling for help. She doubted they'd be willing to just sit by and do nothing if there was a chance to save Zinni; she just hoped they hadn't gone and done anything stupid.

Once she made it past the spaceport, traffic began to thin out and she accelerated. The clouds on the horizon were starting to turn brilliant shades of pink and orange and she knew it wouldn't be long until daylight. She'd spent plenty of time roaming Zylka during the day, but with so many unknown factors at play, she preferred a more secretive approach in the dark. Her window of time for one was closing rapidly.

She guided the car down a side street, her eyes fixed on the counter that displayed the distance to her destination. She began to decelerate as she neared, sweeping her gaze around and keeping an eye out for any structures that could be the apartment complex Ray had described. The area was almost entirely residential, so she wasn't sure if—

*There.* Her eyes fell upon a figure wearing a set of all-too-familiar black armor. She steered the car to the side of the road and came to a complete stop, watching as the man came to the edge of an alley, took a cautious look around, then beckoned to someone behind him. That someone turned out to be a some*thing*, a large groundcar piloted by two more Durutian soldiers. The vehicle turned her way, and Ziva sank lower into her seat, watching with her peripherals as it passed. But when she saw who the passengers were, she couldn't help but give it her undivided attention. Even through the transport's tinted windows, she recognized Skeet's orange hair. He was slumped against the door with his eyes closed, and the silhouette that held a similar position on the other side of him could only be Aroska. Another pair of armed Durutians rode in the third row of seats.

Ziva swore and slammed her palms against the steering controls. Four 'borgs would be easy enough to deal with, but even if she managed to take them out, she'd have her two unconscious agents to deal with *and* the rest of the Durutians would be on her tail in no time. If they were going somewhere more secluded, she might be able to wait until then to make a move. But time would still be limited; with the force field in place, they'd have nowhere to run. They'd be trapped in the city unless she could get them back to the *Zenith*.

She sat still until the large vehicle was an adequate distance away and then turned her own car around, following in its wake. Confident the truck would be easy to spot in traffic, she turned down the next side street and wove around the block, flying parallel to it until they reached one of the city's main thoroughfares. She stopped the car, using a cluster of other parked vehicles for cover, and waited.

She wasn't entirely sure what she'd been expecting the Durutians to do, but it certainly hadn't been *turn left*. She glanced around—the spaceport and anything else of consequence could be found deeper in the city to the right. The only things they'd find to the left were junk yards, more apartments identical to the ones they'd just come from, and...one of the portals.

*The desert.*

"Damn it," she muttered, pulling her car back out onto the road and resuming her tail. There was no reason for the 'borgs to be taking Skeet and Aroska to the desert—no good reason, anyway. It didn't take a genius to figure out what had happened. They'd been investigating the Durutians' compound—it could have only been a recon mission for all she knew—and they'd been discovered, captured, and probably interrogated. Now they were being taken to the desert to be disposed of per Ronan's orders.

Ziva could see the portal ahead, a wide, circular opening at the base of the force field created by a disruptor that could be switched on and off by city officials. There were at least ten throughout the city, one at the end of each of Zylka's main roads. There was no way she'd be able to follow the truck through without being noticed. If she remembered correctly, there should be another portal just a kilometer to the north.

She swerved around a slow-moving vehicle and pushed her car to its top speed, darting in and out of traffic until she came within sight of the second portal. It was light enough now that she'd be able to see the Durutians' vehicle without any trouble, but they'd be able to see her just as easily if she got too close. She steered the car through the portal and angled south toward the one the 'borgs had taken Skeet and Aroska through, catching sight of their truck over the crest of a sand dune. She glanced toward the sun and found, to her surprise, that it wasn't nearly as bright as she'd expected it to be. It was hardly more than a pale yellow disk, choked out by the roiling brown wall rising up on the horizon. The wall stretched farther than she could see from where she sat, and at the speed it was moving, it would be upon them within twenty minutes.

"*Sheyss.*"

# · 14 ·
## DESERT
### OUTSKIRTS OF ZYLKA, AUBIN

E ven if Skeet hadn't been shoved into a kneeling position, he would have fallen to his knees anyway. Whatever the Durutians had used to paralyze him had finally started to wear off, but they'd shot him full of something else just before leaving the compound. His head felt like a boulder resting on his shoulders and his arms and legs were like jelly. It was all infuriating, really—the cyborgs were threatened enough by him and Aroska that they felt the need to take extreme measures to subdue them. He would have been flattered if not for the fact that those extreme measures were working splendidly.

Even at such an early hour, the sun's lethal rays were already excruciating. Without the force field to protect them, they'd be dead within a couple of hours. In that sense, Skeet welcomed the thought of a bullet or plasma bolt through his head. Their Durutian captors sported full armor and helmets, sufficiently shielding them from the sun, but his sensitive Haphezian skin was already starting to burn and itch after the mere minutes he'd been exposed to the light.

After close to ten years in spec ops, he was no stranger to near-death experiences. Sure, he tried his best *not* to die on any given mission, but there was always that knowledge in the back of his mind, that unspoken understanding that it was bound to happen sometime given the gravity of his work. He'd never imagined going out like this, though. He hated to admit he'd accepted his fate, but he'd spent a lot of time contemplating his options—at least when he'd been lucid enough to do so—and he saw no way out. With a useless body and blurry vision, it was impossible for him to defend himself against the Durutians, much less make an offensive move. Even if he was able to move his arms and legs, he would be sluggish at best, and he'd still be outnumbered. Either option—holding still and waiting, or trying to fight—would draw the same results: death.

For a moment, Skeet felt as though he were falling, though with his current proximity to the ground, there was really nowhere to fall to. A rough hand grabbed his shirt and yanked him back into an upright position, and he realized the momentary blackness he'd just experienced had been the result of face-planting in the sand. The coarse grains scraped at his burning skin and he shook his head as best as he could, but the motion only made him dizzier.

Muffled footsteps approached behind him, and another person dropped down beside him with a grunt. Though a mere meter away, Aroska was hardly more than a dark shape against the endless yellow backdrop of the desert. Skeet blinked several times, but a combination of sand, sweat, and foggy vision rendered him nearly blind. He leaned forward and retched.

"I'm sorry," he croaked, though he was unsure if the words had even been audible. He didn't really know who the apology was directed at: Aroska, for dragging him into this mess; Zinni, for allowing her to be taken in the first place and then failing to save her; Ziva, for getting himself killed when there was nothing she could do about it.

He heard a plasma cell being exchanged behind him, followed by a moist *thump* that seemed entirely out of place given the circumstances. The sound seemed familiar, but he couldn't quite place it. For a moment, he thought it might have just been his mind playing tricks on him, but then a split second later, he heard the telltale *crack* of a projectile rifle echoing across the desert.

*Thump. Crack. Thump. Crack.* Whoever had been hanging on to him released their grip and crumpled into a heap, and he once again fell facedown into the sand, unable to support himself. *Three shots in succession*, he thought, *and four Durutians*. He had no idea who the shooter could be, but if the gun was anything like the ones he was familiar with, the person would have to stop and reload now. The fourth Durutian knew that, too; he could hear the man scrambling for cover somewhere behind him.

The shooter was good, that much was clear. Three bullets...three men...all within a split second of each other. The fourth shot came sooner than Skeet had expected. The last guard must not have been quite concealed because he heard the slug strike flesh just before the rifle cracked again. The man howled in pain but was silenced by one last shot.

The knowledge that he was no longer about to be executed at point blank range allowed Skeet to relax, and for a moment, he felt himself succumb to the faintness that had been threatening to overtake him for the past few minutes. Rather than the gritty, blistering sand, he was lying in his own bed in his loft in downtown Noro, a far cry from the cots and cheap bunks he'd been forced to use for the past few weeks. The window was open and a cool breeze blew in, though in reality it was probably just the sweltering desert wind meeting the perspiration on his face.

The sound of an approaching vehicle drew him out of his stupor and back to the present. He tried to open his eyes, but the chapped skin on his face restricted the movement of his eyelids to what seemed like only a few millimeters. A shape moved toward them across the sand, and something on the front of it reflected the sunlight. *That must be the car.* No, it was a bird, flying out over the Tranyi River—he could see it through the open window.

*Stay awake*, he told himself. *You're not in the clear just yet.*

By the time the car reached him, there were four—no, five—copies of it, all swaying back and forth and disappearing at intervals behind a veil of black nothingness. A door slammed and he could hear soft footsteps moving through the sand. He pried his eyes open once more and could just make out a figure sprinting toward him. Tall, muscular, head shrouded by brown cloth, huge black eyes. Or were those goggles?

The last thing he remembered was the sensation of floating.

## · 15 ·

## APARTMENT COMPLEX

### ZYLKA, AUBIN

Taran unconsciously reached out to brace himself against a supply crate as the massive wall of sand struck the force field. A hush fell over his squad as they stood in the courtyard, watching the cloud swell up and wash over the shimmering dome above them. The sun blinked in and out for a moment until it was obscured completely, leaving the city shrouded in dusky brown shadows. He didn't fully understand the technology of the force field and how it could allow ships to pass through but not microscopic sand particles, but quite frankly, he didn't care as long as those sand particles remained outside. He wasn't sure how long the field had been in place—only a few decades, he thought—but whoever had implemented it was a genius; not only did it protect Zylka's citizens from the unforgiving sun, but it saved city officials from days of cleanup every time a sandstorm came along.

The soldiers around him began to relax and go back to their business, and Taran released the breath he hadn't realized he'd been holding. Mae moved up beside him and slipped her hand into his as she too watched the cloud.

"It's done," she said with a sigh.

"It is," Taran murmured, envisioning the Haphezian agents' bodies being engulfed by the sand. "I hope our truck made it back into the city in time. Have we received an update yet?"

Mae shook her head. "Storm likely interfered with comms, though. We'll give them a few more minutes. What's our next course of action?"

"You said it yourself—it's time to start fresh. Let's get everything packed up and we'll get out of here as soon as the storm blows over. See if the Feds have any new leads for us."

"You got it. I'm ready to get—"

The door of the nearest apartment burst open before she could finish her thought. Cowen appeared in the doorway, wide-eyed and breathless. "Sir! Priority transmission for you!" His face went pale. "It's from a Haphezian network."

Taran's heart thundered in his chest, and he cursed under his breath as he and Mae took off at a dead run for the control room. He pulled up short before stepping onto the communication pad, swallowing hard and taking a moment to wipe away the sweat that had gathered on his brow. Was there some way HSP could already know about what he'd done? He cleared his throat. "This is Sergeant Taran Reddic, Durutian Special Forces. To whom am I speaking?"

He had to suppress a gasp as the silvery-blue hologram rendered on the console in front of him. There stood Devani, looking as striking and regal as ever in the same diplomat robes she'd been wearing the last time they'd spoken. Her long, dark hair hung in straight sheets, framing her similarly dark face. The three-dimensional image was so clear Taran could see her optical implants adjusting to the light of whatever room she stood in.

"Devani," he said, overcome by some mixture of joy and confusion.

"Hello, brother," she replied. "I'm terribly sorry about the delay. Just wanted to check in. How goes the hunt?"

*Just wanted to check in?* "What have they done to you? Are you hurt? Do you need help?"

Judging by her outward appearance, the Haphezians had done nothing to her. She appeared unharmed, and her voice was steady. She scowled and tilted her head. "What are you talking about? I'm fine."

"Five days. It's been almost *five* days since we've heard from you. Where are you now?"

"Just leaving HSP Headquarters. There isn't anything here. There never has been."

That same lump that had formed in Taran's throat before

descended into the pit of his stomach. "What?"

"Let me explain. I went to meet with HSP's director when I got here, just like we planned. But something happened. There was an attack—" she held her hand up for silence when Taran opened his mouth to speak "—on their military base, and the entire agency was on lockdown. It's precisely what it sounds like—nobody enters or leaves, and nobody communicates with anyone on the outside. They kept me in a comfortable holding room, more for *my* protection than anything else. They took good care of me, okay? Stop worrying."

"So you didn't find anything? No sign of the Resistance or Ronan?"

"Nothing," Devani said, "and according to the director, their government still has strict laws in place prohibiting any Resistance presence. They're still trying as hard as possible not to involve themselves in this mess. But I'll stick around for a couple more days and see if I can find any more information."

Taran swallowed and glanced to Mae; her face displayed the same anxiety he was feeling. It was exactly as she'd said earlier: *"Why would they be allied with the Resistance now, after all this time?"*

"What's wrong, little brother?" Devani said. "You look like you're going to be sick."

"I'm fine," Taran answered, rubbing a hand over his face. He couldn't help but smile a bit in response to the childhood nickname. She was a whopping six minutes older than him, and she'd never let him forget it. She'd stepped up after the deaths of their parents, always taking charge and mothering him. Now here she was again, trying to take care of him from halfway across the galaxy. "We just had a little bit of a...rough night here."

"Still on Aubin, I see."

He nodded. "We're getting ready to head out, though. We've exhausted all our leads."

"Have a safe trip, then. My car is about ready to leave. I'll see you soon."

Devani's hologram fizzled away, leaving Taran standing alone on the comm pad. For a while, all he could do was stand there staring into empty space as his mind attempted to process everything his sister had just said and compare it to their current situation. "What have we done?" he whispered.

Mae watched him with wide eyes, wearing an expression that read of something between regret and 'I-told-you-so.' "You didn't say anything."

"You expect me to tell my sister I just killed two HSP agents while she's *on* Haphez?" he shouted. "Then they'd really take her. Then we'd *really* never hear from her again."

Somehow, the fact that Mae didn't even flinch made him feel worse about raising his voice. "The agency will eventually realize those men are missing. What do you plan to do?"

"They'll be buried under three meters of sand by the time the day is over," Taran said, "and the bodies won't last long in this heat." He slumped down in the same chair he'd sat in as he'd puzzled over Devani's disappearance a couple of days earlier. "And anyhow, I'm still not convinced we're wrong. Those men were checking us out for a reason. They wanted something. They could be rogue, maybe double agents of some sort."

"I suppose that's true," Mae said, eyebrows furrowed as she checked her wrist unit. "Still no word from the truck. They should have been back by now."

Taran had almost forgotten about the execution squad—his mind had been focused solely on the men they were supposed to be executing. This was just one more complication in a situation that had already become far *too* complicated for his taste. "Comms can't be down if Devani's transmission was able to get through. Maybe they didn't make it back to the portal in time. Come on."

He led her out to the nearest parked groundcar and started it up, taking off so fast the repulsors sprayed sand over all their other vehicles. The majority of the city's traffic had come to a standstill thanks to the storm; with the portals closed, no ground vehicles could leave, and no space-worthy vessels were permitted to pass through the force field in these conditions. He maneuvered with ease past all the other cars that could do nothing more than sit on the edge of the road and wait.

They arrived at the nearest portal, though with the disruptor deactivated, the only things marking it as such were the two metal pillars on either side of the road and the nearby security shack. The force field now extended down to the ground, sealing what was normally open space. Seeing the billowing cloud of sand up close was surreal—the warm gusts of wind permeated the field, swirling past Taran and Mae as they walked up to the security building, but the sand itself was kept at bay.

"The portal is closed!" one of the officials called when he saw them approaching. "Nobody gets through until this thing blows over."

"Did a heavy-duty groundcar come through here?" Taran asked, glancing around for any signs of their missing truck.

The man shook his head. "One went out this way, but it's been at least half an hour. No vehicles have entered through this gate all morning."

Taran kept his eyes on the flying sand as he once more attempted to hail his men via comm. And once more, there was no response. Surely the Haphezian agents hadn't been able to fight back, but he could think of no other reason why the soldiers wouldn't have been able to return before the storm hit.

Angry, confused, and at a loss, all he could do was shake his head. "What the hell is happening out there?"

# · 16 ·
# HSP HEADQUARTERS
## NORO, HAPHEZ

Emeri looked up when he heard the knock on the frame of his office door. With the lockdown in place and the number of people coming to speak to him, he'd opted to leave the door open for once. Now that the threat level had been reduced to Code Orange, he imagined he should probably lock it again.

Aura Stannist stood there, her face scrunched as she eyed him distastefully. It was the same hostility she'd regarded him with since she'd realized Ziva was gone. Emeri had denied any involvement in her disappearance, but he could tell there was no fooling the probation officer—or Disciplinary and Personnel Control Specialist or whatever absurd title she went by. Still, for one reason or another, she hadn't reported him to the Royal House. She'd been involved with HSP at some point—he vaguely remembered hearing of her transfer to the Royal Offices just before he'd been named Prime Director—so perhaps, in a way, she understood the camaraderie among ops agents and, subsequently, why he'd allowed Ziva to leave.

"Agent Stannist," he said, straightening. "How can I help you?"

She strode toward him, as rigid as ever, with the light from his massive picture window reflected in her pale-yellow eyes. "The last of the VIP detainees has been released following the lockdown. Any word from Payvan?"

It was almost as if she kept asking just to rub it in his face—surely she knew the answer. "As I have already explained, there's no way to hear from her or the rest of her team until Condition Black has been lifted."

"But Condition Black *has* been lifted."

"All off-world agents are bound by the protocol until they return to base."

"And you have no way of knowing how long that will take?"

Emeri shook his head. "Typically, the agents will return to the system and use outside resources to gather intel before even approaching the planet, much less Headquarters. The protocol has only been in effect for six days—typical return time is two weeks."

An exasperated growl escaped Aura's throat. "You know I could say two words to the Royal Officer and have you thrown out on your ass for this."

"And yet," Emeri said, tilting his head and not bothering to finish his sentence. She'd already threatened him, almost verbatim, on the day of Ziva's departure. She was right—it probably wouldn't be difficult at all for her to get him fired—but if she hadn't made good on her threats yet, she likely never would. He just hoped Ziva would be able to track her team down and return in a timely manner; he may have offered to cover for her, but that didn't mean he planned on enjoying the experience.

His comm system buzzed, cutting off Aura's next words before they could escape her mouth. "Priority transmission from Na for you, sir," one of his aides announced. "It's originating from the medical center."

Emeri stood, relieved by the interruption, and strode to the communication pad at the head of his conference table. In his peripheral vision, he could see Aura still standing in front of his desk. Her crossed arms and cocked hip told him she wasn't planning on going anywhere.

The hologram of Doctor Anson Baez materialized on the projection pad across the table. The man was an old friend who had essentially been his liaison to the military for the past two months, but now that Ziva's rehab and trial were over, hearing from him was troubling. The worrisome look on the doctor's face confirmed that the news he bore wasn't good.

"Anson. What can I do for you?"

"I'm afraid we have a problem." Even in the hologram, Emeri could see the sheen of sweat glistening on Baez's forehead. The man was breathing hard as if he'd been in a hurry. "We've been monitoring all the soldiers involved in the attack the other day, paying special attention to those who were exposed to the gas to the highest degree."

"I'm glad our analysis of the blood samples was helpful," Emeri said. "Has the higher exposure brought about any unique physiological developments?"

"You could say that," Baez answered, wiping his brow. "The priority patients we identified via the blood tests began show-ing...*adverse* symptoms this morning. Extreme confusion, loss of motor control, seizures. Initial studies showed the gas—whatever it is—had the chemical composition of a nerve agent, but at the time, nothing had happened to the victims to indicate such. I guess now we know for sure."

"But they haven't showed any symptoms before now?"

"Some reported minor headaches, but the med center gave them basic treatment and wrote it off as a reasonable side effect considering the trauma they'd undergone. But you want to know the really strange part? Brain scans show that there's still internal neurological damage, and the headaches have reportedly gotten worse, but they're all virtually fine now, at least on the outside. Functioning almost like normal."

The knot that had been forming in Emeri's gut tightened. His thoughts drifted to Kat Reilly's data and the substance the young woman had been injected with. Following the attack on Na, a comparison had revealed that it was nearly identical to the gas released at the base, just in a liquid state. The minor differences between the two substances still had scientists stumped, and they had yet to be identified. But these symptoms? These seizures and headaches followed by relative normality? Emeri shuddered—this sounded all too familiar.

"What about the other victims? Those who were exposed to a lesser degree?"

"The med center is rounding them all up as we speak," Baez said.

"Specialists have already had a chance to examine some of them. These people are also reporting headaches, but so far, they aren't exhibiting any of the major symptoms. Still, their scans show heightened brain activity, and they're recognizing some of the same patterns they saw in the other victims. I hate to say it, but based on the reports I'm reading, I have a feeling the symptoms *will* start manifesting, just more slowly."

"You're telling me *anyone* who was exposed is at risk to some degree."

"That's correct. The decontamination processes they went through following the attack rendered them non-contagious, but the chemical had already been introduced into their bloodstreams by then."

"*Sheyss*," Emeri muttered, dropping his palms to the table. "Ziva was there."

"I know," Baez said quietly. "That's why I contacted you. It's crucial that she return to the base so the neurologists can examine her and keep her under observation. Until we figure out what this chemical is, I'm not sure what all we can do for the victims, but I'd hate for her to be out in the field when the symptoms begin to manifest."

"Captain Payvan *is* in the field," Emeri said, pinching the bridge of his nose. He could almost feel Aura's cold glare boring into his back. "She's currently operating under Condition Black, a protocol that involves zero communication with Headquarters. She has severed all ties until further notice. I have no idea where she is."

Baez remained silent for several long seconds. His shoulders sagged and he swallowed. "That's...problematic."

Both men stared at their feet as they each contemplated the gravity of the situation. It seemed, in the past few months especially, that nothing could ever go smoothly.

Emeri sighed; standing there wasn't going to help them find Ziva and her team. "Thank you for contacting me, Anson. I'll send Payvan your way as soon as I hear from her."

Baez dipped his head and rushed away, effectively ending the transmission. Emeri steeled himself and turned to face Aura, who was no doubt reveling in the fact that she'd been right. *You win*, he thought.

"I suppose it would be inappropriate to say 'I told you so'," she said, sliding her hands down to her hips and shifting her weight to her other leg.

The look on her face had been sufficient enough for Emeri to tell exactly what she'd been thinking. "And yet that didn't stop you," he said, brushing past her as he returned to his desk. "What the hell kind of mess have we gotten ourselves into?"

"I think you mean what kind of mess have *you* gotten us into," she snapped. "Whatever kind of mess it is, it's yours to clean up. On the authority of Royal Officer Jan Ganten, I'm ordering you to devote any resources not dedicated to the Ronan investigation to finding Payvan. Right now, I don't care how precious she is to this agency. She's *mine* for the next year, and I want her back here, with or without her team."

# · 17 ·
# SAFE HOUSE
## ZYLKA, AUBIN

The room he was in was ill-lit and dusty—Aroska could tell that much before he even opened his eyes. He was fairly certain he was lying down, though he didn't remember how he had gotten there. The last thing he *did* remember was falling face-down into the sand in the middle of the desert.

He was suddenly aware of a strange pressure in his arm, and he pried his eyelids apart long enough to glimpse a needle penetrating his skin before the light—however dim—forced him to close his eyes again. A pounding headache raged throughout his skull, and the thought of having to wake up nearly made him sick. But considering where he was and the things he'd been investigating, having an unfamiliar needle stuck in his arm was the last thing he wanted.

Gritting his teeth, he willed his eyelids to part once more and dragged his right hand over to his left arm. The needle was attached to a thin tube that ran up the wall and into a sack of clear fluid hanging above him. His fingers found the needle, but he refrained from pulling it out as his mind continued to process the situation. The realization that he wasn't in any danger hit him just as a voice rang out across the room.

"Don't touch that."

His foggy mind struggled to ascertain the identity of the speaker as he rolled his head back across the pillow and strained to see. The first thing he noticed was Skeet lying on a cot a short distance away; he too had a makeshift drip line attached to his arm. A figure sat at a small table, obscured momentarily by a wave of blackness that washed through his vision.

He realized it was Ziva just a split second before his eyes finally managed to focus on her. She sat at the table cleaning pieces of what appeared to be a large rifle. The tabletop was covered in a fine layer of sand, and piles of the stuff had gathered under the area where she was working. He suddenly remembered being dragged out to the desert, dazed and sick, and passing out just before he was supposed to be executed. Considering her rifle and the fact that he was still alive, it wasn't a stretch to assume she'd had a hand in his rescue.

Aroska tilted his head back and looked up at the tiny window above the kitchen counter. A dark cloud swirled by high above, blocking out the light from the sun. The force field held fast, keeping the cloud at bay, but he could still hear the wind howling as it rushed through the streets, and he could feel the building shudder.

"Sandstorm," Ziva said before he could even ask what was going on.

He didn't remember anything about a sandstorm, and he was beginning to wonder exactly how long he'd been unconscious. Images of the sprawling desert and scorching sun flashed through his mind, but nothing else. "You got us out...." He wasn't quite sure what he was trying to say.

"The wind was in our favor—that might have been the only thing that saved us. I brought you in through a different portal than the one the Durutians took you through, and that took extra time. The portal was already closed by the time we got to it, but they opened it back up when they saw us coming."

He vaguely remembered riding in a vehicle, though whether it was the Durutians' or Ziva's, he wasn't sure. He could picture her tearing across the desert, pushing the car to its limits while the roaring sandstorm closed in. He didn't know how she'd found them or taken out their Durutian captors, but he knew if she hadn't, he and Skeet would now be buried under mountains of sand, never to be heard from again.

"Thank you," he murmured, attempting to prop himself up on his elbows. The movement was almost nauseating; the room began to spin, and his throbbing headache intensified.

"Lie still and rest," she snapped, though there was a certain tired quality in her tone. "I'll strap you down if I have to."

Aroska tried to scowl but the skin on his forehead felt tight and brittle. He reached up to touch it and found it peeling off in flakes, leaving tender pink flesh behind.

"Yeah, you're not looking so hot right now, pretty boy," Ziva said, setting the rifle down and coming to loom over him with crossed arms. "That sun is hell, isn't it? You're dehydrated and burned. Like I said, don't touch that drip line. The fluids have been infused with caura extract that should get you all fixed up within a few hours."

He ignored her and continued his quest to sit up. "Let me at least—"

"I said lie down," she growled, halting his movement with a solid hand and pushing him back onto the cot. "Just lie there and shut up. Please."

"*Sheyss*, Ziva," Aroska said, settling into a more comfortable position. He watched her stride back across the room and sit down hard in the chair, resuming her cleaning with a certain aggression that seemed to be directed more at him than the rifle. He imagined it was her way of telling him she was angry that he'd gotten into her strongbox...and also that now was not the time to talk about it.

More rest did sound appealing, and he didn't have the energy to argue with her. He turned onto his side, making sure not to disturb the drip line, and watched her past drooping eyelids. With as busy as he'd been for the past few days, his fear for her safety had gotten pushed to the back of his mind. Part of him was okay with that, the part that still wanted to be angry with her for everything she'd done to him. But now she'd gone and saved his life again, and he once more felt his resolve weakening. He did care about her—he'd even admitted it to Kade Shevin—but he was finally starting to understand why that was a problem. It was exactly what she had always talked about, the reason she tried so hard *not* to care about people. In a way, he still thought her behavior was ridiculous, but at the same time, he realized where she was coming from. He pictured himself scouting the Durutians and being ambushed while lost in thought worrying about her. He knew he wouldn't have stood a chance.

Now that it was over, he felt all the suppressed fear bubbling to the surface, despite the fact that they were all safe and sound. He recalled the day they'd received the news about the attack on Na and was glad he'd been out and about so Skeet couldn't see his initial reaction. Thankfully, the prospect of chasing Ronan's ship had given him something else to devote his energy to, but for a brief moment, the thought of losing her had been debilitating. The feeling was identical to what he'd felt that day in Argall as he'd sprinted toward her lifeless body on the landing pad. All that blood, her deathly pale features…the fear that he was too late had rendered him completely numb. He'd realized he hadn't felt despair on such a scale since discovering Saun Zaid was a traitor. The fear. The *fear*. First Saun, the woman he loved, then Ziva, the woman he…what, exactly?

Skeet's raspy voice snapped him out of his thoughts. "Where the hell are we?"

"Zylka Base," Ziva answered as she began piecing the rifle back together. "You've been unconscious for a couple of hours."

Aroska could see Skeet reach up and touch his face, feeling his own peeling skin. He groaned and muttered something about the force field, then he turned his head and seemed to process Ziva's presence for the first time.

"Z," he breathed. The word was somewhere between a question and a sigh of relief. "How'd you get here?"

They both listened as she repeated her story, including new details Aroska hadn't heard yet. She'd arrived in the city early that morning and hadn't found them here at the apartment. Ray, the man who'd given Skeet intel earlier, had mentioned the Durutians and had given her the address of their compound. She'd followed their truck out to the desert, where she'd managed to take out all four of the 'borgs before Skeet or Aroska could be killed. She'd gotten them back into the city, barely managing to avoid the sandstorm, and the brown cloud still swirled by on the other side of the force field.

The more Aroska heard, the more he was beginning to remember. He could still feel a tender, tingly spot at the small of his back where that redheaded Durutian woman had hit him with the stun baton. He remembered being struck by the cyborg leader and subjected to that awful sedative; he probably still had some of the stuff in his system, just one more factor contributing to his current state of lethargy.

"Wait," Skeet said, furrowing his eyebrows and immediately wincing as his crusty skin stretched. "You asked Ray about the Durutians? How did you even know about them? How did you even know to come here?"

"Emeri suggested I go to Niio first, considering that's where you were when Condition Black was implemented," Ziva replied, fitting the last couple pieces of the rifle back together. She bit her lip and grimaced in embarrassment, and unless Aroska was mistaken, she was trying not to smile. "I may or may not have struck a deal with Tobias in order to find you."

Skeet's maniacal cackle was startling and almost seemed out of place, but as he listened to the other man laugh, Aroska couldn't help but crack an incredulous smile himself. No, now that he thought about it, there was nothing to be incredulous about. Ziva was exactly the type of person who would waltz in and demand help from the head of the Niiosian Mob.

"You struck a deal with Tobias Niio," Skeet cried, still laughing. "One of these days, I might finally stop being surprised by the things you do."

Aroska had never had the pleasure of meeting Tobias, but the mobster's reputation preceded him. "And he just told you what you wanted to know?" he asked, trying once more to prop himself up on one elbow.

"I owe him a favor now, if that's what you're asking," she answered, sending him a scolding glare for daring to move. "And believe it or not, he's looking for Ronan, too. The Durutians who took Zinni killed some of his men." She stood up and moved around to the near side of the table, leaning up against it with her arms crossed. "Tell me about the group you've encountered here. Are they the same ones?"

"Based on the timetable, we thought they might be," Skeet said, coughing a bit as he finally recovered from the fit of laughter. "Ray said they'd been here about three weeks. There wasn't any sign of Zinni in the compound, at least that we saw, but these people were definitely interested in us. They had eyes on us the moment we arrived."

"They're good," Aroska admitted, thinking of how the redheaded woman had managed to take him from behind in the alley. "Probably special forces of some sort, considering the way they move."

Ziva directed her gaze toward him, regarding him with that familiar cold, calculating stare he'd seen during their very first encounter in Emeri's office. It was the same condescending look that had made him want to strangle her for the majority of the Dakiti mission. "I assume they tried to question you."

That was it. "Okay, enough!" he said, sitting up before she could protest. "What the hell is your problem?"

"Oh, I don't know, possibly the fact that I got done with rehab only to be sentenced to a year of disciplinary probation, caught up in a chemical attack, and told that one of my only friends had been captured *four weeks earlier* by some mysterious entity nobody can find. Then I sold my soul to the Niiosian Mob and chased you two halfway across the galaxy, arriving here just in time to take out a squad of 'borgs in the middle of the damn desert before they could execute your sorry asses." She paused and heaved a sigh that sounded almost apologetic. "Let's just say it's been a rough few days."

*You're not the one who was paralyzed and dragged out to be buried by a sandstorm*, Aroska thought. "Look," he said, "blame me for all of this if you want, but I'm not sorry I took that data pad and syringe. The majority of the agency is on board right now, and we're a lot closer to finding Ronan than we ever would have been if you'd kept this all to yourself."

She stared him down for several more seconds, regarding him in a way that would have sent him running for cover in the past. But the days of letting her manipulate him were over. Part of him regretted ever wasting his time being worried about her.

"What did the Durutians want?" she asked with another sigh, unfolding her arms long enough to massage her tired eyes.

"Not a lot," Skeet replied, glancing between the two of them. "They asked who we were, who we worked for, but that was about it. I don't think they were huge fans of the face time—they'd kept their distance for the past two days, but they were forced to take action when we took action. They were careful about saying things or letting us see anything that might give away who they were working for. One of them called the leader 'Taran,' but that's all we know."

"The guy seemed distraught," Aroska added, "almost like he was taking our presence personally. He also said something about starting fresh, like we weren't of any further use to him."

Ziva gnawed at her lower lip and nodded to herself as she listened. "Starting fresh. If these people took Zinni but were ready to cast you both aside...." She didn't need to finish the sentence for them to know what she was thinking. Things weren't boding well for the intelligence officer, assuming she was even still alive.

"What do you propose we do?" Aroska murmured, settling back down on the cot as another bout of lightheadedness began to set in.

Ziva shrugged as if there was only one option. "First, we wait until you two are on your feet again." She checked the time. "Give it a few more hours. The storm should've run its course by then. And then? I think we'll go pay this Taran a visit."

# · 18 ·

# DESERT

## OUTSKIRTS OF ZYLKA, AUBIN

"Stop the vehicle!" Taran ordered, his eyes glued to the tracking device's viewscreen. The groundcar slowed to a stop and came to rest on the soft sand. He leaped out, immediately taken aback by the heat. Without the protection of the force field, the sun was not only beating down on the ground—the rays were also bouncing back off the sand, making everything twice as hot and, it seemed, twice as bright. The sudden need for fresh air was overwhelming, but he didn't dare lift his helmet visor for fear of what the sun would do to his skin.

He'd gathered a small team to investigate the disappearance of the execution squad, and they'd spent the last hour or so of the sandstorm waiting directly in front of the portal. The Gatekeepers had opened it just moments before, and he'd wasted no time in bringing his team through. They'd managed to establish locks on the communicators of the missing soldiers as well as the truck they'd taken. All five signals had been immobile for the duration of the time they'd been tracked, tying Taran's stomach into an uneasy knot.

A strong breeze still whistled over the desert and small clouds of sand still swirled by every so often, but the storm was effectively over. It had been over eight hours since the soldiers had gone missing; that was a long time for sand to be piling up on top of them.

"Got one, right here!" Taran hollered, coming to a halt as the tracker zeroed in on one of the target communicators. He continued moving, listening as Mae got out and directed the operation of the digging equipment they'd rented from the city officials. His viewscreen beeped progressively faster and lit up in green, indicating that he was standing on top of the truck. "Got the vehicle!"

Another few moments of searching revealed that the other three men were a short distance away, no doubt to secure the prisoners and perform the execution itself. With the amount of heat reflecting off the sand, using infrared to check for the Haphezians' bodies was futile. He pocketed the viewscreen and stepped back as his team moved forward with the machinery. They'd find out what was down there soon enough.

A good ten minutes of careful digging passed before they caught a glimpse of the truck. The massive shovel moved down along the edge of the vehicle, scooping out mounds of sand and casting them aside as quickly as possible.

"Start looking for the other three," Taran ordered the soldier operating the machine, waving him toward the markers he'd set up several meters away. "We'll take it from here."

Mae tossed him a handheld shovel and, along with young Cowen, they slid down into the depression and began to dig more precisely toward the spot the viewscreen had indicated. Taran's shovel struck something solid; the sand began to slide away, revealing black cloth. He abandoned the tool in favor of his own hands and began clawing at the material until it was revealed to be a pant leg. He established a grip on it and pulled, finding a boot and clumps of bloody sand.

"Help me with him," he said, continuing to pull. The man's other leg became visible; Mae and Cowen took hold of it, brushing away sand as they all dragged him out into the open.

None of them said a word as they stood there staring at the body. The bloody sand was the result of a gaping hole that had been blown through his left thigh. Judging by the trail of dark brown clumps, he'd been shot and had attempted to drag himself to safety behind the truck before being struck again in the chest.

Mae and Cowen both swore and turned around, but Taran couldn't pry his eyes away from those gory holes. All the members of his squad wore uniforms made of lightweight fiber mesh so they were virtually plasma-resistant. Whatever this man had been shot with had completely obliterated the material, and the entry wounds screamed *high-caliber projectile.*

"Sir, over here!" called another woman in his squad.

Taran peered over the edge of the crater and could see her crouching on the edge of the hole the machine was currently digging. "How many?"

"Just the three, sir." With her helmet obscuring her face, it was impossible to see her expression, but in her voice, he heard the same dread he was feeling. "No sign of the Haphezians."

Taran scrambled out of the depression and jogged over to find the rest of his team hard at work clearing the sand away from the three bodies. One had been hit in the chest in the same manner as the first. The other two had been shot cleanly through the head; not even their anti-ballistic helmets had stopped these rounds.

"What the hell happened here?" Mae murmured somewhere behind him.

It was doubtful he would see anything of interest after eight hours, but Taran swept his gaze over the surrounding landscape anyway, looking for odd shapes, reflective objects, anything that didn't belong. But that was the thing about the desert. Even without the presence of powerful sandstorms, it was always changing, shifting in the breeze. With the amount of sand the storm had dumped on his soldiers, he imagined the landscape looked completely different than it had that morning. It was impossible to know where the shots had come from.

The guilt he'd felt about killing the Haphezian agents was now being overtaken by sheer anger—anger at himself for not simply ending them right there in the apartment complex, and anger at whatever unknown elements were at play here.

"Those two men couldn't have done this," he murmured, half to himself and half to whoever bothered to listen. It was the one thought that brought him some comfort. "They were too heavily-drugged."

"You think they had backup?" Mae asked. "Were there more of them in the city that we didn't know about?"

Taran shook his head. "Possibly, but they arrived alone and hadn't been in contact with anyone but each other. Maybe they already had contacts in the city. What became of the data your team recovered on Ronan?"

"I've had a tech working on it," Mae replied, "but so far, he hasn't managed to break in."

All Taran could do was crouch and gaze off into the distance, but he found he wasn't focusing on any particular point. Devani was safe—the Haphezians hadn't captured her like he'd feared, and so far, she'd found nothing tying them to the Resistance. But these HSP agents were on the planet, stalking his unit, and they possessed heavily encrypted data on the Res's highest-ranking individual. Something didn't add up.

"Who are we dealing with?" he muttered.

As if on cue, the comm unit in his helmet buzzed, indicating a transmission from one of their men at the base. "Go ahead."

"Sir, we have a problem," said a shaky voice.

"What's going on?"

"S-s-standby."

The silence lasted just long enough to make Taran sweat—it was a cold, sickening sweat that bore distinct differences from the perspiration caused by the heat.

"Hello, Taran," said a female voice. It sounded vaguely familiar, like he'd heard it before and should know it from somewhere. Based on the way his stomach turned over when the woman spoke, he knew any previous encounter with her hadn't been pleasant.

"Who the hell is this?" he demanded.

"Why don't you come see me? We need to have a chat."

The transmission went dead.

# · 19 ·
# RAY'S CAFÉ
## ZYLKA, AUBIN

Ziva perked up when the sounds of voices and approaching footsteps reached her ears, as did the Durutian soldier sitting across the table from her. Aroska nodded from his place at the tinted window, confirming that the noises were originating from the visitors they were expecting. She nodded back and gestured at the Durutian. "Stand up."

They stood in Ray's café, a location that had been deemed suitable neutral ground after a bit of consideration. The rest of the 'borgs had done exactly what she'd expected them to do: returned to their base, found the man who had summoned them back to be mysteriously absent, then traced his location to this shop. Based on the way he was dressed, this young man wasn't combat-ready; he was merely a tech, maybe a communications officer, and as such, he'd been easy to grab while the rest of the group had their attention devoted to the bodies in the desert.

She, Skeet, and Aroska had stormed into Ray's shop with the Durutian in tow, informing the few customers that the establishment was closed until further notice. Ray himself remained in the kitchen, insisting he at least be allowed to continue fulfilling call-in orders if they were going to steal his business for half the day. Aside from the sizzle of the stove and the clanging of utensils, the space had been dead silent until the group arrived outside.

Skeet and Aroska stepped away from their places at the windows to flank the door, weapons held low but ready. Ziva drew her own pistol and moved around the table to stand behind their captive, pressing the barrel of the gun to his spine and closing her free hand around the back of his neck. "Open a transmission," she hissed in his ear.

The man did as he was told, holding his communicator up so she could hear and participate in the conversation if desired. "Sir?"

The footsteps outside ceased abruptly. "You okay, kid?" the Durutian leader asked after a brief hesitation.

"I just want to talk, Taran," Ziva said before the soldier could respond. "The front door is open. You and one of your people may enter. If anyone else so much as looks like they're trying to get in, I'll shoot them, and then I'll shoot your man here. Understand?"

There was a bit of muttering in the background followed by a heavy sigh. "Yes."

The atmosphere within the restaurant was tense to the point of becoming unbearable as the door slid open. The interior lights were dimmed, giving Ziva a better view of those entering than they initially had of her. A man stepped inside, followed by a woman with curly red hair—no doubt the one Aroska had described. Both remained armed, but neither had drawn their weapons.

Keeping herself hidden behind her prisoner, Ziva took advantage of her superior position and studied the man for a split second before his implants could adjust to the shadows. He was exactly who she'd expected him to be after hearing his name, and she allowed a small fraction of the tension in her body to release. "Reddic."

His face hardened as if he'd simultaneously recognized her and managed to place her voice. "Payvan."

There wasn't time to stop and examine the shocked looks Skeet, Aroska, and the woman were displaying. "Shut and lock the door," Ziva said. "Can we agree to remain civil, or should I have your weapons confiscated?"

Skeet and Aroska moved in behind them as the door closed. In response to her question, both Durutians lifted their hands and stepped forward, their silver eyes flitting between her and their captured squadmate.

"Sergeant Reddic—if it is still *sergeant*—would you kindly join me at the table?" Ziva waited until he began to move then leaned forward to whisper in the captive soldier's ear. "Walk."

She gave the man a light push and stepped back, keeping her pistol pointed down but not loosening her grip on it. She skirted back around to her side of the table and slipped into her chair, watching as Reddic did the same across from her. Aroska and Skeet holstered their weapons and took up positions on either side of her; the other two Durutians followed suit with their own leader, clearly uncomfortable with the fact that their backs were to the door.

"What do you want?" Reddic growled.

"Let's forget for a moment that you tried to have my agents here executed," Ziva began. "I seem to recall demonstrating what happens to people who get in my way—" her gaze shifted to his cybernetic arm "—and I would have thought you'd learned your lesson."

"What's she talking about, Taran?" the redheaded woman asked through clenched teeth. She stood with tense muscles, no doubt itching to draw one or both of the pistols she was packing.

"Remember that story I told you about the Haphezian assassin who was chasing the same target as me a few years back?" Reddic answered without removing his eyes from Ziva. "The one who blew my arm off when I got too close to taking her bounty?"

Ziva ignored the woman's ice-cold glare and drummed her fingers on the tabletop. "You're in my way again, Reddic. Do I need to take your other arm?"

"You murdered my men."

"Because they were about to murder *my* men."

He shook his head, cracking a disingenuous grin. "I gave them a chance. If they'd just told me what I wanted to know, told me why they're working for Ronan—"

Ziva had always been careful not to allow her facial expressions to betray her thoughts, but whatever flashed through her eyes just then made Reddic hesitate. She took advantage of the silence and slapped the table with an incredulous snort. "You think *we're* working for Ronan? You're the ones who captured our agent on Niio!"

"*What?*" the woman exclaimed.

Reddic's face mirrored her confusion. "We don't even have a team on Niio. We're the only unit in this sector." He scowled. "How do you explain the Durutian Special Tasks Unit that went missing near the Noro system?"

"I can't. I don't know anything about that. How do *you* explain these, taken at the Niio spaceport a little over four weeks ago?" Ziva produced her data pad and slammed it down in front of him, displaying Tobias's surveillance photos.

The room was quiet for a couple of minutes as he studied the images, zooming in, zooming out, comparing them side by side. He finally muttered a rough Durutian curse and beckoned to the woman. "Mae, look at these."

"Those are your people," Skeet said. It wasn't a question.

"Yes. Well, no," Reddic said. The tone of his voice had softened significantly. "This is our armor, and that symbol on the shoulder pads designates this group as the Delta Patrol, the unit that went missing right outside your system." He paused and swallowed. "But this isn't them."

"The weapons are all wrong," Mae explained. "We don't carry anything like that. And nobody's worn their uniforms this formally for years."

Ziva lifted an eyebrow. "What are you saying?"

Reddic reached out and took Mae's hand as he answered. "I'm saying we've thought Ronan was responsible for the disappearance of our people all along, and we were right. But it wasn't you." He returned his attention to Ziva. "And you thought Ronan's people captured your agent, and you're probably right. But it wasn't us."

"If you're not working for Ronan, then how do you even know what it is?" Aroska said.

"I could ask you people the same thing," Reddic answered, giving them each a wary look in turn. "You first."

Ziva cleared her throat—curiosity was getting the better of her. "A freelancer friend on Chaiavis was investigating one of Ronan's facilities after a colleague of hers was held captive there. They're both dead now, but we have their data and we've been trying to continue their investigation. At this point, we're still trying to figure out what Ronan even is." It was as much of the truth as she was willing to reveal at the moment.

"That's the data you recovered from our hotel," Skeet said, crossing his arms. "We went back to check the place out this afternoon. Thanks for tearing everything apart—looks like you owe HSP some new long-range communication equipment."

Both Reddic and Mae shot him unimpressed looks. "Well, we're currently one of several Special Tasks Units the Federation hired to patrol the Fringe for Resistance activity."

"You're working for the Feds?" Ziva said.

Reddic nodded. "You said you're still trying to figure out what Ronan is? It's a person. Tav Ronan, leader of the entire Resistance."

Ziva heard Skeet swear behind her. *Well, things just got a lot more interesting.* "Leader of the Resistance. You're kidding."

The man shrugged. "And that's all we know. The Federation dossier is incomplete. We have very little information, no photo. Just the name."

"That explains why we haven't been able to find anything," Aroska mused. "If the Feds don't even know anything about Ronan, how is anyone else supposed to?"

"Why don't they have any data?" Ziva asked. "The Feds and the Resistance have been going at each other for years. Surely they have spies who could have gathered more intel."

"They do have spies," Reddic replied. "The intel is just new. The Feds have suspected there was a sole figure at the top of the Res's food chain for a while, but it's like Ronan is just now coming out of hiding for some reason. The name only started cropping up about four months ago."

*About the time Kat was looking into it,* Ziva thought.

"One of the biggest issues is that the Resistance has been trying to expand farther out into the Fringe, away from Federation presence," Reddic said. "We can't get intel on them if they're not around to give us any. That's where our unit comes in—we're supposed to be driving them back toward the Core systems where the Feds can keep a better eye on them."

Mae's eyes were still glued to the images on the data pad. "But now that they've taken our people, probably killed them—"

"This has become personal," Reddic finished for her. "This is no longer simply a battle between the Federation and Resistance. It's a battle between us and Ronan, and I intend to avenge our soldiers by any means necessary."

Ziva bristled. "And I can't let you do that until we've recovered our agent."

One thing she hated about the Durutians' optical implants was that it made it harder to read their eyes. Still, there was a certain amused twinkle in Reddic's that she didn't care for. "How sweet. I never thought you people were the no-man-left-behind type."

"This has become personal for us, too," Ziva snapped. "HSP is considering it an act of war against the agency. I'm not going to let you go destroy some Resistance facility if there's a chance my agent is inside."

"It's been over four weeks, Payvan. My people are probably dead. What makes you so sure yours is still alive?"

It was a reasonable question, really. Ziva told herself this was a unique situation; Zinni had been taken by an unknown entity that posed an unknown threat level, so in a way, no news was good news. Besides, Kat and Corey had both survived their encounters with Ronan, though for a limited amount of time. Still...if Zinni was alive and had the means to do so, Ziva knew she would have made contact by now. The chances she'd survived until this point were slim, and they grew slimmer with each passing moment.

"That's what I thought," Reddic said when she didn't reply. He stood up and pushed his chair in. "This has been a lovely chat, but we should really be going. We've just wasted over three weeks on this rock." He turned to Mae and leaned down to speak quietly in her ear. "Call Devani. Let her know Haphez is a dead end."

Ziva stood up as well, not the least bit comfortable with him looking down on her. "You've got an agent on Haphez?"

"A Representative," Reddic replied. "What's it to you?"

She turned slightly, addressing Skeet and Aroska as well as the Durutians. "A foreign dignitary would have been taken into protective custody by the agency. If she can be reached by comm, it means the lockdown is over. Call her."

"And talk about what? The weather? Why don't you call in yourselves? Like you just said, the lockdown is over."

"You seem to forget someone smashed our comm equipment," Skeet muttered.

Ziva had yet to holster her weapon, and she reestablished her grip on it. "*Call* her."

"And say what?" Reddic asked again. Despite his gruff tone, he reached for his communicator.

"Ask about the agency, about the lockdown. Ask about Na."

He seemed confused but heeded her instructions, keeping a distasteful eye on her as the transmission connected. "Devani?"

"Remind me to go away more often," said a woman's voice. "We don't even talk this much when we're on the same planet."

"I hate to break it to you, but it's time to go home. New intel—Haphez is a dead end."

"I did not spend five days sitting in a holding room for you to tell me that."

"I know, I'm sorry. We just learned from a new...*source*—" the way he said the word made Ziva fume "—that the Haphezians are hunting Ronan just as much as we are. There's not going to be a Resistance presence there."

The woman sighed. "Well, thank you for letting me know. Are you headed home or back to the Core?"

"Back to the Core," Reddic said. "We'll see if the Feds have any new information we can act on. But hey, before you go...is anything interesting going on there? Heard anything more about that attack on the base you were telling me about?"

"Nothing much. Why?"

"Just curious."

"Let me check the local news feeds." There was silence for a moment, interrupted only by some faint shuffling in the background. "They said the lockdown was in effect until they could determine whether there was still a threat to HSP Headquarters or the military base. If it's over, that must mean they didn't find anything...." Her voice was quiet, distant, like she was talking to herself. "Oh, this is interesting."

Ziva tensed.

"There was some sort of gas released during that attack, and it looks like the people who were exposed are starting to show what they're calling 'adverse symptoms'."

A shiver ran down Ziva's spine and she took a step forward, clenching her jaw to keep her facial expression from changing. There was no need to say anything to Reddic; her eyes did all the talking. *Go on.*

"Like what?" he asked.

"Headaches, numbness, partial paralysis, seizures. Sounds like it was some sort of nerve agent."

The pressure of Skeet and Aroska's collective gaze was almost tangible. They knew better than to say anything right now, but Ziva refrained from turning around all the same. A lump was beginning to form in her throat as she silently mulled this new information over. Unless she was mistaken, the gas on Na was the same substance Kat had been injected with, just as she'd feared. And that, in turn, meant only one thing: Ronan—the Resistance—had been behind the attack.

In the back of her mind, she could still hear Reddic speaking with the woman, discussing when they'd see each other again, but all she could focus on were the chilling words: *"the people who were exposed are starting to show what they're calling adverse symptoms."* If the manifestation of these symptoms had been so delayed and the onset so sudden, there was no telling when hers might start. The prospect terrified her.

"Satisfied?" Reddic asked, ending the transmission. "Now, if you don't mind, we've got a job to do. Under normal circumstances, I might wish you the best of luck. But seeing as how you're once again trying to go after one of my targets, I can't bring myself to do it. I might also say I hope you find your missing agent, but you killed four of my people—good soldiers with families—so maybe it's only fair that you lose someone, too."

"*Huhren shouka souhn!*" she growled, raising her pistol and taking aim for the man's head. She wasn't entirely sure what she was hoping to accomplish. Shooting him was out of the question when there was a whole unit of Durutians waiting just outside. Skeet and Aroska had drawn their own weapons behind her and no doubt had Mae and the technician in their sights. Neither Reddic nor the woman had had a chance to pull their own guns, and a simple wag of Ziva's head told them what the consequences would be if they tried to.

"You can show yourselves out," she muttered.

Each party exchanged one more wary glare before parting company. She waited until Reddic, Mae, and the tech had all exited and shut the door before turning to face Aroska and Skeet. Their intense defensive expressions disappeared altogether as they shifted their attention from the departing Durutians to her.

"Don't try to tell me you weren't involved in that attack, Z," Skeet said. Something verging on fear flashed through his eyes. "We'd hoped you were nowhere near it, but I see it in your face. You were at ground zero."

Was she really being that careless with her body language, or could he just read her that well after all these years? "I was there," she murmured as the implications continued to weigh down on her. "I was exposed."

"Well then, we have to go home!" Aroska said as if the solution were that simple.

Ziva shook her head. "We can't just leave Zinni hanging."

Both men were quiet for a moment. The way they stared at the floor and refused to make eye contact told her two things: they recognized the merit of her point, but they'd also begun to give up on the prospect of finding the intelligence officer. None of them, including her, wanted to say what they were really thinking.

"These symptoms sound exactly like what Kat described," Aroska said, more softly this time. "If that's the case, maybe you can get help in time. Maybe they can synthesize a cure."

"The labs have been studying that syringe since you found it," Ziva replied with a wag of her head. "They still don't know what the hell the stuff even is."

The room was silent once again. Even the sounds of Ray's bustling had ceased; perhaps he had gone out the back door for a smoke.

"He's right, Z," Skeet finally said. "We've been out here chasing false leads for close to five weeks. It was pure coincidence that we even found the Durutians here. It's time to go home."

"If we stop now, Reddic is going to find Ronan first and that bastard is going to wipe out everything in his path, including Zinni."

Skeet took her by the shoulders. The ferocity of his grip told her he knew that as well as she did, and he was devoting all his energy to staying focused. "The Durutians have to regroup, too—it will be a little while before they can cause any damage. We're a three-person team with limited resources and no current means of contacting our agency. If we try to press on right now, the outcome probably isn't going to be pretty, and who knows what could happen to you in the meantime."

Going home and recuperating a bit did sound nice, especially after such a quick turnaround upon returning from Na. But going home also meant wasting what could be valuable time and possibly receiving health-related news she didn't want to hear. And it meant facing Aura Stannist again. Ziva didn't blame the woman one bit for—*how had she put it?*—fighting fire with fire, but dealing with her didn't seem the least bit appealing right now.

"Okay," she finally said. "Where's my ship?"

"Docked in a secure landing bay at the port," Skeet replied.

"One of us will need to fly the *Zenith*. If we cut across one of the Core FTL lanes, it'll get us to Haphez in a little under four days." Ziva heaved a sigh and glanced between the two of them, glad she'd found them and wasn't going back completely empty handed. "Let's go home."

## · 20 ·

## UNKNOWN LOCATION

### FRINGE SPACE

*W*hat do you know?

She was lying flat on her back; that was about it. She was in the same small, dark room, or at least she assumed it was the same one. It smelled the same—like stale air and cold metal—and it looked the same—nothing but blackness. But realistically, there was no way to tell.

*My name is Zinnarana Vax. I'm an HSP agent. They took something from me.*

She wasn't sure who 'they' were or what that 'something' was, but there was a certain emptiness inside her that told her something was missing. It was a very small amount of something, possibly something she didn't need or something that would grow back. The difference left her feeling weaker than usual.

*I can't move.*

As far as she could tell, she wasn't being restrained by anything except her own weight. Her arms rested on the floor at her sides and were rendered numb by an ache that throbbed just above each elbow. Rather than lift them to perform a self-exam, she mentally took herself through the process, focusing on each body part and thinking, feeling... *is something different?*

She reached her toes without finding anything of interest. Unless she was mistaken, she'd had this peculiar feeling on other occasions sometime in the past, but with the way the hours ran together and the way she slipped in and out of consciousness, she had no idea when. She hadn't been able to pinpoint the Difference then, either. Hadn't been able to focus long enough to think about it. Maybe she was a little more lucid now, or maybe the Difference had somehow become more significant.

*What is everywhere but nowhere? Skin, maybe? No...would feel that on the outside. Blood? Did they take my blood?*

The thought made sense, though she had no idea why. She didn't have enough information about her situation or surroundings to know whether it made sense in relation to her circumstances, so she decided it only made sense in relation to her body. Yes, some of her blood had been drawn—not enough to kill her, of course, but more than what was necessary for a typical blood test, hence the severe weakness and ache in her arms. *Well, the weakness is nothing new.*

Satisfied with this conclusion for the time being, she shut her eyes—or maybe they'd been shut the entire time—and let the subtle swaying of the floor carry her off into a dream-like state that really felt no different than when she was awake.

*My name is Zinnarana Vax. I'm still alive.*

## · 21 ·
# HSP Headquarters
### Noro, Haphez

"*That's* your probation officer?" Aroska said as the three of them left the *Intrepid* and *Zenith* behind and moved across the landing platform toward the cluster of people gathered at the door.

"Disciplinary and Personnel Control Specialist," Ziva corrected with a roll of her eyes. The picture was all too familiar; she couldn't believe it had already been over a week since she'd crossed this same landing pad and found Aura Stannist waiting for her. The woman's outfit was even the same, and she wore the same thick braid draped over her shoulder. At their first meeting, she'd stood tall and erect with a very dignified air hanging about her. This time, she stood with one hand resting on a cocked hip, clutching her data pad with the other. One foot tapped impatiently at the ground.

"Even before the trial, there were rumors the Royal Offices would be sending a stiff," Skeet said, "but damn. The only other eyes I've seen that are that cold are yours, Z."

Ziva could only scoff. There *was* something rather unnerving about Aura, no doubt the reason she'd been selected to come here. The woman's icy glare could be felt from across the platform, and for a moment, she wondered if this was what people felt like when *she* stared at them. If so, she was pleased it had the desired effect, but she wasn't enjoying being on the receiving end of it.

Emeri moved toward them, mercifully giving her something else to focus on for a moment. She extended her hand to shake, but he bypassed her arm entirely and came closer still. For a split second, she thought he might hug her for some inexplicable reason, but he simply took her by the shoulders and looked her up and down as if searching for injuries or abnormalities.

"I'm fine," she said, surprised by the fatherly concern he was showing. "We heard about what's going on, but I swear I'm fine."

"How did you know it was clear to come home? We weren't expecting you for at least another week."

"We ran into some Durutians on Aubin who had a contact here on the planet. It's kind of an interesting story, one that may shed some light on everything that's been happening. I think it's time for a long, thorough—" her gaze flitted past him toward Aura "—and private debrief."

He nodded. "I understand, though I'm not sure if it's possible. She hasn't reported either of us to the Royal Offices yet, but she doesn't hesitate to remind me that she *can* and *will*. She's been obsessed with getting you back since we heard about what was happening with the attack victims, so I doubt she'll want to let you out of her sight. I'd tread lightly if I were you."

As tired as she was, Ziva had half a mind to heed his advice. Upon thinking harder, however, she knew she'd never give in to the probation officer. Maybe it was partially out of spite, but she also knew if she'd remained on the planet where Aura could keep an eye on her, Skeet and Aroska would probably be dead, they'd be no closer to finding Zinni, and they would never have learned the truth about Ronan or the Resistance. She'd defy the woman again in a heartbeat if that was what it took to keep the people she cared about alive.

The four of them proceeded toward the door where Aura waited with Adin Woro and his team. Based on his placid demeanor, Ziva guessed someone had finally briefed him on the situation, successfully quashing the fear he'd felt after Skeet and Aroska's disappearance. She gave him a respectful nod, throwing one toward Mari Rebek and Colin Zier as well before bracing herself and turning her attention to Aura.

To her surprise, the woman wasn't looking at her at all. Her eyebrows were arched and her focus remained on her data pad as she made a show of entering something into it. *So much for a clean slate*, Ziva thought as she continued inside behind Emeri. She cringed when she heard the *clack clack clack* of Aura's shoes chasing after them.

Adin, Mari, and Colin broke away from the procession and returned to the field ops squad floor, armed with the new data Skeet had compiled on Ronan during the trip home. The rest of them continued on to Emeri's office, where the doors were immediately locked and the windows tinted.

"Doctor Baez requested that I send you to Na for observation forthwith upon your return," Emeri said, glancing across the conference table at Ziva as they all gathered around. "We shouldn't waste any time here."

Ziva nodded toward Skeet and Aroska, who began updating the director on everything that had happened since the implementation of Condition Black. They'd picked up emissions signatures from the ship that had taken Zinni right around the time they'd received the order to cease communications. They'd gone to investigate those signatures near Bectin, but the trail had been cold by the time they'd arrived, so they'd continued on to set up a new base on Aubin. Ziva was already familiar with most of what had happened after that. She listened as they talked about scoping out the Durutians, unable to help but notice the unimpressed look on Aura's face when they confessed to being captured.

She waited until they got to their would-be execution to chime in. "That's when I got there. I'd started by checking out Niio, just like you suggested." She thought it best to not mention the part about owing Tobias a favor as long as Aura was in the room and opted to leave her visit with the mobster out of the story entirely. "I traced the *Intrepid's* trajectory and headed for Aubin, hoping for the best. A local contact confirmed my team's presence and pointed me toward the Durutians' stronghold. I arrived just in time to see them transporting Lieutenant Duvo and Sergeant Tarbic to the desert for execution. I followed them out and neutralized all four of the 'borgs before they could act. We barely made it back into the city before the sandstorm hit."

"You killed four members of the Durutian Special Forces," Aura muttered, aghast. She tapped furiously at her data pad. "I cannot believe this."

"It was either that or allow them to kill two of our people," Ziva retorted. "Which would you have preferred?"

"Payvan," Emeri said, his voice quiet but firm.

She whipped her head toward him, jaw clenched. The message in his eyes was clear: *Please be careful.*

"We thought they were working for Ronan," she said, struggling to maintain composure. She produced the data pad with Tobias's photos. "It made sense considering it appeared to be a group of Durutians who took Officer Vax from that warehouse on Niio."

"Except it turned out they weren't working for Ronan," Skeet said.

Both Emeri and Aura stood in stunned silence. The probation officer once again went about entering something into her data pad. Ziva could only imagine what kind of memo she was compiling—*"murdered four members of a neutral foreign military who actually weren't conspiring with the enemy."*

"If they weren't working for Ronan, why the hell were they going to execute you?" Emeri said.

"Because they thought *we* were working for Ronan," Ziva answered. "I arranged a meeting with their leader. Turns out we've met before—he was the Durutian operative I injured on that solo mission on Vellom a couple of years ago." She caught herself before elaborating further, and her eyes shifted toward Aroska for a split second. *The mission I left for right after I killed Soren.*

"Long story short," she continued, "this particular group of 'borgs is currently employed by the Federation. And Ronan, as it turns out, is the leader of the Resistance. The people who took Zinni on Niio were Resistance agents dressed in the uniforms of a Durutian patrol they captured. It happened just outside our system, yet another reason Reddic's group was so suspicious of us."

"*Sheyss,*" Emeri muttered. "You're saying the *Resistance* was behind Kat Reilly's illness and Vax's capture?"

"And, unless I'm mistaken, the attack on Na."

Based on the look on the director's face, he'd already begun to form that theory. "We've confirmed that the substances from the base and Reilly's syringe are nearly identical," he said with a nod. "The purpose is clear: attack the nervous system. The gaseous state obviously allows for a larger, faster distribution. But this particular chemical composition isn't in any of our databases."

To Ziva's surprise, the sour look on Aura's face had abated in the last few moments. "Is Ronan some kind of scientist, then? Records indicate that the name was printed on Reilly's syringe."

"Could be," Aroska said, "or at least the person in charge of this chemical's development and distribution."

"Forward me the data, please." The woman paused and shot Ziva a glance that looked almost apologetic—perhaps she was beginning to realize the merit of their encounter with the Durutians, however unorthodox. But the flicker was gone in an instant, replaced by her usual impassive expression. "It would be best if we kept the media completely out of the loop on this, but I need to go connect with Haphor and alert the Royal House to the situation. Excuse me."

They all watched in silence as she strode out. Ziva couldn't help but notice how similar she and Aura were; it was no doubt the biggest contribution to their continual clashing. They both thrived on making threats until they got their way, but their drive to learn the truth often kept them from making good on those threats. To the Royal Officer's credit, Aura was the perfect candidate for this assignment. A lesser agent would have crumbled under the pressure and Ziva would have taken delight in running circles around them. It was almost a relief to be babysat by someone for whom she could muster up some semblance of respect.

"Are you sure you're feeling okay?" Emeri said after a moment.

"I'm fine," Ziva reassured him. "We heard the news from a Durutian diplomat who was held here during the lockdown."

"Ah yes, Devani Reddic. I spoke with her at length regarding the Resistance presence—or lack thereof—in the region. Some relation to this Taran Reddic you encountered?"

Ziva raised an eyebrow at the mention of the woman's last name. "I assume so. The way she spoke, it sounded like things were getting pretty bad on Na. I half expected to get sick on the trip home, but I kept a close watch on my vitals and ran myself through a series of cognition and motor tests during the flight. Nothing out of the ordinary."

"You haven't experienced *any* of the symptoms?" Emeri said. "No numbness? No headaches?"

She shook her head. "No more than…" She stopped when something clicked in her mind. A series of memories presented themselves all at once, and she struggled for a moment to sort them all out. "…normal," she murmured.

She took a step away from the table, staring straight ahead at Emeri and Aroska. "Skeet, will you excuse us?"

"What?" He crossed his arms. "Why?"

"Just do it. I'll brief you later."

"But Z—"

"Lieutenant! Do not make me tell you again!"

He hesitated for a few more seconds, clearly unnerved by the request. Then he spun on his heel and went out, walking with heavy footfalls Ziva could still hear even after the door had shut. Emeri and Aroska kept their focus on his departure for a moment before warily turning their attention back to her.

"It's nostium," she said.

Both men watched her with gaping mouths for a beat before speaking simultaneously: "What?"

Ziva looked around until her gaze fell upon a crystal award on Emeri's display shelf across the room. She extended her hand and called to it with her mind, and it was in her grasp in the blink of an eye.

"It's *nostium*," she repeated, unable to suppress a shiver as the telltale surge of energy rushed down her spine. Several seconds passed and she felt no stabbing pain in her head. She held up the crystal statue. "Before that attack, I probably wouldn't have been able to do what I just did. Even if I could, I would've been left with an excruciating headache."

"But why is it having such a negative effect on everyone but you?" Emeri asked as if he were speaking to some ethereal being.

"Gamon—my trainer, master—never elaborated on the science of it all, but it's possible that my brain is conditioned to the chemical and everything it does. I remember the first time I received a real infusion. I was dizzy and sick for hours before my body started to adapt. A little dizziness is normal—happened with every infusion after that—but it's immediate and temporary. These symptoms the Na victims are showing are abnormally delayed and severe. This isn't how it's supposed to work."

She caught herself when she realized what she was saying. She'd never talked about any of this with anyone, not even Gamon. The closest she'd ever come was the conversation over dinner while the team had Jayden Saiffe in custody, or maybe when Aroska had teased her in the kitchen with the kytara. Both men were currently watching her as if she were speaking some foreign language neither of them could understand.

"You really are one of them," Emeri said, shaking his head. "That man you killed—he wasn't trying to kidnap you at all. He was your teacher."

"He *was* trying to take me," Ziva spat. "Everything I told HSP during that time was true, except for the fact that I knew him. He was trying to persuade me to come with him to a new Resistance base, and when I refused, he tried to take me by force. It was self-defense."

She stopped when she heard her own words. She'd forgotten much about that final conversation with Gamon, but one part had always stuck with her: the part where he'd tried to treat her as an object of his own creation. His voice echoed through her memory: *"You have no future here. Come with me to Forus. There's a new Resistance hideout there, and they're trying to develop a new nostium formula. As a Haphezian, you'd be an invaluable asset. Come put your talents to good use and help us make a difference. I've spent twelve years creating the perfect warrior—don't tell me it was all for nothing."*

"By the five moons," she murmured. "Forus."

"Forus?" Emeri repeated.

"That's where he wanted to take me," she said with a scoff and a wag of her head. "He said there was a new Resistance base there. And that GA fighter that crashed at the base?" She had to suppress a curse as her voice rose in volume. "Major Sheen told me it was one of several ships presumed lost in a battle near Forus a few years ago. The auto-pilot system was online, but it still would have needed a carrier to bring it to the area. Sheen said they had people trying to salvage what was left of the internal computer—any news on that front?"

Emeri shook his head. "There was too much damage. No way to review the ship's flight path or see who engaged the autopilot system. They did find evidence of sabotage in the engine compartment, though. Looks like a small charge was detonated remotely to cause the crash."

"You're saying the Resistance captured that fighter and had it all this time?" Aroska said. "Then they brought it back here and used it against us?"

Ziva shrugged. "It worked, didn't it? No one at the base even noticed anything was wrong until it started coming down. I'm lucky they noticed when they *did* or that thing would have landed right on top of me."

Aroska's reaction to her words took her by surprise. Concern flashed through his eyes, akin to what she'd seen in the brief moments of clarity while lying on the Argall landing pad in a puddle of her own blood. "You were that close?" he said quietly.

"I was. Could have been inside the mess hall—that would have been interesting."

Emeri spoke up again before Aroska could respond. "If Ronan has had this fighter for all these years and sent it back here for the sole purpose of crashing it on the moon and exposing people to this…this *nostium*, that leads me to believe there's been a plan to attack us all along."

"Why the hell would they want to attack us?" Aroska said with a grunt. "We've been nothing but neutral throughout their entire war with the Federation."

"No, no, that doesn't make any sense." Ziva massaged her temples. "Nostium isn't lethal. They wouldn't have used it if the intent was to kill. Unless…" She looked to the director, wide-eyed. "You said Kat's substance and the gas were *nearly* identical? There were differences?"

He nodded. "The labs have reported subtle differences in the molecular structure. It's clear the two substances were designed to have the same effect, but they are, nevertheless, different."

"*Sheyss.* These are new formulas."

"What?"

"Gamon said they'd been working to develop a new formula after the Federation destroyed all their former development facilities. And Jayden!" Ziva whirled toward Aroska. "You were there! At dinner that night, Jayden Saiffe said something about Nosti resurfacing around the galaxy. I just ignored it because that's what we always do, and let's face it, he was trying my patience. But they're resurfacing because they've got a *frouchten* new formula."

He crossed his arms. "If they've been working on it for over ten years, why is it still causing so many problems?"

Ziva paused when she realized she'd begun pacing back and forth in front of the table. "Imperfections, or maybe these are just bad batches," she said, talking more to herself than anyone else. "The Feds hunted and killed any known Nosti—that's why Gamon came here to begin with—and the Resistance facilities were all demolished. They would have had to start developing a new formula from scratch. That would take time and involve a lot of trial and error." She crossed her arms and stared vacantly at the tinted picture window for a moment. "It almost seems like this formula is too strong. The one Kat was injected with acted more slowly but still overwhelmed her nervous system. The gas on Na was quicker, though still not as quick as nostium is supposed to be, and again, it's proving to be too much for the victims to handle."

It seemed like Emeri hadn't stopped shaking his head since the beginning of the conversation. "Clearly some Nosti managed to survive. Why not take blood samples from them and synthesize a new formula that way?"

"It doesn't work like that. Nostium is supposed to be undetectable in the bloodstream. This stuff *is* detectable, which is just one more factor that leads me to believe it's too strong. Too potent, if you will. I never learned much about how it works, but I know it only stays in the bloodstream until it reaches the brain. It's been engineered to pass through the blood-brain barrier and it essentially 'sticks' in the brain, stimulating the subject until it wears off. Standard procedure was to receive a fresh nostium infusion every six years, but it's been...*had been* over nine years since my last infusion, and I could still feel traces of it."

Emeri and Aroska could only stare at her as if they still couldn't believe what they were hearing. She doubted either of them had ever taken much time to really consider the weight of her secret. Neither of them had ever expected it to end up playing such a pivotal role, especially not in agency matters. She hadn't, either.

"Then there's no 'cure,' per se," Emeri said. "Even though the nostium isn't hurting you, we can't, say, draw your blood and distribute it to the other victims."

Ziva shook her head. "That wouldn't accomplish anything."

"What about a scan? You said your brain has already been properly conditioned. We can see how this stuff is supposed to be working, compare it to the scans from everyone on Na, maybe figure out some way to counteract it."

"Could something like that be done in time to save those people?" Aroska asked.

"It's doubtful," Emeri replied. "They're in bad shape. Many of them are already starting to exhibit the same symptoms Ms. Reilly documented in her friend's final days."

"Then what would a scan accomplish?" Ziva said, finally resigning to a nearby chair.

"We're not going to take the Resistance's actions lightly. This has never been our fight, but whether we like it or not, it is now. If this thing escalates, or if Ronan decides to try anything else, we need to be prepared."

"And who would do the scan? One of you? It's not like I can waltz into a med center and tell them everything I know."

"I know that." The director pulled up another chair and sat down in front of her. "But this is information the government and military need to know. Everyone has to understand what we're really dealing with here. We can have the scan done by someone we trust, and nobody will have to know exactly where the information came from."

"And who exactly do 'we' trust enough to do something like that?"

He shrugged as if the answer were obvious. "Anson Baez."

Ziva tilted her head, staring him down through slightly narrowed eyes. "Look, I liked the guy and all, but not enough to go spill my life secret to him."

"You think he doesn't already know, Ziva?"

Her train of thought came crashing to a stop and she saw Emeri bristle in response to the look she gave him. "*What?*" she said through her teeth, standing back up.

"Just listen for a minute before you blow up on me," he said, speaking with the same authority as he had upon her arrival home from Na. He rose to his feet as well. "Baez is an old friend. He was the field medic assigned to the unit of marines I accompanied back during the Fringe War. Saved my life twice. We've kept in contact ever since."

"But—"

"You think I had you dragged all over the planet after Argall for no reason? I wanted you back here at HSP's med center so we'd have control over the situation. Once they'd confirmed your head injuries, I wanted someone trustworthy to handle them. We couldn't have just anyone monitoring your brain activity. Baez had already agreed to oversee your rehab, but I brought him on board early so I could have him running point throughout your entire treatment process. He's owed me a favor for the past couple of years, and he has made good on that favor by maintaining confidentiality."

Baez *had* struck her as being someone she could trust, a trait she often had trouble finding in people. At the moment, however, Ziva's attention was divided between the fact that the doctor had known her secret the whole time and the fact that Emeri had managed to pull one over on her. As tempting as it was to yell and threaten to never trust him again, she knew he'd made the right move. Briefing a single, dependable ally was better than having the whole planet find out while she was incapacitated in the hospital, and to Baez's credit, she hadn't even picked up on the fact that he was keeping something from her.

Aroska had been looking rather lost for the past couple of minutes, but he stepped forward and shrugged. "If that's the case, I'd have to agree that bringing him into the picture now would be a smart move. Even if it's too late to save the soldiers who were exposed, we need to be able to defend ourselves against potential Resistance attacks in the future."

"I'll contact Baez and have him come down here," Emeri said. "He's probably still expecting me to send you back to Na for examination. We can have him run the tests at our facility and then send the results back to the GA's neurologists under an anonymous name."

"And what happens when people start wondering why I haven't shown any symptoms?" Ziva said.

Both men were silent for a moment as if neither of them had given it much thought yet. "We'll think of something," Emeri assured her. "Not that many people know you were on Na in the first place, and even fewer are aware you were at ground zero. For now, we can just say there's been a delay in the manifestation of the symptoms."

"That's probably not going to fly for very long," Ziva said. "But while we're contacting the military, I'd suggest withdrawing the garrison stationed at Tantal. If the Federation doesn't even know about this new nostium formula, I shudder to think of how Jayden Saiffe knew the Nosti were resurfacing. Tantal claims to be an independent colony, but if I didn't know any better, I'd say the Tantalis have been involved with the Resistance to some extent. We shouldn't take any chances."

"Duly noted," Emeri said. "Let's not waste any more time." He moved to one of the comm pads at the table, dismissing the two of them with a dip of his head.

Ziva could hear him initiating a transmission as they walked out. She stiffened a bit when she felt Aroska place a reassuring hand on the back of her shoulder. It was more startling than anything; she *did* feel...well, reassured.

For a moment, she tried to imagine what the situation would be like if she'd never saved his life at Dakiti. He'd be dead, Emeri wouldn't know about her Nostia, and right now, she'd either be confessing everything for the first time or standing by and letting people die. She had to admit it felt good to have someone backing her up.

"We've gotten ourselves caught up in quite the *sheyss* storm, haven't we?" he muttered.

She sighed. "We sure have."

# · 22 ·
## MEANWHILE...
## PATROL FRIGATE *VIGILANCE*
### FRINGE SPACE

Regardless of how many times she saw it, the wide view of open space through her cabin's viewport took Commander Sadey Payne's breath away. She caught herself when she realized she was staring and returned her attention to the workbench in front of her. The repairs to her kytara were nearly complete; a few more minor tweaks were all it would take to realign the left blade and keep it from catching on the inside of the grip every time it engaged. The damage had been done during a practice duel nearly a week prior, leaving her with only a single functional blade the previous day when she'd faced a real threat. She cursed herself for having been too busy—and maybe even too lazy—to fix it sooner.

The PF *Vigilance* drifted through empty space as her crew awaited the all-clear signal from Forus Command. To any passersby, they were a trade ship transporting businesspeople and merchandise to and from the hundreds of manufacturing plants and conference centers Forus boasted. As such, they had to actually do some transporting every so often in order to maintain a legitimate façade, but much of that transportation was between the various companies controlled covertly by the Resistance. Very few people paid them any mind out here so far from the Core worlds, but on the off chance they were stopped by a Federation patrol, they had a legitimate shipping manifest and carried legitimate clients with legitimate destinations. It just so happened that most of those clients were Resistance agents.

In reality, the *Vigilance* was a battle-ready vessel with thirty guns—for protecting valuable cargo and passengers, as far as the authorities were concerned—a crew of two hundred trained soldiers who could double as civilians at the blink of an eye, state-of-the-art anti-plasma shielding, and two hidden cargo bays that had been retrofitted to house up to three shuttles and ten fighters simultaneously. The entire ship was one big undercover operation, and Sadey couldn't have been prouder of the job her crew was doing keeping it that way.

She allowed an exasperated growl to escape her throat and swiveled in her chair to search the cabin for the tiny set of pliers she'd been holding only minutes before. Just as she'd suspected, they were sitting on the corner of her desk across the room, right where she'd set them when she'd gotten up to respond to an incoming transmission. With a sigh, she stretched out her hand and called to them with her mind. They were in her grasp a split second later, and a faint tingle continued creeping over her skin as she went about putting the finishing touches on the kytara.

She set the restored weapon down but only got to admire it for a full two seconds before there was a knock on her cabin door. Performing the delicate repairs had kept her mind occupied as she'd waited for Ronan's instructions, and the sudden presence of another crewmember reminded her that they had a job to do.

"Enter," she called, rising to her feet.

The door hissed open and a striking young man with jet-black hair and pale blue eyes entered—just the man she'd wanted to see. Lieutenant Jalen Gero stopped and stood at attention, giving her a quick salute. "You said I should report to you at sixteen hundred, ma'am," he said in a clipped, efficient tone.

Sadey offered a salute in return, chagrined that the time had managed to creep up on her. "I wanted to make sure you've been fully briefed on all the mission parameters."

"Yes ma'am," he replied, clasping his hands behind his back. His blue eyes had taken on that same cold quality Sadey often recognized in her covert operatives. He was only in his mid-twenties, but he'd become one of the finest soldiers under her command. He'd already donned a black stealth suit in preparation for his upcoming assignment, and he stood there watching her with a calculating gaze and certain attention to detail that told her he was well-versed in his field. Like many of their people, he was of average-verging-on-small stature but no less capable for it. The smaller build made them all more effective in the realm of melee combat, an art which valued speed, agility, and dexterity over brute force and size.

"I'm confident you understand the 'what' of this mission," Sadey said, "but do you understand the 'why?' It's important to me that you do."

Jalen hesitated. "I understand the basics."

It wasn't quite the answer Sadey wanted to hear. "The operation on the Haphezian moon didn't work—we've established that much. Yes, the distribution method worked splendidly, but this particular nostium formula still isn't having the desired effect on its subjects. It's acting more quickly than what we developed on Chaiavis, so progress is being made on that front, but we can't have it killing everyone who is exposed to it. It needs to be a supplement, not a detriment."

"Then what's the point of exposing multiple people at once? Why aren't we just testing revised formulas on a single person like we used to?"

"You've seen the news feeds, Lieutenant. Over ninety people were exposed to some extent at the base, which means we have ninety new data points, ninety new sets of results. That's also ninety less people who can retaliate against us, assuming they ever even find out who attacked them."

"And what happens when one of these formulas works?"

"Well then, Haphez won't be a neutral world anymore, will it?"

That was the key. Assuming the chemical engineers managed to design a nostium formula that didn't cause its subjects to drop dead, select groups of Haphezians would suddenly become Nosti without even meaning to. Sadey took that back—they'd never be *real* Nosti. The act of wielding Nostia and a personalized kytara was an art form they'd never understand. Still, the Federation wouldn't see it that way. One anonymous tip to the Feds would be all it took to start a war with the

Haphezians and leave the rest of the galaxy oblivious to Ronan's intentions. The Haphezians were really nothing but a scapegoat in this situation, and unfortunately for them, they'd set themselves up perfectly for it thanks to their desperate attempts at remaining uninvolved and independent over the years. Once the Federation got wind that something was amiss, that neutrality would be gone in a heartbeat.

"The Haphezian military is the perfect candidate for this experiment," she continued. "If bad nostium doesn't wipe them out, the Federation will. Either way, we don't have to worry much about them coming after us."

"And the purpose of my mission is to cut the head off the snake," Jalen said. It wasn't a question; he *did* understand.

A smile crept onto Sadey's lips. "Exactly. If nothing happens, we'll know we have a successful formula, and the Feds will be out here to clean up in no time. And if it doesn't work, it will further cripple the military, and we can revise the formula accordingly. Either way, it's a win for us."

Jalen mimicked her sly grin. "I'm proud to have been chosen for this assignment, ma'am. I won't let you down."

"Glad to hear it, Lieutenant. We're trying the formula in a gaseous state again—that way, it has the most chance of affecting multiple people. Inserting it directly into the ventilation system and trapping it in an enclosed space may be helpful in terms of ensuring a consistent degree of exposure in all victims."

"Understood."

"The nostium won't affect you, of course, but I want you to get out of there as fast as you can anyway. The high-profile target is going to draw a sizable law enforcement presence. This is not a suicide mission. We want you to come back alive if possible, but if you *are* captured and escape is not an option, I assume you have a contingency plan."

Jalen nodded and tapped the small pocket on the left shoulder of his stealth suit, the same pocket where they all kept their choice of suicide pill. Ever since the war with the Federation over twenty years prior, the Nosti way of life had hinged on its ability to remain a secret.

In the rest of the galaxy's eyes, they were simply common people, ordinary inhabitants of various Resistance-affiliated worlds. But being captured—by anyone, not just the Feds—likely meant their secret would be revealed, and over two decades of hard work and planning would be down the drain. None of them were strangers to the idea of giving up their lives for the cause.

"And I assume you have some sort of odor-masking spray? You know how the Haphezians are."

"I do, ma'am."

Sadey allowed her features to soften a bit. "Just listen to me, going on about things you've already been briefed about."

"It's all right," Jalen replied with a smile. "I'm glad to know you've got my back."

"Well, then. Don't let me keep you from your preparations. You'll find the capsule containing the nostium down in the medbay. I'm expecting mission confirmation at any moment. When that happens, it will just be a twenty-minute FTL jump to the Noro system. Go make us proud, Lieutenant."

"Yes, Commander," Jalen said, the confidence rolling off him in waves. He gave her another hearty salute and strode out, once more leaving her alone in the silence of her cabin.

Satisfied with the state of her kytara, Sadey bypassed the workbench and moved straight to the viewport, standing at rest as she let herself get lost in the view again. She'd never been to Haphez; this mission was the closest she'd ever come. Before Ronan's plan had been set in motion, most Resistance fighters had steered clear of the planet for fear that they'd be discovered by the Haphezians and turned over to the Federation. The Nosti especially had kept their distance, not fans of the idea of being executed on sight.

Jak Gamon had been the only one of them to ever effectively establish himself on Haphez. At the time, Phase One of their plan hadn't been scheduled to start for another five years, but he'd insisted that starting early would increase the chances of their little experiment succeeding. Not to mention, an independent world like Haphez was a perfect place to hide from the Federation immediately following the war.

He'd been right about starting early. That little girl he'd stumbled upon had ended up being the perfect recruit. Naturally strong and intelligent, but driven by anger and the desire to fight, she was everything they'd been hoping for and more. Gamon had kept the rest of them updated on her progress but had suggested withholding the truth about her purpose from her until it was time to come join the rest of the group. Sadey and Ronan had both warned him against it, but he'd feared the girl's allegiance would be underdeveloped if he told her any sooner.

In the end of course, they'd been right. They'd waited a full day after Gamon was scheduled to bring Ziva Payvan to them before accessing the Haphezian news feeds. Sure enough, he was dead, overpowered and killed by his own student. Sadey had petitioned to try again, citing the overall success of the project despite the outcome, and had even volunteered to go to Haphez herself. But Ronan wouldn't hear of it, not after that incident. The Haphezian authorities had become hypervigilant and sending another Nosti to the planet was far too risky. So instead, they'd spent the past ten years quietly working through the remaining phases of their plan, struggling through the parts that had originally relied on Gamon and Payvan's contribution.

No one had ever discussed the details, but Sadey knew some of her counterparts in Resistance leadership had considered hunting Payvan down after all these years and still finding a way to work her into their scheme. Up until a couple of months earlier, she hadn't even known where to start looking, but then they'd caught wind of an assassination Payvan was wanted for and had found her name in various news networks throughout the Fringe. She was nearly thirty years old now, an operative for the Haphezian Special Police. That alone effectively rendered her too hot of a target; any attempts to go after her would draw far too much attention, assuming they could even find her in the first place. The woman was trained to disappear, and according to the news, she'd done just that after the assassination.

Sadey sighed and turned away from the window. Having Payvan and being able to study a successful Haphezian nostium infusion would have been—and would still be—immeasurably helpful to their efforts, but alas. They were doing just fine without her; things were just moving more slowly than any of them had wanted. The original plan had been to recruit one Haphezian to their cause and then essentially blackmail the rest of them into joining unless they wanted the Feds to come after them. The idea was that there was strength in numbers. A single civilization, regardless of its military prowess, would be obliterated by the Federation, so joining the Resistance would give the Haphezians a chance to defend themselves. But following Gamon's death, they'd instead focused their efforts on converting as many remaining Resistance members as possible to Nosti. The Feds had sent them limping back to their side of the Core after the war, and even now, over twenty years later, they were still trying to rebuild. They may have had inferior numbers, but when the vast majority of those people had covertly become skilled Nosti, the odds began to tip back in their favor.

Her comm system came alive the moment she turned and laid eyes on it. She rushed over and watched with bated breath as a blinking light on the console flashed yellow then turned green. Ronan hadn't wanted to risk voice transmissions for this operation—the crew of the *Vigilance* had literally been waiting for a green light.

Sadey tapped out a quick *message received* code and picked up the comm receiver, opening a direct line to the ship's navigator. "We're a go."

# · 23 ·
# PALACE OF THE ROYAL GENERAL
## HAPHOR, HAPHEZ

"Rotera," Jada Jaroon answered after pausing for a moment to consider the question. "The different minerals in the soil there make it turn all sorts of colors. There's an overlook where you can stand and see out over these rolling hills, and it looks like the ground has been painted in shades of red and purple. Gorgeous." She nodded to herself and took a bite of the shredded warco meat that had been stuffed into a piece of folded flatbread. "What about you? Where's your favorite view away from home?"

Vonn, head chef for the Jaroon household, folded his thick arms across his chest and leaned against the kitchen counter. "I'd have to go with Osari," he answered. "What can I say? I can't get enough of the ocean. Osari has some of the most breathtaking coastlines I've ever seen, maybe even better than ours."

That was quite the declaration coming from him, considering he hailed from the Mairo Region that bordered the Sea of Haphez on the opposite side of the planet. These late-night conversations always somehow gravitated toward the topic of travel. Vonn had done a lot of exploring before being employed by the Jaroons. He'd been to every civilized Fringe world and even to some of the Core worlds, picking up various ethnic recipes and cooking tips along the way. He always laughed when Jada asked for a simple warco wrap.

As a member of the Royal House, she rarely got the chance to travel for leisure, so she enjoyed listening to his stories as much as he enjoyed telling them. She wasn't sure when the man ever slept; he was always working in the kitchen, at the beck and call of anyone who ever needed anything regardless of the time of day. He was probably lonely, and she guessed he liked having someone to talk to, someone who actually listened. Jaril and Jazel were always so rude to him during meals.

This routine of coming to the kitchen for a midnight snack had become the norm over the past month or so. Jada never had been able to successfully adapt to the Haphezian custom of only eating every other day. Her puny single stomach craved nourishment more often, especially since she'd begun a new nighttime exercise routine. One of Vonn's warco wraps—with some secret ingredient he refused to tell her about—made the perfect snack before calling it a night.

"Never been to Osari," she said with a smile. "I'll have to put it on my list."

"Be sure to send a holo when you get there."

"Will do." She swallowed the last bite of her wrap and stood up, insisting she be allowed to put the plate through the washing system herself. Vonn did enough work as it was, and she was already encroaching in his supposed off-duty time by being there. "Thanks, Vonn. You're the best. Good night!"

The man beamed. "No problem, my lady. Good ni—"

Jada paused, disconcerted by the look that had come over his face in just a fraction of a second. Nothing else about him or their surroundings seemed to have changed. She opened her mouth to ask what was wrong, but he held up a hand to stop her. Judging by the tilt of his head, he was listening to something.

The urgency with which he moved compelled her to comply. There were times when she'd been tempted to have some sort of hearing aid implanted so she could be on par with her Haphezian counterparts. Not being able to hear everything they could drove her mad, especially in situations where her safety was potentially at stake...like now. She glanced around, unable to pinpoint the sound Vonn was hearing and unsure where it could even be coming from.

She didn't need a sensitive Haphezian nose to pick up the scent that suddenly wafted into the kitchen. It was something she'd only smelled on a few occasions, but it had been quite unforgettable: *cha'sen*.

The stench sent a wave of nausea rolling through her stomach and the warco wrap threatened to come back up. She and Vonn both turned toward the small service hallway that led to a door off the back patio. The scent seemed to be coming from just beyond that door, and the intensity was enough to make her wonder if someone had died.

Vonn's reaction confirmed that theory. "Stay back, Jada," he said, stepping between her and the hallway. She couldn't bring herself to care that he hadn't called her by a proper title. At the moment, she could only be envious of the fact that the *cha'sen* was nothing more than a musty body odor to him.

Unsure if it would be a help or a hindrance, she reached to the nearest wall panel and shut off the lights. An emergency light remained on at the end of the hallway; if anyone tried to come through the door, they'd have ample warning. That exit would be locked at this time of night, but if someone had managed to kill a guard, Jada didn't doubt their ability to break through a locked kitchen door.

"We need to move," he whispered. His large hand wrapped cleanly around her entire upper arm, and he nudged her toward the door into the dining room.

Jada needed no persuasion. There'd be a guard stationed in the foyer for the night and they needed to get to him, warn him about what was happening.

They broke into the dining area and found the man already headed their way, wide-eyed. "Lady Jada, you need to come with me. There's been a breach in security."

She nodded as she and Vonn fell into stride behind him and made their way out into the foyer and sitting area. Njo and Namani Jaroon were being hustled down the massive spiral staircase by another member of the security detail, and Jada rushed toward them as they reached the bottom. Her mother looked her up and down and placed an arm around her shoulder, and her father gave her a reassuring pat on the head before moving forward to address the guards.

"What's the situation?" he asked. His voice was surprisingly calm, but his furrowed eyebrows and steely features spoke of confusion and concern.

"Man down outside the kitchen access door," the head of security replied, finger pressed to his ear as he listened to the reports flooding his earpiece. "Repeat last transmission." He nodded and beckoned for them to follow him toward the front door, where two more of the guards covered the entrance. "We have someone in custody, but we need to get you all somewhere safe—"

They hadn't made it three steps before a cloud of greenish-gray smoke erupted from the nearest air duct. The man spun around and herded them back in the opposite direction, only to lead them straight into another cloud billowing from the vent above the dining room doorway.

"Get down!"

Jada was already in the process of diving to the floor. She kept her face as near to the ground as possible and tugged the collar of her shirt up over her nose and mouth, though she doubted it would do much good—she could already feel a tickle in her throat and had to resist the urge to cough for fear of inhaling more gas. It had an odd smell to it, some quality that seemed almost metallic. She crawled forward a few meters, holding her breath as best she could, then paused when she realized no one seemed to be following. She could hear them coughing and sputtering, but the sounds all remained in one place and carried an unnatural, desperate tone that compelled her to look back.

The sight behind her rendered her completely numb and her hand fell away from her face. She'd been walking past her father's office a couple of days earlier and had stolen a peek through the open door just in time to glimpse some footage from the Grand Army's med centers. It had showed one of the soldiers from the attack on Na, strapped to his bed, eyes crazed but vacant. The man's body had been overtaken by spasms and the medical staff had been attempting to hold him down and insert something into his mouth that would prevent him from biting his own tongue. This was, apparently, what was happening to all the troops who'd been exposed to the gas after the fighter crashed. As much as the sight had disturbed her, she hadn't been able to look away, and the memory of it had kept her awake later that night.

Now here, in her own home, with her own family, she was seeing the same thing again.

# · 24 ·
# HSP MEDICAL CENTER
## NORO, HAPHEZ

The corridors of the HSP med center's neuroscience wing were eerily quiet at this hour. It was late at night—no, the time-stamp on the nearby monitor showed it was actually early morning—and all the medical personnel had gone home, leaving only a skeleton staff to govern the building. They were all in their offices, making rounds, or tending to patients, and the labs and exam rooms were left alone. Emeri had insisted they wait until now to bring her in, partially from a privacy standpoint and partially because Baez had been tied down helping with the situation on Na and hadn't been able to get free any earlier.

The chair Ziva sat in was designed to tip backward until she was flat on her back. It would then slide on smooth rails until her head passed under a translucent, semi-circular band. How that fragile band could actually be the scanner, she didn't know, but it seemed non-threatening, and it appeared she'd actually be able to see through it during the test. Regardless, she had no desire to lie back and stick her head under it until it was time.

"Are you going to tell Skeet?"

She looked up from staring at the floor and found Aroska still leaning against the wall just inside the doorway. They had two mem-bers of Emeri's personal security detail standing guard outside, but he'd remained nearby as well, adding one more layer of protection if any nosy hospital staff came around. He'd never technically asked to accompany her into the room, but neither had she asked him to leave.

"I don't know. He's pretty pissed at me."

"If I were him, I'd probably be more pissed the longer you made me wait."

She shrugged and returned her gaze to the floor. "He'll find out sooner or later. A lot of people probably will."

"If he's as angry as you think, it would be best if he heard it straight from you."

"*Sheyss*, what are you? My therapist?"

He held his hands up in mock surrender. "Just saying."

"I think he's been angry for quite a while. He knows something happened at Dakiti and it bothers him that I won't tell him and Zinni what it was. I think he also wished I would have put more confidence in them when I was in trouble with Dasaro. It's not that I didn't trust them—I just couldn't get to them without exposing myself. Now there's this." She sighed and looked back up at him, shaking her head. "And I don't think he likes the fact that *you've* been the common factor in all of these situations."

Aroska scoffed. "What, is he jealous?"

His tone made her bristle, and she stood up. "Possibly, because I've known him for almost ten years, and I should be able to trust him wholeheartedly. Instead, I'm putting my full confidence in a man I've only known for four months, one who wanted nothing more than to kill me for the past two years."

For a moment, he almost looked remorseful. "Okay, okay," he said, shuffling his feet and folding his arms across his chest. "Why *did* you trust me, anyway? You're always going on about not getting close to any more people than you have to, so it seems like you've been breaking your own rule."

"I told you before, I didn't trust you. You were just one of the only people HSP didn't already have eyes on."

"Don't give me that, Ziva. When you came to my house, the first thing you did was go take a shower. You can't get much more vulnerable than that. What if I'd called HSP while you were in there? After all, I didn't really have a solid grasp on my mental faculties at the time.

Couldn't really reason, right? Calling the police is the logical thing to do when there's a wanted criminal in your house. They would have come, and you would have had nowhere to run."

"I knew you wouldn't turn me in. I wouldn't have even come to you in the first place if I thought you would."

"And there you have it."

Okay, so maybe there *had* been a small element of trust involved. But there was also a big difference between trusting someone to do the right thing and knowing they were likely to do the right thing based on past experiences and behaviors.

"Well," Ziva said, "don't think 'trust' had anything to do with it at Dakiti. I saved you on that landing pad because I'd just busted my own ass trying to get you out of that place, and I wasn't going to let it all be for nothing."

He only laughed. "Wow."

"What?"

"Do you remember when you came in and got me out of the harvesting room? I'd expected you and the others to be long gone, but you just said—"

"Of course I came back, you idiot," she muttered in perfect synchronization with him as he completed the phrase himself.

"I was completely shocked you had even bothered to come back for me. Like I said before, it would have been so much easier for you to just let me die. But you said that like I should have expected you to come, and it has taken me a long time to understand why. You came back for me because it was the right thing to do, and that's also exactly why you saved me out on the landing pad."

Ziva crossed her arms, unsure how to argue. Her previous explanation had merit—she hadn't wanted to let all her hard work go to waste—but he also had a point. She wasn't one to stand by and let a fellow agent get crushed by a toppling pillar, especially when said agent had kept her from plunging over a cliff to her death. Her Nostia had simply been a tool, a quick fix for a rapidly deteriorating situation. It had seemed like the most efficient thing to do, and there were times when she'd wondered if there might have been a way to save him without revealing her secret. Dwelling on it was pointless, though. She'd rescued him, he knew about the nostium, and now they were both caught up in a much bigger mess neither of them had seen coming.

It was almost as if he were reading her thoughts. "You're doing the right thing now, too. We'll try to keep this all under wraps as long as possible, of course, but you're potentially sacrificing your secret in order to give future victims a chance to live."

"I just want to know how to defend ourselves against Ronan," she said. "The Resistance picked the wrong people to screw with."

"I got to thinking—if you hadn't been on Na, we would never have known the gas affected you differently and we may have never figured out what it was. I mean, it's awful that you had to be involved in the attack, but I'm still glad you got to go there after Argall and regain your strength." He hesitated a moment, and unless it was Ziva's imagination, his cheeks flushed ever so slightly. "You look good."

To her chagrin, she felt her own cheeks flush a bit in return. Emeri hadn't been kidding when he said they'd vetted Aroska thoroughly before bumping him to full-time spec ops. Part of that process included intensive physical conditioning and fitness testing. He'd managed to gain back much of the muscle mass he'd lost during his funk, and he no longer had the stench of govino and alcohol hanging about him. Modern rehab techniques were as effective as they were fast, a good thing considering he'd probably have been fired if the agency ever caught on. Keeping the short haircut had effectively turned him into a new and improved version of his old self. *Aroska Tarbic 2.0.*

"You, too," she admitted with a shrug.

In the silence that followed, Ziva picked up the sound of approaching footsteps echoing in the hallway. Aroska turned toward the door as well, moving aside to allow Doctor Anson Baez to enter. The man looked frazzled, and his lab coat and military uniform were both missing, leaving him in a simple set of dark blue medical scrubs. He perked up when he saw her standing there alive and well.

"No offense, Baez," she said, "but I had kind of hoped to never see you again."

"Likewise, Lieu—*Captain*. And I mean that in the best possible way. But with the circumstances as they are, perhaps it is, in fact, a good thing that we have to meet again."

She knew exactly what he meant. She could be dead or dying like all those other soldiers on Na. Instead, she was alive and even thriving, all thanks to a life-threatening secret she held, one he'd helped keep.

"We should get started," the doctor said, shooting a nervous glance toward Aroska.

"He's okay," Ziva said. "He knows why we're here."

Aroska nodded and stepped forward, offering his hand. "Sergeant Aroska Tarbic."

"Ah, Sergeant Tarbic." Baez gave his hand a quick squeeze before turning to Ziva and motioning for her to take a seat. He tilted the chair back and began to slide her toward the scanner. "Ziva told me all about you."

In her peripherals, Ziva could see the mischievous glimmer flash across Aroska's eyes. "Oh she did, did she?" he said, addressing her rather than Baez.

"I may have mentioned how you pulled me up off that cliff and how you saved my life in Argall," she said, studying the inside of the scanner as the chair came to a stop.

Baez adjusted the width of the band until it shielded her entire face. "Sergeant, if you could please come over here with me," he said, leading Aroska toward the control board behind a glass wall on the far side of the room. "This won't hurt a bit, Captain Payvan. Just try to remain as still as possible."

Something clicked behind her and the chair's headrest folded down, leaving her head to balance on a narrow, cushioned bar. The band was, in fact, a full circle, and she watched it light up as the scan commenced. She could see the three-dimensional model of her head being rendered on the control panel where Baez and Aroska stood.

"Won't someone recognize my face?" she murmured, unsure exactly how still she was supposed to remain.

"The faces on these busts are all generic," Baez answered. "The size and relative shape of the head can vary by patient, but the internal image of the cranial cavity is the only thing that's truly unique." He was quiet for a moment, and Ziva could see him staring intently at the model as he captured individual images every few seconds. "I'm no neurologist, but this looks very similar to what we were seeing in the other patients. If you could perhaps use your...ah..."

"Nostia," she sighed.

"Yes," he said, clearing his throat. "If you would."

Other than the bulky, expensive medical equipment, the room was virtually empty. Not wishing to look around and ruin the scan, Ziva focused on the first small object she could think of: Aroska's sidearm. She closed her eyes and stretched out her hand as the flood of energy coursed through her. The gun slid out of its holster, summoned by her thoughts, and before she knew it, it was in her grasp.

"Oh, *sheyss.*"

She honestly wasn't sure which one of them had spoken—Aroska in response to the theft or Baez in response to the sudden burst of activity the scanner picked up. She could hear the doctor tapping furiously at the controls, capturing images as fast as he could. Aroska only stared at her in disbelief, just as he had when she'd snatched her kytara out of his hand that night in his kitchen. She released her grip on the pistol and left it suspended in mid-air for a moment before pushing it back toward him. For a while, he regarded it like it was a thermal grenade with a flipped primer switch, but he finally took it and slid it back into the holster.

"That should be enough, thank you," Baez said, just as unnerved by her display. "You can go ahead and come out now."

Ziva slid the chair out from under the scanner and sat up, remaining motionless for a moment as she waited for a bout of lightheadedness to pass. From an upright position, she had a much better view of the model and was impressed by what she saw. A holographic head floated above the small projection pad, rotating in a slow circle as Baez flipped back through the captures he'd taken. The face was nondescript, just as he'd said, with a generic nose and mouth and small indentations for the eyes. Any viewer's attention was automatically drawn to the colored patches inside the hologram that represented each lobe of the brain and any corresponding activity.

"Let me just get this data sent back to the GA's neuroscience division," Baez said, bundling the images into a single file and marking them for transmission. "Here's hoping they can use it to make some sense out of what's going on."

"Indeed," Ziva muttered.

She wanted to ask about the status of the other victims, particularly Major Sheen, but the sharp chirp of her communicator interrupted her train of thought. She glanced down at the device, unnerved by the red light that indicated a priority message from Emeri's office.

"Yeah," she answered, leaving the transmission open so the two men could hear.

Rather than the director, she found herself listening to Aura Stannist's abrasive voice. "Captain, please report to Headquarters at once. The Royal House is requesting your immediate presence in Haphor."

*Damn it.* This had to be about her undermining Aura's authority by leaving the planet. Or worse yet, maybe the Royal Officer was already wanting an explanation as to why she hadn't gotten sick yet. Surely the entire Royal House had been made privy to the fact that she'd been involved in the attack. Still, why call for her in the middle of the night?

"What the hell for?" she demanded.

"The order came from your mother, Captain. There's been another attack on the Royal General's estate. Your family has been exposed, and they're already showing symptoms."

She froze, staring straight ahead as her mind sorted through the information and established the facts. Who was her family? Her mother, stepfather, half-siblings, Jada. To what had they been exposed? Nostium. What were the symptoms of nostium exposure? Seizures, headaches, loss of motor control, all things that declared a breakdown in the nervous system. And what did a breakdown in the nervous system mean? Death. Her family…nostium…death. It was that simple, yet she still struggled to comprehend it.

*Stay calm. People are watching.* "Status report?" she said, suppressing a shiver as the hairs on the back of her neck stood on end.

"I don't have details," the probation officer replied. "I've only been instructed to escort you to Haphor. Report to HSP Headquarters immediately. There's a shuttle waiting to transport us."

"Copy that." The words felt mechanical, forced. She killed the transmission and swept her gaze from Baez to Aroska; both were watching her as if they expected her to panic and rush away. "Excuse me," she said quietly, striding from the room and ignoring Aroska when he called after her.

*You know it's probably too late to help them.*

*But Jada is there.*

*These people have done nothing but hurt you for most of your life. Why waste your time being concerned?*

*Have to get to Jada.*

The thought prompted her to pick up her pace and she broke into a steady jog. Somewhere in the back of her mind, she heard Aroska's hurried footsteps as he rushed to catch up.

"Ziva, stop!"

The only reason she complied was because she came to the elevator and was forced to wait for the door to open. "This is insane," she said, giving up on the idea of leaving him behind. "What the hell is Ronan trying to accomplish here?"

"Hey," Aroska said as he came to a stop behind her. He took her shoulder and spun her around to face him. "I know you've had some issues with your family, but it's okay to be concerned about them right now."

"What are you even talking about?"

"Look at you, running away like this. You don't have to pretend you're not worried."

A beat.

"I'm not pretending. I was running because I'm in a hurry." She swallowed past the lump threatening to form in her throat.

"There's nobody around to put on a show for," he said, spreading his arms and looking up and down the hall. "I'm the only one here, and I know you better than that."

"No," Ziva said, stepping into the elevator as the doors finally opened. She held her hand out to stop him from following her inside. "No, you really don't know me at all, so stop acting like you do. Yeah, sure, you got me. I'm concerned about Jada. But I'm not running or trying to hide anything, okay? And all that *sheyss* you said back there? I'm not a good person—I've told you that before. I'm trying to do whatever it takes to survive. I need you to back off."

He didn't try to enter the elevator, but neither did he make any move to leave. "I was going to see if you wanted me to come with you."

"Stay here," she answered, allowing her tone to soften a bit. "Make sure that data gets transmitted safely to Na and then report to Headquarters and find Skeet. Tell him I'll explain everything in due time. Just see what you two can do to help with the investigation, and I'll be back as soon as I can."

His features were still stony, but he gave her an affirmative nod and turned back down the hall, moving with a stiff gait. The elevator door slid shut as she watched him go. She was glad she didn't have to look at him anymore, and glad he wouldn't turn around and notice the involuntary trembling that had set in the moment he turned his back.

She whirled and slammed a fist against the elevator wall before burying her face in her hands and screaming into them. She wasn't sure if Aroska himself was infuriating or if the fact that she didn't know how to handle him was infuriating. Either way, he wasn't helping the situation. He'd been hovering ever since she'd confessed to being involved in the attack on Na—he and Skeet both had—and, granted, she should expect to rely a bit more exclusively on him as long as he was one of the only people aware of her Nostia. But this business of acting like he knew her, acting like he knew what was going through her head...that was too much.

*He's pushing, so push back. Don't do it. Don't let him in.*
*Are you kidding? He's already in and you know it.*

She hit the wall again for good measure and turned around as the elevator reached the ground floor. Aura's transmission echoed through her mind, drawing her back to the present, and she took off for the parking bay as fast as her legs would carry her.

# · 25 ·

# HAPHOR–NORO TRAFFIC LANE

## TASMIN FOREST, HAPHEZ

T aking Aura's shuttle effectively reduced the trip to Haphor from four hours to two, but it was still beginning to feel like one of the longest journeys of Ziva's life. Not only was she concerned for Jada's safety and angry that the Resistance had managed to launch another attack, but seeing her family again was a bit unnerving in itself. It had been at least a year since she'd spoken to her mother, and Njo and the twins had despised her since childhood. Some of that was probably her fault; she hadn't been very welcoming when her mother remarried after her father's death in the Fringe War, especially not after she'd run away to Noro and begun her clandestine training with Gamon. She was content with seeing as little of the Jaroons—with the exception of Jada—as possible.

On top of everything, Aura had been sitting there silently scrutinizing her for the entire flight. The probation officer had spent a while on comm with someone from the Royal Guard, but she'd kept her eyes fixed on Ziva for the duration of the conversation, almost as if she thought she might somehow disappear from the ship. As far as Ziva knew, Aura still wasn't aware of the reason she'd been at the med center, or that she'd been at the med center at all. She figured she'd have to tell the woman about her Nostia at some point...if she didn't find out on her own, that was. She imagined it wouldn't be too hard to put the pieces together, considering HSP had contacted the Royal House about the nostium immediately following a private meeting at which only she, Emeri, and Aroska had been present. Nobody would have to try very hard to figure out where the tip had come from, and she was glad only a few people knew she'd been there.

Aura was on comm again now, and unless Ziva was mistaken, she was speaking to the Royal Guard's Supervisory Special Agent Luko Zona. At least she hoped that was the case. She'd never cared much for the pretentious agents who made up the RG, but Zona had a good head on his shoulders. Their introduction had been a fleeting one in Argall, but if he'd taken the time to submit his data to the magistrates to help her trial end favorably, he was all right in her book.

"Everyone who was involved in the attack has been quarantined inside the house," Aura said as she ended the transmission. "That includes your family and all household staff and security personnel who were present at the time. Lord Jaril and Lady Jazel were attending a social function and were not involved. They're currently in the care of the Royal Guard."

"Of course they are," Ziva muttered with a wag of her head. "You said they have someone in custody?"

"Yes. A man was apprehended as he fled the property just after the gas was released. He was shot in the leg by security forces, and the injury was enough to keep him from taking some sort of suicide pill before he was captured."

"And they're sure this is Ronan? It's the same as the gas from the Na base?"

"Initial findings seem to indicate so. The labs are working on it now."

"But it's got to be a different substance if it acted so quickly." *Almost like regular nostium*, she thought, *but still too potent.*

Aura tilted her head.

Ziva hesitated for a split second before continuing, mentally running back through what she'd just said to ensure she hadn't tipped the woman off. "The substance from Na was slightly different than what Kat Reilly was injected with," she continued, "and it also acted much more quickly. If what we're hearing is accurate, exposure to this gas tonight produced almost instantaneous results. It makes sense that it would be different as well."

The look the probation officer gave her just then was rather unsettling. Ziva bristled as she stood up and strode across the cabin, holding one of the grab rings above the seats to keep her balance as she clutched her ever-present data pad in her free hand. "Don't think for one second that I don't know, Payvan."

So she had figured it out. "Know what?" Ziva said anyway, rising.

The height of Aura's shoes allowed them to see nearly eye-to-eye. "As an admin within the Royal Offices, there are certain things I'm kept in the loop about. One of those things is the fact that we're dealing with nostium here." To Ziva's surprise, she shot a cautious glance toward the cockpit to ensure they weren't being overheard. "I don't know who figured it out—you, Tarbic, or Director Arion—but it's pretty clear to me that it happened right after I left that office this evening, right after Lieutenant Duvo told me *you* asked him to leave."

Ziva felt her pulse spike but forced her countenance to remain unchanged, not daring to break eye contact. She pictured it as giving Aura a taste of her own medicine. *Two can play this game.*

"Considering the fact that you haven't shown any of these symptoms yet, I'm beginning to think you're the one who told the director. I think you know something about this stuff, and for one reason or another, Tarbic and Emeri are the only ones you've shared that knowledge with."

"So tell everyone," Ziva muttered, staring the woman down through narrowed eyes. "Tell them all about this theory of yours. Watch me get arrested again. Then I wouldn't be your problem anymore. It's a win for you, right?"

"No."

"Oh, okay. You just want to make sure we're aware of the fact that you could fry us all alive if you wanted to. You're like the Royal Officer's pathetic pet guhr hound, Aura. So far, your bark has been a lot worse than your bite."

Aura shook her head, letting the insults roll off her. "Payvan, you are so lucky you're as important as you are." She took a step closer still, lowering her voice to an agitated whisper. "I don't know exactly *what* you know or *how* you know it, but if the Royal House finds out you were the source of this information, they will crucify you. Now, the way I see it, this knowledge you have makes you the only person on this whole damn planet who's qualified to go up against Ronan. That's why I'm keeping my mouth shut. I don't like it one bit, but I want this all to end as quickly as possible, even if that means loosening my grip on your leash."

So, Ziva had been right about her after all. It was in her nature as a former agent to bend rules for the sake of addressing a bigger picture. She tried to maintain this cold demeanor, wanted Ziva to think she was only using her as a tool to fulfill her own agenda. No, she was doing this because deep down, she knew it was the best way to get the job done and save lives. She was doing this because she was a good person.

Ziva caught herself. *Oh, bloody hell, Tarbic.*

The shuttle pilot's voice rang out from the cockpit, disrupting her train of thought. "We're starting our approach into the Royal City, ma'am."

"Thank you," Aura said. She stepped back to give Ziva some space, but not before giving her another frigid once-over.

The ship swooped down over downtown Haphor and angled toward the massive cluster of white buildings rising up out of the middle of the city. Even from a distance, Ziva could look through the front viewport and see the swarms of police vehicles hovering in the sky above the Royal City, sweeping their spotlights to and fro just as they'd been doing the night she'd broken in after her arrest and escape. Every building within the private community was illuminated, even at this hour. Security obviously wasn't fooling around.

A space had been cleared for the ship to touch down on the Jaroons' front lawn. Massive lighting panels had been set up, illuminating the area as if it were the middle of the day, and Ziva had to shield her eyes as she made her way down the boarding ramp with Aura hot on her heels. The whole yard was one big maze of RG cars, vehicles from the Haphor field office, hazardous materials response units, and a dozen other organizations with important-looking logos and flashing lights.

"Agent Stannist?" a voice called out as the speaker made his way toward the docked shuttle. A man emerged from the crowd and jogged over.

Ziva stopped. "Kade?"

Kade Shevin's eyes grew wide, but he didn't break stride. He let out an incredulous chuckle as he approached. "Ziv—er, Lieutenant Payvan! What are you doing here? I was told Agent Stannist would be escorting Lady Namani's daught—" He stopped as the realization hit him. "You?"

"I don't believe it myself sometimes," Ziva said. "And it's Captain now, actually."

Kade hesitated for a moment as he processed the information. "Oh," he said with a slow nod, telling her he understood she'd taken Dasaro's place. "I'm glad that all turned out okay."

"Thanks in no small part to you and Zona's files," she replied. "Is he here?"

"This way," Kade said, turning and carving a path through the crowd.

Ziva and Aura followed. Most people moved aside upon recognizing the Royal Officer's insignia on Aura's suit, though Ziva had a hunch most of them had also been anticipating her arrival and noticed the family resemblance.

"Look who crawled out from under her rock."

The overbearing female voice made the hairs on the back of Ziva's neck stand up and she turned toward the sound. Jazel and Jaril were huddled together on a bench near one of the fountains across the yard, their bright green eyes fixed on her. Sitting there with their tousled party clothes and tear-stained cheeks, they looked so pitiful she almost felt sorry for them. The sour looks on their gaunt faces were a sufficient reminder that they were two of the reasons she avoided this place as much as possible.

Against her better judgment, she veered toward them. "Of all the people to walk away from this thing unscathed, it had to be you two."

The majority of Jazel's makeup was smeared down her face. "Figured you'd come over here and play hero?" she spat.

"I'm here because Mother sent for me," Ziva retorted. That was more or less a lie. It was the official reason for her presence, but in truth, she was there for Jada and Jada alone.

"Why?" Jaril demanded, leaping to his feet. "Why would she call *you* here? And since when do you ever listen to her?"

Ziva had never been a fan of the fact that he'd grown to be taller than her. Still, with an advantage in age and maybe even weight, she hardly cared that she had to look up to meet his gaze. "This is part of an ongoing investigation, okay? I came here to see if everyone was all right."

"We're not all right," Jazel muttered, adjusting the jacket of some Royal Guard agent she had draped over her shoulders. "This is probably all your fault. Anything bad that ever happens to us is your fault."

Ziva could only shake her head as she brought her hands to rest on her hips and shifted her gaze between the two of them. Aroska had described the way Jazel blamed her for her misery during the lockdown following Tachi's murder. Her thought process lacked any logic whatsoever. But now the young woman's words struck Ziva in a manner she hadn't expected. In a way, this *was* her fault. She'd brought Kat's data home, hadn't hidden it well enough. These attacks were probably Ronan's way of retaliating against an investigation she'd inadvertently sparked.

Jada's voice rang out somewhere behind her before she had any more time to reflect. "Ziva, over here."

Ziva turned and found the girl standing on the front walkway where Kade and Aura waited. Her large brown eyes were wide with worry, but she appeared unharmed. Then again, initially so had everyone who'd endured the attack on Na. The idea didn't bring Ziva much relief.

"I thought you were all quarantined," she called, abandoning Jaril and Jazel in favor of her adopted human sibling.

"We went through a decontamination process," Jada said, coming to meet her halfway across the lawn. "They just let us out."

Ziva took her by the shoulders and looked her up and down, unsure what she was even searching for. "They said the symptoms set in almost instantaneously," she said quietly.

Jada nodded and glanced around. "Everyone's fine now, just like what happened with the soldiers." The look on her face was almost guilty, and tears began to well up in her eyes. "But Ziva, nothing happened to me."

Ziva blinked. "*What?*"

"The others...they just started convulsing, and I could only sit there..."

In her peripherals, Ziva saw Aura's eyes widen in response to Jada's words. *Another person unaffected by the nostium.* She wasn't sure where Jada had lived before being brought to Haphez as a toddler, but if it had been a world controlled by the Resistance, it was certainly possible she could have been exp—

"*There* you are."

Ziva looked up to find her mother approaching with the Royal General. They too appeared normal on the outside, even normal enough to maintain their usual condescending facial expressions. Njo spared her a few seconds for a distasteful glare before heading toward Jaril and Jazel. To Ziva's surprise, Namani barely gave the twins a second glance.

Aura and Kade moved away, leaving Ziva and Jada alone with their mother. Ziva shrugged and shook her head. "Well, I'm here."

"I heard those soldiers on Na weren't surviving long after their symptoms set in," Namani said, voice devoid of any sympathy. "With as fast as ours manifested, I figured I didn't have long, and I wanted a chance to see you."

"So you demanded I come over here in the middle of the night?"

Unless she was mistaken, Ziva saw something that might have been fear flash through her mother's eyes, but with as good as Namani was at hiding her emotions, it was impossible to tell. They'd always been too much alike, both hurting but unwilling to give in to each other. Ziva knew good and well why she'd been called here: Namani was afraid of dying. She would never admit that, of course, and Ziva would never admit that now that she thought about it, the thought scared her a bit, too.

"You really haven't changed, have you?" her mother said.

"Neither have you."

"Ziva, I'm going to die. Doesn't that bother you at all?"

Jada let out a small whimper and rushed away.

"You can't expect me to suddenly start caring after all this time," Ziva replied, her voice hardly more than a whisper. The words hadn't emerged with as much ease as she'd hoped. Aroska had been right—she may have spent most of her life loathing these people, but they were still family.

She wasn't entirely sure which one of them was more at fault when it came to the breakdown in their relationship. After the War, her mother had dealt with her grief by moving on and starting a new life as quickly as possible. Ziva had dealt with hers by running away to escape the pain, then subsequently throwing herself into her training with Gamon. Neither agreed with the other's method, especially since Ziva had been considered a missing child for a full year after escaping to Noro. They'd found her and brought her back to Haphor only to have her run off again. The pattern had continued for another two years, but once the twins were born, Namani had given up trying to make her stay in the Royal City. They both continued to distance themselves, and neither one of them was willing to admit they were wrong.

"I know you've got work to do, so I'll make this fast." Namani reached out and took her by the hand, and somehow Ziva managed to avoid pulling away. "Put an end to this, okay? You're strong." She hesitated for a moment before adding a sharp nod. "Your father would be proud of you."

Would he be? Enough time had passed that it was growing increasingly difficult to remember him. Ziva had only been six years old when he'd been killed, but one thing she did remember was his kind spirit and the utter selflessness with which he lived his life. That's what had gotten him killed, after all: sacrificing his own life to save the Royal General, the very man her mother had ended up marrying. Somehow, Ziva couldn't imagine Kalim Payvan approving of the way she constantly bent the rules, the way she could kill without hesitation, the way she regarded everyone she met with such apathy. But those things were all necessary in order to function in her line of work, practically requirements. No, she decided, her father would most definitely *not* be proud of who she had become.

She realized she'd given Namani's hand a squeeze only after the fact and quickly loosened her grip. "I will," she said, turning her attention back to the crowd to locate Kade. He approached when he saw her looking and she broke away from her mother to meet him by the front door. "I heard you have someone in custody."

He nodded and beckoned for her to follow. "I'm sorry about your family," he murmured, leading her downstairs toward the safe room.

"Don't feel sorry for me," Ziva said. "This house...these people... they've caused me a lot of pain over the years."

*Don't forget all the pain* you've *caused* them.

They entered the security room that served as a foyer for the emergency bunker below the house. Several RG agents were gathered around the control board listening to a man who must have been the Jaroons' Captain of the Guard, fresh out of quarantine. He gestured toward one of the small security offices on the opposite side of the room as he recounted his story, and Ziva caught sight of Luko Zona standing inside. The agents guarding the door moved aside as she and Kade approached.

Ziva leaned into the room and found Zona staring down at a young man seated haphazardly at an empty desk. His jaw was set, and he slouched with one leg extended in front of him. Yet another RG agent stood behind him, maintaining a firm grip on his shoulder. Ziva could smell blood from the gunshot wound but no disinfectant; they'd only patched up his leg well enough to keep him from bleeding out during interrogation. Upon further consideration, she couldn't smell *anything* other than the blood. The man appeared human, but he wasn't giving off that odd sour scent most humans did. Judging by the high-quality stealth suit he sported, she guessed he'd been well equipped to infiltrate their culture and wore some sort of odor-masking spray.

Zona threw a quick glance her way then did a double take and gave her a nod of approval. She sent him a look that she hoped did an adequate job of thanking him for submitting evidence for her trial, and he managed a faint smile that said *you're welcome*.

"Captain Payvan," he said, stepping aside to give her more space in front of the desk. "Perhaps you'd like to have a go at our new friend here."

It was a petty thing, but speaking to someone high enough in the chain of command to acknowledge her new rank was a bit of a relief. According to Emeri, Zona's supervisory position within the Royal Guard had also earned him a spot on the initial list of people who were briefed about the nostium and Ronan's connection with the Resistance. Ziva was glad he was there.

"Who do we have here?" she said, crossing her arms as she studied the man in the chair. It was always hard to tell how old the humans were; perhaps he was in his mid-twenties. He had dark hair and tanned skin, but his eyes were a pale blue. A patch of his suit had been cut away from his shoulder, no doubt where this suicide pill had been stashed.

"Won't give us a name. Won't tell us who he's working for, either, but it's a safe bet he's a Resistance agent."

Unless it was Ziva's imagination, the man tensed a bit at the mention of the rebel organization. It was difficult to tell for sure thanks to the periodic grimaces he made in response to the pain, but something in his eyes told her he was interested in what Zona had just said...and not in a good way.

"Does he have a way to contact his people?" she asked.

"No communication devices were found on his person. He's been scanned for implants, too, and we came up with nothing. This was a dark mission."

Based on the agent's reaction to Zona's words, the Resistance likely had no idea the Haphezians knew they were behind these attacks. He seemed surprised to hear them talk about it, and he had good reason to be. After all, the government only knew what it knew because Ziva had told them, however indirectly. The fact that he'd been carrying and willing to take a suicide pill told her he hadn't wanted to risk capture, which meant Ronan and the Resistance were trying to keep their presence under wraps. The existence of the Resistance as a whole was obviously no secret, but the fact that nobody—including the Federation—

had even heard of Ronan until a few short months ago made her wonder exactly what kind of clandestine operation this person was running.

If her theory was correct and the Resistance didn't realize the Haphezians knew they were involved, she imagined HSP and the rest of the government should attempt to keep that information secret for as long as possible. She agreed with Aura's suggestion to not let the media into the loop, and she was glad this agent had no means of contacting his people. Considering the way Ronan had reacted when Kat was investigating Corey's captivity, she couldn't imagine the Resistance would take kindly to the entire Haphezian population knowing what they were up to.

Unsure how many of Zona's people knew the gas was nostium, Ziva opted to err on the side of caution before proceeding and dismissed the guard with a jerk of her head. She shut the door behind him and turned to survey all the items in the room. Zona had retreated to the corner and stood in front of a table upon which all the former contents of the desk had been piled. One of those items was a comm receiver that looked like it belonged on one of the consoles outside. She picked it up and looked it over for a moment before hurling it as hard as she could toward the Resistance agent's head.

Just as she'd expected, it came within centimeters of hitting him in the face before veering off in another direction, propelled by what could only be Nostia. Even with the way he was slumped in the chair, there'd been something about the way he held his head and shoulders that reminded her of the way she'd carried herself in her teens—and had carried herself for the past several days, now that she thought about it. Something about that tingle at the base of the skull prompted a person to hold their neck a little straighter, regardless of where you were or what you were doing.

The agent's eyes widened as he realized what he'd done, and he looked up to meet her gaze. Deflecting objects was one of the most basic skills she'd ever been taught, and after a time, it had become a simple reflex, something she did without really thinking. If she hadn't been forced to keep her abilities secret and go years without a real nostium infusion, it would have been a skill she'd have used on a daily basis. Breaking the habit after Jak Gamon's death had been harder than she'd anticipated. The fact that this agent's first reaction had been to deflect the comm receiver told her two things. One, he had received a successful nostium infusion at some point in the not-too-distant past, and it hadn't had any lasting negative side effects. Two, he'd been properly trained as a Nosti, and if his instincts were still so sharp, it had probably been recently.

Zona drew his service pistol and stared the man down over the barrel. Ziva had half a mind to draw her own weapon and shoot the agent then and there, but he represented an opportunity that needed to be taken advantage of. "I hope you've got a good grip on that gun, Special Agent Zona," she said, moving around to the other side of the desk to keep a better eye on the Resistance fighter's hands. "This man needs to be properly secured. Get a restraining block in here, now!"

Zona went to the door and relayed her instructions to the men outside while she stepped behind the agent and seized him by the shoulder, digging her fingers into the space above his collarbone. It was unnerving to think he was capable of attacking anyone in the vicinity without moving from the chair. If he'd been so intent on taking a suicide pill, she wondered why he hadn't just used his Nostia to grab someone's gun; it would have been a surefire way to earn a bullet or plasma bolt between the eyes. She assumed the only reason he hadn't done such a thing was fear of revealing he was a Nosti and thus who he was working for. He'd exposed himself by unconsciously deflecting the comm receiver, and now that he knew *they* knew who he was, she thought it reasonable to once again consider him a suicide risk.

"I know exactly what you're capable of," she hissed in Standard, leaning down to whisper in his ear. "I'd threaten to kill you, but I'm sure that's exactly what you want. So how about this: you move a muscle, and I shoot your other leg. We're going to do everything we can to keep you *alive* until you tell us how to find Ronan."

She felt him tense up at the mention of the Resistance leader's name and he swallowed. "You people have no chance," he muttered. He turned his head to address her, watching her in his peripherals. "So, you're Ziva Payvan."

Without hesitation, she drew her pistol and brought the butt of it down hard against the back of his head. He fell forward with his face resting against the desk, a trickle of blood running from his hair and down his neck.

Ziva stood there motionless for a moment, willing her pulse to slow as she attempted to process all the new information that had presented itself over the past several minutes. This man was a Nosti; there was no doubt about it. That meant the Resistance had to have an effective nostium formula, one that had been working for a reasonable amount of time. Why, then, was the gas having such an adverse effect on everyone who came in cont—

She stopped when it dawned on her. Kat, Corey, the GA soldiers, her family...all the victims they knew of were Haphezian. This agent—a human—was unaffected. Jada—a human—was unaffected. These experimental nostium formulas were tailored specifically to Haphezians. But why?

On top of that, this man knew her name, which had to mean others in the Resistance did as well. It made sense when she thought about it. Gamon had clearly been in contact with other Resistance survivors throughout the course of her training, albeit unbeknownst to her until that fateful day when she'd finally killed him. They'd been waiting for him to bring her to them. She wondered for a moment if she was the true target in all of this, and the thought tied a sickening knot in her stomach.

This all registered with her in a split second and she looked up as Zona returned to the room carrying a restraining block. He didn't even ask her what had happened as he began fitting the device over the unconscious agent's hands, rendering them immobile. It wouldn't stop the man from using his mind to move or throw objects, but at least he wouldn't be able to hold said objects.

"I want him transported back to Noro Headquarters with me," she said. "We should have his brain scanned and see how the results compare with the soldiers." *And my family*.

She had to admit she was surprised when Zona nodded; the Royal Guard had always had a reputation of being so egotistical when it came to jurisdiction and any matters pertaining to royal families. "Good idea," he said. He glanced briefly toward the door and lowered his voice. "How did you know he would do that?"

"Just a hunch," she replied matter-of-factly. "We know the gas is nostium, we know he's one of Ronan's agents. I wanted to see his reaction, and I think it proved that we're not just dealing with the Resistance here—we're dealing with a new wave of Nosti."

"Do you have any idea where this intel about the nostium came from?"

"No clue." The lie rolled off her tongue just as easily as it had every time she'd ever been questioned about her connection with Gamon. "I was just briefed on it this evening." She jerked her head toward the agent. "How did he get in?"

"We don't know for sure yet," Zona answered. "The gas was stored in a canister with a timed detonation mechanism and inserted into the ventilation system from the maintenance room. As near as we can tell, he killed a guard on his way back out. Nobody could smell him, but security forces heard the commotion and pursued him, wounding him before he made it out of the yard." He shook his head. "It should have been impossible for him to infiltrate this place."

*It's not impossible*, Ziva wanted to say. *I did it once.*

"What matters is that we have him now," she said instead.

"But at what cost?"

"I have the utmost confidence he can provide us with information that will make up for what he's done." She almost felt bad saying it, but it was the cold truth. "We need to make security a top priority for him. His hands—hell, his whole body—should be kept immobile. Any objects in a room that aren't bolted down will be fair game for him. And I want him sedated for the trip back to Noro." *So he can't blurt out the wonderful fact that he somehow knows who I am*, she thought.

She stood and massaged her eyes as Zona began arranging for a prison transport. She'd never imagined finding herself in the middle of a situation of this magnitude when she'd taken Kat's data pad and agreed to look into Ronan. It seemed, perhaps, that the entire Haphezian military—or maybe the entire *civilization*—was in the middle of the situation. If only they could figure out exactly what that situation was.

She stared down at the back of the unconscious agent's head, feeling the telltale tingle building up in the back of her own head. Clenching her hands into fists, she strode from the room with the intention of finding Aura and leaving this place. It had already been a long night, and it was about to get even longer.

## · 26 ·
# PATROL FRIGATE *VIGILANCE*
### FRINGE SPACE

It had been too long. Something was wrong.

Sadey strode out of the elevator and onto the *Vigilance's* bridge, taking a moment to collect herself before approaching the communications officer. He glanced up when he saw her coming and gave his head a subtle wag as he removed his earpiece.

"I'm sorry, Commander. Still no word."

Eight hours had passed since they'd heard from Jalen. He'd sent a coded message upon arriving in Haphor, informing them that he'd acquired a vehicle and would be ceasing all communication, just as planned. Upon completing the mission, he'd been scheduled to report back with a single binary value, just as Ronan had done before. A green light indicated a successful mission, while a red one announced failure.

*There's more than one type of failure*, Sadey thought. In the best-case scenario, a failure simply meant that, for one reason or another, the nostium hadn't been distributed and Jalen had been left with no choice but to bug out. But if he'd been forced to take his own life to avoid capture—or worse, had *been* captured—there'd obviously be no way for him to contact them. She'd notified Ronan about her concerns but had been instructed to wait a bit longer before jumping to conclusions. There were a number of reasons Jalen could be taking extra time. He could have simply had trouble getting in or out of the Royal City and needed to take a more circuitous route. Or the vehicle with his comm equipment could have been towed away. Or maybe that equipment was simply malfunctioning.

*Or maybe he's dead.*

By now, it would be nearly dawn in Haphor. Jalen was a skilled operative who wouldn't have wanted to risk conducting the mission in broad daylight. If the job hadn't been done by now, it probably wasn't going to be. And if they hadn't heard back from him by now, Sadey doubted they ever would. She hated for the Resistance to lose a soldier—especially one under her command—when numbers weren't on their side in the first place, but it was better than having a whole squadron wiped out.

"I'm writing him off as a casualty," she said, wishing she didn't have to speak the words.

"Shall I prepare to transmit a 'mission failure' to Ronan?" the officer asked.

Sadey shook her head. "We don't know for sure if it *was* a failure. Do we have access to the Haphezian news networks yet?"

The *Vigilance* floated on the outskirts of the Noro system as the crew waited to move in and rendezvous with the small shuttle Jalen had taken planetside. "Looks like we're too far out of range to pick up any local news signals," the comm officer answered. "But if they have anything streaming on an interplanetary network, we should be able to see it."

Sadey watched with bated breath as he sifted through news feeds on the large viewscreen above the control panel, irritated that they'd lost not only a soldier but a shuttle as well. All the shuttles and fighters docked on the *Vigilance* were either stolen or registered to legitimate organizations, so there was no reason to be concerned about someone finding it. It was just one more lost resource.

"I've got something," the officer announced, pausing on one particular news feed with Haphezian text scrolling across the bottom of the screen.

"Circulate this," she ordered.

The man manipulated the controls and the news report appeared on every viewscreen on the bridge. All the crewmembers in the vicinity stopped what they were doing to watch.

A Haphezian woman stood outside a large white gate speaking into a recording device as several hovercams floated around her head. The timestamp in the corner indicated the feed was live, and the sky behind the reporter was already beginning to lighten. The translation program kicked in and a feminine voiceover began relaying everything the woman was saying in Standard. The scrolling banner read "Breaking News."

"...have been working through the night to clear the air inside the house so authorities can continue the investigation. The Royal Family and their staff were kept under quarantine pending an initial examination then put through a decontamination process before being released. I've been told the Royal General and Royal Lady are currently resting comfortably and aren't in any pain."

A tingle of excitement made Sadey's skin crawl. So the mission had been a success, then? She listened as someone thanked the woman for her report, then the feed flashed over to a previously-recorded interview. A man who appeared to be a member of the security detail stood amid the crowd of law enforcement personnel, and according to the report, he'd just been released from the quarantine.

"It all happened so fast," he said. "We hit the floor, but that stuff was already in the air. Even if we could have made it outside, it would have been too late. Once the seizures kicked in, there was nothing anyone could do."

Sadey's eyes widened and a grin spread across her face. Seizures, of course, meant the nostium had done too much damage to the brain to be effective. But if she understood what the man was saying, the symptoms had set in mere minutes—maybe even seconds—after exposure. The infusion may not have been a success, but they'd still managed to take out the head of the entire Haphezian military, and they now had confirmation that they were headed in the right direction with the formula.

The news feed returned to the woman at the gate. "Initial findings suggest this was a follow-up attack performed by the same group responsible for the incident at the Na Base over a week ago. Police are still searching for leads as to who is behind these attacks. Meanwhile, authorities do have a suspect in custody—"

And just like that, everything went to hell. Sadey's heart leaped into her throat; the reporter kept speaking but she didn't hear a word the woman said as she focused on the previously recorded clip spliced into the feed. It showed a group of HSP agents escorting a man up the boarding ramp of a prison ship, towering over him as they went. His head was covered by a hood, and he had some sort of restraining contraption fitted over his hands and arms, but the black stealth suit he wore was unmistakable. Jalen Gero was alive, and he was currently in the custody of the Haphezian Special Police.

She stood and watched with a gaping mouth for another few seconds, taking in every detail she could. The pocket containing the suicide pill had been ripped from his sleeve, revealing bare skin underneath, and the agents were practically carrying him up the ramp thanks to a poorly treated wound on one of his legs.

"You're recording this?" she asked.

The communications officer nodded. "Yes, ma'am."

"Play that back."

He backed the footage up several frames then played it back at half speed. Sadey took a step closer, though it really did nothing to enhance her view of the screen, and studied one of the agents walking with Jalen, a tall woman with deep red stripes running through her dark hair. Another wave of dread and uncertainty swirled through her stomach. They were the same red stripes that ran through Ziva Payvan's hair in the mugshot that had circulated on some of the Fringe's news networks after the Haphezian Royal Officer's assassination. After her reported disappearance, Sadey had never expected to hear of her again, but there she was, alive and well and very much involved with the same agency that had been hunting her.

Part of Sadey felt a glimmer of hope at the sight of Gamon's former student, but the other part was stricken with terror at the thought of Payvan interacting with Jalen in any way. He was smart enough—and trained well enough—to not divulge any information during an interrogation, and the absence of his suicide pill told her he'd already tried to take it. But with Payvan's experience as a Nosti student, however long ago it was, Sadey doubted it would take the woman long to figure out who he was.

"Are we going to launch a rescue, Commander?" asked a young officer who had been watching from a nearby workstation.

"No," Sadey replied without hesitation, though it pained her to say it. "He knew the risks, and I'm confident he'll do whatever is necessary to make sure his identity and Ronan's operations remain undisclosed." She looked around and found that everyone in the area was looking at her. They all knew she meant Jalen would kill himself. No point in wasting resources to rescue a man who was as good as dead.

She leaned down and spoke in a hushed voice to the communications officer. "I want a copy of this footage forwarded to Ronan forthwith. Once we're out-of-system, open a direct line to Forus Command and reroute the transmission to my quarters."

Sadey pivoted and strode back across the bridge, pausing long enough to instruct the navigator to plot a new course out of the Noro system. She entered the elevator and returned to her cabin, where she sat down at her private terminal and began to draft a written memo with orders on how to proceed. Having Payvan in the picture changed everything. The agent might not recognize Jalen's affiliation right away—and maybe she never would—but Sadey had no desire to take any chances. They'd already had to move through the plan at an accelerated pace, but now that there was an increased risk of being discovered, they'd have to move even faster.

*Calm down*, she told herself. *You know how the Haphezians are— even if Payvan realizes who Jalen is working for, they may not want to involve themselves in Resistance matters.*

No, she decided, that wasn't going to fly anymore, not after their military and political leader had been attacked. Regardless of whether Payvan kept her mouth shut or not, there was no time to waste. The time for subtlety was coming to an end; the next stage of the plan would have to be put into motion immediately. She relayed her orders in the memo, requesting a slight alteration of the most recent nostium formula in hopes that it would be less potent. They would also need a smaller ship. The *Vigilance* was far too large, and the other two shuttles it carried weren't adequately equipped for this upcoming mission.

What they needed was a freighter-sized vessel, and Sadey smiled as an idea presented itself. They'd been scheduled to rendezvous with the *Titania*, a Resistance ship masquerading as a medical transport, near Sardonis following Jalen's mission. The *Titania* was due to report back to Forus Command after spending the past several weeks on assignment on the other side of the Fringe, and the two ships had planned on traveling home together. They could still make the rendezvous happen but alter the timetable. The *Titania* was perfectly equipped for this phase of the plan, and unless Sadey was mistaken, they were already transporting one of the Haphezian test subjects. If they were still on schedule, they'd only be about an hour away from the Noro system at the moment.

Feeling better but still apprehensive, she went to the viewport and gazed out at the stars until the transmission from Ronan came through.

# · 27 ·

# GALACTIC FEDERATION
# MARTIAL COMMAND
## JUNIA, EDEAN

E legant cities like Junia always overwhelmed Taran after spending time on Duruta, Aubin, and all the other backwater planets he frequented. A person began to grow accustomed to all the rocks and dirt, so being in an environment composed entirely of shiny white and silver surfaces was almost surreal. He tried not to touch anything if he could help it; the citizens of Edean didn't actually have anyone following him around wiping up the dust and sand that fell from his clothes and boots, but he always got the feeling they wanted to.

He and Mae strode down the same white hallway toward the only office they ever visited when they came to the Federation's military headquarters in the galactic capital. Neither of them had much interest in exploring further, and as mere contractors from an independent world, the Feds didn't want them doing much exploring anyway. They were always told to enter the same elevator, walk down the same corridors, and enter the same empty office space whenever they arrived to meet with the Federation's Colonel Adrian Matney.

As usual, a security guard met them at the door, let them inside, then vanished. The office was well-furnished, but if Taran had to guess, meetings like this were the only thing it was ever used for. The far wall consisted of a large window that looked out over the Junia skyline. Perpetually sunny. Blue sky stretching as far as the eye could see. Sparkling, intricate architecture. The place almost seemed artificial.

Navigating back to the Core from Aubin had taken a bit of doing.

The arrival of the Haphezians—Ziva Payvan in particular—had been an unwelcome twist, and having to spare the extra time and manpower to finish recovering the corpses of his slain soldiers in the desert had complicated matters further. He'd ended up sending most of his unit back to Duruta with the bodies while he, Mae, and a couple of their men returned to Federation space to discuss recent developments with Matney and receive new instructions. That meant having to meet back up with the rest of the unit later, which in turn meant more wasted time. *More time for the Haphezians to get to Ronan first.*

"Payvan really got to you, didn't she?" Mae said, as if reading his thoughts.

It always amazed him how perceptive she was. This was the first time they'd really been alone in a quiet place since leaving Aubin four days earlier.

"This may sound weird," he said, looking down at his hand as he opened and closed the mechanical fingers, "but it always kind of bothered me that she didn't kill me outright. The surgeons said I should be grateful that my arm was all I lost, that she'd allowed me to live. But it was almost like she was taunting me, showing me that she could have taken my life if she'd wanted to. Yes, she took my arm, but she also *gave* me that knowledge, and it's something I have to live with for the rest of my life." He took a moment to examine the cybernetic appendage again. "That's the kind of person we're dealing with here."

Mae reached down and took his hand, interlocking her dexterous fingers with his prosthetic ones. The neural sensors embedded in the metal registered the warmth of her palm, and it brought him some comfort.

"Why haven't you ever talked to me about this before?" she asked.

"It's not the most pleasant of subjects, if you can believe it," Taran answered, arching his eyebrows. "And never in my life did I imagine running into Payvan again. It's one of those things you try to forget and move on from." He sighed and wandered over to the window, gazing out at the dazzling mid-day view of the city. "She's good, I'll give her that. But I can't let one person affect me."

The office door opened before he could say any more and in

walked Colonel Adrian Matney. He was a muscular man in his late forties with a sharp nose and black hair that had begun graying at the temples. Rather than a formal military uniform, he was dressed in a plain black shirt, gray fatigue pants, and spotless combat boots. The Special Tasks Units were his project within the Federation armed forces; all the Durutian contractors currently employed by the Feds reported directly to him.

"Sergeant Reddic, Corporal Nasser, a pleasure to see you again," he said, giving them each a nod. His voice was smooth and calm, but he never smiled. Taran always wondered if it really *was* a pleasure to see them.

"We've got nothing. We just wasted weeks on Aubin—it was a dead end, and the Haphezians are a dead end as well."

"Yes, I received your message," Matney answered, waving them toward some plush white chairs in the center of the office. "Why don't you have a seat, and we'll talk."

For a moment, Taran felt guilty about soiling the flawless furniture, but the feeling was a fleeting one and he sat down without another thought.

Matney seated himself across from them and consulted a data pad. "You said you tried to track the Resistance ship that took the Delta Patrol but lost track of it in the Achiuq sector of the southwest quadrant."

"Correct," Taran said.

"You set up a base on Aubin—" Matney's eyes roved over the information on the pad "—and encountered a pair of Haphezian operatives whom you believed were employed by Ronan."

"Considering the Delta Patrol was captured just outside the Noro system, we suspected the Haphezians may have been responsible. That theory was reinforced when we lost contact with the representative we sent to investigate Resistance activity on Haphez." He went on to explain that Devani's silence had in truth been due to a lockdown of the Haphezian Special Police headquarters following an attack on their military base. "It was a procedural thing. They were protecting her, not detaining her."

"So the Haphezians still have no affiliation with the Resistance,"

Matney said. "But you said in your report that a third operative arrived and murdered four of your men. Why?"

"To her credit, she was only defending her agents," Mae said. She squeezed Taran's arm with a firm hand when he tried to interject. "We captured those Haphezian men on Aubin because we thought they worked for Ronan. Turns out they were spying on us because they thought *we* worked for Ronan. She was merely protecting her people from a hostile force."

Taran scoffed. "I can't believe you're defending her."

"I'm stating facts," Mae replied. She kept her voice calm, but her face was rigid. "You know you would have done the same thing if you were in her place."

"Why the hell are the Haphezians looking into Resistance matters?" Matney demanded.

"They didn't know who Ronan was," Taran said. "They were continuing an investigation for some colleagues who had stumbled onto a Res facility on Chaiavis."

Matney sat up a little straighter. "And what became of these colleagues?"

"Both dead. Payvan didn't give us details, but based on the way she talked about it, I kind of assumed Ronan was responsible for killing them. She said she had 'their data,' but I don't know what all that entailed."

"And none of your representatives have found anything on Chaiavis before?"

Taran shook his head. "It's always been a bit of a problem area for our patrols, though. With no single governing entity, it's difficult to determine law enforcement jurisdiction and figure out who's in charge of a given area of the city. Our representatives can ask around at the embassies all they want, but the chances of those people actually knowing anything are slim. The only way to get solid intel is to send recon teams into the city, but we can't devote the time and manpower to an operation like that without leaving holes elsewhere."

Matney nodded and jotted down a few notes. "You mentioned Niio in your report. What's the deal there?"

"A member of Payvan's squad was captured by Res agents there. Surveillance footage showed that these people were wearing Durutian armor. That's where the Haphezians got the idea that we were in league with Ronan."

"That armor belonged to our missing Delta Patrol," Mae added.

The corners of Matney's lips curled downward. "Are you telling me the Resistance has now taken a number of soldiers from the Durutian Special Forces *and* a number of Haphezians, including a member of their law enforcement?"

Taran shrugged and nodded.

"Damn it." Matney was on his feet in an instant, pacing back and forth in front of his chair. "What's the Resistance doing attacking civilizations from independent worlds?"

"At first, I assumed our patrol was taken because of our affiliation with you. That could very well still be the case, but their apparent interest in the Haphezians makes me wonder if they've been going after other Fringe cultures as well. There could be a bigger picture we're not seeing yet."

"Like what?"

"You know as well as I do that the farther they go out into the Fringe, the harder it is to keep an eye on them. The Special Tasks Units are helping, but we can't be everywhere and see everything at once. There hasn't been any suspicious activity on any of the Resistance-controlled Core worlds?"

"Not that we've seen, no," Matney admitted. "Just the usual riots, homemade bombs, supply chain raids. Nothing we can't handle. Someone on Yotune tried to turn a house into a makeshift nostium lab, but we've destroyed it and are keeping a close eye on them now." He clicked his tongue and shook his head. "You'd think they'd have learned their lesson years ago."

"But now we have confirmation that Ronan had some sort of project running on Chaiavis," Mae put in, "and it's safe to say there's been a Resistance presence on Niio. These are both independent Fringe worlds. For all we know, they could be targeting us and the Haphezians specifically because we're not part of the Federation. They know you don't care. They know they're free from your shadow out there and can do whatever the hell they want while you're not looking."

"Are you suggesting we look, Corporal?" Matney growled. His face flushed and a vein in his forehead was becoming more prominent by the second. "Are you suggesting we leave established Resistance groups to their own devices while we go out and search the Fringe for leads that may or may not actually tell us anything? We may have superior numbers, but that doesn't mean we can cover the entire galaxy. Our forces are stretched thin enough as it is, and I'd rather not have a bunch of Fringe races pissed at us for sticking our noses in their business. It would violate neutrality agreements."

"Ronan is *attacking* those Fringe races," Taran said, bristling a bit. "You're willing to just sit by and let it happen?"

"Look, I know it's difficult to hear, but you, the Haphezians, all the other Fringe worlds—you all knew what it meant when you became neutral. You were too far away to make a valuable contribution to the societal structure of the Federation, so you were granted independence. That means we don't meddle in your affairs as long as you don't meddle in ours, namely by associating in any way with the Resistance."

Taran sighed and nodded.

"Now, I realize that you and many of your people are bound to us by contract, but that doesn't mean your entire civilization is or *wants* to be affiliated with us. And the Haphezians? Everyone knows they've spent decades trying as hard as possible to avoid any Federation or Resistance association. I can guarantee they don't want us coming out there searching for Res activity, and with the size and strength of their military, you can be damn sure they'll take action against anyone who interferes. We could wipe them out eventually, but the last thing we need right now is to go to war with someone other than the bloody Resistance."

"While you make a valid point, my question still stands," Taran said, rising to his feet. "You're going to sit by and let Ronan kill these people, *our* people?"

"We're supposed to be the good guys here, the foundation that holds the galaxy together," Matney replied. "We can't compromise that by violating neutrality agreements. No one—including our own people— would trust us again, and we don't need more Federation worlds trying to break away and join the Resistance. I'm sure the president and the rest of our military leaders would agree."

"Then what do you propose we do?" Mae said, standing as well.

"Here's the thing. We can't directly offer protection to you or the Haphezians. Who knows if they'd accept it anyway? But we *can* combat the Resistance. Ergo, if you can find the connection between your people and the Haphezians and figure out what Ronan is planning, we can stop it on our end. We can help you, just not through official channels. Understand?"

Taran wasn't a fan of the idea of doing all the leg work, and the last thing he wanted right now was to be directly responsible for helping the Haphezians after what Payvan had done to his soldiers. But this was better than nothing.

"Do we have any new intel on Ronan?" he asked with another sigh.

Matney sighed as well, and a bit of the redness that had appeared in his ears and cheeks began to dissipate. "I'm afraid not. A couple of new transmissions that mentioned the name were intercepted recently, but that's it." He paused a moment to gaze out the window and murmured to himself: "Tav Ronan."

"Still no indication as to why the name cropped up when it did?" Mae said.

"Our theories suggest that Ronan has been in hiding for some time. If the Resistance has been openly snatching members of Fringe cultures, I would guess it's getting harder for them to conceal whatever they're doing, but they're still trying as hard as possible to hide their actions from *us*. Maybe, for one reason or another, Ronan couldn't hide anymore, either."

Taran nodded. "Next course of action?"

"Go to Chaiavis on my order," Matney said. "Go ahead and take the time to search for this facility the Haphezians told you about. If all else fails, go back and confer with this Payvan woman and see what her friends' data entails."

Taran's hands curled immediately into fists.

"I'll dispatch another STU to Niio to take a closer look at the situation there. In the meantime, I've authorized payment for your time on Aubin to be transferred into your team's account. I trust you'll take care of dividing it accordingly." He paused and gave them each a look that almost struck Taran as being sincere—there was even a hint of an understanding smile on his lips. "Now, if you'll excuse me, I must prepare to leave for my next tour tomorrow. There's an officer outside who will escort you back to your ship."

With that, he turned and strode out, once more leaving Taran and Mae the sole occupants of the office. Taran took one last look out the window, glanced down at the sweaty stain he'd left on the white chair, then beckoned for Mae to follow him out the door. They moved down the spotless corridor in silence and were herded back to the landing area by the same guard who'd opened the office for them.

"I don't like this," Taran growled as they climbed the boarding ramp of their vessel.

"I don't, either," Mae said, "but he was right. The situation is delicate. Offering help to Fringe civilizations would do more harm than good at the moment. This all goes a lot deeper than we ever realized. I know you don't like the thought of it, but finding Payvan again might be our best move. Her friends encountered the Resistance firsthand, and at this point, she may know more than we do."

"I'll keep that in mind," Taran muttered, sitting down in the pilot's seat and priming the ship's engines. "Let's explore our other options first. We'll go see if we can find anything on Chaiavis. Then I want to talk more with Devani, see what else she knows about what happened while she was being held. I'm beginning to wonder if Ronan wasn't behind that attack she told us about."

"Why would the Resistance attack a Haphezian military base?"

"That's what we need to find out. Are you ready to go save the galaxy?"

# · 28 ·
# PAYVAN RESIDENCE
## NORO, HAPHEZ

I t was mid-morning by the time Ziva set the *Zenith* down in the underground landing bay beside her house. She'd opted to leave the *Intrepid* docked at HSP Headquarters and bring the borrowed ship home instead, at least long enough to unload all her supplies from it. It felt odd to be landing a strange ship there; she'd hardly had a chance to touch her own vessel over the past few months.

The escapade to Haphor had taken all night. It had been daylight by the time they made it back to Noro and deposited the Resistance agent in a stark holding room with constant supervision. Last she'd seen him, he'd been lying on a table, rendered completely immobile by the multiple straps and clasps pinning him down. His hands were covered, and the agency had even fitted him with a muzzle. Officially, it kept him from trying to ingest anything, though Ziva had a hunch Emeri ordered it after she told him the agent knew who she was.

He'd also ordered her to return home and get some rest. For the sake of appearances, it seemed like the logical thing for her to do after her family had just been involved in an attack. But as tired as she was, sitting around at home was the last thing she wanted to do, especially when they were dealing with a person who could spoil her secret in a heartbeat. Emeri had assured her everything would be fine—they'd start by running some tests and wait to start any interrogations until after they had a clearer picture of what exactly had gone down in Haphor. The agent was too big of a security risk to take to a med center, so mobile equipment would have to be brought to HSP Headquarters. That would take a while, he said, and he wanted her rested up after a long week. Besides, he'd already sent Skeet and Aroska home.

Ziva secured the ship and made her way into the house with her backpack over her shoulder, once again feeling like a stranger in her own home. At least her security code worked on the basement door this time. The last time she'd set foot in the house was when she, Aroska, and Kat had made a brief stop for supplies before heading for Argall. She hadn't seen Marshay and Ryon since the day she'd awakened in the hospital after being shot.

Voices could be heard on the ground floor as she made her way down the corridor and up the stairs. To her surprise, she found Skeet and Aroska in the living room talking with Ryon while Marshay contributed to the conversation from the kitchen. All four of them went silent the moment they saw her.

"Z," Skeet said, standing up. "How is it?"

She shrugged and set her bag down. "They've all been exposed," she said quietly, certain they'd already heard everything through agency channels. "The symptoms set in immediately. There's not much else to say."

"Everyone?"

"Njo, my mother, all the staff and security personnel present in the house. Another guard was killed by the intruder. The twins were at a party and are unharmed. Jada is—" she glanced at Aroska "—unaffected."

She had honestly hoped to catch a few minutes of sleep after coming all the way home, but now that Skeet and Aroska were both present, there was much that needed to be discussed. One look at Marshay and Ryon was all it took to dismiss them from the room. Their faces were rather downcast, but they went without fuss as they always did, each stopping to give her a pat on the shoulder before vanishing into their rooms.

"Emeri briefed all the spec ops lieutenants," Skeet said once all had become quiet again. He crossed his arms. "He told us this stuff is nostium. You want to explain to me why everyone else is dying but you and Jada haven't been affected?"

Ziva didn't care for his tone. "Jada is safe because the formula is tailored to Haphezians."

Aroska's eyes widened. "What?"

"The man we took into custody is a human Nosti," she answered. "The Resistance obviously has a working formula somewhere if he's using his power without any problem. Think about it—the only victims we know of right now are Haphezian, and Jada is immune. It makes sense."

"Does that mean there are more Nosti out there somewhere?"

"I'm sure it does," she said. "It's one of the things we'll try to determine when—"

Skeet's harsh voice cut her off. "Ziva, answer me!"

When she looked at him, she felt crushed under all the pent-up frustration she'd sensed in him since Argall. Being stared at by an angry person was nothing new, but never before had it been someone she was so close to. Even without breaking eye contact, she could feel Aroska watching her as well. *"If I were him, I'd probably be more pissed the longer you made me wait."*

She was tempted to pull rank and berate him for speaking to her in such a way, but despite his unforgiving tone, she knew he was addressing her as a friend. "What do you want me to say?"

"Explain to me how you know all of this. Explain to me why you sent me out of Emeri's office. I'm not stupid—you're the one who told him this is nostium. I can't help you if you keep me in the dark. I want you to tell me what the hell is going on." His eyebrows were furrowed, but his eyes glistened with emotion. As much as he wanted an explanation, Ziva could tell he was afraid of what one would entail.

"I hate to actually call myself a Nosti," she began, pausing as he swore, turned in a circle, and ruffled up his hair, "but that's the gist of it."

He looked at her as if he didn't believe her. "How long?"

"Since I was seven."

"*Frouchten hehle*," he muttered. "Why didn't you tell me?"

"It's not exactly something I want to share with everyone," she scoffed.

"But of all people, *he* knows?" Skeet waved his hand toward

Aroska, who stood quietly with a chagrined expression. The fact that he hadn't spoken up or been shocked by her words was all the explanation Skeet needed. "That's what happened at Dakiti, wasn't it? That was the 'breach of protocol'."

Ziva nodded. "I was going to tell you sometime."

Skeet forced an incredulous chuckle and cursed again. "Can I talk to you for a minute?"

He stormed by, knocking his shoulder against hers, and disappeared down the hallway toward her bedroom. She sighed and shot Aroska an unimpressed glance before turning and chasing him down.

In addition to her weapons cache, all her computer and communications equipment remained aboard the *Zenith*, leaving the room bare. But there was hardly time to stop and look around at all the empty space. She slammed a fist against the wall panel to shut and lock the door and then turned, arms crossed, to find Skeet standing in a similar position a couple of meters away.

"What the hell is your problem?" she demanded.

"*My* problem? Listen to yourself, Ziva. One of our teammates is missing, your family is going to die, and on top of everything, I find out you've been wielding some insane magical power since you were little. We're supposed to be able to trust each other. You know I would have never betrayed a secret like this."

"I know that, Skeet," she said, trying as hard as possible to keep her voice low and even. "But you've got to understand—I didn't want to tell *anyone*. What you didn't know couldn't hurt you."

"But I assume Emeri knows. And Tarbic obviously knows."

"Because I saved his life!"

He remained silent for a few seconds before heaving a sigh. "So that's why he got you off the hook when you were scheduled for execution."

She nodded.

"I still don't understand it. Why did you even go back for him that day?"

Ziva had asked herself the same question on several occasions. How had Taran Reddic put it? "*I never thought you people were the no-*

*man-left-behind type."* She had to admit it was true. They'd rescued Jayden, gotten what they'd come to Dakiti for. Every HSP protocol dictated that she should have left with the team, should have considered Aroska a casualty of the mission. After all, spec ops agents—even temporary ones—should always expect to be treated as expendable in the field. And yet, she'd chosen to go back and find him, despite not knowing what condition he'd be in, and she'd done it without a second thought.

*Of course I went back, you idiot.* The answer seemed that obvious, though she didn't understand why.

The look on Skeet's face told her he was unimpressed by her silence. "Well, Zinni is as good as dead thanks to this investigation he started."

"Don't you even go there!" Ziva said, advancing toward him. "I know you're pissed, but you're being completely irrational. No single person can be blamed for any of this. If you're bent on picking someone, then pick me. I should have put that damn data pad somewhere else."

"I'm not going to blame you, Ziva. That wouldn't even make sense—you were away on Na for over two months. And yet here you are, trying to shift the blame away from the guy who wanted to kill you for what you did to his brother, the guy you used to take pleasure in mentally tormenting. You're acting like he's the only person you can really trust. What's changed?"

"*Sheyss*, Skeet. You're telling me to listen to myself? I think *you* need to listen to *yourself*. Without him, who knows if I would have survived the whole debacle with Dasaro? Trust me, I wanted so badly to come to you and Zinni for help, but I couldn't risk exposing myself. If I hadn't gone to him, we wouldn't have gone to Chaiavis to find Bosco, wouldn't have met Kat, wouldn't have heard about Ronan. We'd be caught in the middle of these attacks right now and wouldn't have a clue what was going on."

Now he looked hurt. He sat down in the chair that belonged at her desk and ran his hands through his hair again before resting his elbows on his knees. "Sorry," he said softly. "Just…sorry. I'm being totally out of line here. I'm tired. I'm starting to give up on Zinni. I'm looking for someone or something to blame and I'm choosing the wrong things." A short chuckle escaped his throat. "You know, I told him once that he'd never get you to open up to him, and trying was just going to get him killed. Looks like he achieved the impossible."

"Come on, Skeet," Ziva murmured. "You know how I get." Her skin crawled and she sent him a look that suggested they avoid the subject.

He gave her an understanding nod. "You're right, though," he said after a moment. "We wouldn't have a clue about Ronan if he hadn't been so adamant about investigating Reilly's data. And I guess we really wouldn't know what was going on if not for you and your...what is it, exactly?"

It was like the word was some sort of curse nobody wanted to say out loud. "Nostia," she answered.

He watched her for a moment, eyes filled with that same mixture of awe and fear both Aroska and Emeri had regarded her with. "I can't believe you've kept it a secret for all these years. Why hasn't the gas hurt you?"

"We're guessing my nervous system is just conditioned to its effects already."

"So you got injected...or exposed, or—"

"They're called infusions."

"How have you hidden all of this for so long?" His eyes widened as the realization hit him. "That guy you killed—that was no accidental encounter, was it? You knew him."

Ziva nodded. "But everything else I told HSP was true. Tell you what. When we've made it through this—stopped Ronan, found Zinni—I'll explain everything." *Assuming the Royal House doesn't eat me alive first.*

That did an adequate job of calming him down for the moment. As he stood up, she could still sense a bit of frustration and animosity directed her way, but his breathing had evened out and his formerly clenched facial muscles were beginning to relax.

"You know you can trust me, right?" he said.

"I know. And I do."

"And you know I can't help you unless you let me."

"I know." Just because she knew didn't mean she had to like the idea.

"Okay then. Let's go figure out how to stop Ronan."

The air in the hallway seemed especially calm and still after the heated exchange. Ziva had half expected to find Aroska lurking there when she opened the door; she'd heard the floor outside the room creak at one point and assumed he'd been eavesdropping on at least part of the conversation. Instead, she found him in the living room pacing back and forth with his communicator pressed to his ear. He ended what sounded like a very curt transmission and looked at them with dread in his eyes.

"There's been another attack."

# · 29 ·

# UNKNOWN LOCATION

## NORO SYSTEM, FRINGE SPACE

*W*hat do you know?

For once, it was a struggle to sort out her thoughts. Usually, there was so little going on—so little to think about—that it took no effort whatsoever.

*My name is Zinnarana Vax. I'm an intelligence officer at HSP. Something is very different. Something is very wrong.*

The subtle swaying of the floor had now escalated to full-out rocking. It wasn't enough to throw her around or even really jostle her, but after being so disoriented for the galaxy only knew how long, the sensation was certainly noticeable.

After a few moments of consideration, she realized she was neither sitting against the wall nor lying flat on her back. She was lying in what felt like a semi-fetal position in the center of the room. At least she guessed it was the center of the room—in the pitch blackness, it was impossible to tell. The odd empty feeling she'd noticed in the past was nothing but a whisper in the back of her mind. That in itself was what told her the situation was *different*. The Emptiness was always the first thing she was aware of when she regained consciousness—or whatever happened—and the absence of it left her feeling almost rejuvenated.

Or maybe it was just the adrenaline surging through her in response to the change in her surroundings. In addition to the tremors in the floor, the vague hum in the walls had risen to a dull roar; it was almost as if something somewhere had come alive and was currently working at full capacity. The sense of urgency was what told her the situation was *wrong*.

*My name is Zinnarana Vax*, she thought again as she struggled to roll onto her back. She began her self-examination routine, forcing her brain to focus on one thing until it could process the rush of new information. Her arms both felt like lead, but she pushed them into action anyway, running her hands over her face, torso, and what she could reach of her thighs. She wiggled her toes for good measure and was satisfied that her legs were in working ord—wait. No shoes? Had her feet always been bare?

She lay there for what seemed like several more minutes—her sense of time had long since been lost—and did her best to examine each detail of the situation and sort out the facts. For the first time, she felt alert enough to investigate her surroundings. She'd been awake plenty of times previously but had only been lucid enough to realize that and that alone. Nothing outside of the space she occupied had been within the realm of comprehension. But even now, despite her desire to know more, it took all her strength to lift her head, and the slightest movements sent a cold fog swirling through her mind. She had to settle with remaining as still and quiet as possible, devoting all her energy to listening, smelling, feeling, just as she'd done before. Any moments of clarity needed to be taken advantage of.

For the first time, she wondered if she might be inside a vehicle of some sort—a ship, maybe. That would explain the movement in the floor, especially if she were in a cargo space. The hum in the walls could be the rumble of engines. So she was on a ship, and they had taken her blood. *But why?* And why had the movement become more violent now? Why was the hum so much louder? She felt panic encroaching as her mind began to stray from what she did know and dwell on the things she didn't know.

*Stop it. Calm down. Think. What do you know?*

*...I don't know!*

In that instant, the rocking in the floor ceased altogether, and the hum of the engines—it made sense to call it that—reduced itself to a mere vibration. She lay still and listened, but she imagined she was deep enough within the ship's bowels that she'd be sufficiently isolated from any activity. The only sound she could hear was her own heartbeat, and she was amazed by how real, how *strong* it sounded.

*I'm still alive*, she told herself.

The mental celebration was cut short when her surroundings shuddered and the engine noise rose once more to an angry roar, louder and more powerful than ever. She felt the need to brace herself and dug her fingers into the cold metal floor despite the fact that she wasn't moving. One thought still plagued her: *something is very wrong.*

A metallic screech echoed through the room, startling her. Red light streamed in as the door opened, but she was forced to squeeze her eyes shut before she had a chance to ascertain its location. The light burned even through her closed eyelids, and she felt the familiar wave of nausea set in.

*Voices. Footsteps. So many footsteps. Someone is yelling. Whimpering, crying. Body heat. Movement.* The sudden overload of information made her want to scream, but when she opened her mouth, only a hoarse squeal emerged.

*Smells. Scents. Specific scents. So many of them. Haphezians? Five, six, eight, ten...eleven. Eleven scents. Eleven people. It's crowded in here.* Someone stepped on her arm, tripped, fell on top of her. It was a small person, but the elbow that jabbed into her ribs was no less painful.

The door slid shut and the red light disappeared, casting the room into darkness once more. She opened her eyes but was met with only a black void, just as she'd grown accustomed to. The sounds and smells around her hadn't gone away, and the darkness had only aggravated them.

*Cha'sen. So much crying. Legs moving, hands reaching. Small voices.* She did her best to wriggle out from under the individual who had fallen on her, and in turn, the person wriggled away from her. *Can literally smell the fear. Small people. These people are children. Eleven small children. They're all terrified.*

*I'm terrified.*

Mustering all the strength she could, she ran her tongue over her lips and swallowed. "My name is Zinnarana Vax," she said, her voice hardly more than a whisper. "Who are you?"

# · 30 ·
# HSP Headquarters
## Noro, Haphez

"What do we know?" Skeet and Ziva said simultaneously as they approached Emeri in the detention corridor. Skeet couldn't help but steal a quick glance at her. Her eyes remained on the director as she waited eagerly for an answer. It was like nothing was different, nothing had changed. Everything was strictly business, as always. The fact that she could act this way after everything she'd just revealed only showed him how easily she'd deceived everyone over the years.

"Witnesses say a freighter-sized ship flew into Salex and touched down in the middle of the plaza," Emeri answered. "Five or six armed men emerged and grabbed eleven children who were on an educational trip to the processing center. Shot their instructor and took off."

"*Sheyss*, kids?" Skeet said.

To Ronan's credit, Salex was the perfect location to abduct someone and get away with it. It was a small community nestled among the farming plateaus east of Noro, about an hour's journey by car. Many of the surrounding small towns had been absorbed by the city over the years, but Salex was isolated enough to garner its own recognition. It was separated from the Noro valley by a range of heavily forested hills and was the location of the region's largest govino orchards. Most people considered it a resort of sorts; the small population there was well-off, and the banks of the Tranyi River were lined with vacation homes where wealthy visitors could lounge in the sun sipping govinolin or freshly pressed govino juice all day. The little town was manned by an HSP outpost, but if the ship had touched down as fast as Emeri said, none of the agents would have had time to react.

"What would Ronan want with a bunch of kids?" he asked, running his fingers through his hair.

"No idea in hell," Emeri replied. He jerked his head toward the nearest holding room. "I'm hoping our friend in there can shed some light on the situation when we begin questioning."

"Now, wait a second," Ziva piped in. "How do we know this was Ronan? There was no gas involved. It could have been pirates looking to make off with the children of wealthy govino farmers."

Emeri nodded. "That's what the Salex HSP office thought at first, too. But when they attempted to trace the ship's exit path, they sent the data back to us and—"

The way he hesitated made Skeet's stomach turn over.

"—the emissions signatures match the ones you've been trying to track for the past five weeks. This is the same ship that abducted Officer Vax on Niio."

The ability to speak eluded both Skeet and Ziva as they processed what the director had just told them. It was almost inconceivable that the same ship they'd been chasing for weeks was suddenly present again, here, now. Then came the realization that whatever had happened to Zinni could be happening to those children.

Ziva spoke up first. "What do you mean they *attempted* to trace the ship's path?"

"After leaving Salex, it entered orbit and merged with traffic departing from Noro Spaceport," Emeri said. "The agency had a fix on it until it broke off from the group and performed an out-of-lane FTL jump. We didn't have a strong enough lock on it to calculate trajectory and possible destinations."

"An out-of-lane FTL jump?" Skeet exclaimed. Not only did the Resistance have possession of eleven Haphezian children, but they were performing one of the deadliest maneuvers in intragalactic travel while transporting them. He hated to admit it, but things already weren't boding well for those kids.

"They must not be going far, then," Ziva said, as calm and collected as ever. "They wouldn't risk jumping outside of an established travel lane unless their destination was close by."

"There are probes sweeping the system now," Emeri said, "but we're running into the same problems as we did when looking for the source of that fighter that crashed on Na. Noro is the last major spaceport in this sector of populated space, so there's an incredible amount of traffic traveling through the system at any given time. Identifying which vessels are threats and which are harmless—quickly and efficiently, anyway—is nearly impossible. By the time we got a fix on the target, it would either be long gone or back here engaging in another attack."

Skeet felt a cold sweat break out on his forehead as he imagined Zinni alive aboard this ship. Five weeks was a long time, especially considering the things they'd seen on Na and in Haphor, but one could always hope. "Why don't we just hit them at the source? You told me the Resistance is on Forus." He stole another glance at Ziva; she'd no doubt been the source of that information, and he still couldn't quite wrap his head around how she knew all this and how she'd kept it from him.

"If only it were that simple, Lieutenant," Emeri said with a sigh. "There have already been talks taking place on Na, but I don't see how it's feasible. Ronan and the majority of the Resistance's military strength may be located on Forus, but they've also got upwards of twenty other planetary systems on their side. I know we take pride in the Grand Army, but we'd be no match for a combined force of that size, especially if some, most, or—galaxy forbid—*all* of them are Nosti."

"We have help," Ziva said, taking both Skeet and Emeri by surprise. "I know one person with a small but motivated force who has already offered to assist. Another is emotionally invested, and I'm sure it wouldn't take much coercion to get him on board."

Skeet wasn't sure who the first person was, but he assumed the latter individual was Taran Reddic. His first instinct was to vote against involving the Durutians since they seemed so hell-bent on wiping out everything that got between them and Ronan, but as long as the team got Zinni back first, he didn't much care how Reddic went about attacking the Resistance. Perhaps they could send the Durutians to Forus while the agency continued the search for this elusive ship.

Emeri remained silent for a moment, and Skeet couldn't tell if he was sending Ziva an unimpressed glare or looking slightly behind her as he contemplated her words. "We'll keep that in mind," he said quietly as if he were still lost in thought. "Forus is about a day and a half FTL trip from here, so we'd have to coordinate arrival times with the rest of this help you speak of." He sighed again. "I'll let Na know we've got limited support in the event that they decide to launch a counterstrike."

Ziva dipped her head and wandered over to the viewscreen on the wall outside the holding room. The monitor was divided into six sections, each of which streamed feeds from one of the cams inside the room. From the hallway, they had a perfect view of the Resistance agent from multiple angles. The man had been sedated with a paralytic similar to what the Durutians subjected Skeet and Aroska to on Aubin. They couldn't risk knocking him out entirely for fear of compromising brain activity for the cranial scans. The paralytic wouldn't stop him from using his Nostia—or whatever it was called—but at least he'd remain completely immobile during the tests. As if the physical restraints weren't enough...

"What do we know about this guy?" Skeet asked, moving up beside her to look at the viewscreen himself.

"At this point, not a lot," Emeri replied. "He's a Nosti, which means there must be a successful nostium formula out there somewhere. I have to agree with Ziva's theory that the nostium used in these attacks is tailored specifically to us, though we don't know why. We're guessing he's an underling and received orders to target the Royal General from someone of higher rank, possibly Ronan. We have agents from the Royal Guard and the Haphor field office combing the city looking for any sign of a vehicle he may have arrived in, but we've come up short so far." He turned and looked at them both, lowering his voice a bit as if he didn't want to speak the words. "And the fact that he managed to take out a member of the Jaroons' security detail tells us how dangerous he is. It's not every day you see a human that size who can best one of our soldiers."

He grew quiet and rested his face in his hand for a moment. When he looked back up, Skeet could tell how tired he was. His perfectly combed hair and impeccable uniform couldn't hide the dullness in his eyes. All the questions and uncertainty surrounding the situation were beginning to take their toll on everyone.

"*Sheyss*, this is a mess," the director muttered. His tone gave Skeet the impression he was speaking to them as old friends rather than subordinates. "The media was already in an uproar after realizing the attacks on Na and the Royal General came from the same unnamed source. Now they know we've got a suspect in custody and they're starting to demand more information on that front. It will get progressively harder to keep this man's identity a secret."

"How many people are in the loop so far?" Ziva asked. "I know Luko Zona is."

Emeri nodded. "As of right now, the ops captains and lieutenants are the only people who know exactly *what* and *who* we're dealing with here, along with other key agency personnel we've advised. Then there are, of course, the few officials in the government and military who have been briefed. We're still working hard to keep everything as restricted as possible, but we're briefing additional people on a need-to-know basis. Everyone has agreed that it's best to continue operating under the pretense that we're oblivious to Ronan's presence in all this. If the Resistance finds out we know and decides to launch a full-scale attack, well...the simple truth is that we're not ready."

"Let's hope this guy can help us get ready," Ziva muttered, eyes still fixed on the monitor. Based on the way the muscles in her jaw twitched, Skeet could tell she wished she'd just killed the Nosti agent while they were in Haphor. At the same time, he imagined it must be rather surreal for her to come face to face with one of...*her kind* after so many years.

"How long until we can begin an interrogation?" he asked, trying hard to stay focused on the task at hand. Now was the time to be thinking about Zinni and the ship that took her, not about Ziva and all her secrets.

"The tests should be nearly finished," Emeri said. "I want to keep any interrogation completely in-house to avoid premature disclosure of certain facts." He threw a glance at Ziva. "I'd prefer if one or both of you did it. I'll question the bastard myself if I have to. The point is, the information we need is delicate, but time is of the essence."

The sound of approaching footsteps echoed down the hallway and the three of them turned to find Aroska moving toward them. Skeet wasn't sure where he'd been for the past ten minutes or so. The man had been glued to his communicator since they'd arrived at Headquarters, speaking at length with someone out in Salex. Perhaps he had a soft spot for children; after all, these most recent developments had the entire Noro region in a frenzy.

Tarbic held up the comm unit as he drew closer. "Salex was wondering if we'd be willing to send someone from ops out to take another look at the abduction site," he announced, pocketing the device. "I went ahead and volunteered. Figured having prior experience tracking the ship might come in handy."

"Good," Ziva said. "Let us know what you find."

"Actually, I was wondering if you would come with me. It wouldn't hurt to have an extra set of eyes."

Ziva tilted her head. "Why me?"

"Come on, Ziva," he said. "You came halfway around the galaxy and found us on Aubin. You of all people should be able to recognize the little details, see things the rest of us are missing. Finding things is what you do best."

Skeet couldn't help but feel that there was something odd about the request. Aroska seemed rushed, preoccupied. Based on the skeptical look on Ziva's face, she could sense it, too. Then again, the man had a point; she *was* good at finding things, especially things that didn't want to be found. Besides, they'd all been preoccupied about one thing or another as of late. Skeet dismissed the behavior as normal considering the circumstances.

"Fine," she said after another moment of silence. She didn't appear completely convinced, but her desire for efficiency always seemed to trump any uncertainty. "But I don't want to take too long. I want a piece of this guy." She turned once more to stare at the viewscreen.

"Sure," Aroska said.

"Want me to save him for you?" Skeet asked.

She shook her head and moved over to stand beside Aroska. "We need information, and we need it fast—there's no time to wait around. We'll be back as soon as possible, but in the meantime, he's all yours. Get something out of him before we return."

With that, she and Aroska turned and took off at a brisk pace down the hall. Skeet watched them go for a moment before fixing his eyes on the monitor and cracking his knuckles.

"With pleasure," he muttered.

# · 31 ·
# HSP Headquarters
## Noro, Haphez

They stopped on the squad floor long enough to pick up their field packs. For a moment, Ziva couldn't figure out why there was no locker assigned to her, but then she remembered what Emeri had said about having Dasaro's old office at her disposal. She had yet to even set foot in the room, so she was surprised to find the door open and the light on when she approached. A second desk, currently occupied by Aura, was situated across from the one Dasaro had used. The woman shot Ziva a glance as she entered but said nothing. Tufts of hair had come loose from her braid, but she'd brushed it behind her shoulder without bothering to fix it. Rather than a formal suit, she now donned a casual jacket and pants, and dark circles enveloped her eyes. She looked like every other agent in the building.

Ziva ignored her and angled toward the locker against the far wall. All of Dasaro's personal effects had been removed, leaving the space bare except for the basic field supply pack all the ops agents' lockers contained. She had no idea what had become of her old one. Not that it mattered—all the packs contained exactly the same things anyway. If you wanted something more than what was there, you had to pack it yourself. She went ahead and filled it with a few of her own items.

She removed the bag from the locker and slipped her arm through one of the straps, taking a moment to look around the rest of the office. The desk and walls were completely empty, and the computer terminal and wall monitor were powered down. She doubted that would ever change. She had little interest in even using the space, much less turning it into her own.

"Where are you going?"

Ziva turned to face Aura, who hadn't removed her eyes from her computer. The question hadn't been gruff, nor had it contained a shred of genuine curiosity. An answer—a fact—was all she desired.

"Salex."

Aura's gaze flitted toward her for a split second. "Stay in contact."

Ziva went out without so much as a nod. She had to admit she was beginning to warm up to the probation officer—at least they were both trying to achieve a common goal. Still, fighting Aura was like fighting a copy of herself, and she didn't like it. Even the simple request to stay in communication rubbed her the wrong way.

She found Aroska already waiting for her in the parking bay beside an idling agency groundcar. They both got in without a word and he piloted the vehicle out into traffic and pointed it toward the hills to the east.

Part of her felt bad for having spent so much time lying to everyone about her past, particularly Skeet and Zinni. Even the word 'lying' sounded so negative—it was more like withholding the truth. It wasn't that she'd given them false information; she simply hadn't given them any information at all. Then she'd proceeded to continue withholding that information, living the majority of her adult life as if Jak Gamon had never existed. If what she was doing should indeed be called lying, then she'd technically been doing it since she was seven years old. She'd gotten rather good at it over the years, and it didn't just apply to her Nostia. She could lie to others—and herself, for that matter—without so much as a second thought.

"Good liars are better at detecting *other* liars," Gamon had told her once. She didn't doubt it. It was one of the reasons she'd been able to pick up on his charade just in time to defend herself, and why she now knew Aroska was being less than truthful about why he wanted her to come to Salex. Well, no, it wasn't so much *why* he wanted her to come—having her employ her tracking skills seemed like a perfectly reasonable explanation. Even if that were the truth, there was still

EJ FISCH

something he wasn't telling her, information he was withholding. Normally, it would have bothered her to no end, but right now, she was more concerned with getting to the little resort town and finding clues—finding Zinni—as quickly as possible.

They had made it out of the city and were zipping along a trade route that cut through lush farmland before Aroska spoke. "How do you get?"

Ziva turned her attention away from the view of the Tranyi River off to their right. "What?"

"Back at your place, Skeet asked why you'd been able to open up to me, and you said, 'you know how I get'."

"Please tell me you didn't want me to come just so you could ask me that while I'm trapped in here," she said, attempting to regulate a sudden increase in heart rate.

To her relief, he shook his head, but when he spoke, his tone was gruffer than she'd expected. "I want to know what you meant by that."

"You know, you have a bad habit of eavesdropping outside closed doors," she muttered, reveling in the rather shocked look he gave her. "Yeah, I know that's how you found out I killed Soren. It's going to get you in trouble one of these days."

For once, the mention of his deceased brother didn't make his cheeks flush with anger. Something that looked like either dread or guilt flashed through his eyes, though with his gaze directed straight ahead at the road, it was impossible to tell for sure. He tightened his grip on the controls and clenched his jaw, refusing to say more.

At least it had gotten him to shut up. Still, it bothered her that saying Soren's name hadn't produced the usual results. In the past, mentioning his brother had always been a surefire way to keep Aroska at bay, keep him angry enough that he *wanted* to distance himself from her. Ziva wasn't sure what to think of his current reaction, or lack thereof.

On top of that, she could tell the question he'd just posed hadn't been what he was hiding after all. He was still keeping something from her. He'd been growing bolder lately, and part of her was glad. It made him a more efficient agent, after all. But part of her hated it. Hated the way he could actually tell what she was thinking and feeling. Hated the way he no longer caved when caught in her glare. Hated the way he seemed to be developing immunity to her manipulation tactics. The idea that her primary defense mechanism was no longer one hundred percent effective terrified her.

She sat there watching the landscape whiz by outside, trying to blame Aroska for her troubles while simultaneously wondering how she'd lost control. She finally decided it was pointless to worry about him and directed her focus down to the data pad on her lap. The Salex office had forwarded all the information on the children and missing ship for them to review on the trip over, and she busied herself reading through it, taking everything in as fast as her mind would allow.

"If the kids were taken here in the plaza, we should start by investigating ground zero," she said. "I'm sure there are plenty of people there who saw or heard something. The next step will be to look for surveillance in the area, maybe a security cam that has some footage of what went down. We can't really do much else after that other than reexamine the ship's flight path. This should take four or five hours tops, and we can be back in Noro before—"

"Ziva."

The first thing that struck her was that it was the first time Aroska had spoken for at least twenty minutes. The second was his tone. "What?" she said, immediately snapping to attention. In past experience, that kind of tone always meant one of two things: something significant was going on ahead—a glance through the windshield ruled that out—or the speaker was about to share something they doubted she wanted to hear. Her eyebrows immediately slid together and she set her jaw, waiting for him to continue.

Aroska's knuckles were white as he gripped the steering controls. "My family lives in Salex."

"Excuse me?"

"My father, mother, brother, his family—they run one of the most successful govino orchards in the entire Noro region."

Ziva shook her head, raking her hand back through her hair. She felt her heart rate spike again. "Pull over."

"Ziva, please, I—"

"Just pull over."

"Will you just listen for a minute? This—"

Without another word, she drew her pistol and shoved the barrel against his temple. "I said pull the damn car over!"

He swallowed and complied, and the vehicle settled to the ground and skidded over to the shoulder in a great cloud of dust. Ziva stuffed the gun back into its holster and gathered up her pack, flinging the passenger door open before Aroska could get a word in edgewise. She slung the bag over her shoulder and began to trudge through the dirt back in the direction from which they'd come.

She heard the pilot's door slam behind her. "Where do you think you're going?" Aroska shouted.

"Not to Salex, that's for sure!"

"Oh, come on!"

She heard his footsteps approaching quickly behind her and turned, shying to one side just before he could grab her arm. "Why the hell didn't you tell me?"

"Because I knew you'd never come with me if you knew the truth!" He respectfully took a step back but placed his hands on his hips, refusing to back down. "My nephew was one of those kids who got taken. He's mentally handicapped and takes medications he can't survive more than a couple of days without. Ziva, he's only seven years old. As soon as I heard, I knew I needed you with me. You're the best chance we have of finding him and any of those other kids."

For a moment, she wondered what her response would have been if he'd just asked. "You seriously think your family is going to let me just waltz in and help? Are you insane?"

"Ziva, they don't know who you are."

She threw up her hands. "How?"

"Because I never told them. I may have been angry about Soren, but I'm not stupid. Telling anyone outside the agency who the Cleaner was would have gotten me fired, and at that point, I knew keeping my job was the only way I could ever catch up to you and confront you." He sighed and rubbed a hand across his forehead as if the memory were unpleasant. "They don't know who you are," he murmured again.

For a long time, the only sound to be heard was the whistle of air as traffic whizzed by on the road. Ziva kept a firm grip on the strap of her pack, having half a mind to just keep walking. She shifted her gaze periodically from Aroska to the land ahead, the land where the little settlement of Salex lay. An odd sensation coursed through her stomach—it had been a long time since she'd been so genuinely uncomfortable with an idea. It was one thing to have to face Aroska on a daily basis, but Soren's entire family? It didn't matter whether they knew who she was. The thought made her sick.

On the other hand, this was one of their freshest leads thus far. If they could make it to the town soon enough and find some clues, it might bring them one step closer to finding Ronan and Zinni. And if rescuing some kids was part of the deal, everyone could go home satisfied.

She clenched her jaw and walked back to the car. "Fine, let's go. But I hope you understand how much this is *not* okay."

If Aroska was surprised by her choice, he masked it well. It was tempting to not go simply to deny him the benefit of being right about her. She wasn't sure how he'd become so adept at knowing what she was thinking, and it was infuriating. But there were lives on the line here, and she reminded herself that Ronan and the Resistance would just keep coming back until they got whatever they wanted.

"Does the Salex office even know we're coming?" she asked, massaging her temples as the car lifted from the ground and merged with the flow of traffic.

"I told them we were coming to look around and that we'd be in the area if they needed anything."

"So you lied to Emeri."

"He knows my family lives out here. That's why he contacted me first."

"But when I…" She paused, aware there was no way to sugarcoat what she was about to say. "When I was reviewing Soren's cleaning order, it said all of his next of kin were in Noro."

"They all moved out here right after that," Aroska replied in the same clipped tone she usually spoke to him in. "My dad's parents were ready to sell their orchard but wanted to keep it in the family. He also thought it would be best to get everyone out of the city after Soren's death and the failed attempt on his own life." His eyes shifted toward her for a split second.

"I told you before—I had nothing to do with that!"

"I know." He stared straight ahead without speaking for several seconds, and the look on his face transformed back into one of guilt. "I don't understand, though. If nobody knows who you are, why are you still so worried about this?"

She directed her focus toward a single tree atop a nearby hill and didn't look away. "I form connections," she murmured.

She heard the pilot's seat creak as Aroska turned toward her. "What?"

"That's 'how I get'." She met his gaze for a moment before returning hers to the road. "When I have a target, it's my job to learn everything there is to know about them. It helps me predict what they're going to do, where they're going to be. When the time comes to take the shot, it's almost like I'm killing someone I've come to know. Maybe it's morbid, but I've formed a connection with them." *Even with the ones I wasn't supposed to kill*, she thought. "The only way to move on and continue doing my job is to forget them, shut them out of my memory. Sever the connection. Do you understand where I'm coming from?"

"You can't dwell in the past," he replied with a shrug, though he sounded hesitant.

"Exactly. But I have to deal with you on a daily basis. You're a constant reminder of Soren. I don't need any more."

When he turned to look at her again, she couldn't tell if it was sorrow or apathy she was seeing in his eyes. "We need to find those kids," he said bluntly.

She crossed her arms. If he thought she'd let her feelings get in the way of her work, he was dead wrong. "Then let's go find them."

The two of them continued the journey in silence. Once they passed through the mountains, the Salex valley opened up ahead. Acres upon acres of govino trees stretched as far as the eye could see, their branches heavy with ripe pods. Ziva tried to keep her mind occupied counting the symmetrical rows as they flew by, but it was of little use.

The closer they drew to the town, the clammier her hands got. It was disgusting; she could stroll into a place like Dakiti with a totally clear head, but here she was getting worked up over a meeting with civilian strangers. At least she tried to convince herself that's all they were.

*Calm down. What the hell is your problem?*

"My parents took a shipment of govinolin to some convention on Gehiri," Aroska said as he maneuvered the car into the heart of the little town. "They're on their way back, but they're probably still a couple of days out. My brother Maston and his family are the only ones here. His son Chyler is the one who was taken. He said we could use his house as a base of operations as long as we're here."

"Why don't we just use the HSP office?"

He shot her a look that told her it had been a stupid question.

"I'm serious," she said. "I get that you're personally invested in this, but there's more at stake here than just your family." That didn't necessarily mean staying at the Tarbics' house was a bad thing—it didn't really matter where they did their work as long as it got done. That was just the last place she wanted to go.

"These are real people with feelings and fears, Ziva. Maybe that's too difficult for you to understand. Yes, it's my duty as a brother and uncle to be there for them, but it's also *our* duty as protectors of this planet." He pulled the car off the main road and steered it down a narrower lane that led to private residences, most of which were separated by more sprawling orchards.

Ziva's hands curled into fists as they turned onto the front drive of the third house. She had to admit the property was impressive; everything from the exterior décor to the architectural design was elegant yet simple. In truth, it reminded her of the area of Noro she lived in. For a split second, the aesthetic and familiarity allowed her to forget all her concerns, but they all came rushing back like a raincloud over her head as the car came to a stop.

Aroska went to open his door but stopped when she grabbed his arm. "Just remember, we're here strictly for business," she said.

The look on his face caught her off guard. He shrugged his arm away and looked her straight in the eye. "No, we're not."

She sat there speechless for a moment as he climbed out of the car. Up ahead, she saw a face peering at them from a window and knew their arrival was known. Appalled, she jumped out and cut him off as he reached the front of the vehicle, hoping nobody would come outside just yet.

"What did you just say to me?" she hissed.

"You heard me," he muttered, pushing past her and continuing toward the house.

She stood motionless and watched as he walked up the front steps and greeted the man, woman, and two small children who met him at the front door. Heart racing, she spun on her heel and stormed back to the car, retrieving her pack and slipping on a pair of shades as she did so. If the eyes really were the window to the soul, she had no intention of letting these people see them.

Sighing, she took a couple more precious seconds to gather herself before slamming the car door and striding after Aroska. Judging by the uncanny resemblance to his younger brother—*both* of his younger brothers—the man at the door was Maston Tarbic. He broke away from Aroska and descended the steps when he saw her coming, extending a hand.

"Captain Payvan, thank you so much for being here," he said. "Aroska says you're the best."

*Don't feel,* she thought as she firmly grasped his hand and shook. "He's not wrong," she replied.

"Please make yourself at home here. I'm Maston, this is my wife Sedna, and these are our two youngest, Samm and Kasey." He indicated the children, a boy and a girl—neither could have been more than five years old.

If they'd been expecting her, it could only mean Aroska had told them she was coming before he'd even asked her to. The idea made her want to strangle him, and she shot him a vicious glare from behind the shades.

Aroska picked the little girl up as Maston led them inside. Both children appeared frightened, though Ziva doubted either of them really understood what was happening. Sedna's eyes were swollen and red but dry for the moment. The communications console in the living room sat in standby mode as the entire family waited for news from the agency. There were no doubt ten other families doing the same elsewhere in town.

"Sorry about the mess," Maston said, looking around at what Ziva considered a fairly tidy room. "As you can imagine, it's been kind of a rough day."

"Feel free to use the parlor," Sedna said. "There's a comm console and viewscreen, and I cleared off the table. I thought it would be easier for you to—" her chin wobbled "—do your work more efficiently in a quiet place."

For just a moment, Ziva thought she could relate. It wasn't that she didn't want to find the kids, too—she was just looking at the bigger picture. Finding them was a means to an end. It meant they'd be one step closer to stopping Ronan. But the desperation these people were feeling... it was the same thing she'd felt when she'd first heard of Zinni's capture, what she'd felt as she pursued the Durutians across the Aubin desert. In both of those cases, she'd had the power to take matters into her own hands. She couldn't imagine what it must be like for the family to just sit by, helplessly waiting for HSP to find something.

*You were desperate because you cared about your friends.*

*But desperation makes you sloppy.*

"Appreciated," she replied, putting on the sincerest face she could muster, "but I want to go take a look at ground zero as soon as possible."

She heard Aroska sigh behind her.

"Right," Maston said. "I can take you there, show you exactly what happened."

Ziva turned without another word and went back out the door, leaving the Tarbic family to stand in stunned silence. Aroska could make faces and berate her for being brusque all he wanted, but he'd asked her to come because he wanted her to produce results, so she was going to do exactly that.

# · 32 ·
# HSP Headquarters
## Noro, Haphez

T he only thing different about the current scene was that they'd removed the Resistance agent's muzzle. Skeet wasn't sure if he'd actually talk, but at least they were giving him the opportunity. He'd been moved from the exam table to a sturdy chair but was no less restrained. Even his head was fixed in place by a brace; the only things he could move were his eyes and mouth.

They'd brought in Adin Woro and his team due to their prior experience with the Ronan case, hoping to throw the agent off by starting the interrogation process with an unfamiliar face. The three of them had been briefed about the nostium and Resistance connection but, like the rest of the agency, were still unaware of Ziva's involvement in the whole matter. Skeet hoped it would remain that way for a while longer, though if anyone had to find out, he was fine with it being the Alpha field ops team. Adin, Mari, and Colin were all trustworthy, and he imagined Ziva would approve of their presence.

He stood with Emeri in the dark room, watching through the one-way window as Adin calmly directed questions at the agent. They'd hoped his cool demeanor would soften the man up and get him comfortable before Skeet stepped in and employed more forceful tactics, but so far, the strategy didn't seem to be working. The agent hadn't said a single word since they'd brought him to Headquarters, and according to Luko Zona, he hadn't spoken while in custody in Haphor. The only person who had gotten him to talk so far was Ziva, and in that case, he'd addressed her willingly, which was rather unnerving.

"You've known about Ziva since Dakiti?" he said quietly, eyes still fixed on the view through the window.

Emeri grunted an affirmative. "I was ready to have her executed like any other Nosti, but Sergeant Tarbic presented a compelling argument." He sighed and shook his head. "I used to wonder if I'd done the right thing by pardoning her, but now I know I did. She's on our side here. If we'd killed her, she wouldn't be here to point us in the right direction now. She's the key to all of this."

Skeet couldn't even imagine how Ziva must feel about that. As a spec ops agent—and one of the assassins, at that—it was her professional obligation to keep herself out of the spotlight, and he knew her well enough to know that she hated being the center of attention from a personal standpoint as well. Despite the fact that only a handful of people knew she was the source of all the information they were getting, she was still carrying the entire Haphezian population on her shoulders, whether they realized it or not.

"How do you think this guy knows who she is?" he asked.

"If I had to guess, it all goes back to that Nosti she killed ten years ago," Emeri answered. "She told me the only thing she lied about was whether she knew him. If that's accurate, she was telling the truth when she told us he wanted to take her to the new Resistance base on Forus. Someone was no doubt expecting them to arrive. Hell, they could have had an entire dossier compiled on her. I'm betting most of the Resistance knows she exists, but they might not know exactly who or where she is."

Skeet wanted to be angry—half the galaxy had secretly been aware Ziva was a Nosti, but he hadn't—but any anger he felt was trumped by the realization of how much danger that put her in. He still didn't know why the Resistance was trying to expose the Haphezian population to nostium, but he was beginning to wonder if Ziva was somehow a target. Had Ronan known she was on Na and purposely crashed that fighter near her? Had the attack on her family been a manipulation tactic? That didn't explain the abduction of the Salex children, though. Perhaps the Resistance was attempting to create a legitimate nostium formula that would turn the people of Haphez into successful Nosti. If that were the case, he feared they might make a point of seeking Ziva out when they realized she was the only person the formula had worked on. But had the gas on Na worked, or was it whatever she'd been exposed to as a child?

It was time for some answers. Turning on his heel, Skeet stormed out of the dark room and was granted access to the holding room by the guard waiting outside. Adin looked up when he entered and gave him a single nod. Even he knew the time for calm negotiation techniques was over.

"My turn," Skeet said, more for the Resistance agent's benefit than Adin's. He waited for the field ops agents to vacate the room before taking a seat in the chair Adin had been using.

The prisoner watched him from across the room. They were separated only by empty space; any excess furniture had been removed, mostly to make room for all the mobile medical equipment, but also to prevent the man from using his Nostia to manipulate his surroundings. He may have been physically immobile, but that wouldn't stop him from hurling a table at the interrogator or window.

He kept his steely gaze locked with Skeet's, a clear indicator that he had no interest in telling them anything and was, in fact, daring them to even ask. If he'd been so willing to kill himself after the attack in Haphor, he likely had nothing to lose. According to Emeri, Ziva had already suggested that threatening him with death or even bodily harm would be ineffective. If he wanted to die, the worst thing they could do to him was keep him alive. Still, there was no guarantee he'd actually talk.

Perhaps bluffing would be the best way to proceed. Reveal some of the key things they knew. Maybe make him think they knew more than they did.

*Might as well get to the point*, Skeet thought. "You want to tell me why the Resistance is exposing all of us to bad nostium?"

With all the restraints, it was impossible to pick up on many of the non-verbal cues the agent might have shown had he been free to move about. To compensate, they'd attached a series of electrodes to his arms and neck in hopes of seeing some sort of internal reaction instead. His heart rate had been steady while Adin questioned him, and it was still relatively constant now, but the monitor on the wall registered a slight spike in his pulse at the mention of the nostium.

"I haven't quite figured out if you're actually trying to kill us or if you're trying to make it work." Skeet stood up—somehow it felt better to address the man while towering over him. He was strong but small, and there in the large chair engulfed in security apparatus, he looked even smaller. But there was certainly something disconcerting about the way he looked at everyone. He was studying them, looking for weaknesses to exploit, looking for a target. The last thing Skeet wanted was to sit at eye level with him.

"Now, the way I see it, if you people really wanted to kill us, you'd use something that was guaranteed to be lethal. Easy to disperse planetwide. Maybe even contagious. The fact that you've been testing varied formulas on individuals and small groups leads me to believe you actually want to turn us all into Nosti, though I cannot for the life of me imagine why."

He feigned a grimace that turned genuine after a moment as he pondered what he'd just said. Regardless of Ronan's reason for targeting Haphezians, the presence of Nosti on the planet would immediately attract the Federation, which would in turn lead to a war not even the full force of the Grand Army could win. Skeet had no idea if that was the point—and he wasn't sure why it would be—but it was certainly a concern. Despite the loss of life, he was suddenly very glad none of the nostium formulas had worked so far, but it was only a matter of time before the Resistance created the correct one. If the frequency of their attacks continued to increase, that time would be sooner than later.

"*Huhren shouka souhn,*" Skeet shouted, pleased by the look of anguish on the prisoner's face as he pressed the heel of his hand down against his wounded leg. "What does Ronan want with us?"

"You're wasting your time," the man said through clenched teeth, breaking eye contact for the first time. His nostrils flared as he took deep, hissing breaths through his nose. "You can't stop what's coming."

"And what exactly is that, *pesch a sheyssa?*" Skeet leaned down until their faces were mere centimeters apart. The bullet wound was already beginning to fester, and it made a disturbing moist sound as he pressed down harder. "Tell me what you people want with those helpless little kids."

"They know exactly where I am, and they'll kill me if you don't do it first. They'll level this whole building if they have to."

Skeet waited several seconds before giving the wound one last hard push and rising back into an upright position. He hated to treat the agent to any sort of reaction, but if what the man had just said was accurate, he wasn't going to waste time holding a staring contest.

He exited the room and made his way back into the dark room next door, where Emeri was still standing at the window. "You think he's bluffing?"

"He could be," the director answered, gray brows furrowed, "but it's also plausible. If the Resistance keeps coming back, it means they have some way of knowing whether their experiments are working. They could be monitoring our news networks or, galaxy forbid, they could have some sort of inside source. Either way, it's a safe bet they do know we have him in custody, and if he was willing to take his own life, it's also a safe bet that they're prepared to finish the job to keep him from talking."

"Would they risk launching a full-scale attack like that? It would be the end of the stealth tactics they've been employing."

"The likelihood is low," Emeri said, "but it's a very real possibility and we need to be prepared for it."

Skeet sighed and raked a hand through his hair, then gave the director a quick rundown of his thoughts about the Federation getting involved. "That's a very real possibility, too."

"*Sheyss,*" Emeri muttered. "What have we gotten ourselves into?" He stared through the window at the agent for a moment. "First step: leak a story to the press. This man is dead. He killed himself, his injuries proved to be fatal, I don't care. If we get it out in the news feeds, it should be enough to keep Ronan from coming down here and wiping us out. In the meantime, I don't want Ziva anywhere near this place. She may be the only person on this planet who has a clue how to stop all of this, and I'm not going to risk her being here at Headquarters or even in the city if there's an attack. Tell her to wait twelve hours until we've had a chance to clear the system. Sergeant Tarbic is officially on protection detail."

Skeet already had his communicator to his ear. "Oh, she'll love that."

# · 33 ·
## CITY CENTER
### SALEX, HAPHEZ

"**Y**ou've got to be bloody kidding me!"

Aroska risked a glance over at Maston, who waited by the car. "Will you keep your voice down?" he hissed in Ziva's ear.

"My orders, Payvan," Emeri's voice crackled in the background. "It's for your own protection."

"Protection!" she exclaimed. "From what?"

"Our Nosti friend here says the Resistance will come finish him off if they hear he wasn't able to take that suicide pill," Skeet said. "He could be bluffing, but we wouldn't put it past them. Emeri doesn't want you here if there's any sort of attack on Headquarters. Says you're the only person who can stop this thing and that we can't risk losing you right now."

Ziva let loose a string of expletives and stormed away to brood, leaving Aroska standing there alone with the communicator. He sighed. "You said twelve hours?"

"Just to be on the safe side," Skeet answered. "We'll get a story out to the news networks and let you know when you're clear to come back. What's got her in such a twist? With all she's been through, I'd think she'd be okay with lying low for a bit."

Aroska was tempted to comment on how little effort it took to get Ziva in a twist, but he decided now was not the time for sarcasm. "My older brother's son is one of the kids who was abducted. My family is here, and she's pissed."

There was a long pause before Skeet spoke. "Well, yeah."

"I would like to have a word with you when you return, Sergeant," Emeri said. His voice was clearer now as if he were speaking directly into the comm unit this time. "Meanwhile, do your best to not aggravate the situation. Is Ziva still there?"

She approached upon hearing her name, her eyes like crimson flames as she stared Aroska down. "I'm here," she growled.

"Go ahead and get in touch with your contacts. Have them on standby. Maybe even get them moving in this direction. If Ronan tries anything, we'll have no choice but to retaliate, and we'll need help."

"Yes, sir." She kept her fiery gaze focused on Aroska.

"We'll be in touch," Emeri said. The transmission went dead.

Aroska pocketed the device, trying as hard as possible not to break eye contact. "You can't blame me for this."

"Oh, I think I can. You're the one who dragged me out here in the first place."

"To do your job! Even if we were still in Noro, Emeri's concerned enough that he'd probably send you away anyway."

The way she crossed her arms told him she understood his point but still didn't like it. "Okay, fine, we're stuck here. But don't think for one second that being my 'protection detail' puts you in charge. You want me to do my job? Let me do my job." She slipped her shades back on as she turned and strode toward one of the Salex agents who remained in the plaza taking measurements.

"Fair enough," he muttered. He wanted to be disgusted with her attitude, but part of him was beginning to feel sorry about bringing her here. It was true that he thought she could employ her tracking skills and increase their chances of rescuing the children, but he hadn't planned on her reacting quite like this. Her behavior reminded him a lot of the way she'd acted while running from Dasaro. She was lashing out in an attempt to conceal another emotion: fear. He wasn't sure what she could possibly be so afraid of, but being introduced to his family had driven her anxiety levels higher than ever. On top of that, both Emeri and Skeet seemed like they'd expected such a reaction. They all still knew something he didn't, and he was almost afraid to find out what it was.

*"You don't know the half of it! If you believe she killed him just for the hell of it, you're wrong. Think what you will about her, but she would never do something like that."*

Aroska let out another sigh in the form of a quiet growl and wandered over to where his brother waited. *I've been wrong about so many things. I don't want to be wrong again.*

He saw Ziva flash her credentials at one of the Salex agents and ask him something. She stood with her hands on her hips, listening intently and studying the ground where the landing gear had left dark marks on the stone. At least she could pretend to be professional, though Aroska was sure Maston could sense there was an issue.

He'd never been as close to his older brother as he had to Soren. It had much to do with the age difference—Maston was five years older, while Soren had been three years younger—but they also lacked common interests and goals. Maston had always been the enterprising family man, and it certainly showed now. With his work at HSP, Aroska had estranged himself to a degree, especially after the family's move to Salex following Soren's death. But in light of the mess he'd found himself in after Dakiti, he'd opted to reconcile with his loved ones over the past couple of months. Their support had made all the difference in his quest to clean up his act. Temptation was still an issue, but thanks to Maston and a friend with a rehab connection, Aroska had been both clean and sober for over a month.

In the end, dealing with such sensitive subject matter had given Maston plenty of practice telling when something was wrong or even when Aroska was lying. The man's current facial expression indicated that he knew good and well both he and Ziva were upset about something.

"Everything good?" he asked.

"Fine," Aroska lied.

Maston lifted an eyebrow. "You look like you want to kill someone."

"This is all a lot more complicated than I thought it would be. There's an issue at Headquarters and we've been ordered to stay out here for the night. Do you mind?"

"No, of course you're welcome here. Are you in danger?"

Aroska shook his head. "This is actually the safest place we can be right now. And if that ship comes back, we can respond all the more quickly." He forced an innocent smile.

They both turned and watched Ziva for a moment as she broke away from the agent and began her examination of the plaza. One second, she was stooped down, running her hand along the skid marks, sniffing her fingers. Then she was on her feet, gaze directed upward, with the light from the sun reflected in her shades. Watching her work now, Aroska was certain she would have found them on Aubin even without Tobias Niio's help.

"Is she always like this?" Maston asked quietly. His eyebrow remained arched as he watched Ziva go about her work with her face contorted in a perpetual scowl.

"Like what? A sociopathic *shouka*? Not always, if you can believe it." Aroska thought back to their conversation on Kat's balcony, to the things Ziva had said to him in the hospital before leaving for Na, to their exchange at the med center the previous night—all times when she'd almost seemed like a normal person. "Is she always damn good at what she does? Yes. Always."

He may not have agreed with most of her methods, but he couldn't deny that she produced results. She was right; he had to just let her do her job.

He made his way over to where she stood in the center of the plaza, turning in a slow circle as she studied the sky. "Any ideas?" he asked.

She jerked her head toward the man she'd been talking to. "Probably nothing they haven't found already. Six-skid landing system—" she sniffed her fingers again "—and pyranil oil. Means it's manufactured somewhere in the Core. Maybe some type of freighter. Let's see if these people have any footage."

The two of them set off toward the nearest Salex agent, leaving Maston to wait behind the police barricade. They skirted around a large puddle of what appeared to be dried blood on the ground, no doubt the place where the children's teacher had been shot. Aroska paused a moment, attempting to gather his bearings as he examined the scene from the new angle. If the instructor had been shot at the base of the boarding ramp, comparing the puddle's location to the distance between the skid marks might give them more clues about the design of the ship. Having photographic evidence, surveillance footage, or hearing an eyewitness testimony would certainly be more efficient, but he imagined it wouldn't be difficult to measure the vessel's dimensions by hand if the need arose.

"Hey!" Ziva barked at an agent who appeared to be in charge. She displayed her credentials again. "Captain Payvan, Sergeant Tarbic, operations. What do you have?"

The man sighed and wiped his brow, directing a look of relief toward Aroska. "Sergeant Tarbic. We spoke on comm. Thank you for coming." He shifted his attention back to Ziva. "That ship has been gone for four hours now. We've been working nonstop since then, but there were only so many leads. To tell you the truth, we don't really have anything more than we did after the first hour. Eleven children are missing. Their instructor is dead. The ship in question made an out-of-lane FTL jump, and Port Control lost it. We've already reported all of this to Noro Headquarters."

Aroska nodded as Ziva swore under her breath. "Is there any surveillance footage from the area?" he asked. "Any image of the ship at all?"

"Nothing from here in the plaza," the agent said. "We did send out a bulletin asking any pilots who may have crossed paths with this vessel to send in any available front cam footage. Let's see if we've received anything."

They followed him over to the small staging area the other agents had set up. "Any eyewitnesses?" Ziva asked.

"There were over twenty people in the vicinity at the time of the abduction, but most ran when those men opened fire. My people finished interviewing everyone a little while ago—they're probably all back home by now. We do have recordings of each interview though and would be happy to forward them to you."

"Please do," Aroska said.

The man went to work at one of the mobile computer consoles and brought up stream after stream of footage provided by hundreds of pilots. Someone had already started sifting through them and had marked several as relevant. These he displayed on the screen, pausing on the frames that gave them the best view of the runaway vessel.

"These visuals match the descriptions some of the witnesses gave us," he said, perking up a bit. "Many of them panicked so we didn't get clear stories, but this is...something."

"Looks like a *Legacy*-class transport," Ziva said, removing her shades to get a clearer look. "Doesn't Solea Technologies manufacture those? They're based on Kovis, aren't they?" The glance she shot at Aroska silently completed her thought: *a former Federation world currently controlled by the Resistance.*

The sight of the ship made Aroska's throat tighten, and he balled his hands up. Neither he nor Skeet had gotten a good look at it on Niio, so they were really only familiar with its emissions signature. It was maddening enough to know that its crew had managed to grab Zinni. Now here it was again, five weeks later, still wreaking havoc. The idea that they hadn't been able to stop it yet sent rage boiling up inside him.

"Port Control never did get any readings from it," the agent said. "No name, no origin code. Couldn't get any crew to respond to our hails, either. By the time we scrambled HSP ships for a pursuit, it had disappeared in traffic and, well, you know the rest. We picked up one last emissions sig in an area just beyond Na before we lost it."

"I'd like a copy of all of this footage, too," Ziva said, holding out her data pad to receive the files. "Forward it to Director Arion as well."

"Of course."

"Thank you," Aroska said. "We'll sit down and take another look at everything, and we'll let you know what we find." He wasn't entirely sure what else they *could* find at this point, but trying was better than sitting idly by.

He and Ziva turned and began to make their way back across the square. Maston remained just on the other side of the barricade, arms crossed but face twisted with worry. Telling him they hadn't found anything new was the last thing Aroska wanted to do at the moment.

"You know *Legacy*-class ships are designed to be medical transports," Ziva murmured.

"I know," Aroska replied, trying in vain to maintain a positive countenance for Maston's sake. After hearing Kat's story and seeing firsthand what kinds of things Ronan was doing and producing, he dreaded to think of the implications.

"We'll find it." In her tone, he could hear the same apprehension he was feeling.

His attention remained on Maston until they reached the barricade. He had no idea what the Resistance hoped to accomplish by kidnapping children, but involving innocent civilians in this mess was the final straw. At least the military and Royal House were powerful enough to fight back to an extent, and at least they knew who or what they were fighting against. These people here in Salex didn't even know what had hit them.

Maston's eyes glistened as they approached, but he continued to stand tall. "Now what?"

Aroska didn't want to tell him they had nothing, nor did he want to lie. He settled on a happy medium and gestured down at Ziva's data pad. "Now, we get to work."

# · 34 ·
## PATROL FRIGATE *VIGILANCE*
### FRINGE SPACE

The shimmering figure standing on the projection pad was indeed impressive. Full Nosti armor with polished kytara firmly attached to the belt. Glossy black hair. Average stature but strong, just like the rest of them. Tav Ronan embodied the perfection all Resistance fighters should strive for, in Sadey's opinion.

"You've got to stop contacting me like this. Voice communication is too risky with all the people we've got looking for us."

Sadey dipped her head and shifted her feet on the comm pad. "With all due respect, we're too short on time to keep up this encryption game. Yes, there's a greater risk of a voice transmission being detected, but the slower we move, the more time someone has to catch up to us. Anything is risky at this point."

Ronan sighed. "Point taken. I assume you have a specific reason for calling."

"All eleven subjects have successfully received direct infusions of the updated formula," Sadey answered. "Blood samples from the *Titania's* prisoner were analyzed and we believe direct infusion may still work best after all. The gas works well for mass exposure, but it's absorbed differently by the body, faulty formula notwithstanding. A direct injection into the bloodstream is more efficient."

"And just how do you plan to subject that many Haphezian individuals to a direct infusion?"

"We don't, although I'd certainly like to. I know we're running out of time—that's why we started targeting larger groups in the first place. But I propose reverting to our old methods, at least for a little while longer. We'll focus on individuals and small demographic groups, and when we find the correct formula, we can try the gas again."

It was difficult to tell thanks to the flickering of the hologram, but Ronan may have looked chagrined. "And exactly *how* long do you propose we do this?"

"We're getting close," Sadey answered. "The last test proved successful from a latency standpoint. The adverse symptoms still manifested, but it was almost immediate."

"Those symptoms are still the issue."

"I know, but we've made some precise changes to the formula since yesterday and none of the current subjects are having any problems yet. They look promising."

"You think it has to do with level of brain development?"

"Possibly. That's what we were hoping."

Ronan nodded. "What about the captive Haphezian agent? Has she been exposed?"

"No," Sadey said. "I was able to go in and see her, and her brain is still healthy. The *Titania* has been using her strictly for blood analysis. She has proven quite useful thus far. The data they've compiled on her blood composition and circulatory system has helped us design the most efficient formulas."

"Except none of those formulas have worked yet."

Sadey did her best to keep her shoulders straight even as her gaze drifted to the floor. They'd already managed to create successful formulas for the rest of the major Fringe civilizations. The Elsara were docile enough creatures that it had required almost no effort whatsoever to swoop down to Lathia and test the nostium on them. The Durutians could just be infused with the same formula the rest of the human-dominated worlds were using; brief experimentation had proved that their cybernetic implants made no difference. They'd even designed formulas for the Sardons and the pointy-eared Rama way out on Xater Prime. The Haphezians had been put on the list first due to anticipated difficulty, but there they remained after all these months.

In hopes of challenging herself, Sadey had volunteered to oversee all Haphezian-related operations, but she was beginning to wonder if she'd bitten off more than she could chew. They had a schedule to keep, and she dreaded the thought of being the person responsible for throwing that schedule off.

"Any word from Lieutenant Gero?" Ronan asked.

Sadey shook her head. "We don't know any more than we did the last time you and I spoke. Last we heard, he was alive and in HSP custody. He's a good agent, well-trained. I doubt he'll give us away, but there's always a remote chance. The Haphezians are known for their ruthless torture tactics and should not be underestimated. It worries me, but there's nothing we can do about it without exposing ourselves."

"We can start by giving them something else to focus on," Ronan said. "Divert their attention away from Jalen. Take the subjects back."

"But the plan was to keep them—"

"Plans change, Commander. You should know that as well as anyone. At this point, we need to focus on strategy, and right now, our best strategy is to keep them stunned, confused. Is the *Titania* still traveling with you?"

"It is."

"Have it take them back. Wait until dark and employ stealth measures. The Haphezians won't know what hit them."

The hologram fizzled away, leaving Sadey standing alone on the comm pad. Classic Ronan…always so terse and to-the-point. It wasn't the first time one of their conversations had ended like that. The leader of the Resistance and restorer of the Nosti culture had more important things to worry about.

Shrugging the behavior off, Sadey picked up the comm receiver and opened a transmission directly to the bridge. "Change of plans. Reroute course back to the Noro system."

# · 35 ·
# TARBIC RESIDENCE
## SALEX, HAPHEZ

"It's Payvan. Put me through." Ziva held the communicator away from her ear and rolled her eyes as the voice on the other end of the transmission let out a coy chuckle. "Damn it, Cole, just do it."

His laugh trailed off and she waited in silence for several moments before Tobias came on. "Yes."

"It's time," she said. "Ronan's people are here. Head for Haphez, and I'll contact you if there are any developments."

"We'll be there," Tobias said, ending the transmission abruptly.

It was all that needed to be said, and in a way, Ziva was glad. She hadn't had the opportunity to tell him Ronan was part of the Resistance, and she wasn't sure how he'd take it. Niio was independent and just as fanatical about remaining that way as the Haphezians were. She doubted Tobias had any interest in involving his small army in Resistance-versus-Federation matters. On the other hand, Ronan's people *had* killed members of the Niiosian Mob, and the Resistance represented a direct threat to that independence he craved, so maybe there wouldn't be a problem motivating him after all.

She turned and looked across the parlor at Aroska, who stood over the table staring vacantly at all the information scattered across it. The viewscreen on the wall behind him displayed still images of the missing ship provided by the Salex office, but he no longer paid them any mind. They'd revised their strategy a bit; in hopes of finding clues about where the ship had gone, they were now attempting to figure out where it had come from, where it had been since they'd picked up its emissions signature near Bectin. The task would have been a lot simpler if they had all of HSP's databases and computing power at their disposal. Ziva added that to her ever-growing mental list of things she hated about her current predicament.

She returned her attention to her communicator and sighed, forcing her fingers to input a comm code she'd had no intention of ever calling again. She'd entered Taran Reddic's code into her own device while on Aubin, mostly in case she ever needed to remind him who was in charge again. The thought of using it to strike up a conversation with the man seemed absurd.

It took a while for him to answer. "Go for Reddic."

"Hello, Taran," she said, unable to help but address him in the same manner as she had on Aubin.

"Go to hell," he growled.

The transmission ended before she could say another word. She stood there staring at the communicator for a moment, contemplating whether she should try again. To her surprise, the device chirped and the screen lit up, displaying the very code she had just called. She lifted an eyebrow and accepted the message.

"That really wasn't very polite," she said.

"Payvan." Rather than Reddic, Ziva found herself listening to that woman who had been with him. Mae something. "What do you want?"

"Where are you?"

Based on the long hesitation before Mae spoke again, Ziva imagined the question had caught the woman off guard. "On our way to Chaiavis to search for signs of Ronan. Why?"

"You won't find anything there," she answered. "You can bet that warehouse is long gone. But I know where you're guaranteed to find something. Remember the attack on our military base Devani Reddic told you about? It's Ronan. It's the Resistance. They're coming after us."

Mae went silent again, and Ziva could hear soft murmuring as something was discussed in the background. "The Federation can't get involved in matters on independent worlds," she finally said.

"I'm not asking the Federation to get involved. I'm doing you a courtesy here, telling you about this because you've also had people fall victim to Ronan. I'm not even asking for help. I'm only asking that the Durutians as a people take action."

"What do you mean by that?"

"You've got a formidable army. Use it to fight for yourselves for once, not just the Federation or whoever else you've got your people loaned out to."

Ziva heard a man's voice say something in the background. "Why should we help you after what you've done to us?" Mae said.

"You shouldn't, you're right. But I told you, you're *not* helping us. You're helping yourselves. The Resistance is as much of a threat to you as it is to us. The Federation is what controls our independence, brings balance and order to the galaxy. If Ronan were to take control, all of that will be compromised." She hesitated for a moment. "We're dealing with nostium here, okay? That's what the gas is, and they're testing it on us. It could be why they took your people, too. The Resistance is a lot more powerful right now than anyone realized."

The silence on the other end of the transmission lasted so long this time that Ziva checked to see if the call was still live. "You struck me as being the voice of reason, Mae," she continued. "There's more at stake here than our differences. Think about this. I hope you'll make the right choice."

This time, it was Ziva's turn to end the transmission without warning. She clenched the device in one hand and massaged her forehead with the other, wondering what the chances were of winning any sort of battle with the Resistance without help. She wasn't sure how large Ronan's army was. A single fleet she could live with, though the thought of all the enemy soldiers being Nosti gave her chills. But if the Resistance was combining firepower from all their inhabited worlds, that would be a problem. Granted, the attack on Na had only affected a tiny fraction of the Grand Army's soldiers, so her people still had a significant force at their disposal, but with the Royal General incapacitated, she knew morale would be low. Tobias's men would make a valuable contribution, albeit a small one. Having a battle-ready civilization like the

Durutians on their side would certainly help.

"Will they come?" Aroska asked, still staring down at the table.

"I don't know," Ziva said.

"Was that Reddic or that *shouka* who knocked me out?"

"Believe it or not, *she* may be our best shot at getting the Durutians on board." She sighed. "I'm beginning to think we know more than they do about the whole situation. They were on their way to Chaiavis to look for that warehouse Kat told us about. I don't think they know anything about the development of a new nostium formula."

"To be fair, we only know it's nostium because of you," Aroska said, finally looking up. "The same goes for that Resistance agent. Just picture it—if you hadn't realized who he was, he'd probably be sitting in a holding room restrained only by a pair of reinforced handcuffs and nobody would have a clue what kind of damage he was capable of causing."

A quiet knock cut Ziva off before she could respond. Sedna appeared in the parlor doorway, eyes still puffy but face still dry. Her shoulders sagged and she wasn't even trying to conceal the trembling in her hands, but her voice was surprisingly steady when she spoke.

"Sorry to interrupt. I'm putting some food out for the little ones. You're our guest, Captain Payvan—will you join us for dinner?"

Ziva froze, clenching her jaw to keep her facial expression from changing. She still felt her eyes widen a bit, and the nervous energy that coursed through her made the hairs on her arms stand on end. She'd done well enough so far; she and Aroska had spent the entire afternoon secluded in the parlor, and she'd managed to avoid dealing with any of the other Tarbics. The thought of sitting down at a dining table face to face with the family of one of her victims was unbearable.

"I, ah..." *Get a grip, Payvan. What's wrong with you?* She felt herself start to sweat and her eyes shifted to Aroska.

He cleared his throat. "Actually, we were just about to head back out to town. We thought it might be good to check out the abduction site again and see if anyone is hanging around now that it's dark."

His words caught Ziva by surprise just as much as they did Sedna. The woman looked perplexed for a moment but shrugged. "You sure?" she said. "Don't want to grab a bite first?"

Aroska shook his head and picked his jacket up from where he'd tossed it onto the couch, slipping it on before handing Ziva her own. "It's fine. Shouldn't be gone too long, but don't wait up for us."

He placed a hand on Ziva's shoulder and guided her out of the parlor and through the living room to the front door. She pulled her jacket on and followed him to the car. As glad as she was to get away, confusion still gripped her mind and she felt a wave of inexplicable anger swelling up inside her. "What's going on?"

"You needed to get out of there," he replied matter-of-factly, gesturing toward the passenger door as he slid into the pilot's seat. "Besides, I still owe you a meal after Dakiti."

Ziva hesitated a moment, part of her pleased that he'd been able to perceive her discomfort and part of her wondering why he'd bothered to do anything about it. The problem with his family was *her* problem, something she was responsible for working through on her own as far as she was concerned. Involving himself in her struggle would only distance him from the people he'd finally managed to connect with again.

She was hungry though, so she was glad he'd renewed the offer he'd made after bringing her Emeri's pardon document. She got in the car and rode in silence until they came to a stop in front of a small restaurant not too far from the plaza they'd been investigating mere hours before. It was packed with other tourists having dinner, but they found an empty table near the back and seated themselves, Ziva keeping her eye on the front door and Aroska keeping his on the rear.

"Maston and I have been here a few times since I've started coming out here," he said absentmindedly as he touched the controls to display the menu. "Their warco stew is pretty good. Not as good as yours or Marshay's—a little spicy for my taste—but decent."

They stared at the menu without speaking for several minutes, eventually placing two orders for the warco stew and fresh govino juice. The food was delivered within moments by a sleek serving bot, a far cry from the rusty old one they'd encountered in the café aboard the transport to Chaiavis.

"You didn't have to do this, you know," Ziva said, methodically scooping at the stew to help it cool faster. "I would have been fine."

"No, you wouldn't have," Aroska said with a cynical chuckle. "You would have done everything in your power to make sure everyone *thought* you were fine. You're the one who told me you want to be the only person who knows you're afraid." He began stirring his own stew. "Don't worry about it. Like I said, I still owe you dinner."

"You don't owe me *anything*," she muttered.

He was quiet for several seconds. "Actually, I do," he said, staring down at his dish. "I never did thank you for...for saving me from Saun. I know I'm the one who fired the final shot, but when you said something about—how did you put it—'taking Saun out before she could blow my head off,' it almost made me sick. I didn't want to acknowledge the fact that I was only alive because you'd once again managed to hurt someone I...loved. It was wrong of me to ignore that."

Ziva thought back to their charade on the riverbank at the relay station outside Haphor. He'd confessed later that subconscious anger about Soren's death had made it easier for him to pull the trigger, so she guessed there'd also been a measure of genuine bitterness behind the comment he'd made about her shooting Saun.

"She was special to you."

"Yeah," he snorted. "A lot of women have come and gone in my life, and I used to be fine with that. But when I met Saun, it was the first time I'd ever really hoped for something more, you know?"

She lifted an eyebrow and lowered her gaze. *Not really*, she thought.

Aroska shook his head. "Right, I forgot you have no concept of emotional attachment." He stuffed a spoonful of stew into his mouth.

The only response Ziva could muster up was a half-hearted scowl.

"I was devastated after I thought I'd lost Tate and Jole," he continued. "Somehow, working with Saun in the Solaris Control Unit made everything a little better. Life was almost okay again, and even though my goal had been to get back into ops, all I wanted when I got assigned to your team was to go back to the SCU. Everything about her seemed so...authentic, so sincere." He paused a moment, his amber eyes burning with anger. "And then to find out it was all a lie, that she was probably the *least* sincere out of all of them...I guess I don't know what's real anymore." There was silence for several long seconds before he scoffed and let his hand fall to the table, rattling their utensils. "I'm sorry, I'm not sure why I'm telling you all of this."

Ziva wasn't, either. She blew on a spoonful of stew before taking a bite, savoring the salty taste of the meat. She was terrible at giving advice—she thought that had been established during their conversation on Kat's balcony—and her only real interpersonal talent was lending an ear. "Because you needed to let it out or it was going to eat you alive?" she suggested.

That prompted a hint of a smirk, and the hard lines across Aroska's forehead began to fade. "Maybe so."

"Would you want to stay in ops if you had the opportunity? Permanently, I mean."

He appeared pensive for a moment. "I think so. Working with your team has been a life-changing experience, to say the least. I'm finally starting to feel like I belong again. But if we don't find Zinni, or if she can't come back...."

He didn't need to continue for Ziva to know what he meant. She was safe in her cozy new position as unit captain, but if Zinni couldn't return to work for one reason or another, they'd find themselves in the very same situation that had prompted Aroska to join the team in the first place. With just two members, the Alpha team would be disbanded, and he and Skeet would most likely be reassigned to a different division or even a different office.

They were quiet as they each finished eating. He'd been right; the stew here was just a little on the spicy side, but it was warm and satisfying and the familiarity brought Ziva some comfort after an entire day of being *un*comfortable. The fresh govino juice was a bit of a treat as well, more flavorful than the processed stuff she was used to drinking at home and in the employee canteen at work. Despite the rather awkward conversation and interaction, she had to admit she was glad he'd brought her here.

She downed the last of the juice and set the glass down with a *thud*, guiding it around in a slow circle until she felt Aroska's gaze come to rest on her hand just as it had in the transport café. "You know the chances are slim that any of those kids are still alive," she murmured without looking up.

He took a breath but hesitated before speaking, telling her that he did indeed know. "I'm trying not to think about it," he said. "I just try to remember Kat and Corey—they both survived their encounters with Ronan, and now that we have scans from both you and that agent, we might be able to come up with some sort of countermeasure. But...you're right. I thought we'd find more clues here. To be honest, I wanted to get out of the house tonight, too. It's hard to stay positive around hopeful family members when you know the news probably isn't going to be very good."

"I'm sorry I couldn't be the miracle-working hunter you thought I could be," Ziva said, wincing at the slight edge she hadn't meant to include in her tone.

If Aroska noticed or cared, he gave no indication. "Don't be. I had no idea what—if anything—we'd find here. Now all we can do is wait and see what happens. I figure we'll stay the night here, and if we get the all-clear from Emeri, we can head back to the city first thing in the morning."

Although Ziva wasn't sure she liked the idea of him dictating what they would do, she nodded in agreement. The thought of spending the night in his family's house was unnerving, but if she was lucky, she wouldn't have to interact with anyone.

"Now," he continued as he fished out his credit chip and waved it over the table's scanner, successfully paying for their meal, "why don't we go at least do a fly-by of ground zero just to be on the safe side? That way I won't have completely lied to my family."

She dipped her head and they returned to the car.

# · 36 ·

## DURUTIAN SCOUT SHIP *DEONIDA*
### FRINGE SPACE

The interior of the FTL tunnel flew by in shades of blue and silver as the ship rushed forward, still on course for Chaiavis. Taran sat in the pilot's chair with his feet up on the control board, hypnotized by the view outside, trying as hard as possible not to think about anything. There were plenty of things he *should* be thinking about, but he feared his head would explode if he didn't allow himself a few minutes of peace.

The transmission from Ziva Payvan had shaken him, and the only thing that kept him from trembling was the fact that his implants had kicked in and were working hard to regulate his heart rate and blood pressure. *"Hello, Taran."* There was something about her voice that unnerved him. It probably had much to do with the fact that every time he heard it, something terrible was happening. He couldn't shake away the images of his troops in the desert, their bodies torn open by her weapon. Memories of his own injury came creeping to the front of his mind as well. The worst part was that her shot hadn't fully detached his arm; it had dangled by a few measly strands of flesh and muscle tissue, and he'd been forced to lie there staring at it until he'd blacked out. The memory still sometimes kept him up at night, and the sight of detached limbs bothered him to this day.

His cochlear implant picked up the sound of Mae's footsteps approaching before she even made it into the cockpit. He heard her stop just inside but he didn't turn around. Her presence lingered there for a moment, and he could feel her gaze boring into his back.

Finally, she sighed. "Are you ready to talk to me yet?"

Just like that, all the things he'd been trying to shut out of his mind came flooding back. The Haphezians. Ronan. The missing Delta Patrol. This warehouse on Chaiavis. Matney's warnings about the Federation getting involved. The rebirth of nostium...*what the hell?* Taran pulled his feet down and swiveled in the chair to face Mae, who stood against the cockpit's back wall with her arms crossed. Her hair was untied, so her red curls had free rein of all the space within, it seemed, half a meter of her head. That combined with the way her optics were focused on him gave her a very wild look. This was an exhausted, irritable woman who was not to be trifled with.

"What is there to talk about?"

"Damn it, Taran. Listen to yourself. I seem to recall you asking me if I wanted to save the galaxy when we left Edean. *That's* what this is about, okay? You heard Payvan on comm—we'd be doing ourselves a favor. I understand why you don't want anything to do with her, and believe me, I don't, either. But this is a lot bigger than some petty race to find Ronan. Ronan found *us.*"

Taran knew she was right, but he wasn't ready to admit such a thing yet. They'd just spent weeks and countless manpower hours searching for Ronan and any signs of the Delta Patrol, and he had half a mind to just leave the Haphezians to their own devices. Payvan had vowed to find Ronan first, after all, and she'd gone and done exactly that. But he knew she was right, too. If the Resistance was allowed to rise to power—especially if this business about the nostium was accurate—they'd destroy the galactic structure the Federation had spent so long creating.

"What did Payvan mean when she said Ronan was 'testing' the nostium on the Haphezians?" he finally asked.

Mae shrugged. "No idea. They've had over twenty years to develop a new formula. Matney even mentioned that small lab the Feds found, so they've had to have something brewing behind the scenes. But I don't know why they'd need to be testing anything on anyone at this point."

Taran looked down and studied his cybernetic hand as he opened and closed the fingers, a motion that had helped him focus in recent months. "If the Haphezians were exposed to nostium, the Federation wouldn't hesitate to retaliate, especially since Haphez has always claimed to have nothing to do with the Resistance."

Mae's eyes widened and she straightened, clearly stricken by what he'd just said. "Do we know of any other Fringe civilizations that have reported disappearances or kidnappings?"

"Not that I've heard. Devani and the other Representatives might know of something. Why?"

"The Haphezians have had people taken by Ronan. *We've* had people taken by Ronan. What if we're not the only ones? We already established that the Resistance has operations running out in the Fringe where the Feds can't reach them. Like you said in Matney's office, they could be hitting *all* the independent systems."

Taran sat up a little straighter. "They could be targeting us specifically because we're not part of the Federation," he murmured, repeating what Mae herself had said during the meeting on Edean.

"You just said the Federation wouldn't hesitate to retaliate if an independent world showed signs of Resistance activity. What if that's the goal? Infuse Fringe civilizations with nostium, make it look like there have been dormant Resistance cells hiding there the whole time." She began pacing back and forth across the cockpit and her voice rose in volume the longer she spoke. "You heard Matney—the Feds are already having trouble controlling the Res presence within the Core. If you tacked a bunch of Fringe worlds onto their current workload, they'd be spread too thin to be effective. Ronan could come up from behind and completely blindside them while they were focused on fighting people like us and the Haphezians."

The thought prompted Taran to stand up. He'd always been impressed by how Mae's mind worked. She saw moves and counter-moves in every aspect of life, just one more thing that made her one of the best soldiers in the Durutian Special Forces. Her analytical way of thinking had helped save the day on numerous occasions, and it was exactly what made her—as Payvan had put it—the voice of reason.

"That still doesn't explain what Payvan meant by 'testing' a formula," he said.

"I know," Mae said, stopping mid-stride and turning to face him, "but if this theory is anywhere close to being right, we have a huge problem on our hands, and probably not a lot of time to solve it."

"I'll contact Devani and see if she can gather information from any of the other Reps. If we can determine whether other Fringe civilizations are involved, it may help us nail down Ronan's strategy."

"And I'll contact Matney," she said. "Warn him about the nostium and this endgame."

"He said the Federation can't get involved."

"He said they can't offer assistance to independent worlds. What they *can* do is keep the Resistance under control within the Core while we deal with Ronan out in the Fringe."

The way she said the word 'we' sealed the deal for Taran. "If we're going to get involved in this, we're going to need all the firepower we've got. We may not have a formal fleet, but we have plenty of ships. Payvan was right—it's time to fight for ourselves for once." It almost made him sick to say the words, but he knew it was true.

That sharp, focused look returned to Mae's face, and she made herself comfortable in the co-pilot's chair. "I'll get in touch with as many of our Special Tasks Units as possible and bring them up to speed."

Taran cut in the sub-light engines and the view outside faded from swirling silver and blue to the black void of space. "Good. I'll have Devani address the politicians, and I'll see what can be done about mobilizing Durutian forces." He calculated a trajectory to a new FTL lane and guided the ship in that direction. It was still close to a two-day journey to Haphez from their current location—they would need to move fast. "Setting course for the Noro system."

Mae reached over and took his hand. "Are *you* ready to go save the galaxy?"

# · 37 ·

# TARBIC RESIDENCE

## SALEX, HAPHEZ

Despite the fact that it had been days since they'd been on Aubin, Ziva's eyes felt like they were full of sand. She blinked several times and tried to rub the scratchiness away, but it was no use. Her body was so tired, but her mind simply refused to sleep. When it had become clear that they'd have to stay the night in Salex, she'd vowed to not let her eyes shut lest she somehow leave herself vulnerable to the Tarbics. She'd finally caved and given sleep a shot, much to her own surprise, but the sofa in the parlor wasn't very comfortable. After a couple of hours of restlessness, she'd returned to the table to stare half-heartedly at the HSP materials they'd spent all afternoon studying.

Even if she wasn't sleeping, closing her eyes at least made her feel like she was resting, and it helped subdue the scratchy sensation. She sat there in silence for a few minutes, listening to the creaking in the ceiling above her. She wasn't sure who else was awake at this hour; she doubted Maston or Sedna would be able to sleep while Chyler and the rest of the kids were still missing, but the sheer emotion and exhaustion the day had brought could have very well overtaken them. Whoever it was, they were pacing back and forth in the room directly above the parlor.

Driven by curiosity and maybe a little by boredom, she stood and made her way out into the darkened house, hesitating for a minute or two at the bottom of the staircase. She could still hear the creaking somewhere above her, but nobody else stirred. Taking one last look around, she began to ascend the stairs, moving as she might if she were approaching a target on the second floor.

To the left at the top of the steps, she found what appeared to be the master bedroom with the door slightly ajar, something she'd found to be a common occurrence whenever she infiltrated households with small children. If both Maston and Sedna were in their room, it could only mean Aroska was the one doing the pacing. She turned to her right and moved toward the three other bedrooms. Dim light seeped out from under the door of the one at the far end of the hallway. It must have been the guest room the Tarbics offered her. For all they knew, she was still using it, but once they'd retired, she had demanded that Aroska take it and let her sleep alone in the parlor. She wondered what he was doing awake, or, more specifically, why he wasn't downstairs pestering her if he couldn't sleep, either.

Two other bedroom doors lay between her and Aroska's. Both stood open, and she could hear quiet snoring within the nearest room. She softened her steps even further and risked a peek inside. Both Samm and Kasey slept soundly in their tiny beds, and a nanny bot stood against the far wall in standby mode. Ziva wondered if either of them were old enough to remember their uncle Soren. Most likely not. They would only hear stories about how HSP had killed an innocent man... how *she'd* killed an innocent man.

She moved on to the next room. Even if she hadn't already seen Samm and Kasey, she wouldn't have had to guess whether it was Chyler's. No one had gone into detail about what exactly his handicap consisted of, but a guardrail lined his bedframe, and a viewscreen for monitoring vital signs was mounted on the wall above the headboard. A second dormant nanny bot stood in the corner. If the boy's condition was serious enough that he needed his own bot to watch him in the night, Ziva couldn't imagine how he was faring in the hands of the Resistance.

The pacing within the guest room stopped, and she sensed Aroska watching the door. She doubted he could have heard her approaching, but he could most likely smell her. She took a step back when she heard him come to the door. The light that poured out into the hall when it opened made her wince, but despite the glare, she could see he was already wearing his jacket.

"Let me show you something," he whispered. It was difficult to tell since he'd spoken so quietly, but his voice might have been a bit gruff.

He was already halfway to the stairs before she made any move to follow. Just as they began to descend, Maston appeared in the master bedroom doorway, groggy but still dressed in the same clothes he'd been wearing all day.

"Do you have news?" he asked, not making much of an effort to remain quiet.

To anyone else, it probably looked like they were heading out to respond to new intel from the agency. "No, sorry," Aroska replied. "We'll be back in a bit."

Ziva followed him down the stairs and out the front door. "And where exactly are we going?" she said, coming to a halt on the front step. He was antsy, agitated, and she got the feeling that whatever he wanted to show her was somehow worse than just staying at the house. The fact that he seemed to be losing sleep over it and was willing to take her out in the middle of the night didn't help, either.

"Ever heard of the Night Sky of Salex?"

"I've seen pictures," she said as her eyebrows dropped into a scowl. The phenomenon known as the Night Sky of Salex was in fact the migration of the aeromids, bioluminescent insects about the size of a grown person's thumbnail. They had become quite the tourist attraction in Salex over the years, putting on a light show every evening during the summer months as millions of them moved from the govino orchards back into the forest. Rather than the govino pods, they feasted on other pests that were a threat to the crops, so they were both beautiful and useful to the farmers. But as impressive as they were, Ziva knew they wouldn't be out at this hour, and she hadn't the foggiest clue why Aroska would bring them up now.

"Don't tell me you're dragging me out in the middle of the night to look at some bugs," she added.

"Just let me show you something," Aroska said again, gesturing for her to simmer down. He waved her toward the car. "Come on."

Ziva could think of way too many times in recent months when she'd allowed curiosity to get the better of her. She took several hesitant steps forward before striding the remaining distance to the car and sitting down hard in the passenger seat with her arms crossed.

Aroska got in as well and piloted the vehicle out to the main road for the second time that evening. Rather than turn toward the plaza and the restaurant where they'd eaten, he guided them out of the town and toward the hills surrounding the valley. Two of Haphez's five moons—Et and Lo—lit up the night sky, but the forest was still shrouded in shadows.

They glided along in total silence for a good fifteen minutes before Aroska set the car down in a clear spot on the side of the road and took a small handheld spotlight out of the storage compartment. "We walk from here."

Traipsing through the forest in the dark wasn't exactly what Ziva had had in mind when she'd followed him out of the house. She got out and stood still for a moment, listening. There wasn't a sound to be heard in the immediate vicinity—no birds, no insects, not even the trees rustling in the wind. No matter how quietly they walked, their movements broke the silence.

She hung back several strides, partially because she had no idea where they were going but mostly because Aroska was sending off a strange, defensive vibe that made her entirely uncomfortable. She continued listening to the forest around her so she wouldn't have to remove her eyes from him, and she felt the rest of her senses come alive as her body subconsciously prepared for the unknown. She shook her head and stuck her hand in her jacket pocket when she realized it had been resting on the butt of her pistol. Surely Aroska wouldn't give her any reason to shoot him, but self-preservation instincts weren't something that could just be shut off. *Calm down. Take a deep breath.*

She bristled and froze when he stopped and turned around. So far, he hadn't even bothered to check and see if she was following; he just knew she would, and it drove her mad. He shone the light on her for a moment without saying anything, then he sighed.

"There's not much farther to go," he said, all signs of his restless behavior suddenly absent. Unless Ziva was mistaken, he almost sounded excited. "You'll probably hate me for this, but will you close your eyes?"

She crossed her arms, staring straight ahead and refusing to blink against the glare of the light. "You've got to be kidding me."

He lowered the light beam and took a couple of tentative steps toward her. "At the risk of sounding clichéd, this is kind of a surprise."

"I don't care." Confusion left her numb. First, he'd been uptight, pacing around his room in the middle of the night. Then he'd asked her about the aeromids out of the blue. Now, he was almost giddy, as if he were just as excited for this surprise as he wanted her to be. It was impossible to read him at the moment, and not just because it was dark. "I'm not closing my eyes. I don't even want to be here."

"I don't think that's true."

"Why?"

He only laughed. "Because you *are* here. If you didn't want to come, you could have just refused. It's kind of like telling me you don't trust me even while you're standing in my house asking me for help." He took another step toward her and extended a hand. "Come on. Trust me now."

*Don't you dare take his hand—he's still hiding something from you.*

*But he's right. You do trust him.*

*You let your guard down and you'll have to face the consequences.*

Ziva slapped her hand into his open palm and heaved a dramatic sigh in hopes of concealing the slight tremor in her breathing. She shut her eyes, immediately diverting all her energy toward smelling, hearing, feeling. The forest was still silent, and the air was warm and sweet. She followed a heel-toe pattern with each methodical step, searching the ground in front of her for obstacles and hoping Aroska wouldn't lead her straight into a tree. If he let her run into anything, she'd kill him.

His hand shifted around hers and she sensed a change in his position. "Log."

She paused, sliding her foot forward until the toe of her boot met rotting tree bark. She poked at it, testing its height, then stepped gingerly over it, teetering for a moment while she regained her balance.

"We're almost there," he said, reestablishing his grip on her hand as he dragged her along. "Watch out for this thorny bush on your left."

She sidestepped to avoid the bush and used her free hand to probe the space around her. It was one thing to go hiking through the forest in the middle of the night—guided by Aroska of all people—but it was something else entirely to do it all blind. It felt like some sort of sensory deprivation.

"Where exactly is 'there'?"

"Almost there," he repeated, nearly whispering. It was hardly the response she'd wanted.

She felt a sudden change in the air, like they'd emerged from the trees and were standing in a clearing of some sort. The moonlight now seemed to reach them uncontested, casting a bright glow she could sense even through closed eyelids. She stopped short, not the least bit comfortable with waltzing out into an open area while she couldn't see.

He moved around behind her and placed a hand over her eyes. With the other, he pushed and prodded until she took a couple of steps to the left.

"I'm going to cut off your arms and have them mounted in my office," she muttered.

Aroska removed his hands. "Oh, shut up."

She opened her eyes and blinked several times. As she'd suspected, Et and Lo hung in the sky to the south, washing the landscape in silvery hues. They stood on the edge of the tree line, looking out over a large patch of some of the thickest grass Ziva had ever seen. The ground sloped gently downward for fifty meters or so before dropping off abruptly. Below them lay several large govino orchards, and beyond those, the Tranyi River sparkled in the moonlight.

"It's beautiful," she said, lifting an eyebrow. She meant it—it was one of the best views of the river she'd ever seen—but she still wasn't sure why Aroska felt compelled to bring her here.

"Move forward," he suggested, "slowly."

She complied after only a slight hesitation, shifting her attention down to the grass. As soon as the sole of her boot settled in it, she realized what was different about it. The hum of a thousand tiny wings filled her ears. The grass wasn't actually that thick; it was occupied. For a moment, it looked like the very ground was crawling, and then, one by one, each blade of grass began to light up in shades of blue and green. The first lights appeared in the area surrounding her feet, spreading outward like a wave until the entire hillside was aglow.

The feeling of Aroska's hand at the small of her back prompted her to take another step forward. The moment she did, every single aeromid on the hill took flight. Hundreds, thousands, maybe even millions of the tiny insects came together in mid-air to form a single massive, swirling pillar that stretched hundreds of meters into the sky. Their glowing green and blue abdomens—determined by what Ziva could only guess was gender—cast the meadow and surrounding forest in varying shades of turquoise as the pillar undulated, constricted, and expanded.

"Ever wondered where they go after they fly over town?" Aroska said, grinning.

The thought had never crossed Ziva's mind. She stared upward, mouth slightly open, and assumed her speechlessness was an adequate answer. She had seen pictures of the Night Sky of Salex, had heard people go on and on about what a spectacle it was, but never in her life had she even given it a second thought, much less expected to see it in person. This could hardly be considered the regular show, either. This was a once-in-a-lifetime experience presented to her by someone with a backstage pass.

"Come on."

She looked down to find Aroska sitting in the grass a couple of meters in front of her. The fact that she'd been too distracted to even notice him move made her shiver.

He patted the ground next to him then settled down on his back, folding his hands behind his head. "Sit down. Trust me when I tell you you'll destroy your neck if you try to stand there the whole time."

She moved forward and settled down beside him, keeping about a meter between them. He was right; leaning back was not only more comfortable, but it gave her a better view as well. The pillar of aeromids broke apart into several smaller clusters, each still composed of thousands of the bugs. Those clusters narrowed and stretched out into long lines that swirled around each other in a triple helix formation that supposedly helped the little creatures maneuver against the strong winds coming in off the river. They reminded her of massive luminescent ribbons someone was twirling through the sky.

"This place has always been kind of a family secret. Soren and I used to come up here all the time when we were out here visiting our grandparents."

A tingle ran down Ziva's spine, immediately breaking the trance the light show had put her into, and she turned to look at him. He stared straight upward, with the light of the aeromids reflecting off his face. There'd been something in his voice—a certain emphasis on his brother's name—that told her he'd had ulterior motives for bringing her up here.

He was toying with her, beating her at the same head games she'd played with him since they'd met. First, he'd forced her to face his family, and whether it had been his intention or not, she'd shown the very emotion she'd sworn she'd never let him see. Now here they were, sharing an experience he'd only ever shared with a man she'd killed. In a way, she couldn't help but be proud; this was exactly the type of thing she'd do to him if she wanted information. But that pride quickly transformed into a sickening lump that settled in her stomach.

"Tell me about it," he said. It was a simple statement rather than a demand.

"About what?" she snapped.

"You know."

It was true—she did know. He spoke of Soren's execution, the last thing she ever wanted to talk to him about. "Why now?"

She made a point of directing her gaze upward as she sensed him roll over and prop himself up on one elbow. The last thing she wanted was for him to see the regret that flashed across her face.

His voice was strained when he spoke. "When we first met, I was convinced you'd crawled straight out of hell. Trust me, there are times when I still wonder, but like I told you after Dakiti, I've now had several opportunities to see that there's more to you than that."

"That doesn't mean anything," she muttered through her teeth, attempting to single out a particular aeromid and track its movements. It was futile; the sight of the insects had completely lost its charm, but it was still better than having to look at Aroska.

"The way people have talked about it.... 'You don't know as much as you think you do.' 'You don't know the half of it.' I'm clearly missing something, but after spending over two years of my life wanting nothing more than to kill you, I was determined part of me had to continue hating you. I didn't want to be proven wrong again." He leaned forward and nudged her shoulder, forcing her to give him her attention. "And don't think you're fooling anyone. Maston just thinks you're a hardass, but I can tell how much being here is upsetting you. I want to know why. I want to know the truth."

She wanted to yell, but her throat tightened and the only words that came out were a choked 'please no.' She sat up in hopes of distancing herself a bit. He had already developed immunity to her manipulation tactics and had even gone so far as to turn them against her. Now with...with *this*, he was trying to break through her final defense.

*Hang on a little longer. Don't let him in.*

*You know it's pointless to even try to fight anymore.*

"You ruined my life, Ziva," Aroska said. "And those people down there? The ones who invited you into their home and are relying on you to find their son? You ruined their lives, too. I think I deserve an explanation."

Ziva heaved a sigh. She fixed her gaze on one of the moonlit hills across the river and silently counted down from ten before turning to face him.

# · 38 ·
## 2 Years Ago
## City Center
### Noro, Haphez

I t was one of those days where the sun was hidden by thick clouds but its warmth still managed to reach the earth. When combined with the sticky summer humidity, the heat trapped under the cloud cover had turned the spaceport city of Noro into a massive sauna. Worse yet, there wasn't even the slightest of breezes to get the stagnant air moving. Even with the window open, she was still sweating as she sat there assembling the rifle.

A noise drew her attention to the door. She held perfectly still for a moment, watching as a pair of shadows passed by outside. The majority of her jobs took place in old, abandoned apartments and warehouses, so it was odd to be taking a shot from a building that was still in use. It was the headquarters of some obscure financial firm she'd never heard of. This particular block of offices was shut down as the ventilation system underwent some routine maintenance—another contribution to the room's stifling temperature—but there were still the occasional passersby heading toward the employee lounge down the hall.

She'd made herself comfortable in the conference room, where she'd locked the door and dimmed the lights to her liking. Looking out with her naked eye, her target was nothing more than a bipedal speck moving across the open-air bridge connecting two buildings several blocks away. In fact, the only thing that told her it was actually him was the flashing yellow dot creeping across the geographic display on her viewscreen.

His name was Soren Tarbic, a young military engineer wanted for the murder of his superior officer and subsequent theft of classified documents. She'd only been assigned to him the previous evening—he really wasn't even her target. The agent tasked with eliminating him had picked up a mission at the last minute and had asked her to take over. She didn't particularly like being chosen as a Cleaner, especially because she too had a priority mission she needed to prep for, but if the man was a threat, he needed to be taken care of. She'd spent much of the night immersing herself in his file, learning all there was to learn about him and his case, and she was looking forward to getting this over with.

She finished piecing the rifle together and climbed up onto the long conference table, settling down on her stomach behind the scope. She paused a moment to study Tarbic's relative position on the viewscreen before locating him with her sights. It appeared he had stopped at the outdoor café on the opposite end of the bridge, the destination he'd specified when he hailed a cab earlier. According to the original Cleaner's intel, this was the first time he'd left his house since his hearing. When someone was wanted for murder, they tended to avoid going out in public. Logical.

The trouble was that nobody was quite sure whether he was really guilty. More accurately, he was guilty on some level, but possibly not to the extent to which he had been charged. According to the file, his family members were his only grace period sponsors, and they'd been working feverishly for the past week trying to prove his innocence. Unfortunately, they hadn't managed to scrape together enough evidence for a second trial. His father and oldest brother were both persons of interest in the case so anything they had to say was taken with a grain of salt anyway.

Today was the last day of his weeklong grace period, and technically the deadline had been two hours ago. The Cleaners could take as long as they wanted to take out a target, though they weren't known to wait more than a couple of days past the deadline. She took a moment to study him through the scope, watching as he sat there drumming his fingers on the café table. It was odd that he had chosen to come out in public today, considering he was now fair game to whichever Cleaner had been assigned to him. A guilty man would certainly have bolted by now, and the thought occurred to her that maybe he really was innocent. She checked the time, noting that she needed to be on a transport to Vellom in less than five hours. There wasn't time to stick around and find out, and that wasn't her job anyway.

She drew in a deep breath and slowly let it out through her nose, letting everything fade into the background except what she could see through the scope. A serving bot approached Tarbic and offered him a drink, which he promptly declined. It seemed he wasn't there to enjoy a nice meal before his impending execution. Was he meeting someone? Things could get messy if he was. It was rare for a Cleaner to take a target down in a place as public as a restaurant, much less when there was someone else with them. She hated to rush, but she dreaded to think about what would happen if someone decided to drop by.

The shot would be clean; there were no obstructions and there was little air traffic. HSP's Cleaners used soft projectiles as their signature ammunition, a mark to show any uninformed investigators that the hit had been sanctioned. They were cheap and lightweight and did a good job of staying embedded in the targets' bodies once they entered. On the off chance that the round passed through-and-through, a low decorative wall would keep it from traveling out into traffic and grazing an engine or another civilian.

It appeared Tarbic wouldn't be going anywhere soon—he'd reluctantly started sipping at a glass of water the serving bot had brought him despite his refusals. It was time to make her move. A clean headshot would do nicely. Her round would enter through his right temporal lobe, severing his optic nerve before breaking up within his brain. His death would be painless, and the cleanup crew wouldn't have much work to do.

Drawing in another deep breath, she placed the pad of her finger against the trigger and tightened the muscles in her hand. "*Tsufein sieda,*" she whispered. *Find peace.*

Movement on the edge of her sights caught her attention at the exact moment Tarbic looked up and smiled with relief. She immediately lifted her finger, shifting the scope over to study the person who had just arrived. It was another man, a relative judging by the amber-colored streak running down the center of his head. He was also armed with a typical HSP service weapon. This must be the middle brother. She couldn't remember his name—something weird, started with an A.

Well, this was a fine mess. She sighed and closed her eyes for a moment before readjusting her sights. The brothers appeared to be caught up in heated conversation. Aroska—right, that was it—had handed Soren a data pad and was leaning forward in anticipation as the younger man read over it with an uneasy look on his face. She guessed the device contained information regarding the case. Her files stated that Aroska had been benched by HSP for the duration of the investigation due to his relationship with the convict, which prohibited him from even visiting his brother's home. That explained the random meeting location and the urgency with which the two of them seemed to be interacting.

She growled under her breath, unhappy with this inconvenient turn of events, and looked down at the military tags lying on the table beside her rifle. They belonged to Soren; she'd taken them in the wee hours of the morning when she'd broken into his house to place a tracker on him. The majority of military officers wouldn't be caught dead without their metal—she snorted at her own joke—but judging by the stench in his room and the bottle on the nightstand, he'd spent most of the night drinking himself into a dazed stupor pending the end of the grace period. She doubted their disappearance had even registered. She fingered the tags. Even in the heat of the room, the thin metal still felt cool against her skin. Specialist Soren Tarbic, age twenty-five—merely a year her junior—Sehale Engineering Unit. She wasn't entirely sure what she'd do with them; she imagined the family might like to have them someday, and then she kicked herself for being sentimental. There was work to do here.

She settled back down behind the scope and took another few seconds to study the two men sitting at the table. Aroska watched his brother expectantly, and Soren continued studying the data pad, alternating between looks of relief and suspicion. She wondered what was so important about the information that the older brother would risk his career to share it. Unless she was mistaken, he could easily be tried for treason if he were caught. Reporting him was pointless, though, considering Soren would be dead in a minute anyway. He was only trying to help his brother, and part of her regretted that Soren had to die in front of him. But that was his own fault—he knew good and well that a Cleaner could strike at any time. Besides, HSP was a big place. She doubted she would ever see him again.

It appeared the conversation was drawing to a close; this secret meeting, whatever it was for, hadn't taken very long. The lieutenant took the data pad back and leaned forward, saying something to which Soren responded with sharp nods of agreement. She locked her sights on him, hoping desperately that he would remain seated for a few more seconds.

She saw the older brother stand up on the edge of the scope. She went rigid.

"Take it," said a voice inside her head.

She pulled the trigger without another thought. Despite the suppressed barrel, the *pop* of the rifle discharging still seemed loud against the quiet of the room. She fixed her sights once more on the café table and took just a split second to stare at the cloud of red mist drifting about in the place Soren had been sitting. As she pulled away, she caught sight of Aroska as he dove to the ground, trying to keep his head down and reach his dead brother. It wouldn't take him long to figure out where the shot had originated.

A few seconds was all it took to disassemble the weapon and fit the pieces neatly back into their compact carrying case. She wiped the table down, clearing it of any sweat and residue from the rifle, and returned the decorative centerpiece to its place. She paused a moment at the door and surveyed the room; everything was still and quiet as if it had never been touched. It was time to move on, time to put this job behind her and focus on the next one. That was how it worked; one had to erase their presence in both a physical and mental sense.

She turned and slipped out the door, almost able to feel Lieutenant Tarbic's frantic gaze as he searched the surrounding buildings for any sign of his brother's killer. She locked the door and continued silently down the hall. In more ways than one, it was as if she had never been there.

# · 39 ·

# HILLSIDE

## OUTSKIRTS OF SALEX, HAPHEZ

A roska remained in his place on the ground, too numb to move as her story sunk in. He wasn't sure when during the narration she had stood up, but she paced back and forth a couple of meters away, looking at anything but him. One of the things that had always bothered him the most about Soren's death was the fact that Ziva had killed him while the two of them were sitting there together. In his mind, anyone who killed a person in front of his family—regardless of the circumstances—was a monster. Part of him still felt that way, but the sudden dump of new information was making it hard for him to sort out his thoughts. And based on what little he could see of her face, she was on the verge of tears. Monsters didn't show remorse.

"It was an accident," he murmured, almost not wanting to say the words. He'd been right; there was more to the story than he'd ever realized, and the truth made him feel sorry for Ziva, just as he'd feared.

"Think of it however you want," she said. "I was left out of the loop. I didn't get the memo. HSP received the data you sent in. You weren't even supposed to be part of the investigation, and you'd already missed the deadline for a trial, but they accepted it and called off the Cleaner, at least until the evidence could be studied more closely." She hesitated. "But they sent the order to the wrong person, the agent who was supposed to take the shot."

"She wasn't even supposed to be there," Aroska whispered, repeating what he'd heard Emeri say on comm that day. At the time, he'd assumed that meant Ziva was some sort of sadist who took pleasure in defying orders. The reality didn't by any means condone Soren's death, but now it felt as though a certain weight had been lifted from his shoulders.

"I called it in," she continued, "and when HSP had no idea what I was talking about, I knew something was wrong. I'd assumed the other agent had briefed them on the task delegation, and maybe it's my fault for not double-checking. You know, I was probably in Emeri's office when you came to the door." She finally turned around, and in the light cast by the aeromids, he saw that by some miracle she'd managed to keep the tears at bay.

For the next couple of minutes, all Aroska could do was sit there with his elbows resting on his knees, head resting in his hands. He wasn't sure whether to be angry, sad, sorry, or just confused. Angry that someone somewhere had made a mistake big enough to result in the loss of innocent life. Sad that Soren was still gone. Sorry he'd jumped to conclusions before trying harder to learn the whole story, and sorry he'd wasted so much of his own life wallowing in anger and self-pity. Still, the truth didn't explain a lot of Ziva's behavior; in fact, it did the exact opposite. If she had essentially killed Soren by accident, why had she spent so much time playing up his death? What was the purpose of all the manipulation and mind games? The word 'monster' began to bounce around inside his head again.

"Why not just tell me?" He looked up to find her staring blankly down at him.

"I couldn't," she answered.

What was that supposed to mean? She was physically incapable of telling him? He wondered how many other people knew what had really happened. Probably most of the spec ops division. Emeri, Skeet, and Zinni for sure. Regardless, there were plenty of people who could have filled him in. No explanation could have changed the fact that he'd watched Soren die, but it might have saved him two years of suffering and rage.

He scrambled to his feet, only to drop back into a kneeling position as all the blood drained from his head. "Why didn't you *just tell me?*" he shouted. The sound echoed off the surrounding hills, shattering the silence, and the swirling cloud of aeromids relocated to a higher altitude farther out over the cliff.

Ziva didn't even blink. "All Cleaner activities are kept confidential—you know that. Not even the unit captains are made privy to cleaning orders. With your emotional involvement in the matter, Emeri was afraid you'd share the information with a third party if you were briefed. You were deemed an intel risk."

Aroska stood back up, trying to ignore the way she'd just referred to his family as a third party. "No Ziva, *you*. Why didn't *you* just tell me the truth in the beginning? Why the act? Why keep calling attention to what you did?"

She didn't look at him with sympathy, concern, or even guilt. She just looked at him. "You remember what I said in the car about forming connections?"

He managed a wary nod.

"Think for a minute. How many people do you think are still alive after I've had them in my sights?"

"Not many."

"Not many," she confirmed. "But I saw you. You may not have been the target, but you were there. And Soren may have only been my mark for one day, but I still treated him like any other target. I studied his file front to back, found out where he lived, who his friends and family were, you name it. But it's all just words on a screen until I see the person with my own eyes. At that moment, they become real, more than just a story. That connection has formed, but I never have to worry about it because it's severed a moment later when I put a *bullet* through their head."

He couldn't tell what gave him chills—her words or the sudden breeze that came up off the river. "What are you saying?"

"It happened with you, okay? You were in the file. You were there that day. The connection wasn't as strong because the intel wasn't about you, but when you're watching someone through your scope, the knowledge that their fate is in your hands brings about a sense of—" She paused as if she didn't want to say the word. "Intimacy. Familiarity."

She threw her hands up and took several steps away, looking out over the orchards. "I thought the chances of ever running into you again were so remote that I wasn't even concerned." She turned and forced a short, disgusted laugh. "Imagine my surprise when I found out you were being assigned to my Solaris task force."

For just a moment, Aroska thought he understood. She was so accustomed to severing her connections that she didn't know how to handle one that was still intact. There were things about Ziva Payvan that never ceased to amaze him, in both good ways and bad ways. This was a woman who could shoot a man's arm off to keep him from reaching one of her targets. She could stroll into Niio Spaceport and demand help from the head of the Niiosian Mob without a second thought if it meant getting the job done. But when it came to inter-personal relationships, she was so broken, so emotionally damaged. It was almost...well, 'pitiful' was the first word that came to mind. He was surprised by how sorry he felt for her.

"You were using Soren's death as leverage," he said. The look on her face told him it was strange to hear someone finally put her thoughts into words. "I reminded you of him, so you were trying to push me away, keep me at arm's length."

Ziva sighed and brought her hands to rest on her hips, taking a single step toward him. "I want you to listen very carefully to what I'm about to say because I'm not going to repeat myself. Right here, tonight, in this spot on this hill, I'm admitting that I care. About people. But I've told you before—in this line of work, I can't afford to care. The more people I care about, the more ways someone could hurt me. The more lives I feel responsible for. The more distractions I have. That's why breaking these connections is necessary. When you showed up again, I knew I had to figure out some way to cut you off before I could start to care. But no matter what I did, you wouldn't go away."

"How could I after you saved my life?" he said. Once it had become apparent that she was more than a bloodthirsty murderer, curiosity had taken over. She was like a puzzle, and he had to assemble all the pieces in order to see the big picture. Solving puzzles and mysteries was what he did for a living, so solving the mystery that was Ziva Payvan had become a personal goal of sorts. The more she fought him, the more he knew she had something worth finding. "This is why you came back to get me at Dakiti. And it's why you saved me on the landing pad."

She nodded.

"I don't understand, though. After Dakiti and everything we accomplished while bringing Dasaro down, why keep this up? Why keep fighting me?"

Ziva blinked. "Because you terrify me."

The nonchalance of her response was startling. It was the last thing he'd ever expected her to say, and he couldn't help but let out an incredulous snort. "What?"

Her voice had risen in volume as the conversation progressed. "I mean, listen to me. I'm telling you things I can't even tell myself. I don't know how, but you seem to have me figured out, and you have from the beginning. Out of all the awful things in this galaxy, that might be what I'm most afraid of: having someone figure me out." She shrugged and shook her head, and unless it was Aroska's imagination, her jaw trembled ever so slightly. "*Sheyss*, I can't believe I'm even saying all of this."

He had to laugh to himself; he wasn't sure if he'd ever heard her talk so much at once, especially about herself. These things she was telling him…he would have never guessed she'd been fighting such a brutal internal battle for so long, and in that sense, he had to give her credit for being able to push through it and even function in her role at HSP. He still couldn't wrap his mind around the fact that the great Ziva Payvan was afraid of him, even if she'd meant it figuratively. Once upon a time, it would have flattered him to know he scared her, but at the moment, the idea made him feel terrible.

He stuffed his hands into his pockets and moved over to her, relieved by the sincerity he now saw in her face. It seemed so foreign after seeing nothing but indifference there for so long. In fact, her demeanor as a whole was unusual—her shoulders sagged, and she sported dark circles around her eyes. She seemed smaller than usual, tired, defeated. But realizing how much she'd been hurting almost made him miss the familiar Ziva, regardless of the things she'd done. As enlightening as it was to see this side of her, he needed her to be strong now as they faced Ronan. All of Haphez needed her to be strong.

"What happened when the agency found out about the miscommunication?" he asked.

Some of the tension in her body visibly released. She was no doubt glad to answer a question not directly about her. "I spent a week on disciplinary leave for accepting an assignment from a fellow agent rather than Emeri," she answered. "The man who was supposed to take the shot was dishonorably discharged from the agency and all its affiliates—not even spaceport security could hire him. A few days later, he was mugged in an alley. Somebody took a bar of eograde steel to his knees, shattered every bone in his legs. They also said he'll never be able to reproduce again. Very unfortunate." The corners of her mouth twitched upward ever so slightly.

The thought coaxed a full smile onto Aroska's face. "Well, thanks for that." He almost didn't want to smile, not while the anger over Soren's death and Ziva's behavior was still so fresh. But merely knowing the truth made him feel like he could finally understand everything. He may not have agreed with the extent to which she tried to lock herself away, but he knew why she did it, why she didn't want to care. He could almost understand why she hadn't wanted to let him get close to her and, subsequently, why the fact that he *had* gotten close made her so angry. And knowing the full story about Soren's execution...he'd always told her he'd never be able to forgive her for killing his brother, but after hearing her account and realizing how guilty she felt about what had happened, well.... He wasn't sure if he was ready to admit it out loud just yet, but maybe there was room for forgiveness after all.

He thought about shaking her hand but decided it seemed rather silly. Instead, his attention drifted to a large blade of grass that had lodged itself in her hair when she'd settled down to watch the aeromids. He'd almost forgotten that was why he'd brought her up here in the first place.

"You've got..." He gestured half-heartedly at the side of his head.

Her hand went to her own head, probing the area he had indicated, but her fingers bypassed the grass and it remained stuck there. She bristled when he reached out to help but eventually lowered her hand, allowing him to pluck the blade from her hair and let it fall to the ground.

A cluster of black strands came loose from her ponytail, and he gently swept them away, tucking them back behind her ear. He began to withdraw his hand, brushing his fingers along her jaw before pausing for a moment and resting his palm against her cheek. She stood motionless, eyes unblinking, and he could feel her racing pulse in her neck.

"Please don't," she whispered.

He closed his eyes and nodded, running his thumb over her scar once more before giving her cheek a slight pat and returning his hand to his side. "Okay."

They both turned and watched the aeromids in silence for another few minutes; the swarm had formed a massive spiral that swirled just a few meters above their heads. One by one, individual insects broke away from the group and floated back down toward the grass. The glow from their bioluminescent abdomens slowly faded until the bugs themselves once more became invisible in the darkness, just as they'd been when the two of them had arrived.

Ziva sighed and shifted her gaze down to the ground for a moment before turning and making her way back toward the trees. "We should go."

"Hey." Aroska took a couple of jogging steps to catch up, slipping his arm around her shoulder and giving her a quick squeeze as he fell into stride beside her. He felt her stiffen, but she didn't pull away. "Thank you for telling me the truth."

"Thanks for bringing me up here," she muttered. The familiar irritated tone had returned to her voice, and he couldn't help but smile again.

Both of their communicators chirped within split seconds of each other. The incoming code was Skeet's; at this hour, a transmission from him was unnerving. They stopped moving and Ziva plucked her comm unit from her belt, leaving the call open so they could both hear. "Yeah Skeet."

"It's back, Z," his voice crackled. "That ship is back. There's a fresh emissions signature just outside Noro airspace. The thing came out of nowhere—must be employing some sort of stealth technology that allowed it to get away so easily last time."

"Where is it now?" Aroska asked.

"We don't have a visual," Skeet answered. "Wait, they just found another emissions trail. If this trajectory is any indication, it's headed straight for Salex."

Both Ziva and Aroska broke into a steady jog. "What action is the agency taking?" she asked.

"I'm boarding a shuttle now. They're scrambling gunships and strike teams to chase it down. We'll make it to Salex within half an hour."

Aroska entered Maston's code and had his own communicator pressed to his ear even as Skeet and Ziva continued talking. It took mere seconds for his older brother to respond to the transmission.

"Look, don't *do* anything," he said after giving the man an abbreviated rundown of the situation. "Just go to the plaza, find somewhere to lay low. All I need you to do is watch for it and let us know what's going on. We'll be there as soon as we can. Do not engage with these people. Do you understand me?"

"On my way," Maston said, ending the transmission without confirming or denying.

"*Sheyss!*" Skeet's voice carried through Ziva's communicator. "Unidentified freighter, hold your fire!"

"What's happening?" she shouted, quickening her pace.

"Some nimrod pilot spotted it and is trying to take matters into his own hands. Must have seen the bulletin we sent out earlier today. I think he hit our target. Can you see anything from where you are?"

Aroska looked up at what little he could see of the starry sky through the trees. "Nothing," he said.

Skeet swore again. "The Salex office is on the lookout. We're on our way. See if you can pinpoint its destination and keep us updated."

"Got it," Ziva said, killing the transmission. She glanced toward Aroska as she continued moving. "You shouldn't have contacted Maston. This could get ugly real fast."

"He can help us," he replied. "He's got a stake in this, too."

She only shook her head. There wasn't time to argue as they reached the car and jumped inside. Aroska wrenched the controls around and sent the vehicle screaming back down the hill toward town.

# · 40 ·
# UNKNOWN LOCATION
## HAPHEZIAN AIRSPACE

*W*hat do you know?

She knew a lot. Her eyes were wide open, a sensation that felt totally foreign after spending so long struggling to even pry her eyelids apart. It was still far too dark to see anything in the tiny room, but being able to feel her facial muscles working somehow made her feel more alive. The remainder of her body was still weak and moving was a chore, but the adrenaline that continued rushing through her veins kept her awake and alert.

The floor of the ship had stopped rocking not long after the children were placed in the room with her. They'd traveled along for a while, only able to feel the same subtle tilt as before, until there'd been a loud grinding sound that rattled Zinni's very bones and the movement had stopped altogether. She didn't remember much after that; the door had opened and several figures had entered to take the children away. She wasn't sure if they'd sedated her with something or if she'd just fallen asleep after being overwhelmed by all the relative excitement. Either way, by the time she'd awakened again, the kids were back in the room and the floor was once again shifting ever so slightly.

She wasn't sure what it was—her nose was still trying to recover from having anyone but herself in the room—but there was something about the children that smelled different than it had when they'd first arrived. Unless she was mistaken, it bore similarities to how the crew of the ship smelled. She dreaded to think of what had been done to the kids while they were out of the room. They were just as confused as she was, and the only thing they'd been able to tell her was that they'd been injected with something.

There were at least three of them clinging to her at the moment. Zinni had worked her way into one of the room's corners in order to support herself better and currently had a child under each arm. She still wasn't strong enough to actually hold them, but the physical touch seemed to bring them comfort. The other nine were gathered around her legs; some hung on to her, but the rest were hanging on to each other per her instructions. She had no idea what was causing the turbulence or why it had only happened for the first time just hours before, but she imagined they should all brace themselves and prepare for the worst.

"Shhh," she said when someone whimpered. "It'll be okay." Her voice was still hardly more than a croak—the galaxy only knew how long it had been since she'd last spoken—but being able to communicate was at least a start.

The floor shuddered and tilted to the right before straightening out again. Zinni's head swam, and she diverted all her meager strength toward tightening her grip on the two children she held. Several of them shrieked and shuffled around her. None of them could see any better than she could, but at least they still had their strength. The last thing she needed was for them to be up running around when for all she knew the ship could be crashing.

"Hang on to each other," she wheezed. Speaking, trying to track each child via sense of smell, even holding their hands—it all required more mental capacity than what she'd used in what felt like years. As long as there were things going on, the adrenaline would carry her through. But adrenaline rushes only lasted so long. She could already feel herself getting tired again and wondered what would happen to the children if she were to pass out. Not that she could do much to protect them even while she was conscious...

She hadn't quite completed the thought when something struck the vessel. All eleven kids screamed. Zinni didn't need to be fully awake to realize the ship was going down.

# · 41 ·
## ORCHARDS
### OUTSKIRTS OF SALEX, HAPHEZ

"HSP is setting up in the plaza," Ziva said, clicking out of the latest transmission. "They're hoping to hit this thing with a dampener of some sort to keep it from taking off again. They don't want to take lethal action if there's a chance those kids are aboard."

Even with her gaze directed skyward, she sensed Aroska turn toward her with a scowl. "You say that like you *want* them to take more drastic action."

Had he paid attention to a word she'd just said up on the hill? "I never *want* people to get hurt, but we need to stop Ronan," she said, unable to suppress the slight bite in her tone. "The ship has already been hit anyway. I'm not sure how much sense there is in even being optimistic at this point."

Before he could argue, a massive object passed by overhead, mere meters above the tops of the govino trees lining the road. Fire and smoke trailed from the rear end, and it went careening out of sight somewhere off to their left.

Aroska swore and yanked the controls around, taking the car into a tight spin and maneuvering back onto a small service road they'd just passed. They could still see the ship ahead, and it appeared to be heading straight for one of the distribution centers out on the edge of the orchards. *So much for setting up in the plaza*, Ziva thought as she reopened the transmission with the Salex HSP chief and filled him in on the developments. "We've still got a visual and are currently in pursuit."

Each distribution building was identical, a square structure situated around a loading dock built into a central courtyard. The Resistance ship angled for one of those loading docks, clipping the edge of the building as it descended and sending chunks of metal and concrete flying into the night sky. Ziva had to give them credit for at least managing to crash-land in a smart location; even if their ship was damaged beyond repair, they still had a positional advantage. The design of the building offered them protection that would make it more difficult for a strike team to get the upper hand.

Aroska turned onto another small road and accelerated, cutting through the nearest orchard on a diagonal path that would get them to the distribution area in half the time. Ziva couldn't be sure—it was hard to tell in the dark surrounded by identical trees—but she thought they were back in the area of the Tarbics' house. It was for the best. The farther away from the town and the people this all went down, the better.

She had to admit she was glad to see some action, and not just because she'd been bored and at a loss for the majority of the afternoon. The past hour or so had been one of the most uncomfortable experiences she could remember, and Aroska knew she hated talking about herself in general, much less about her feelings. Getting some of those things off her chest was rather liberating, but it felt good to get back to doing something she was good at, something she could focus on. Based on the way he'd looked at her a moment earlier, he was disgusted by the way she could turn her feelings on and off with the flip of a switch. But it was necessary in order to function, necessary in order to survive.

Floodlights around the exterior of the complex revealed a pillar of smoke billowing up from the loading docks in the center of the largest distribution building. It had been there for a good two minutes by now. "Target is down in Building Three," Ziva relayed through the comm as they passed by several outbuildings and came within sight of the entrance. A door already stood open, and an unoccupied groundcar hovered outside with the engine still idling.

"*Sheyss*, that's Maston's car!" Aroska said, bringing their vehicle to an abrupt halt. "He must have seen the ship headed this way."

Ziva called after him as he leaped out, but it was no use. This was exactly why she'd thought it unwise to involve Maston in the first place. Aroska had been correct in saying that he too had a stake in all of this, but that was precisely the problem. People went to insane lengths to protect their loved ones, especially when those loved ones were mere children. The thought of a civilian trying to take on any of Ronan's soldiers was preposterous, even more so if all those soldiers turned out to be Nosti.

Going in without backup was idiotic, but she wasn't about to let him rush into this on his own. She jumped out and ran after him, checking her pistol as she went, and caught up to him just as he reached the open door.

As they burst through the opening, a fresh rush of adrenaline shot through her veins and time seemed to slow to half-speed. Her body moved independently as her eyes took in all the crucial details of the surrounding space. The back-to-back cracks of projectile gunfire across the room. Multiple sets of footsteps racing by on the catwalk above them. Maston lying in a pool of his own blood. The stack of shipping containers just to her left. The surprised man running past the doorway with a large rifle.

Her mind processed each of these details and began to prioritize them as she continued moving inside. *The surprised man running past the doorway with a large rifle.* Their entrance had clearly caught him off guard, and in the time it took him to turn around and take aim, Ziva had already put a sizzling plasma bolt through his chest.

*The stack of shipping containers just to the left.* She ducked to the side and dropped into a crouch behind them, sparing a few seconds to listen and make note of any enemy activity she'd missed. Another armed man emerged from a doorway on the far side of the loading platform that connected to the landing pad outside, and several repetitive shots from her pistol sent him diving for cover. A hail of gunfire from behind her reminded her of the steps she'd heard on the catwalk, and she slipped around the corner of the shipping containers, catching a glimpse of another pair of shooters descending a steep metal staircase. They found themselves in both her and Aroska's sights and were silenced in seconds.

*The back-to-back cracks of projectile gunfire across the room.* She waited for a lull in fire before darting toward the next stack of crates and taking out the man she found hiding behind it. She abandoned her half-dead pistol in favor of the assault rifle he'd been carrying and was pleased to find it fitted with a thermal scope. Peering through the space between two containers, she located the first of the two remaining hostiles. He wasn't much more than a pale pink humanoid shape crouching behind a piece of dark gray loading equipment, but she didn't need a clear picture of his face to know where to shoot. The moment he lifted his head to find her, her plasma bolt struck him between the eyes, sending him back to the floor behind the machine.

Unsure where the original shooter with the projectile weapon had gone, Ziva directed her attention to the final item on her list: *Maston lying in a pool of his own blood.* From her current vantage point, she could only see his legs protruding from behind a large box. But in the thirty seconds she and Aroska had been in the room, he hadn't moved.

She began moving back toward the door through which they had entered, keeping the rifle aimed toward the loading platform and stealing periodic glances at the body. She dropped to her knee behind her original stack of crates and listened. Aroska was nowhere to be found, but faint, raspy breathing reached her ears. Stealing a peek around the edge of the pile, she could barely make out the slight rising and falling of Maston's chest as he struggled to breathe. He was alive, but she doubted he would remain that way for much longer.

Lowering her eye to the rifle scope, she scanned the platform again, still unable to locate the shooter. Had he left the room? Or had he just retreated deeper into the forest of storage containers? Maybe he'd—*wait.* She paused and shifted the scope, watching as a pink form emerged from behind a piece of loading equipment and took cover behind a thick steel pillar. *There you are.*

Before she could draw a bead on him, another door slid open, and she immediately shifted her sights toward the first of the three armed men entering. But just as her finger pulled back on the trigger, a blurry bipedal shape—much closer than the others—filled the scope. Aroska. She twitched, hoping the subtle movement would be enough to throw off her aim, but the plasma bolt was already in flight. She could only watch helplessly as Tarbic dove behind the crates that had previously been blocking Maston's body from her view, paying no attention to the hole she'd just drilled through his left bicep.

*Bloody idiot!* She ducked down to avoid the spray of plasma bolts the newcomers sent her way, glad she didn't have to look at Aroska for several seconds. Granted, the backup had taken her by surprise as well, but he knew better than to run into the middle of an open space before it had been cleared, regardless of who was down or how many hostiles there were. Gritting her teeth, she rose back up and took aim for the first man she laid eyes on. Her first shot struck him in the shoulder, halting his advance, and her second sent him to the ground for good.

Aroska remained crouched behind his stack of crates, his back to the shooters and his dying brother. Ziva ignored him and resumed her journey toward the door, startled when she heard more footsteps approaching from outside. She raised the rifle, expecting the worst, but instead of more of Ronan's men, she found herself face-to-face with an HSP entry team from the Salex office. She recognized the supervisory agent they'd spoken to in the plaza and gave him a terse nod.

"Two hostiles at fifteen meters," she called as they filed in and took up cover positions. "Another at twenty."

"Headquarters wants these guys taken alive," the agent said, indicating the stunner pistols he and his men carried.

She nodded and lowered her weapon, watching from cover as the side doors burst open and two more HSP teams entered. Rather than run for cover, the Resistance soldiers on the floor immediately opened fire and the one on the platform turned his gun on himself before any of the agents could reach him.

The shooting stopped abruptly as the two remaining hostiles were hit by stun beams. Ziva heard two weapons clatter to the floor followed by two bodies. She lifted her head and looked over the scene; Aroska was just emerging from his hiding place, and two of the Salex agents appeared to have taken minor hits, but the coast was clear.

Free to move forward at last, she beckoned for the agents behind her to follow and rushed toward the platform and the massive loading door that would lead them to the downed ship. "On me!" she hollered, gesturing toward Aroska and Maston as she passed them. "And we've got a man down! Let's get some help in here!"

Aside from the adrenaline rushing through her body and the anger she still held toward Aroska, she was beginning to feel the onset of some other emotion...fear, unless she was mistaken. Fear of the unknown. Fear of what, if anything, they would find in this ship. Yes, it was the ship that had taken Zinni, but that had been over five weeks ago. The chances that she was even still alive, much less aboard, were next to nothing.

Flanked by four Salex agents, she climbed up onto the loading platform, keeping her weapon trained on the Resistance soldier she'd shot as she passed him. There was hardly any need—her plasma bolt had burned deep into his brain, and the hole in his forehead was still smoldering. The one who had shot himself was sprawled nearby, but she didn't give him so much as a second glance as they arrived at the loading door.

They'd killed six—well, seven—men and were taking two into custody. She wasn't sure if a ship this size would realistically have a crew of only nine. Perhaps they were the only ones mobile enough to get out when the vessel crashed, or perhaps there were more men aboard securing prisoners. Either way, she treaded carefully as she ducked through the boarding hatch. None of the landing gear had been deployed in the crash, so the entire ship rested on ground level. That combined with the fire that engulfed most of the aft section made for rather unstable footing inside.

The Salex agents had come prepared with spotlights mounted on their rifles. With these, they swept over the walls and floor of the corridor they'd entered. Sure enough, it was a medical transport manufactured by Solea Technologies, but it appeared to have been heavily retrofitted. As she moved along with a pair of agents, Ziva found additional lab space in areas that should have been designed for patient bunks. One section they passed through looked like a legitimate infirmary, but another contained an alarming number of tables with straps and clasps that reminded her all too much of the ones they'd encountered at Dakiti. This may have been a medical transport, but its uses went far beyond that.

"The fire crew is en route," one of the agents said, tapping his earpiece. They all paused and looked ahead to where a dead man lay sprawled on the floor at the end of the corridor. Beyond him, smoke roiled and wires sparked and snapped. The ship's onboard fire suppression systems were doing a decent job keeping things under control, but with the shape the vessel was in, there was no telling how much longer those systems would stay online.

Ziva beckoned for them to follow her down another corridor and light her way. Faint voices could be heard elsewhere in the ship, and unless her ears were playing tricks on her, the sounds were coming from somewhere below them.

"Look for a hatch, a ladder, anything that might lead to a cargo space," she instructed.

"Here!" one of the agents called, shining his light down a steep staircase that appeared to descend into the hold.

She nodded and followed him down with the other agent hot on her heels. The corridor below was narrow and lit only by dim red lighting panels. Their layout told her they were the primary light source for this passage and weren't merely safety lights that had been activated following the crash. She was glad they had the spotlights; the red hue was already giving her a headache, and she couldn't imagine what reason the crew would have for keeping the cargo hold so dark.

She took that back. There wasn't a *good* reason to keep the cargo hold so dark. She didn't need to hear the muffled cries to know this was where Ronan's troops kept their prisoners. Those cries grew louder the farther she and the agents progressed down the corridor. They seemed to be coming from within what would have normally been a storage room had this been a legitimate vessel. Smoke from all the fires on the deck above was seeping through whatever crevices it could find, and the entire space smelled of hot metal. Whoever was in that room needed to get out *now*.

Ziva motioned for the agent in front of her to hit the control panel. She and the man behind her rushed inside as the door opened, drawing screams of alarm from the people within. They shied away from the light, covering their faces with their hands. A quick glance around revealed no other source of illumination; it was impossible to know how long they'd been locked away in total darkness.

"HSP!" she called. "Everyone stay still!"

The smell alone told her they were all Haphezian, but with all the movement and only one light as of yet, it took her a moment to realize they were children. *The* children. They all appeared unharmed at first glance, though judging by the angle of the floor, they'd probably been tossed around a bit during the crash. The other agent entered with his light, giving her a clearer picture of the room. Yes, eleven Haphezian children were present and accounted for.

Another familiar scent reached her nose just as she caught sight of a twelfth figure in the back corner. A flicker of blue in the dark ignited a similar flicker of hope that managed to burn through the disbelief she was feeling. "Zinni," she whispered.

A second pair of Salex agents arrived and made their way into the already-crowded room, helping the dazed children to their feet and escorting them to the door. Ziva pushed her way through the group to the corner where Zinni lay crumpled in a heap with a child under each arm. One of them wriggled away and stumbled blindly out the door with the rest of them. The other, a little boy with amber stripes running through his tousled black hair, remained in his place and tried to bury his face farther into the folds of Zinni's shirt. Ziva didn't need to look at his *gesh punti*—even with his head partially obscured, she could see he had the same facial structure as all of the Tarbic men.

"Chyler," she said, closing a hand around his arm. He perked up upon hearing his name but shied away from the unfamiliar touch.

"We're here to help, son," one of the agents said, reaching down to help him to his feet. "We're going to take you home."

The boy whimpered and struggled as they took him to the door, but at least he seemed to understand. For a moment, Ziva's thoughts were drawn to what had just transpired in the warehouse, and she wondered what exactly home would be like from now on. She hadn't gotten a close look at Maston, but things hadn't appeared to be boding well for him.

She returned her attention to Zinni and dropped to one knee, examining the intelligence officer for obvious injuries. She found none except for a trickle of blood oozing from a lump on her forehead. Based on the dent in the smooth metal wall beside her, she'd hit her head in the crash. She wore a sweat-stained tactical outfit, likely the same one she'd been wearing on Niio, sans the armor plating. Her hair was tangled and greasy, and her sunken eyes were squeezed shut to escape the light.

Ziva pressed her fingers to Zinni's neck and was pleased to find a strong pulse. "Zin? Are you with me?"

"About damn time you showed up," the intelligence officer murmured. The words had barely been audible, but at least she was talking.

Ziva suppressed a smile, glad her friend seemed to be okay. It wasn't until she slipped her hands under her arms and began to drag her to the door that she realized what bad shape she was in. Though Zinni was still a far cry from the prisoners they'd discovered at Dakiti, Ziva had to fight away an image of herself dragging Jole Imetsi out of the murky holding cell they'd both been locked in. The woman was malnourished and could barely do anything to help herself along. Ziva considered carrying her over her shoulder, but one of the other agents appeared at her side, and together the two of them moved her out into the red corridor and back up to the main deck.

Several Salex agents passed by as they emerged, escorting two more Resistance soldiers at gunpoint. Both were limping and their faces were bloodied, and they were of the same general height and stature as the man who had been captured in Haphor. Their armor even bore similarities. It was difficult to tell thanks to the way they were walking, but they may have been Nosti as well. The thought gave Ziva chills. She imagined they might attempt to keep their abilities a secret in order to hide their affiliation, just as the other agent had done at first. But now there were at least four new soldiers in custody. Four new Nosti on the planet. Four *too many* Nosti on the planet.

She and the Salex agent transported Zinni around to the front of the building where an HSP shuttle was just touching down beside the still-idling car she and Aroska had arrived in. Skeet was on his way down the boarding ramp before it had even hit the ground. He sprinted toward them and all but shoved the other agent out of the way in his quest to take hold of Zinni.

"She's weak but seems to be hanging in there," Ziva said before he could ask for details. "She was even talking a minute ago, but it looks like she banged her head pretty good."

"And the kids?" Skeet said, beckoning wildly to members of a medical team as they arrived on the scene.

"All eleven are accounted for, and they're all mobile and coherent. Ronan's men were holding them all in a storage room in the cargo hold."

"Any idea what's been done to them?"

Ziva shook her head. "We need to give them all a full medical workup and have them checked for..." She hesitated as the medical team drew nearer and mouthed the word 'nostium.' "If you ask me, whatever they've done to the kids is different than what they've done to Zinni."

Skeet looked down at the intelligence officer as the medics placed her on a hovering stretcher, torn between staying by her side and discussing confidential matters. He risked a couple of steps away and lowered his voice. "Emeri was on comm with Baez just before we picked the ship up. Thanks to the scans you provided and the data they gathered on the prisoner, the engineers on Na have managed to whip up a countermeasure. It's temporary at best—it's just designed to slow down the effects of the nostium—but that could buy them time to come up with the real thing."

Ziva nodded, relieved that her sacrifice was proving to be of some use. "You oversee the treatment process. I want all the kids and Zinni given priority admission to HSP's med center, checked for nostium exposure, and treated accordingly. I'll finish up out here and rendezvous with you in a couple of hours."

"Got it," Skeet said, taking a couple of jogging steps to catch up with the med team. He paused after a few strides and turned back to her with that telltale crease cutting across his forehead. "You all right?"

She wasn't sure if he was asking about the shootout with the Resistance soldiers or about her surprise visit to the Tarbics' house. Her answer was the same either way. "I will be."

He gave her an understanding nod and rushed off, leaving her to wonder about Aroska for the first time in over ten minutes. She resumed her journey toward the door through which they'd entered the warehouse and found him standing just outside, staring helplessly at the emergency transport that was just taking off on the other side of the parking area. He clutched his bloodstained jacket in one hand and a medic stood beside him, trying to get him to sit down so she could examine his injured arm.

He didn't pay Ziva any mind as she approached. Upon closer inspection, it appeared her shot had merely grazed him. There was still a sizable chunk of flesh missing, but the plasma had cauterized the wound on impact and only small bits of blood oozed from the edges.

She had no idea what to say, so she stepped in front of him and said the first thing that came to mind. "Are you okay?"

His eyes shifted down to her and remained glassy for a moment as he struggled to focus. He made no move to respond and looked at her as if he hadn't even understood the question.

"What about Maston?" She doubted he would reply, and his behavior was already giving her a sufficient answer as it was.

Sensing the awkwardness, the medic looked up and gave a subtle wag of her head. "Three projectiles to the chest. They were struggling to stabilize him. It doesn't look good."

Ziva sighed. Of course they'd had no way of knowing the ship would land here, or that Maston would be here for that matter, but this was exactly the sort of thing she'd feared would happen.

"We found the kids," she said. "They all seem to be okay. Zinni was aboard, too."

Aroska's eyes had gone out of focus again, and she wondered if he'd heard a word she'd just said. Her attention was drawn to the blood smeared across his cheek in the rough shape of a handprint. The fact that it was on the side of his face opposite his own wound told her it wasn't his.

She reached into the medic's bag and took out a sterile caura cloth. "Here," she said, removing the wadded-up jacket from his hand. Based on the extent to which it was saturated with blood, she guessed he'd tried to use it to stop Maston's bleeding. She replaced it with the cloth and closed his fingers around it to ensure he was holding it. "Clean yourself up, okay? You're a mess."

Her lifelong quest to keep people at arm's length had resulted in a successful career, but if there was a downside to not letting herself care about people, it was that she had no idea how to properly console someone. Not only was Aroska hurting, but he was also in shock. Sympathy and impatience vied for control as she stood there waiting for him to react, and she didn't know which one she should grant priority to.

"Come on, Tarbic," she said, sighing again. She set the jacket down on a nearby crate, bothered by the blood that now covered her own hand, and took the cloth back from him. Not wanting to be too gentle—she had to admit she wanted him to snap out of it—but also not wishing to be too harsh, she set about wiping the blood from his face. It was still wet, so the damp cloth only smeared it and made a bigger mess. She gritted her teeth and pressed harder.

The increase in pressure finally seemed to pull him from his stupor. "*Sheyss*, Ziva," he muttered, snatching the cloth away from her. She imagined he'd intended to sound gruff, but his voice had been hoarse, strained.

She stood there and watched his pitiful attempt at wiping his own face before turning and cleaning her hands with a fresh cloth the medic offered. "I want him taken back to Noro, given a full workup."

"Yes, ma'am," the woman said. "That's the plan."

"Captain Payvan!"

Ziva turned, expecting to find one of the Salex agents or a member of the strike team Skeet had arrived with. Instead, she saw Sedna Tarbic rushing toward her from the edge of the parking area. A pair of HSP officers halted her advance.

The same anxiety she'd felt when Aroska had revealed his family's presence in Salex seized control of her mind, and for several seconds, she couldn't move. *Get a grip and just tell her the truth—there's no time for subtlety.* Ziva curled her hands into fists and strode forward, locking all other thoughts and feelings away for the time being.

"Captain Payvan!" Sedna called again. "What's happening? Maston said something about the ship and then he just left and then I could see the fire from the house so I left the kids with the bots and I didn't know—"

"I need you to calm down and listen to me," Ziva said, harsher than she'd meant to. Now was not the time for tact. "We found the kids. They all seem fine, but they're currently on their way back to Noro to be looked at by the agency's physicians."

The tears that had been absent from Sedna's eyes all day finally made an appearance. "By the five moons, thank you," she said, wiping at her face with her sleeve. She stole a peek over Ziva's shoulder. "Is Aroska hurt?"

Ziva turned and watched as the medic led Tarbic over to one of the emergency transports. "He was shot," she replied. "The wound is superficial, though—he'll be fine." *At least in a physical sense.*

"And where's Maston? He said something about following the ship to the plaza, but if it's here..."

Her voice trailed off when she saw the somber look on Ziva's face. She shook her head, and the tears immediately turned from ones of joy to ones of terror, of heartbreak.

"It doesn't look good," Ziva said, simply repeating what the medic had told her.

Based on the way Sedna had maintained some semblance of composure throughout the afternoon, the sudden fit of hysteria she threw herself into was totally unexpected. Ziva couldn't understand what she was saying or even if she was saying anything specific. She thought she heard her call to Aroska, beg him to do something, but the two HSP agents began dragging her away and her words were unintelligible.

"Take her home, get her kids, and make sure she gets to Noro," Ziva instructed. One of the officers responded with a quick salute.

"Captain Payvan!"

She bristled and closed her eyes, drawing a deep breath before turning around to locate whoever had called to her this time. The stress of venting to Aroska combined with the stress of the past few minutes was beginning to take its toll on her already-exhausted body, and it was growing increasingly tempting to just leave the scene.

"Captain, you need to see this." It was the Salex agent who had first showed her around the abduction site the previous afternoon. He beckoned to her and took off at a jog toward the docks and the downed ship.

The look in his eyes—some mixture of excitement and dread—was all the encouragement she needed. She wondered what they'd found that had evoked such a reaction in him.

They arrived back at the ship in a matter of moments; it appeared the fire crews had the situation under control, but the rear end of the vessel was still smoldering. They entered through the same hatch as before and angled toward the cockpit rather than the labs. Several other agents were already gathered there, eyes fixed on the readouts displayed on the control board's viewscreens.

"Take a look at this, Captain," someone else said, stepping aside to give her a better look.

Ziva moved forward, sweeping her gaze across the screens as she looked for a starting point. According to the internal computer, the ship was called the *Titania*, and just as they'd suspected, it was registered to a medical facility on Kovis. She doubted it was actually used by that facility—having a legitimate registration was just an added layer of protection from Federation police. The galaxy only knew where it had come from and where it was headed.

Based on some of the readings she could see, the *Titania* had been designed with clever shielding technology that kept it from being identified by any scanners that weren't set to a certain frequency. It was no wonder Port Control had been unable to get any readings from it. It was likely that the only ships that could communicate with it were other Resistance vessels.

"This is what we found most interesting," one of the agents said, indicating a specific screen. "This vessel has been in contact with a trade ship from Forus called the *Vigilance*—"

Ziva's heart skipped a beat at the mention of Forus.

"—and they've been communicating only via encrypted text-based messages. No voice transmissions, no holo-communication. Must be a security precaution. According to the logs, this ship came from a rendezvous with the *Vigilance* just outside our system. They stuck close enough to the major FTL lanes that we didn't pick them up. A memo from a Commander Payne states that the *Titania* had orders to return the children before meeting back up with the *Vigilance* as it passed through the system."

Why would the Resistance risk bringing the children back, especially if the entire Haphezian population was on the lookout for their ship? Perhaps that was the key. Give HSP and the GA something they wanted to see. Force them to focus on a specific thing while something else went down behind the scenes. The extent to which Ronan had gotten the best of them was already demeaning, and Ziva dreaded to think of what else the Resistance might be planning.

"So the *Vigilance* is here? Somewhere in the system?"

"We believe so, yes."

"Then forward this data to Na and HSP Headquarters immediately," she said. "We need to find this ship and take it out."

"Will do, ma'am. But there's one more thing."

She'd started to turn and leave, but his words stopped her dead in her tracks.

"According to the computer, the *Titania* sent out a distress signal during the crash. Payne's original orders stated that no one was to be taken alive."

Ziva had expected as much, but she swallowed as what he was saying sunk in. The agent they'd captured in Haphor…his bluff about the Resistance coming to finish him off to keep him from talking hadn't seemed too far-fetched. But he was just one man, a skilled Nosti agent who had no doubt undergone vigorous training to withstand even the most brutal of interrogation tactics. In the grand scheme of things, Ronan probably wasn't worried about him giving out any information.

But these men aboard the *Titania*? They were mere soldiers. No better than Tobias's thugs. Maybe not even all Nosti. They were each good with a gun and probably knew a thing or two about the medical equipment aboard the ship, but they were by no means covert operatives. None of them wore stealth suits with hidden pockets for suicide pills. On top of that, there were now at least four of them in HSP custody, which meant the chances of Ronan's secrets being revealed were four times more likely. If the *Titania* had sent out a distress signal, it meant the *Vigilance* knew exactly where it was. And if this Commander Payne didn't want the soldiers talking, there was no telling how the Resistance might react to their capture.

"We need to move away from this area," Ziva said.

"What? Why?"

"Because I doubt the Resistance is going to take kindly to us having possession of not only their men but one of their ships as well. Get a copy of this data sent off and get everyone away from this warehouse."

She stared at them until they leaped into action and then strode out of the ship, not entirely sure what she expected Ronan to do. All she knew was that any action taken to destroy evidence of Resistance presence would be drastic.

That was why she wasn't particularly surprised to see the massive shadow descending from the sky when she stepped back outside. The ship was hardly more than a dark gray shape standing out against the pink light that was beginning to appear on the horizon. This was without doubt the *Vigilance*, responding to the *Titania's* distress call as it traveled past Haphez. She was sure there were plenty of Resistance fighters aboard, but she didn't know how they expected to accomplish anything with a trade ship. There wasn't even anywhere to land a vessel that size in the area.

*Unless the trade registration is just a ruse, just like the* Titania's *medical registration.*

She saw that was exactly the case when the first bombs began to fall.

# · 42 ·
## Patrol Frigate *Vigilance*
### Haphezian Airspace

"**B**ut ma'am, are you sure?" the officer cried, regarding Sadey with a look of horror as he jogged along beside her en route to the bridge.

"We have our orders from Forus," she said, certain her own face mirrored some of the same discomfort the man was showing. "Start dropping charges now. Follow the *Titania's* flight path and knock out any law enforcement vessels that may have been trying to catch it."

The officer gave her an uneasy salute and rushed off, leaving her alone with her thoughts. Never in her wildest dreams had she imagined actually taking the *Vigilance* into Haphezian airspace, much less entering the atmosphere. Bringing the stolen fighter near enough that it could fly to the military base was the closest they'd ever come, but even then, they'd been able to keep their distance. This, however, was suicide.

Ronan had gone insane, Sadey decided. Having them travel through the Noro system to rendezvous with the *Titania* had been risky enough, but sending them in so close—and having them directly engage the Haphezians, at that—was going to render all their efforts toward maintaining secrecy totally futile. According to the news, HSP agents had killed Jalen during interrogation, so there was no need to worry about him giving them away, but now here they were showing themselves anyway. The enemy now had a face, and it wouldn't be long until the Resistance had the Haphezian military on their tail. They might even be willing to involve the Federation, independence be damned.

The handheld holoprojector clenched within her fist buzzed, reminding her of the transmission she'd muted long enough to address the officer. She took another split second to compose herself before reactivating the hologram. The three-dimensional image of Ronan stood there in her hand, less than half a meter tall but as menacing as ever.

"I'm not going to risk someone getting their hands on the data the *Titania* is carrying," Ronan said, picking up the conversation right where they'd left off. "Destroying it is our only option."

"Our scanners are already picking up police activity at the scene," Sadey said. "How do you know they haven't already found the data?"

"Our men are better than that!" Ronan snapped. "They will have put up a fight, bought us some time. Someone down there was in good enough shape to send out the distress signal. They won't have let the Haphezians get that close."

Sadey pursed her lips and moved faster, skirting around a couple of officers who sprinted past her. As some of the only Nosti who had survived the Federation's attacks, she and Tav Ronan had been close friends for over two decades. But once their plan for retaliation had gotten underway, they'd begun to have their differences. Sadey wanted results and she wanted them fast, while Ronan was the patient, calculating type who could sit and wait—for years, if necessary—for the enemy to make the first mistake.

Now, it seemed, their roles had been switched. Sadey was trying to remain levelheaded while Ronan was the one calling for action. The leader of the Resistance had never been one to be reckless, but as their plan reached its final stages, everyone's patience was running thin. Losing the *Titania* had been the final straw.

"I know what I'm doing," Ronan said. "Bomb the warehouse. Destroy the *Titania* and kill anyone in the vicinity, including our men and the prisoners."

"We'll be starting a war with Haphez."

"The nostium was a dead end. Without nostium, the Federation will never come wipe them out like we planned. If we ever want to expand here, war would be a requirement anyway."

Sadey stopped dead in her tracks. "I told you we were close! The children were promising! We just need a little more time." The familiar apprehension began creeping through her mind again. Unless she was mistaken, this was Ronan's way of telling her she'd failed.

"We're *out* of time, Commander. The longer we try to incorporate the Haphezians into the plan, the more time they have to figure out who is behind these attacks. If we write them off, they become just as much of a threat as the Feds."

"Tav, think about what you're asking us to do." Sadey hesitated, unable to remember the last time she'd addressed Ronan on a first-name basis; despite their former friendship, it had been months. "We'll be trapped down here. Exactly how are we expected to get out of this?"

Even with the silvery-blue hue of the hologram, it was plain to see the cold look on Ronan's face. Sadey swallowed past the lump in her throat and forced her feet to continue forward. The answer was clear: they *weren't* expected to get out of this.

"If you go through with this, two decades of work may be wasted," she said.

"It's too late now," Ronan replied, black eyes emotionless. "Your people have been working on a nostium formula for the Haphezians for over a year and you still failed. Do you want to see the plan succeed or not?"

"Yes." Sadey shuffled into the elevator, grateful for the momentary isolation. The *Vigilance's* crew was already confused and anxious as they scrambled to fulfill Ronan's orders, and the last thing she wanted was for everyone to see her so discouraged.

"I'm giving you one last chance to contribute here, Commander. The Haphezians were the final barrier keeping us from putting the plan into motion. We may proceed at any time, but they will need to be dealt with first. The last thing we need is to be fighting them and the Federation simultaneously."

The elevator opened onto the bridge and Sadey strode out, squaring her shoulders as best she could. "Deal with them how?"

"We'll begin by focusing exclusively on them. Target their police and military forces. Use the bad nostium if you have to. Do what we must to cripple them and render them incapable of retaliating. The Federation is unlikely to respond to an altercation on an independent world. I'm currently assembling the fleet and the remainder of our Fringe resources, and we should arrive in the Noro system in less than two days."

Even without looking up, Sadey could sense every pair of eyes on the bridge looking at her. "And in the meantime?"

"That's where your contribution comes in, Commander," Ronan answered in a nonchalant tone that sent chills up Sadey's spine. "You understand how our plan works. We expose Fringe races to nostium. The Federation moves out to investigate. Our forces come around and take them from behind while they're otherwise occupied, and we gain control of the Core. This will be very similar, but *you'll* be keeping the *Haphezians* occupied."

In that instant, Sadey understood what was expected of her. Ronan's plan had always assumed the targeted Fringe civilizations would be annihilated when the Feds arrived to look into the nostium presence. If the *Vigilance* and her crew were the Fringe civilization in this scenario, they would likely be wiped out by the Haphezians before Ronan and the rest of the Forus fleet arrived. The ship's presence *would* keep the Haphezians distracted and allow Resistance forces to sneak up on them, but that advantage came at a higher price than Sadey had ever expected to pay.

"I trust you'll think of something creative," Ronan said. With that, the hologram flickered and disappeared.

Everyone on the bridge had no doubt overheard the last part of the conversation. Ever since the war with the Federation, every Resistance agent had to be willing to give their own life to protect the cause. If the Feds ever found out what they were planning, all the years they'd spent covertly rebuilding the Nosti culture would be wasted. That was why they couldn't let the Haphezians get their hands on the data aboard the *Titania*, why Ronan had sent them into Haphezian airspace in the first place. Everyone understood that, and they were all ready to sacrifice themselves as a last resort.

But this situation was different. Sadey couldn't remember a single time when Ronan had *ordered* Resistance troops to take their own lives. There was a difference between warning people against being taken alive—something she'd done herself a number of times—and blatantly telling them to kill themselves for the cause. Worse yet, this was all her fault. She was being punished because she'd failed to stay on schedule with the nostium development, and the rest of her crew had to suffer because of it.

The bridge remained silent as everyone contemplated what Ronan meant. A low rumble vibrated the ship as the bombs fell, obliterating the warehouse complex where the *Titania* crashed. Sadey had no desire to disobey orders, nor did she have any desire to make two hundred other people pay for a mistake she'd made. If she was careful, she might be able to save them and still buy the Resistance fleet enough time to get there. Ronan hadn't specifically said this had to be a suicide mission, though the idea was implied. The *Vigilance* was a fast vessel; if they were able to leave the atmosphere, they could run. Leading the Haphezians on a wild goose chase was a surefire way to keep them occupied until Ronan arrived. It might even be enough to scramble their military and keep them spread thin enough that the Resistance forces wouldn't have any trouble taking them out.

Her navigator and lieutenant commander approached and stood at ease a respectful distance away. "Your orders, ma'am?" said the latter.

Sadey looked up to find all eyes on her. The only people who weren't paying her any mind were the helmsman and whoever was down in the main battery.

"Orders?" the lieutenant commander asked again.

She stood still for a moment, eyes fixed on the readouts displayed on the viewscreens around her. Each bomb had hit a structure of some sort, effectively wiping out the *Titania*, its prisoners, and, she hoped, any Haphezian police at the scene. The med ship's crew would have put up a fight, successfully keeping investigators from getting too close and discovering evidence before it could be destroyed. In the event that they hadn't been able to take their own lives, the bombs would have destroyed them as well.

They would travel to the nearest city, she decided. It would give the Haphezian military more time to react, but she doubted they'd be willing to shoot the *Vigilance* down over a heavily populated area. If they were lucky, they could slip into one of the busier traffic lanes and use the civilian transports as a shield until they reached open space. In the event that they were unable to make it off the planet, they'd have no choice but to make do with the resources they had available. That included the *Vigilance's* weapons systems and maybe even the ship itself. They had enough firepower to cause some real damage, but they would cross that bridge when they came to it.

"Make sure there's nothing left of the *Titania*," she finally replied, "then set course for Noro."

# · 43 ·
# GOVINO DISTRIBUTION CENTER
## SALEX, HAPHEZ

Ziva ran. She couldn't recall the last time she'd run so hard. Maybe when she and Aroska had been fleeing the main building at Dakiti. At least this time she wasn't carrying an unconscious man on her back.

The charges continued hitting the ground behind her, shaking the earth and making for rather unstable footing. She had counted five so far—no, there went a sixth—and they were getting progressively closer. Just as she'd suspected, the *Vigilance* was no ordinary trade ship.

She hadn't looked back once since she'd taken off from the warehouse. A quick survey of the parking area had revealed that all the emergency transports had taken off already, which meant Aroska, Skeet, Zinni, and the children had made it safely away. The HSP ships transporting the prisoners had still been in the vicinity, and she sincerely hoped they'd avoided the *Vigilance's* plasma cannons. She could hear the massive bolts striking the ground in the lulls between bombs.

There were at least four other agents running along behind her. One of them had stumbled at some point and she wasn't sure if he'd managed to catch back up. She couldn't help but think about what Emeri had said, the reason he'd ordered her to stay in Salex to begin with. As much as she hated to admit it, she *was* important. She had the best idea of who they were dealing with here, so she thought it realistic to allocate a bit more focus toward saving herself. There wasn't much she could do for the other agents anyway other than hold hands and run beside them, and that wouldn't do anyone any good. For the moment, it was every man for himself.

One last explosion, this one stronger than any of the others, rocked the ground and she finally risked a look behind her. The distribution building and the wreck of the *Titania* were engulfed in a monstrous fireball that billowed up into the early morning sky. The yellow-orange light it cast reflected off the hull of the *Vigilance* as the ship banked and altered its course. It was moving away from them. Moving toward Noro.

The other agents stopped and looked with her. She had no idea how many people had been claimed by the explosion, but based on what she could see of the blast radius, anyone who hadn't started running when she had was gone. It was a good thing HSP had been right on the *Titania's* tail; otherwise, they wouldn't have been able to respond as quickly as they had. She pictured everyone arriving just as the *Vigilance* showed up to clean house. The bombs would have claimed the lives of all the first responders as well as the *Titania's* crew and all its prisoners, which was no doubt what the Resistance was hoping for.

Against her better judgment, Ziva began moving back toward the warehouses, removing her communicator from her belt as she went. She opened up a transmission to Skeet, disconcerted by how long it took him to respond. His transport had a decent head start, but she dreaded to think of what would happen if the *Vigilance* caught up to them.

"Little busy here, Z. We've got a tail."

"I'll say," she said, glad they'd already caught on. She broke into a jog, keeping her eyes peeled for any aircars or small ships that hadn't been consumed by the blast. "It just wiped out the entire warehouse."

"*Sheyss.* Did everyone make it out?"

*I doubt it.* "I hope so," she answered. "Divert course. Order all the HSP vessels to get the hell out of the way. It's a safe bet the Resistance wasn't counting on us responding so quickly. If we hadn't already been tracking the *Titania*, we'd probably just now be getting there. If they see you heading for the city, they won't hesitate to blow you out of the sky."

"Already done," Skeet said. She could hear him on another comm confirming the course diversion and advising the other emergency and prison transports.

Several Salex agents who had taken off in a different direction were piling into a response shuttle that had landed farther away to deter curious onlookers. There'd been more bystanders than Ziva would have expected at this hour; the govino farmers were clearly early risers. Luckily, they'd been far enough away that they'd had no trouble escaping the blast radius, and the little ship remained unscathed. She waved an arm as she ran toward it and one of the agents waved back, gesturing for her to join them.

"I've got transport," she said as she arrived at the shuttle and climbed aboard. "I'll rendezvous with you in the city. Stay out of that ship's way."

She clicked off and took hold of one of the grab rings as the shuttle lifted from the ground. It was almost identical in design to the one she and Aura had taken to Haphor. When had that been? Night before last? The days were starting to blur together. What she *did* know was that if it had taken Skeet half an hour to get to Salex, it would take about the same amount of time to return to Noro. If they pushed the vessel to its top speed, they might be able to get there sooner, but she also thought it wise to maintain distance from the *Vigilance* and stay out of range of its plasma cannons.

"See anything?" she called to the agent piloting the shuttle.

"It's hard to miss, ma'am," he replied.

He was right. She moved forward to get a look through the front viewport. The ship, likely some sort of mid-sized patrol frigate, stood out against the increasingly light sky. Even if there had been other traffic around, it would have dwarfed the other ships and vehicles using this traffic lane.

"Keep your distance, but don't let it out of your sight," she instructed.

"My thoughts exactly."

She stepped back into the passenger area and reestablished her grip on one of the grab rings. Keeping her gaze directed toward what she could see through the viewport, she opened a new transmission to Emeri's office.

"I had you stay in Salex to keep you away from all of this," he answered without so much as a hello. The time for formalities had passed.

"A lot of good that did," she said. "Where are you?"

"Agent Stannist and I are just leaving to meet the incoming transports at the med center. We've just received some data from the downed ship. It says you authorized it?"

So they had managed to send the data before the bombs hit. Ziva breathed a sigh of relief. "This incoming vessel is the *Vigilance*, a trade ship from Forus mentioned in those files. It's got substantial firepower. We're on our way back and are maintaining a visual on it."

"We're tracking it as well," Emeri said. "Based on its speed and trajectory, we're estimating it will reach downtown Noro in fifteen minutes."

"*Sheyss*." The shuttle was at least five minutes behind; they'd have to push hard to catch up. "Can we hit it with a dampener? Even shoot it down?"

"The dampener we'd planned to use on that freighter isn't big enough for a ship that size. Noro's AA guns could do some damage, but scans are showing considerable shielding on this thing. They could probably break through eventually, just not before it reaches the city. There are GA ships on the way, but they're concerned about engaging it over a populated area as well. We'd be looking at massive loss of life."

"So you'd rather have it drop more bombs on the city?" Ziva said. "People are going to die either way!"

"I believe they're going to try to force it out over the river in hopes of preventing civilian casualties," Emeri replied, breathing hard as if he were in a hurry. "There's simply not enough time to take it down before it gets here. We're doing what we can."

She sighed. The fact that Ronan had managed to catch them by surprise so many times was humiliating, and for the first time, she wondered if it was perhaps her fault. The Resistance clearly knew the best ways to exploit their weaknesses; what better way to learn those ways than to send one of their own agents to live on the planet and raise a runaway Haphezian girl? Through his interactions with her, Jak Gamon had gotten an inside look at their culture, and living on Haphez for twelve years had given him plenty of time to research their military and police forces. Having the stolen fighter—possibly *multiple* stolen fighters and their pilots—on Forus for the past several years had no doubt helped as well. Granted, Gamon wouldn't have been able to gather much concrete information, but it would have been plenty for any decent strategist to act on.

Part of her also wondered if Ronan had been looking for her this whole time. At first, she'd assumed she'd been the target in all of this—she and her family had been at ground zero for all of the attacks, after all. But after a bit more consideration, she'd deemed it pure coincidence. If they had been looking for her, chances were they wouldn't have been trying to kill her. As far as she knew, she was the only Haphezian who'd ever received a successful nostium infusion. If anything, she imagined Ronan would have liked to study her to see how the substance affected her brain, just like HSP and the GA were doing. She wondered for a moment why the Resistance hadn't just tried to come after her specifically. Her existence was clearly common knowledge if the captured Res agent knew who she was, and after her bout with Dasaro, her face had circulated all over the Fringe. If Tobias knew her true identity, surely Ronan did, too.

There wasn't time to speculate, though, and it didn't really matter anyway. She was still caught in the middle of this whether she liked it or not.

The shuttle crested the hills, and they had an unobstructed view of the *Vigilance* as it swooped down over the flat farmland surrounding Noro. Light from the rising sun glinted off its dark gray hull, and though they were too far away to see details, Ziva detected several protrusions that could only be those hefty plasma cannons.

"Civil Defense is locked on," the pilot announced. "They're picking us up as well and we've been ordered to back off. All our emergency transports made it through the perimeter."

Ziva moved back toward the front of the craft as it slowed,

gripping one of the rings so tightly her knuckles turned white. As long as they could maintain a visual of the Resistance ship, she was satisfied. Once the Civil Defense guns began firing, it was safe to assume this Commander Payne character would order some sort of counterstrike. The last thing they needed was to make themselves easy prey for the *Vigilance*, or worse, take a hit from their own AA guns.

Even from a distance, she could see the bright red heat signatures from the Civil Defense weapons. The Resistance ship slowed, forcing their shuttle to slow even further to maintain distance. But just as Emeri had predicted, the *Vigilance's* shields did a good job of absorbing the onslaught. They wouldn't last forever, but the ship was getting close enough to the city that there wasn't much chance of breaching Res defenses before they were forced to cease fire. She drew closer to the viewport and strained to see up into the sky; two of the GA's own patrol frigates, along with several gunships and fighters, were descending directly over the city. If they were able to lock on soon enough, there was still a chance of stopping this thing.

"Swing out wider," she suggested to the pilot.

He'd already begun guiding the little ship farther out toward the river. "On it." HSP may have known they were there, but it was still their responsibility to stay out of the way of any defensive procedures.

"*Sheyss*," one of the other agents said, looking up at the approaching military ships as well. "They're not going to make it down here in time."

The towering structures of central Noro jutted out of the landscape ahead. It already looked like spaceport traffic was being diverted, and a swarm of white dots that were no doubt HSP fighters hovered over the port itself. Ziva had a hunch they were only there for appearance's sake—the agency had to realize they would be no match for the *Vigilance* in terms of firepower, but they couldn't let Noro's citizens think they were just sitting by doing nothing.

The missile came out of nowhere. More accurately, it had been fired by one of the nearest gunships, but it passed directly over the shuttle, causing them to swerve right and away from the river. It snaked its way through the air and struck the *Vigilance* broadside, sending a bluish ripple across the ship's surface as the impact was absorbed by the shields.

"Stay on this trajectory," Ziva ordered. "Bring us around to the north side of the port, and whatever you do, make sure Civil Defense knows where we're headed!"

The Resistance ship pressed on despite being pelted by thick plasma bolts from the AA guns. They'd have to stop firing within another minute; the frigate had already reached some outlying residential areas and even falling debris would likely cause casualties. Another missile shot through the early-morning air and knocked out one of the *Vigilance's* batteries, but still the ship advanced.

Then everything fell still. To Ziva's chagrin, the AA guns stopped firing altogether. She understood why HSP and the GA were being so cautious, but at the same time, if they didn't stop Ronan's forces now, they could end up with much larger problems on their hands that would result in even greater loss of life. The military ships hung motionless in the sky, forming a barrier that would keep the frigate from leaving the atmosphere. If it moved out of the area, they'd be free to engage it, and they'd be sure to win. For all intents and purposes, it was trapped over the city. Why, then, was it still moving forward?

"It's slowing down," the shuttle pilot announced.

No sooner were the words out of his mouth than the bombs began to fall again. Without warning, the *Vigilance* altered its course, swinging out toward the river and curving back inward toward central Noro, all while leaving a path of utter destruction in its wake. Its plasma cannons were at work as well, firing on the nearest structures and any vehicles unfortunate enough to be within range.

"*Frouchten hehle*, somebody do something!" Ziva shouted to no one in particular.

Someone somewhere must have read her mind. The AA guns turned inward and resumed their bombardment, ignoring the idea of collateral damage for the time being. Plasma and missiles rained down from the GA's ships above, gradually eating away at the *Vigilance's* shields until someone finally scored a direct hit. Black smoke billowed from one of the frigate's engines, but it continued its journey toward the center of the city, dropping charges as it went. Everyone in the shuttle held their breath as it passed over Noro Spaceport, leaving at least three hangars in ruin. Still, it pressed on.

"Where the hell do they think they're going?" someone muttered.

Ziva studied the trail of smoke and the way the ship dipped lower and lower the farther it progressed. She shifted her attention to the structures ahead and her eyes widened.

All anyone in the shuttle could do was stand and watch as the *Vigilance* crashed headlong into the center of HSP Headquarters.

# · 44 ·

# HSP Medical Center

## Noro, Haphez

"Look, Lieutenant!"

Skeet watched as the team of medics pushed Zinni's stretcher inside and then turned to find the speaker. His gaze was immediately drawn to the *Vigilance*—it was close enough that it commanded the majority of the visible sky. A trail of black smoke streamed from its rear end, and plasma bolts pelted it from all directions. It was slowing down, almost as if it were coming in for a landing, but it was still headed straight for them.

He sprinted back to the door, taking cover in the entryway as the massive ship passed directly overhead. Its own guns were ablaze, raining plasma down on the city. At least it had stopped dropping the bombs Ziva had talked about, but it was causing no less damage. A stray bolt struck the landing pad he stood on, flipping the medical transport that had contained him, Zinni, and several of the Salex children only moments before.

Once the frigate was out of sight, he took off at a dead run toward the end of the landing platform, attention directed upward. His advance was slowed when the entire building shuddered and he was forced to duck out of the way of some falling debris. Then a horrible sound reached his ears; it began as a series of sharp cracks combined with some sort of metallic screeching, and it rose in volume until it was nothing more than a deafening roar on the other side of the med center. He regained his footing and continued down the platform until he reached the corner of the building, where the sight before him rendered him completely immobile.

By his estimation, the *Vigilance* was between two hundred fifty and three hundred meters long—small for a military-grade frigate, but large enough that it would have needed to use one of the spaceport's massive intragalactic transport bays in order to land. As such, the idea that it was currently burrowed headfirst into the heart of HSP Headquarters was inconceivable. He reached out to brace himself against the wall of the building and swallowed against the overwhelming urge to throw up.

For what seemed like a long time, he could only stand there staring at the wreck, or more accurately, what little he could see of it through the swirling cloud of smoke and dust. The ship's hull rested flat on the ground, or as flat as it could get with all the rubble beneath it. The scene was just a larger version of the *Titania's* crash site; the ops towers and administrative buildings were still intact, but the docks, training center, and all the smaller structures in the center of the campus had been completely obliterated.

Even from two blocks away, he could hear the multi-toned wail of the alarms rising up throughout the complex. He'd seen a good portion of HSP's air force out over the city already so perhaps many of their pilots and vehicles had avoided the attack. Trying to find a silver lining was almost pointless, though. He couldn't even imagine how many people had just lost their lives, both in the crash and in the preceding destruction.

Without even realizing it, Skeet had his communicator out and was sprinting back across the landing platform. He burst through the doors they'd taken Zinni through and got halfway through entering Emeri's comm code when he spotted the director approaching with Aura Stannist and several frantic security guards.

"What the hell is happening out there?" Emeri demanded, ushering his entourage aside to make way for the same group of emergency responders who had just brought Zinni and the kids inside.

Skeet wasn't even sure how to answer. For the moment, he was just glad the director had made it away from Headquarters unscathed. If he and Aura had already made it this far into the med center, chances were they hadn't seen a thing that had transpired outside for the past ten minutes.

Unsure where to even begin, he heaved a sigh and shook his head. "We're at war."

# · 45 ·
# PATROL FRIGATE *VIGILANCE*
## NORO, HAPHEZ

S adey pulled herself up off the floor and dusted herself off. A trickle of blood ran down the side of her face—the result of striking her head on the corner of her desk—but after a quick self-examination, she found no severe injuries. Her helmsman had done a good job keeping the *Vigilance* level even after they'd lost shields. He'd brought the ship in slowly enough and at a shallow-enough angle that she doubted they had sustained much loss of life, if any. It was a sturdy vessel; chances were the docking bays, labs, and anything located in the lower hull had been destroyed, but if the crew had all moved to the upper decks like she'd ordered them to, they should all be fine.

Crashing the ship into HSP Headquarters certainly hadn't been on the agenda for the day, but she'd had to think on the fly once it became clear they wouldn't be able to leave the atmosphere. She wasn't sure how the Haphezian military had made it down to the city so quickly—it was almost as if they'd had advance warning. Had they found the *Vigilance* out on the edge of the system and tracked it, or worse, had they somehow gotten their hands on the *Titania's* data?

The only way they'd have gotten to the *Titania* that fast was if they'd followed it. She was confident that her agents had taken every precaution against being tracked, which meant the Haphezians had another source of information. The only people who could have told them were people with firsthand understanding of their methods. If

Jalen had been executed during interrogation, only Payvan remained. She was likely to be at HSP Headquarters, the main reason Sadey had chosen it as a target. The chances of actually taking Gamon's former student out by crashing the ship were slim, but somehow the act still seemed appropriate.

Ronan had said to keep the Haphezians occupied, so that's what she planned on doing. Destroying a large portion of their main police facility was a start. Unless she was mistaken, they'd landed right on top of HSP's air patrol docks, severely limiting the extent to which the agency was capable of responding. Even when they could respond, they'd still have to deal with removing a wrecked frigate from their campus...a wrecked frigate containing two hundred well-trained Resistance soldiers, almost all of whom were Nosti.

Sadey's kytara had flown from her grasp upon impact, and she took a moment to search for it. She found the weapon resting against the wall at the base of the cabin's slanting floor and snatched it up, firmly attaching it to her belt. Elsewhere in the ship, the rest of the crew was no doubt doing the same. Everyone had kept their kytaras hidden for the majority of the mission in case the *Vigilance* was boarded by Feds, but now the time for concealing their Resistance affiliation was over. The Haphezians would figure out who they were anyway when Ronan and the fleet arrived in less than two days—a little forewarning wouldn't hurt anything.

The jacket Sadey had set out for herself had also slipped away in the crash. She recovered it and shrugged it on over the plain white tank top she wore under her military uniform, ensuring it adequately concealed the kytara. Along with herself, she'd selected a number of her highest-ranking officers and ordered them to don plain clothes and arm themselves to the best of their abilities. HSP—and possibly even military troops—would no doubt attempt to infiltrate the *Vigilance* at some point. She'd ordered her agents to stay aboard and kill any Haphezians who tried to enter; they had an advantageous position aboard the ship, and they'd likely be able to make a decent dent in HSP's numbers. She and the other officers would escape during the fray and slip into anonymity in downtown Noro, a city that was already renowned for its amount of foreign traffic.

She'd relayed all of this to the crew via intercom the moment she'd spotted the Haphezian military ships hovering over the city. Unless they wanted to be shot down, leaving the area had been out of the question. She had to admit she'd been surprised the Haphezians had retaliated, even after the *Vigilance* began dropping more bombs. Perhaps they simply recognized that their city was already being destroyed so there was no harm in causing a little more damage. Sadey couldn't help but smirk to herself as she went to the cabin's jammed door and manually overrode the controls to open it. Even crippled, her crew could still come together to create a brilliant, destructive force. Ronan would be proud. Ronan had *better* be proud.

The corridor outside her cabin was silent except for the hiss of the fire suppression systems within the ceiling. This high up in the ship's structure, everything was virtually undamaged. If not for the fact that everything was tilted about ten degrees to the left, Sadey wouldn't have even known anything was wrong.

She jogged forward toward the hatch to her personal escape pod bay, silently lamenting the fact that she hadn't had time to commend her crew on a job well done. There'd barely been time to come up with a plan, circulate the idea, and make it back up to her cabin. Everyone had come together as a unit and followed her orders to a T despite the ridiculously short notice. She imagined self-preservation had been a motivating force. Even though there was no one around, she offered a salute to thin air for good measure and climbed through the hatch.

They'd launched all the escape pods amid the bombardment, partially to confuse the Haphezians but mostly so the officers could escape through the empty pod bays. Initially, HSP's scans of the vessel would only show main docking hatches. Chances were they wouldn't even discover the makeshift escape routes until Sadey and her colleagues were long gone.

The stench of burning material overwhelmed her senses as she passed through the airlock and crouched in the empty bay. Through the opening, she saw that the immediate area was completely shrouded in smoke and dust, making her escape all the easier. Based on what little she could see of the surrounding environment through the haze, it would take responders some time to remove rubble before any entry teams could even access the ship. Praising her good luck, she climbed out and inched along a narrow ledge before reaching a set of handholds designed for EVA maintenance. Bits and pieces of the ship's hull had been blown away by Noro's AA guns, providing additional footing options that weren't part of the vessel's original design.

Sadey reminded herself that she her officers weren't merely escaping to save themselves. That was partially the case—they were all ranking Resistance officials who needed to do everything in their power to get back to Forus and maintain organizational structure. But theoretically, they'd also be able to work covertly within the city to help coordinate Ronan's attack, feed the fleet information, and do whatever they could to slow the Haphezians down. Assuming they made it safely away from the wreckage, their physical build and training would allow them to slip in and out of crowds, and their kytaras would make them lethal opponents in close-quarters combat. Sadey imagined herself tracking down Payvan and catching her off guard. Surely killing Jak Gamon's former student—and a potential source of Resistance intel for the Haphezians—would help win back Ronan's favor.

The number of available hand and footholds was dwindling, and after another few moments of climbing, they disappeared altogether. Sadey took a look around to ensure the area was still clear and then glanced down. A good ten meters of hull still separated her from the ground, but the surface was smooth and curved outward around one of the ship's intact engines. Not wishing to waste any more time, she settled down onto her stomach and allowed herself to slide backward, using her palms and boot soles to slow her descent. She crested the curve and fell the remaining couple of meters, tumbling down onto the cracked surface of an HSP landing pad. With a quick roll, she was back on her feet and headed away from the ship. This battle was not over, not if she had anything to say about it. The real war was just beginning.

# · 46 ·

# HSP MEDICAL CENTER

## NORO, HAPHEZ

The sight of the overturned medical transport and plasma scarring on one of the med center's landing pads made Ziva's stomach flop. Never mind the massive frigate lying in the middle of HSP's campus; the crash had no doubt claimed the lives of multiple agents, but *her* agents—her dearest friends—had been aboard those emergency ships. Right now, they were a priority.

"Set us down there!" she ordered, gesturing toward the landing pad.

The pilot directed the shuttle toward the place she had indicated. Ziva had the door open and leaped out before the landing gear had even touched the ground. She sprinted toward the wrecked transport, opening a transmission to Skeet as she went. Relief overtook her when she found the overturned ship to be empty, even more so when Skeet's calm voice answered her call.

"Where the hell are you?" she demanded. Just because he, Zinni, and Aroska weren't aboard the ship didn't mean they weren't still in trouble.

"Right here, Z."

The voice hadn't come from the communicator. She looked over and found him walking toward her from the building entrance with that familiar crease still visible on his forehead.

She waved her arms toward what remained of HSP Headquarters. "Did you see that—?"

"I saw," he assured her. "Glad you made it safely."

"I could say the same to you."

He nodded toward the emergency transport. "It was a close call. If we'd been aboard for an extra sixty seconds...." His voice trailed off and he shifted his attention to the sky. The military ships had resumed their descent into the city, and more were appearing higher up. The smaller vessels—gunships and fighters—were already upon them, flying low over the HSP campus and circling the *Vigilance* like birds of prey.

"We should move inside," he said, hustling her back toward the door.

Ziva was eager to get inside as well, though she wasn't sure if she liked the way he was herding her around. It was one thing to be concerned for her safety, but trying to shelter her was pointless. She'd already been forced to spend the night in Salex for her own protection, and a lot of good that had done.

They entered the building, and she followed him down a secondary hallway while the rest of the agents from her shuttle continued down the main corridor. Emeri and Aura waited off to the side, trying to keep themselves in the loop without being in the way of the frantic medical personnel. Both approached upon seeing her and the director muttered a curse, though his tone spoke of nothing but relief.

Ziva realized he was on comm when he began talking but didn't make eye contact. Based on the nature of the conversation, he was speaking with whoever was in charge of the military's operations outside. Aura watched her silently, and unless Ziva was mistaken, there may have been a hint of gratitude in her eyes. It was always so hard to tell.

"What are we going to do?" she demanded, not caring which one of them gave her an answer.

"'We' aren't going to do anything," the director replied, removing his earpiece as he ended his transmission. "The GA is sending troops in to deal with this situation. After the attack on the base, this is technically their jurisdiction. The Royal House has already declared a planet-wide state of emergency and may impose martial law on the city until this mess is cleaned up."

A pang of some emotion Ziva couldn't pinpoint coursed through her stomach. As Royal General, Njo would have been responsible for any declarations of emergency or martial law, but she doubted the planet's other rulers would have allowed him to continue serving in a normal capacity after the nostium exposure. The thought drew her attention to her family, and for just a split second, she felt legitimate concern. "The Royal House?" she asked.

"Your mother and stepfather have been deemed incapacitated," Emeri replied, picking up on her apprehension. "They're both still functional following their seizures, but scans aren't looking good. The countermeasure Na's neurologists developed may help them, but since their symptoms have already manifested, chances are it's too late. Meanwhile, Royal Officer Ganten is representing the Royal House in both a law enforcement and military capacity, just as General Jaroon did after Officer Tachi's death."

Ziva began to nod but then shook her head, shoving the thoughts of her family to the back of her mind. "We need to get down there! This is our agency!"

"I know," Emeri said, "and we will. The Royal House is coordinating with our Haphor field office to send more support. For now, all we can do is wait until we have a green light from Ganten and the GA. I don't want you anywhere near that wreck until we know exactly what we're dealing with here."

Ziva paused. The way he'd said 'you'—he didn't mean HSP, he didn't even mean her team. He meant *her* specifically.

"You can't be serious!" she exclaimed. "You can't just keep me cooped up in here!"

Emeri dipped his head and sent her a look that compelled her to stand down. "Believe me, I'd love to have my best agent out there in the thick of things, but right now, your mind is your best asset. We have plenty of manpower—what we don't have is firsthand knowledge of how these people operate. You've seen that agent we brought in from Haphor. We're not going to get any information out of our prisoners, at least not soon enough. You're our best shot."

In that instant, she felt the entire weight of the planet settle on her shoulders. As much as she didn't like it, she understood why Emeri was trying to protect her. But never before had she stopped to ponder exactly how much everyone seemed to be relying on her. They may not have known about the nostium or even who she was, but the entire population of Haphez was watching, waiting for someone to do something that would fix all of this. And that someone was her.

"What do you expect me to do?" she demanded, allowing her gaze to flit over to Aura for a fraction of a second. Trying to exclude her from the loop at this point was futile; Emeri may have already explained everything to her by now anyway. She at least knew about the nostium and knew Ziva was involved, and that was enough.

"Help us coordinate our attack," the probation officer replied in a soft, calm voice that made her sound like a completely different person. "You know how to fight these people."

So she did know. "You're all severely overestimating me. I'm *not* one of them." Ziva wasn't sure if it was the newfound realization of her burden, lack of sleep, or some combination of the two, but she suddenly felt as though her legs were going to give out underneath her. She hated being the center of attention in the first place, hated having to live up to other people's smallest expectations. What they were asking of her now was nonsense—surely they had to realize that.

"It has been *ten* years," she said, clenching her teeth to keep her jaw from trembling. She hesitated, silently commanding herself to pull it together, and lowered her voice. "This is a new formula. These are new Nosti. They've had an entire decade to build and organize their forces. I fought one man."

"That's one more than any of the rest of us have fought," Emeri said.

She looked into his eyes and saw he wasn't joking. They truly wanted her at the forefront of this battle, despite the fact that she'd spent her entire career working from the shadows behind the scenes. That was where she thrived, where she could do her work with minimal interruption and outside influence. She was accountable to no one, had no one watching her, waiting for results.

They were looking at her like they expected her to be able to win this fight for them. She was their secret weapon, albeit unbeknownst to her. Had providing her brain scans not been enough? They had a countermeasure, so she'd already made a valuable defensive contribution, and a risky one at that. Anything more and the entire planet would know she was a Nosti.

The alcove where they all stood had fallen silent as she tried to wrap her head around everything they were asking of her. That silence was broken by the whimpering of children, and she turned to find a teary-eyed Sedna Tarbic approaching with Samm and Kasey in tow. The two HSP officers who had escorted her away from the distribution center trailed behind her.

"Where's my son?" the woman asked, voice steady again. "My husband?"

"Come with me," Aura said, leading Sedna and the children away. One of the officers followed.

The other, the one Ziva had addressed in Salex, stepped forward and gave her another quick salute. "Agency materials were recovered from the Tarbic residence," he said. "A couple of gear packs and research on the abduction. We packed everything up and brought it back with us for you to claim."

The thought of this man being able to keep his head despite the chaos in Salex brought Ziva a measure of comfort that, for a moment, allowed her to forget her own problems. "Good work."

"How does it look out there, officer?" Emeri asked.

For the first time, the man seemed to comprehend that he was addressing the Prime Director of HSP. "Not good, sir," he said, straightening. "We got a good look at the damage on the way in. Between the bombs and the plasma cannons, that ship obliterated everything in its path. There's a swath of damage along the river and then it cuts across the city to Headquarters."

Ziva's eyes widened at the mention of the Tranyi. "Are the homes on the river okay?"

"Hard to tell, Captain. There wasn't much left of anything out there."

She turned to Skeet and found that he'd already taken out his communicator. He entered a code and held the device to his ear for several long, uncomfortable seconds before shaking his head. "Transmission's not even going through," he said. The crease across his forehead grew deeper than ever.

It felt a little morbid, but the idea of having something important to focus on made Ziva feel better. Anything to keep her mind off the *Vigilance* and the real reasons Emeri didn't want her anywhere near it.

"Go," the director said before she even had a chance to turn and ask permission to leave. No, inform him she *was* leaving. "Go check on your house. We'll handle things here."

"I'll come with you," Skeet said.

"You have a car?" Ziva said, taking the Salex agent by the arm and dragging him along as they turned and began rushing down the corridor.

"Yes ma'am, this way." He led them back out to the landing pad from which they had just come. Another small shuttle from the Salex office sat idling next to the one Ziva had arrived in, and they angled for it.

The past two days had consisted of one blow after another. Just when it seemed like things couldn't get any worse—or, galaxy forbid, things were actually getting *better*—something else went wrong. Ziva felt the guilt hit her like a punch to the gut when she realized she hadn't even thought of Marshay and Ryon as she'd watched the bombs fall. As usual, she'd been focused almost exclusively on stopping the enemy rather than who all the victims were. Too often, victims were nameless; she by no means wanted people to die, but there was always a disconnect when they were mere strangers. She wouldn't go so far as to say she didn't care about them, but when there was no connection, she preferred to stay in combat mode, not slip into rescue mode.

But these events had been different. All the attacks had involved her, someone she was close to, or someone one of those people was close to. The same feelings that had propelled her out of the med center and to Haphor two nights ago drove her again now as the shuttle lifted from the landing pad and passed over the ruined city.

Skeet had his communicator out again and was attempting to connect to her home comm. He didn't even need to say anything; a subtle wag of his head was all it took for her to know it still wasn't working. Marshay and Ryon carried personal mobile comms but only when they were out of the house. Ziva tried these and drew the same results. She tried to convince herself that a comm tower had simply been taken out in the attack, scrambling communications, but a voice in the back of her mind quietly reminded her of far more gruesome scenarios that were more likely. That voice was rarely wrong.

Skeet once again repeated the process of initiating a transmission, waiting, and disconnecting. The look on his face told Ziva he thought it was a lost cause but that he continued trying for her benefit.

"Everyone made it back safely," he said quietly.

She watched him quizzically for a moment but caught herself when she realized she hadn't asked about Zinni, Aroska, the children, even Maston. She'd been happy to see Skeet and Emeri because they could answer her immediate questions, and that had been enough. She spent a moment silently berating herself before giving Skeet a nod of thanks and returning her communicator to her belt. If nobody had answered by now, she doubted they were going to. Turning back to face the front of the shuttle, she directed all her focus toward what she could see through the viewport.

With the faster vehicle and the air free of traffic, the journey to the homes along the Tranyi River took just under ten minutes. Columns of black smoke billowed into the morning sky at intervals, marking the path of destruction into the city. Some of the larger estates farther to the east appeared to have escaped the carnage, but her own home was located at the apex of the curve the *Vigilance* had followed as it moved toward downtown. She pointed the Salex agent in the right direction and clenched her jaw as the house came into view.

To her surprise and relief, most of the homes in the vicinity had already been blanketed in blue foam retardant. A fire car hovered half a kilometer away, working to put out some of the major structural fires as it moved into a more populated area. An emergency transport, likely from one of the small depots in this sector, was already parked on her front lawn. She wondered if Emeri had perhaps called ahead and sent someone out, though it seemed unlikely considering he was busy coordinating with the military and running HSP remotely. She swept her gaze over the scene again and fixated on a single point. No, they'd been there for a while already. Had probably just been in the area. The two occupied gurneys draped in black cloth confirmed it.

The same adrenaline and slow-motion effect she felt in the heat of combat overtook her as the shuttle touched down, but now it felt wrong, out of place. She stepped out of the ship and strode toward the emergency transport without hesitation, unnerved by how little she was feeling at the moment. The tactic worked—was useful, even—when she had a job to do, but this situation by no means fit that criteria.

One of the medics saw her and jogged over. "Is this your place, ma'am?"

"It is," Ziva replied. The response had been louder in her head. "How long have you been here?"

"Since that frigate got clear," he answered. "We were just finishing up the night shift and were on our way back to the depot when it showed up. We took cover and then headed for the nearest house to see what we could do to help. Had to wait for the fire car to get here before we could do anything."

She struggled to swallow against the lump forming in her throat and glanced past him to where his partner was pushing the gurneys onto the transport. "You found two people."

He nodded and his collected demeanor vanished for a moment, replaced with a look of sympathy. "Male subject was dead on arrival. Female subject only lasted a couple of minutes after we pulled her out. She had burns covering ninety percent of her bod—"

"I understand," Ziva said before he could continue. There was no point in spelling it out for her. "Where are you taking them?"

"The nearest med center we get cleared for. Every clinic and hospital in the region is going to have their hands full. Will you claim the bodies?"

She managed an affirmative nod.

"Thank you. I hate to be curt, but we've got a lot more people to help, so we should be going." He dipped his head and rushed away.

Ziva got one more look at the gurneys as the shield doors closed, and she realized she didn't even know which body was which. Perhaps it didn't really matter. Her eyes followed the transport until it disappeared behind a veil of smoke, then she shifted her attention to the damage before her.

She shuffled forward a couple of steps until her feet reached the edge of the crater that had swallowed the front of her house. Based on the shape, it appeared the bomb had hit the ground just meters from the front door. The kitchen and living room walls had been disintegrated along with all the furniture—and people, she realized—the rooms had contained. Marshay and Ryon were always in the kitchen at this time of morning.

The majority of the house's frame remained intact, though all the windows had been blown out and the walls that were still standing had been blackened by fire. Small patches of flames continued creeping through the ashes despite the retardant, and wisps of smoke swirled by in front of her, turning the morning sunlight an eerie orange.

On the bright side, the *Zenith* appeared unharmed; the landing bay was far enough from the house that it had escaped the brunt of the attack. On the other hand, one of the *Vigilance's* thick plasma bolts had cut straight down the center of her beloved sarmi tree's trunk, sending branches and limbs flying across the yard. Part of it had even caught fire and the pile sat there smoldering, adding more thick smoke to the cloud already hovering above the house.

*This is what you get*, that voice inside her head whispered. *The more you get attached to something, the more painful it will be to lose it.*

It was exactly what she'd been trying to explain to Aroska, the reason she worked so hard to keep the list of things and people she cared about short. The last thing she needed was to be completely debilitated by emotion when she needed to focus. But this went so far beyond that. *This*—she gave the scene another long look—was what Emeri wanted her to stop. This was the work of a single ship and wasn't even a direct result of the crew being Nosti. Somewhere out there, a whole fleet of Nosti-controlled ships was ready to do *this* to anything that got in its way, and people expected her to know how to deal with that.

Her legs finally gave out and she fell to her knees at the edge of the crater. She was certain part of it was sheer exhaustion—the thought occurred to her that she'd only slept a couple of hours in the past two days—but it also felt like she was being crushed by the weight of everything that had happened that morning and the previous night. She sat still with her arms at her sides for a moment, suffocated by the sight before her. The ability to breathe, to speak, to even think...they all eluded her. She couldn't even bring herself to shed tears, though the smoke made her eyes smart, and when she opened her mouth to release the scream she felt building inside her, no sound emerged.

Somewhere behind her, she could hear Skeet speaking quietly into his communicator, reporting the situation to someone back at the med center. She was aware of his voice, aware of the way his boots crunched in the grass but didn't come any closer. Little by little, the scents, the sounds, every visual detail—they began to register with her, bringing order to the jumbled mess in her mind. As they all came together to form one fluid image, she felt something else brewing in the pit of her stomach: sheer anger. None of the people in Noro or Salex deserved what had just happened to them. She pictured Marshay and Ryon going about their morning routine, preparing for the day and oblivious to their impending fate. She should have called them, gotten them out of the house. She should have *known*.

Her hands curled into fists and a fresh surge of adrenaline allowed her to get back to her feet. Her legs were still wobbly as she moved down into the crater and entered what was left of the house. Skeet called after her and she heard him wrapping up his conversation, but she didn't break stride

With any luck, the rooms below ground hadn't sustained much damage, but the rest of the upper floor hadn't fared so well. The fireball had consumed all the furniture and décor, leaving the space empty except for intermittent piles of charred refuse.

She passed through a gaping hole that had been her bedroom door the previous morning, and her thoughts drifted once more to Marshay and Ryon and how she'd only seen them for a couple of minutes before sending them out of the room. Her own room was still empty; if there was a silver lining to all this, it was that all her most important possessions remained outside aboard the *Zenith*. There was one last item she wanted, however, one last item that might have just become the most significant thing she owned.

Most of the decorative tiles had shattered and fallen from the charred wall across the room, exposing the hidden compartment that housed her strongbox. Aside from being just as black as everything else, it appeared to be in prime condition. The merchant she'd bought it from on Quothia had assured her it was the best-quality strongbox credits could buy on the Fringe. Supposedly, it could withstand anything short of a direct hit from a large explosive device, in which case the contents would be destroyed anyway. Even so, she held her breath as she opened it, hoping it had lived up to her expectations.

The kytara sat inside untouched along with a few credits, a plasma pistol, and several other small items she'd been carrying in her backpack on the way to Argall. She had to admire Aroska for being so thoughtful, but the idea of him so much as looking at the strongbox reminded her of the syringe and data pad he'd taken from it. The syringe and data pad that had started all of this. The syringe and data pad she should have hidden somewhere else.

"I don't even know what to say, Z."

She turned and found Skeet standing where the door had been, surveying all the damage for himself. He'd grown up an orphan, so her house had become a second home for him. Marshay and Ryon were just as much his family as they were hers.

"Me, either," she said, reaching in to remove the items from the strongbox. She pocketed the credits and tucked the gun into her waistband, then paused to examine the kytara.

"What is that?"

In response, she flicked her wrist upward, engaging the glistening blades. They were as sharp and polished as ever, despite the fact that the weapon spent nearly all of its time hidden away in a dark hole. She flicked again and the blades retracted with a soft metallic *click*.

The look on Skeet's face told her he needed no further explanation. "What are you going to do with it?"

Ziva looked down at it and shrugged. "I guess I'm going to stop Ronan."

# · 47 ·
# HSP MEDICAL CENTER
## NORO, HAPHEZ

There were a number of reasons Aroska found himself standing in Zinni's room. Perhaps the most obvious reason was that as of about twenty seconds ago, it was now his room as well. The influx of wounded people following the attack and crash had come as no surprise, and between the frantic medical personnel, HSP, and the Grand Army officials who continued arriving on the scene, the place had been transformed into a warzone. They'd moved him into Zinni's room, partly because they were colleagues, but mostly to open up space for victims who needed more immediate attention.

Maston hadn't survived the trip to Noro, they'd told him. He was still having trouble comprehending exactly what that meant. Surely his brother couldn't actually be dead, not after all the trouble he'd gone through to keep him alive there on the warehouse floor. It didn't even make sense. *Maston is dead.* He could repeat those words all he wanted, but they did little more than echo through his head for a moment before fading away. Meaningless. *What is even happening right now?*

In the event that he forgot to remind himself, Sedna had been quick to do it for him. He could still hear her wailing somewhere farther down the hall, another reason he'd opted to stay within the safety of the room. This was *his* fault, she'd cried while they stood outside the operating room where his brother had officially been pronounced dead. *He* was the one who had asked Maston to follow that ship. He'd wanted to argue, but he'd frozen up upon realizing she was right. He'd only been able to stand there listening to her scream at him. The kids had been crying too, though it was probably more out of fear and confusion than anything else. A nurse had finally escorted him to Zinni's room while Sedna was wrestled away by Aura Stannist and one of the Salex agents.

He had yet to receive any real treatment for the wound on his arm, a third reason he remained in the room. The medic had done a decent job patching him up outside the warehouse; the gash wasn't deep, but he'd been told there was damaged muscle tissue that would require a full caura treatment unless he wanted to lose mobility in his arm. Still, the injury was rather insignificant compared to nostium exposure, and he'd opted to give the children aboard his transport priority on the trip back to Noro. He'd managed to get most of Maston's blood off of him, though he imagined he still looked like *sheyss*. The only thing he could do now was wait for someone who could spare the time necessary to begin his treatment. All he wanted was to go home.

At least, that was all he'd wanted until the frigate crashed into Headquarters. It had been on their tail since leaving the distribution center, though they'd thankfully gotten enough of a head start to make it safely to the city without incident. Everyone was calling it the *Vigilance*; apparently there'd been intel aboard the wrecked ship in Salex. The word was it had dropped a series of bombs on the resort town before turning its sights on Noro. He vaguely remembered seeing Skeet leave on a transport with Zinni, but he wondered for the first time if Ziva had made it out. No, now that he thought about it, Skeet's warning about the *Vigilance* chasing them had come from Ziva, so she had to have avoided the attack. Regardless, the crash was another good reason to stay. The nurse had advised him to remain seated, so he'd moved his chair over to the window, where he had a perfect view of the *Vigilance*, the GA's ships, and all the goings-on over at HSP Headquarters.

Agent Stannist hadn't given him details, but she'd stopped by long enough to give him a quick rundown of the situation. Head-quarters—what remained of it, anyway—was on lockdown. Those who were still inside stayed inside, and nobody could get in short of Emeri himself and anyone he authorized personally. The GA was claiming jurisdiction over the crash site and the agency had relinquished control to them, at least until the situation was contained.

From Aroska's place at the window, the *Vigilance* was still hardly more than a dark shape beneath a veil of thick smoke. He couldn't actually see the ground, but he imagined any GA entry teams would have difficulty approaching the wreck until some of the rubble and debris had been cleared away. And then what? Based on its firepower capabilities, this was a military-grade ship, no doubt full of trained Resistance soldiers. Trying to infiltrate it would be like trying to infiltrate the police station in Argall, and they'd be picked off before they made it five steps inside. There was always the option of destroying it from above, though he wasn't sure if Emeri would want to risk an explosion that would damage the rest of Headquarters.

And so he watched and waited. It felt like he'd been there for hours already, though it had only been fifteen, maybe twenty minutes. The sound of Sedna's sobbing eventually died away—he wondered where she would go, what she'd tell his parents when they arrived home from Gehiri. They'd already been a bit perturbed by the way he'd distanced himself after Soren's death, so he didn't have high hopes for the way they'd handle this situation.

At least the room was quiet now. The noise of all the medical staff rushing about had morphed into a dull roar in the back of his mind. The machine providing oxygen for Zinni beeped quietly, but the sound was steady and soothing. He turned to look at her lying in the bed behind him and wasn't sure if she was unconscious or just sleeping. According to the nurse who had brought him in, she'd hit her head when the ship crashed, resulting in a mild concussion. She was malnourished and her captors had drawn a significant amount of blood over the past five weeks, leaving her in a weakened state, but once she received some nutrients and her blood cells had a chance to regenerate, she was expected to recover nicely. There were still traces of some sort of sedative in her system, the nurse had said, explaining why she was still so lethargic.

The relative silence of the room was broken by a louder and more urgent beeping, and for a moment, Aroska was unable to locate the source. He'd forgotten he was even still carrying his communicator. It began to vibrate after several more seconds of beeping and he reached down to remove it from his belt, wincing at the pain that shot through his injured arm. A glance at the incoming code allowed him to break the rest of the way out of his stupor.

"Skeet?"

"Hey."

Even after one word, Aroska could tell there was something wrong. Skeet's voice wasn't frantic or gruff, not like the voices of all the other agents responding to the crash. He sounded subdued, at a loss. Maybe even grief-stricken.

"I couldn't get through to Emeri," the lieutenant continued. "I wanted to let someone know…"

"Let someone know what?"

"It's Ziva's house. It's been hit and there's…there's not much left."

Aroska swallowed, unsure what exactly Skeet was saying. Surely he didn't mean Ziva had been *in* the house. "What?"

"It was right in the *Vigilance's* path. Most of the homes along the river have been completely destroyed."

"Marshay and Ryon?"

There was nothing but silence for a moment. "Both gone."

It was just like with Maston. Aroska could hear the words—the statement, the fact—but he still couldn't comprehend it. It meant nothing. *What is even happening right now?* All he could do was ask himself the same question over and over.

He was glad he'd obeyed the nurse and was already sitting down. At that moment, he felt the full gravity of the situation coming down on him. He'd lost his brother, but other people in the city had lost their homes, their entire families. And one of those people was someone he'd come to care a great deal about.

"And Ziva?" he managed.

"She's…just sitting there," Skeet said. His breathing quickened. "She talked to the medics like nothing was even wrong and then she just…. Her back's to me, I can't see—"

A long silence followed. Aroska was beginning to wonder if they were still connected, but he realized he could hear the whistle of the wind coming up off of the river. If the scene was bad enough to shut Skeet down, he couldn't even imagine what it must look like.

No, he took that back. He could picture everything perfectly. In his mind, he saw the vulnerable, broken Ziva he'd met on the hill the night before staring into the remains of her home, where two of the only people in the galaxy she'd actually allowed herself to care about had just been blown away. For a moment, his own loss seemed rather trivial in comparison. Maston's death had been his fault, after all. It was all his fault.

The realization that there were now hundreds—maybe even thousands—of people currently experiencing what Ziva was experiencing made him feel small in the grand scheme of things. As a veteran HSP agent, he should be focused on the Resistance and all the victims, not his own problems. A quiet voice, the same one that had once urged him to take his own life, whispered in the back of his mind, reminding him that he could never do anything right. *You're wrong again. Now's not the time to be selfish.*

"Skeet?" he said, hoping to drown out that voice with his own.

"She's going inside," Skeet replied quickly as if he'd been jolted awake from a dream. He shouted for Ziva to wait up. "I'd better catch up with her. You might fill Emeri in if you see him."

"I will," Aroska said. There was another long silence before the transmission went dead.

He returned the communicator to his belt and stole another glance at Zinni before turning back to the window. The smoke shrouding the *Vigilance* was finally starting to clear, and the GA gunships were moving in closer.

For the first time, he wanted to be down there, fighting beside the ground marines, cutting down these cowardly Resistance dogs. His arm was stiff and sore, but the overwhelming grief he'd been feeling had been replaced with a new anger that trumped the pain. But regardless of how the injury felt, it would slow him down in a battle, whether he realized it or not. And with the emotional turmoil he'd suffered through since bringing Ziva to Salex, he knew his body and mind were in no condition to fight. He thought back to the way Ziva had tried to go after Dasaro on Chaiavis. Mindset had been her biggest problem; she'd claimed she'd thought things through, but he knew she hadn't, and least not in the right way. He refused to make the same mistake now. He'd take action—there was no question about it—but first he would rest, allow his arm to be treated, and take that time to come up with a plan. Then, Ronan and the Resistance would pay for what they'd done. To him, to Ziva, to Zinni, to Kat, to everyone.

He settled back in the chair, content with his decision, and stared out at the *Vigilance* in hopes of keeping his mind off the events of the morning and shutting those awful whispers out of his head. A couple of nurses rushed in and out periodically to make sure Zinni was still stable, each taking the time to apologize for how long it was taking to get him some help.

"It's fine," he assured them both, leaving out the fact that a longer wait gave him more time to come up with a plan. "Help the people who need it."

He sat quietly, watching as crews began clearing out the rubble around the *Vigilance* while the gunships provided aerial protection. GA troops had been dropped in and currently surrounded the vessel with their weapons up and ready. There was still no indication of how they expected to breach the ship, but it appeared the time to do so was drawing near.

He had been sitting there for close to two hours before he heard heavy footsteps enter the room and stop. He turned to find Ziva standing in the doorway. She was looking at Zinni but shifted her gaze to him when he stood up.

"What are you doing here?" The shock he felt upon seeing her had given his tone a nasty bite he instantly regretted.

She produced a data pad and extended it toward him. "Debrief about what went down in Salex. I already compiled all of my information. Add yours and make sure this gets to Emeri."

For a moment, he wasn't sure if he'd heard her correctly. She had to be joking—this was not the same Ziva he'd been picturing what seemed like only minutes before. She'd just lost her home and all her possessions, he'd just had another brother die before his eyes, and here she was worried about paperwork.

This time, the tone wasn't an accident. "You don't waste any time, do you?"

"Yeah, well, I had nothing better to do," she muttered, offering him the pad again.

He reluctantly reached for it. "You're insane. You just lost everything! You should be grieving right now!"

She tightened her grip on the pad and stepped closer, eyes burning. "Do *not* tell me what I should or shouldn't be doing," she said through her teeth. Her voice wavered and the tears appeared for a split second. Then she blinked and they were gone.

The display of emotion, however brief, gave him a flicker of hope. She was feeling something, but as usual, she was working hard to keep it buried. With everything that was going on and with everything that still needed to be done, maybe that was for the best. Aroska found himself wishing he were capable of doing the same.

She finally released the data pad and turned away, taking several seconds to observe Zinni again before heaving a sigh. "The GA has given the crew of the *Vigilance* several opportunities to surrender and come out," she said. "They just received their final warning. If they don't surrender within another hour, we'll take action."

"What's the plan?" Aroska ventured, giving up on changing the subject.

"Gas," she replied, her voice low and monotone.

The look in her eyes was the same one he'd seen the first day they'd met in Emeri's office: a horrible, vicious, and unwavering stare that told him her thoughts consisted of nothing but malice. He could tell it wasn't directed at him this time around, but it was disconcerting all the same.

"We'll beat them at their own game," she continued. "The agency is hoping to flush some of them out, maybe take a few into custody for interrogation. If you ask me, we should make sure they *can't* get out. The fewer survivors, the fewer potential Nosti we'll have to deal with. Besides, you saw those guys in the warehouse—they were ready to shoot themselves to avoid capture. We're not going to get anything out of these people. We've already got the prisoners from Salex. They'll have to be enough."

Part of him wanted to chastise her for her apparent eagerness to take so many lives. A ship the size of the *Vigilance* probably supported a crew of nearly two hundred. But another part of him agreed wholeheartedly. If even half of that crew were Nosti, he wasn't sure how well the Haphezian forces would hold up against them. Perhaps, in a way, it would be their own fault if they died. When the gas was released into the ship, they'd still have a chance to get out. If they chose to stay inside and die so that any secrets died with them, that was perfectly fine with him.

"Where are you headed?" he asked.

That hateful look in Ziva's eyes morphed into one of simple frustration. "Emeri doesn't want me down by the wreck at all, so I'm joining up with one of the sniper units they've got watching the ship. Skeet's tagging along with the ground teams even though the GA is running point. Someone's got to watch his back." She turned and resumed her journey toward the door.

Aroska wasn't sure if that had been some sort of irrational jab at the fact that both he and Zinni were still incapacitated or a mere observation. Given her level of impatience, he wouldn't have put the former past her, but he deemed it the latter and watched her go. "Be careful."

She waved her hand—either an acknowledgement or an irritated dismissal of his warning—without looking back and disappeared in the hustle and bustle of the corridor.

He stared at the empty doorway for several more seconds before glancing at Zinni again and lowering himself back into the chair. There he sat for the remainder of the morning, watching the activity over at HSP and doing everything in his power to keep his own thoughts from eating him alive.

# · 48 ·
# HSP Headquarters
## Noro, Haphez

A n hour passed. Skeet could feel the marines around him tense up the moment the countdown reached zero. He reestablished his grip on his assault rifle and watched as everyone else did the same. He doubted there was really any point; the *Vigilance's* crew wasn't coming out. It was probably for the best. Like Ziva, he wasn't sure how well he and the rest of the soldiers would hold up if most or all of the crew turned out to be Nosti, even if numbers were on their side.

He looked up to observe the approach of another GA ship and saw the sun reflect off the scope of a sniper rifle on one of the nearby rooftops. He didn't know where Ziva had been positioned, but just knowing she was up there somewhere brought him indescribable comfort. If the Resistance crew did emerge and put up a fight, the sniper units would likely be able to dispatch them with little trouble.

The ship that had just arrived was designed for in-atmo combat and, as such, had guns outfitted for both plasma and massive, armor-piercing projectiles. According to the GA, the plan was to arm several of those projectiles with large gas canisters rather than incendiary or explosive devices and fire them at key points in the *Vigilance's* hull. With the Res ship's defenses offline, they should have no trouble penetrating and would be capable of affecting a much higher number of people than any handheld devices. Skeet had to admit the use of gas was a little barbaric, but so was everything the Resistance had done to them. Entering the ship simply wasn't an option unless they wanted to be picked off one by one. Forcing the crew out was the only way to go; they could either come out and risk capture or stay inside and die. The choice would be theirs.

"Pull back!" someone ordered.

Skeet turned to locate the speaker and saw Sergeant Anden Fay moving toward him. He vaguely remembered meeting the man when he and Zinni had emerged from Dakiti's sewers with Jayden Saiffe and Jole Imetsi in tow. Fay's title had been Sergeant Major back then, if he recalled—the demotion must have been a result of the court martial Ziva had mentioned when she'd told them about meeting Kevyn Sheen on Na. Fay commanded the small group of marines Skeet had fallen in with, and he was glad to see a familiar face when there were so many unknown factors at play.

He and the other soldiers complied, retreating back several paces while the GA ship settled into position overhead. Similar clusters of troops did the same elsewhere in the vicinity, giving the *Vigilance* a wide berth but keeping their perimeter intact. Everyone remained quiet while the Resistance crew received one last warning. As before, it fell on deaf ears, and the destroyer opened fire.

Over the course of the next few minutes, the ship drifted in a slow circle around the *Vigilance*, firing the heavy projectiles into the Resistance vessel's hull at several points the GA had identified as being vulnerable. There was no way to know where the crew was or how many people were inside—any infrared scans had been blocked by the heat shielding built into the ship's armor—but they'd managed to pick out five different locations predicted to result in maximum gas dispersal. Chances were it wouldn't affect every single person and any entry teams might still have to put up a fight, but the odds were certainly now in their favor.

The final projectile tore into the *Vigilance* as if the ship were made of cloth. Every soldier fell silent, eyes peeled for any sign of movement. There were two large airlock doors, one on either side of the ship, as well as a number of small openings that had once housed escape pods. According to Fay, they had been jettisoned elsewhere in the city and troops had been dispatched to investigate them. Skeet had a feeling they wouldn't find anything of use. Nobody would survive an escape pod ejection at such a low altitude; they were likely decoys, possibly even used intentionally as weapons. He only hoped nobody had been able to crawl out through the empty bays, which had been conveniently hidden behind a thick cloud of smoke for at least twenty minutes following the crash.

Several minutes passed and nothing happened. The gas was supposed to be fast-acting, slower than the gaseous nostium that had been used against the Royal General but quick enough to kill anyone who didn't immediately escape exposure. In the event that the gas was utilized, they'd been ordered to wait ten minutes before entering the ship. Some of the soldiers were already putting on their gas masks.

The small demolitions unit moved forward and climbed a makeshift ramp up to the airlock. They positioned their charges around the door and stepped back to wait. There was another palpable shift in the crowd of soldiers as the ten-minute countdown came to an end. The unbearable silence was shattered as the charges detonated and the airlock door blew inward.

Skeet could feel beads of perspiration forming on his forehead as he waited for something—anything—to happen. The demolitions crew cleared out quickly, making room for the first entry team to take position at the base of the ramp. A thin cloud of smoke and residual gas drifted out the airlock, dispersing in the crisp mid-morning air.

*There.* A glint. Something metallic reflecting the light. A figure approaching through the haze. The view of the woman became clear after a moment. She staggered out, coughing and sputtering, her skin a sickly pale green. It appeared as though she was struggling to even remain upright. She was dressed in lightweight but functional black armor, and whatever metallic object she'd been carrying had vanished, replaced with a narrow black bar about the length of her forearm. She held it up as if signaling surrender and allowed the soldiers to approach, doing her best to lower herself to her knees when they ordered her to do so.

Everything after that happened so fast that Skeet didn't even process it all until a few seconds later. The woman had still been holding the bar and she'd jerked her arm in a strange fashion, though the significance of the act hadn't registered with him at the time. Then the discharge of a plasma rifle echoed through the air and the woman crumpled to the ground with a smoldering hole through her chest. Skeet's first thought had been that overwatch was getting just as trigger-happy as the troops on the ground, but then he noticed the long silver blades now protruding from either end of the black bar. The only shooter who would have been able to discern the woman's true intentions, he knew, was Ziva. He risked a peek over his shoulder, tracing the plasma bolt's trajectory with his eyes, and could make out several figures perched on one of the spec ops building's landing platforms. He wanted to offer her a salute but figured she wouldn't notice with her focus on her scope. Fay's voice distracted him anyway.

"Bastards. I'd hoped we could take some of them alive, even after the gas. But not if they're all going to pull *sheyss* like that."

At this point, Skeet welcomed the thought of no survivors. There were already too many Nosti at HSP Headquarters, none of whom were any more willing to talk than the others. And up until this morning, the Grand Army had been busy prepping for a full-scale assault on Forus. Several recon ships were already on their way there. There was no point in capturing any more of these people.

"New orders from Officer Ganten," Fay said, turning to address their little group as he listened to the voice in his earpiece. "Shoot to kill, take no prisoners. We gave these people a chance and they didn't take it."

On cue, the clusters of soldiers—with the occasional HSP agent mixed in—began to converge on the ship, watching carefully for any more movement as the smoke faded. Skeet secured his own gas mask over his face and pulled his goggles down, giving his eyes a moment to adjust to the holographic readouts inside the lenses. They were mostly meant to protect him from the gas, but if the interior of the *Vigilance* was dark or still cloudy, they'd be a great help in locating enemies.

His group was the third to enter through this particular airlock. A few teams remained outside to watch the escape pod bays and prevent any other kind of trouble that might arise. It felt good to finally be doing something; he'd spent most of the previous afternoon in the interrogation room with the Nosti prisoner from Haphor, and by the time he'd made it to Salex in the wee hours of the morning, he'd missed all the action. Upon leaving Ziva's house earlier, the two of them had stopped to assist other HSP units throughout the city, but it wasn't how he wanted to be spending his time. He knew he was contributing, but the heat of battle was where he could actually see and feel the results of his work.

They'd been ordered to travel in pairs upon entering the ship, so he followed Fay down the main corridor to a narrow stairwell leading up to the next deck. With the number of soldiers they'd brought in, it wouldn't take long to search the entire vessel. What they really needed was a manifest to which they could compare the death toll. It might shed some light on who exactly they were dealing with, as well as whether there was anyone missing.

The hallway was already littered with the bodies of men and women dressed in black armored uniforms identical to what the woman outside had worn. Some still clutched various firearms, while others grasped retracted kytaras. Skeet had never seen one in action, but even after the quick glimpse he'd caught of Ziva's, it was obvious they were lethal in experienced hands. He dreaded to think of the damage that woman could have caused on the ramp had she not been shot. Ziva obviously knew, and he was once again glad to have had her watching his back.

"Live one," Fay said quietly, his voice muffled and mechanical behind the gas mask.

Skeet looked ahead to where he had indicated and saw that one of the figures slumped against the wall was still moving. The man clutched at his chest, sucking in raspy breaths through blue lips. He mumbled something that sounded like a plea for help.

"Put him out of his misery," Skeet muttered.

Fay grunted in agreement and fired a plasma bolt through the struggling man's head. Occasional shots could be heard elsewhere throughout the ship, some exchanges longer than others whenever any survivors tried to put up a fight. The presence of those survivors meant someone had gotten ahold of gas masks; there was no doubt enough breathing apparatus aboard for the entire crew, but clearly not everyone had managed to get their hands on it.

The entire ship was tilted to one side, making footing rather tricky. Some of the bodies had begun to slide down the incline, piling up against one wall. Skeet's goggles were still registering their heat signatures, indicating they had expired only minutes before.

"Seen any officers yet?" he asked, glancing at the uniforms of every person he passed. All appeared to be some level of petty officer, with the occasional ensign thrown in. Nobody of significant rank.

"Negative," Fay replied, pausing in front of a small storage room. He hit the controls and stepped aside, allowing Skeet to clear the space. It was empty.

They continued forward, easing past the gaping hole one of the massive projectiles had torn in the hull. It had embedded itself in the deck below, enabling the gas to disperse on both levels. The majority of the people they'd passed had probably been claimed by this single canister. Five had been more than enough to do the job.

The two of them broke out into a large space full of workstations and consoles that appeared to be the bridge. There were fewer bodies there than Skeet had expected. Most of the crew had been positioned in or near the airlock corridors, waiting to cut down any entry teams. The tactic would have worked if not for the gas. Another projectile had entered through the front viewport and still lay in the middle of the ruined floor with a thin trail of brown smoke drifting out of it. Several GA soldiers had already arrived on the scene and were investigating the consoles.

"Here," Fay said, gesturing toward an elevator at the rear of the room.

Skeet forced the door open and peered up the narrow shaft to where the elevator car remained parked another two levels up. The few onboard systems that were still online were running on emergency power, so there was no way to call it back down. The last passenger had to have taken it up just before the ship crashed.

He stepped back and found a hatch nearby. Inside was a slender staircase with steps so steep it was practically a ladder. He secured his rifle strap over his shoulder, beckoning for Fay to follow as he ducked inside and began to climb.

The first of the two levels separating them from the elevator car appeared to be office spaces and crew quarters. Skeet could hear the voices of some of the GA troops as he and Fay climbed past, eyes fixed on the level above.

The uppermost level was significantly smaller. Two doors stood open on their right, revealing cramped officers' cabins. A larger door, this one only partially opened, was positioned farther to the left. They made their way toward it, weapons up, and took cautious looks inside. The room was bigger than the others, though still compact; a quick look around was enough to confirm nobody was there.

"Captain's cabin," Fay observed.

Skeet nodded and looked over the large communications console and workbench the other rooms lacked. The information stored on the comm console would no doubt provide them with some answers. A wide viewport took up the majority of one wall. All he could see through it now was dust and smoke, but he imagined the view must be spectacular while traveling through open space.

When he stopped and thought about it for a moment, he realized the room smelled faintly like Ziva. The idea perplexed him, but then he wondered if it was the other way around—Ziva smelled like the room. Maybe, for all these years, he'd somehow been smelling traces of the nostium in her body. The prisoner from Haphor had smelled so strongly of blood thanks to the wound on his leg, but now that Skeet thought about it, there'd been something strangely familiar about his scent as well. Taking all that into consideration, the occupant of this room was most definitely a Nosti.

He voiced his thoughts to Fay, who was poking at a piece of clothing on the bunk with the barrel of his rifle. The man grunted in response and beckoned for him to approach. "Take a look at this."

The jacket was black and reinforced with flexible armor like what the rest of the crew had been wearing, but the shields on the shoulders were what caught Skeet's eye. "Commander," he said, lifting an eyebrow.

Fay set his rifle down and picked up the jacket to get a better look. "The question is, where is he?" He studied the cut of the garment through narrowed eyes for a moment. "*She*," he corrected himself. "The data from the *Titania* mentioned a Commander Payne. This must be her."

"No sign of one of those swords," Skeet pointed out. "If she has one, she must have it with her."

It was as if they both had the same thought simultaneously. On cue, they each moved back to the door and peered down another narrow corridor that hadn't been visible from the stairwell. At the end, one of the escape pod hatches stood open, revealing another empty bay. Beyond that lay the smoky sky and structures of the city.

Skeet sighed as his mind drifted back to what he'd been pondering outside. That twenty, twenty-five minutes of blindness immediately following the attack...the chaos that had ensued.... If anyone had left the ship during that time, they'd have no idea. And those people would be long gone by now.

Fay vocalized Skeet's thoughts perfectly as he spoke to his superiors over the comm. "Yes, sir. There's a Nosti commander loose in Noro."

# · 49 ·
# RIVER DISTRICT MEDICAL CENTER
## NORO, HAPHEZ

B y the time Ziva exited the small med center in the residential sector of the city, night had fallen. After an entire day of bright lights, raised voices, gunfire, and constant movement, the dark and stillness felt heavenly. She paused on the steps, shutting out all thoughts of the two charred corpses she'd just identified inside, and allowed herself a brief respite.

It was tempting to just sit down then and there and not get up. Aside from the time she'd spent behind the scope of a rifle and behind the controls of a vehicle, it felt like she'd been on her feet all day. One of those raised voices had been Emeri's as he'd finally ordered her to go get some rest. She hadn't wanted to leave Headquarters or the HSP med center; there was still way too much happening. Commander Payne was still at large. The *Vigilance* still lay in the middle of the HSP campus. There were still Resistance bodies that needed to be dealt with. Wounded were still pouring in from around the city. Half of Salex had been destroyed. These things kept her fueled, bolstered her desire to keep working, but she'd also done the math and realized she had nowhere to go if she left. Her home was in shambles, and the two people who had made it anything more than just a house were gone. She needed to keep herself moving.

There was no possible way she could fix all of these problems herself, and when she reminded herself of that, she was almost okay with taking a break. But taking a break also meant unplugging herself from the energy source—the mental outlet—she'd been relying on to carry her through the day. Things had slowed down to the point that she could once again hear herself think. Under any other circumstances, she would have been fine with that, but considering the situation and everything that had happened in the past day, it was the last thing she wanted.

She forced her feet to descend the remaining steps, angling for the unmarked HSP groundcar she'd borrowed. She slid into the pilot's seat, sitting in silence for a long time before pulling the vehicle out into the street. The Royal House had gone ahead and placed certain sectors of the city under martial law while the GA and HSP searched for Payne and the *Vigilance's* other ranking officers, so traffic was minimal. According to the crew manifest someone had pulled from the ship's logs, there were at least twenty people missing, all of them likely Nosti. Any humans unfortunate enough to be passing through the city were immediately searched, and some even detained and tested. Only one lieutenant had been found so far, and he'd been thrown into an empty cell in the depths of HSP's detention wing like the crew of the *Titania*.

So far, none of them had been willing to talk, despite being hounded by Adin, Skeet, several of the GA's favorite interrogators, and even Emeri himself all afternoon. Ziva had to give them credit; short of HSP's best ops agents, she'd never seen any soldiers so adept at withstanding questioning. But it was also terrifying, because it meant whatever Ronan was planning was big enough that they were willing to take their own lives to keep it secret.

They'd find out what that secret was soon enough. Despite the detour planetside to deal with the *Vigilance*, the GA had spent most of the day mobilizing a good portion of their fleet and were scheduled to depart for Forus sometime the next day. At this point, they were merely waiting to hear back from their scout ships, which had taken off for stealth recon immediately following the crash of the *Titania*. Ziva planned on taking part in any assault on the Resistance base whether Emeri liked it or not, so she imagined it wouldn't hurt to get a little rest now after all. The *Intrepid* was still docked somewhere at HSP, and the

*Zenith* remained in her private landing bay. One of them would serve as a fine temporary home. She only hoped sleep—or, if not sleep, thoughts of the upcoming battle—would be enough to block everything else out of her mind.

She'd been flying for close to fifteen minutes before she realized she didn't know where she was going. It wasn't that she was lost; the scenery, despite being dark, was perfectly familiar. She just wasn't sure what she was doing there. Ahead on the left, she saw the abandoned house, still empty, where she'd hidden while on the run from Dasaro. Directly across from it sat another house that had turned into a sanctuary for her, a place for recuperating and building a trust that had eventually saved her life. Aroska's house.

A quiet growl escaped her throat as she pulled over and shut the engine off, giving herself a moment to clear her head. Part of her was still furious with the man for dragging her to Salex in the first place and tricking her into coming up to the hill with him, but then she'd been so short with him at the warehouse and the med center. As much as she hated apologies, she probably owed him one. He was hurting, and now that she had no work to throw herself into, she was starting to hurt as well. There was still an hour left until the curfew the GA had established, so perhaps it wouldn't hurt to go check in on him. And perhaps she'd ended up here because she'd subconsciously been thinking it might be nice to have someone to talk to.

She sat and observed his house for a moment, puzzled by the number of vehicles parked outside and the people coming and going. None of them looked familiar, and she doubted Aroska would want much company after the day he'd had. A thought struck her, and she reached over to log into the car's mobile terminal. She'd spent plenty of time pondering the way he was trying to get a fresh start, but she hadn't considered the possibility that might have included moving. *Leave the old behind*, she thought, entering her spec ops credentials and bringing up her unit's personnel files. *Leave behind the lingering stench of govino and alcohol and the memory of his near suicide.*

As she'd suspected, a new address appeared on his profile: an apartment building in a nice area closer to downtown. She started the car back up and pulled out into the street. There'd be plenty of time to get there, see how he was holding up, and make it back to one of her ships before the curfew was enforced. She was technically exempt from it thanks to her rank at HSP, but it wouldn't keep any overzealous GA officers from stopping her and bombarding her with questions. After everything that had happened that day, that was the last thing she wanted to deal with.

It took a mere ten minutes to reach the apartment building. It was a newer structure, at least thirty stories tall, with an exterior that appeared to be made primarily of glass. She imagined all the tenants had a great view of the city, regardless of what floor they lived on. It was also only a couple of blocks from the nearly identical building Skeet lived in. Perhaps that had been part of its appeal. Maston may have been Aroska's prime source of support, but she had no doubt that Skeet and Zinni had had a hand in his recovery as well.

She checked the apartment number on the display one more time before logging out of the computer and shutting the car off again. She left the vehicle in one of the complex's lower-level parking bays and made her way to the elevator, riding it up to the twenty-sixth floor. Aroska's apartment was located halfway down the long hallway. She paused at the door for a moment before knocking, able to hear muted voices within. It seemed Tarbic already had a visitor.

The door slid open in response to her knock, and she found Adin Woro standing there. He perked up a bit upon seeing her and opened the door wider to allow her entry. "Ziva. Glad to see you're safe. When we heard about Salex this morning, we feared the worst."

It was the same thing he'd said to her upon her arrival home from Na. "Thanks," she muttered, wondering how much time he and his team actually spent worried about her safety.

"What brings you here?"

She peered past him to where Aroska was standing across the room, gazing out the window. He'd glanced her way when she'd come in, but he turned away when he saw she was looking.

"Just need to do a quick debrief about everything that went down in Salex," she said, unsure why exactly she felt compelled to lie.

Adin looked at her as if he thought the idea was ludicrous, but he heaved a sigh and made no comment.

"How is he?" she asked quietly.

"I think he'll be okay," he said, lowering his voice and throwing a quick glance in Aroska's direction. "Docs were only able to administer caura treatment a couple of hours ago. He sat in that med center waiting all day. Finally started doing what he could to help out, and someone took notice of him. He seemed to be fine with it, but it pissed me off. They ended up having to put him through a second round of treatment to make sure there was no permanent muscle damage."

*That's life*, Ziva thought, though she said nothing. There were hundreds of people who had been crushed by rubble or hit by one of the bombs and needed immediate, thorough attention. A graze from a plasma bolt—even a deep one—was low-priority relative to everything else. Still, she was glad Adin was so concerned about his friend; the galaxy only knew how much Aroska needed the support.

"I checked all the cupboards," Adin continued, nearly whispering this time. "Didn't find anything. With all the *sheyss* he's seen today I was afraid he'd want to start up again."

It took her a split second to realize what he was talking about, and she nodded her approval. "Good idea. He's lucky to have you looking out for him."

"I only wish I could have been here for him before. I had no idea things were so bad." He watched Aroska for a few seconds then sighed. "Well, I was just heading out anyway. I'll leave you to your *debrief*."

The way he emphasized the word told Ziva he didn't approve of her timing. Part of her didn't care what he thought, and part of her was glad she wasn't actually there to dredge up memories of that morning. But despite the sting in his words, he offered her a sympathetic dip of his head before exiting.

The door slid shut behind him, throwing the apartment into silence. She sat down in a chair facing the massive window; the night-time view of the Noro skyline was truly spectacular, though it made her uncomfortable to be so exposed to anyone looking in. Aroska remained in his place across the room, staring out at the city lights with his right arm against the glass. She couldn't see his face, but his sagging shoulders spoke volumes. His left elbow rested in a sling, immobilizing his injured arm until the caura treatment had run its course.

"Considering you already gave me the debrief paperwork, you've either lost your mind or that's not actually why you're here." It was the first time he'd spoken since she'd arrived.

She looked up, surprised to find that he still wasn't looking at her. *I've got nowhere else to go*, she thought. That wasn't exactly accurate—she could have just stuck to her plan and returned to her house to settle into the *Zenith*. But somehow being there and knowing nothing would ever be the same seemed unappealing. She thought of the way she'd arrived at his old home without even meaning to. She hated to admit it, but she was running away. That's what she was doing here.

"How are you feeling?" she asked, not prepared to admit how lost she felt.

Several seconds passed before Aroska made any move to respond. "I guess I can take this thing off now," he sighed, sliding the sling's strap off his shoulder. A thick white bandage protruded from under his shirt sleeve.

He reminded Ziva a lot of herself when he was angry. "That doesn't answer my question," she said.

"How do you *think* I feel?" he snapped, choking on his words.

"You should be with your family."

"Yeah, well, they're not exactly my biggest fans right now. Not now that I've gotten another brother killed."

His words took her by surprise. She hated to say 'I told you so' in this situation, but she *had* warned him not to involve Maston. But this was the first time she'd ever heard him try to take credit for Soren's death. He was talking nonsense, of course—she alone was responsible for killing Soren. These were his emotions talking.

"What do you mean?" she asked, certain he knew which brother she was talking about.

"It was my fault he was even out that day. I should've known better than to bring him out in the open before I knew for sure whether he'd been cleared. I was overconfident, too proud of the fact that I'd managed to find that evidence."

She had to admit they were valid points, though they were things she'd never expected him to say. In the end, she'd been the one to pull the trigger, but if anyone were truly at fault, it was the agent who had asked her to take his place.

"I'm going to ask you one more time, Ziva," he said. "What are you doing here?"

She folded her hands in front of her mouth, fixing her eyes on the blinking light on the top of a distant building. "I don't know," she said.

That caught his attention. Without looking up, she sensed him turn and face her for the first time. She continued to sit in silence, kicking herself for even mentioning such a thing.

"What's that supposed to mean?"

She allowed her gaze to flit over to him for a moment. "It means I don't want to be here, but I don't want to be anywhere else. And I can't very well go home, can I?"

It was hard to read him. His face seemed devoid of all emotion, or maybe it was so full of emotion that it was impossible to tell which one he was actually showing. His eyes lingered on her for a moment before he turned back to the window. "I'm sorry for your loss."

For some reason, it struck her as a ridiculous thing to say, considering his circumstances. "Well, it was bound to happen sometime."

Aroska made a noise that sounded like a cross between a cough and a chuckle, a sound that told her he was on the verge of a meltdown. "I cannot believe you just said that."

Her eyebrows slid together. "What?"

"*Sheyss*, Ziva, what's wrong with you? What do you do, meet someone and then immediately start counting down to the day they die? That's disgusting."

"I can't let it take me by surprise," she retorted, rising to her feet and forcing the words out of her mouth. Forcing herself to believe them. "I need to make sure I've got nothing to lose."

He shook his head. "Just when I was starting to think you weren't a heartless *shouka*."

"I told you before, Aroska. Anyone who gets close to me is signing their own death warrant. Someone is going to wind up hurting them if I don't somehow do it first."

"Are you kidding me? That attack left half the city in ruins. You weren't the target. It had nothing to do with you."

"It's my fault the Resistance came here to begin with!"

"How do you figure?"

"I'm the one who told Kat I'd find Ronan. I'm the one who brought that data pad home for you to find."

"Do you have any idea how ridiculous that sounds?" Tears threatened to spill down his face, but his voice was steady. "You know, I've always admired you for seeming so selfless and shifting the blame to yourself, but then I got to thinking—" he turned around to address her directly, and his eyes were colder than she'd ever seen them "—maybe you just can't stand the thought of everything not being about *you*."

"What the hell does that mean?" she spat.

"You're telling me anyone who chooses to get close to you will get hurt because of it. You ever stop and think that maybe things just happen? Maybe people make choices that have nothing to do with what you've said or done to them? You blame yourself for anything that happens, good or bad. You can't be responsible for everything. You can't *control* everything."

She folded her arms. "But it's okay for you to blame yourself for what happened to Maston? Maybe it was *his choice* to help us."

She'd caught him. His mouth hung open for a moment, his next words frozen on his tongue. He had a lot of nerve calling her a hypocrite when he was doing the same thing.

"That was different," he said quickly.

"Not really."

"Yes, Ziva, it was! I specifically told him to go to that warehouse. He was there because I asked him to be."

"No, you told him to follow the *Titania*. You know he would have ended up at the warehouse anyway when he found out Ronan's men were there."

Once again, she'd cornered him. He spun on his heel and stormed back to his place at the window, slamming a fist against the glass. He was probably right about her, about the way she tried to blame herself for everything, but somehow it always felt better to try to take the credit for mishaps rather than admit something was totally out of her control.

The room was silent for a long time. Ziva sat back down and rested her elbows on her knees, staring at the floor while Aroska stared out the window. When it came down to it, she wasn't sure which one of them had lost more. Granted, Zinni was still alive, but right now, there was still no way to know if she'd be able to serve in the field again. All the homes along the cliff overlooking the river had been completely obliterated on top of that, along with their occupants. So she had lost her home, possessions, and two people she considered family, and one of her only true friends was potentially incapacitated. Aroska had lost a member of his actual family, his own flesh and blood, but Zinni had become just as much of a member of his team as she had Ziva's, and Marshay and Ryon had treated him like family from the outset. So maybe they were equal after all. She kicked herself for even trying to make a contest out of it.

It was Aroska who finally broke the silence. "When we first went into that warehouse," he said, so quietly that it took her a moment to realize he was speaking to her, "my first instinct was to run to my brother. I didn't at first, but not because we were taking fire. It wasn't a survival instinct or a sense of duty that held me back. No, I was standing there thinking, 'What would Ziva think?'" He turned to look at her. "'What would Ziva think if I abandon the mission to save my brother?'"

She forced a half-hearted smirk and snorted. "Since when do you give a damn what I think?"

"That's what I finally realized," he said. "That's when I was able to go to him."

"That's when you got yourself shot," she corrected him.

Those tears welling up in his eyes finally broke free, but his voice still didn't falter. "You know, I didn't even realize I'd been hit until it was all over." He sighed. "It was you, wasn't it?"

She nodded, biting the inside of her lip to keep from calling him out on his reckless actions. He'd suffered enough already. "It was stupid of you," she said. "You're lucky."

He shook his head. "I get it, okay? I get why you're always so adamant about not getting close to anyone. When you love someone, you can't make rational decisions. Can't think clearly. You wind up getting hurt." He balled his hands up and clenched his jaw, trying hard not to yell. "But damn it, what the hell did you expect me to do?"

Every instinct she had wanted to scream that he should have followed protocol, should have cleared the area before proceeding. But some part of her, deep down, understood why he'd done what he'd done. It was hardly more than a flicker, but it was enough to make her hesitate before responding.

Aroska sighed. Either he already knew her answer, or he hadn't been expecting her to actually give him one. "Well, we did decide it was your turn to shoot me."

He had a point. "I'm not sure if this counts," she said.

Once more, everything was quiet. Ziva tried her best to put herself in his position. Who did she care about enough that she'd run blindly into the line of fire to save—Skeet, Zinni, *him*? She tried to convince herself that she'd put the mission first, as failure to complete it would no doubt result in death anyway, but in all reality, she wasn't sure. It would depend on the circumstances, she decided. How many hostiles were there? Where had her comrade fallen? How much backup and firepower did she have? Yes, it would just depend.

The discomfort of being there was taking its toll on her, but she didn't know where else to go. The idea of returning to her ship had completely lost its charm. She stood up and angled toward the door, concerned by the fact that she felt so...well, *concerned.*

"Where are you going?" Aroska asked.

*Anywhere other than here*, she thought. "I don't know."

"Don't go."

It took her a moment to realize what he'd said, as it was the last thing she'd ever expected him to say. She hesitated a moment, unnerved and confused by the request. She thought he'd made it clear that he didn't want her there, but when she turned around, she found his glistening eyes pleading with her to stay.

She shrugged and took several steps back into the room. "What do you want me to do?" she demanded, hoping for his sake that she hadn't sounded quite as harsh as she'd initially meant to.

He was clearly hurt, and she kicked herself for making the situation worse. "Everything happened so fast at the warehouse," he said, pulling away from the window. "I'm not the only one who lost something today. I kept thinking...why should I get to grieve when other people lost so much, too? Why should I get to grieve when *you're* the one who lost everything you own?"

The idea that he'd been spending all his time being concerned about her seemed preposterous, but the thought sent a tingle through her body and she suddenly felt very cold. "That's ridiculous," she muttered.

He shuffled toward her, head hanging as he rubbed the bandage on his arm. "I know that now. I just need some time to let it all sink in, and I didn't want to do it alone. Adin is one of my closest friends, but there's no way he could really understand. I'm glad you came by."

How he expected her to help, Ziva had no earthly idea. She wasn't sure what to say, and she had no intention of sitting there listening to him cry. "Do what you need to do, then," she said, her words little more than a choked whisper.

He nodded and wiped the heels of his hands across his eyes. "Thank you for understanding."

He advanced suddenly, closing the remaining distance between them in less than a second. Ziva went rigid as the events from Kat's garage flashed through her memory, but instead of the startling sensation of his lips meeting hers, she felt his arms slide around her shoulders and pull her closer. Trapped there against his body with his arms around her, she felt panic encroaching and her thoughts began to run rampant. It took her racing mind a while to register that this was a simple hug.

*What do you want from me*, she thought, unsure what she could possibly do to make him feel better. Consoling and comforting weren't in her nature—certainly he was aware of that—and it didn't help that all she could do was stand there, frozen.

He wrapped his arms around her even tighter, making it impossible for her to adjust her position even if she'd wanted to. "I'm sorry," he whispered. His voice finally cracked. "I am so, so sorry."

She didn't know what he could possibly be sorry for, especially since he'd just finished telling her he was done feeling sorry for anyone but himself. They stood there in silence for what seemed like a long time, though it had only been a few seconds. Unsure what else to do, she shakily slid her arms around his torso, even going so far as to clasp her hands behind his back.

She was no good at this and he knew it. And yet, of all people, he'd said he was glad *she* was there, even though he knew she was uncomfortable and incapable of bringing him the forgiving sympathy he wanted and needed. Thoroughly confused, she felt her jaw start to tremble and found herself involuntarily wrapping her arms tighter around him.

In all reality, she couldn't remember the last time she'd given anyone a hug, or received one for that matter. It had literally been years. She tended to avoid any situations where it might be necessary, and after her bout with the Cobian pirates, she'd been hesitant to even let anyone touch her. This was how it worked, wasn't it? As unnatural as it felt, it brought her a sense of peace and comfort she hadn't expected. She felt almost guilty, considering Aroska was the one who needed to be comforted. But he wasn't complaining; his grip on her didn't falter, and he had begun to weep softly.

Images from the past couple of days fought their way into her mind—a dying Maston, the charred remains of her home, a weak and damaged Zinni hooked up to all those machines in the med center. Hot tears leaked out onto her face, but for Aroska's sake, she didn't dare make a sound. She suddenly realized that maybe it was a good thing she'd stayed, that maybe she needed this just as much as he did. She needed some time away from everyone else, time where she could just ponder everything in the presence of someone she...someone she...she...

*Don't say it.*

*You know he's right about you. You know you care.*

*Just don't say it.*

His body was warm and solid, and through the stench of burnt material and medicine, she caught a whiff of his familiar spicy scent. Annoyed by how vulnerable she felt, she moved her hands up to his shoulder blades and pounded a fist against his back before resignedly bringing her head to rest on his shoulder. Her house may have been destroyed, her family gone, and her team disjointed, but she felt strangely at home here.

# · 50 ·
# NORO INTRAGALACTIC SPACEPORT
## NORO, HAPHEZ

With HSP and half the Haphezian military searching for her, Sadey had gone to the one place humans could still safely blend in in the city: Noro Spaceport. According to the news reports that streamed incessantly on every screen throughout the port, the authorities knew nothing more than her name and gender. They'd gotten their hands on the *Vigilance's* manifest, which, for appearance's sake, kept an accurate record of every crewmember. Because all their operations were covert, none of the crew dossiers had images attached to them. HSP had a list of missing crew that included her and most of the other officers who had escaped following the crash, but without the ability to put faces to the names, they had no basis for their search. Still, Sadey refused to let herself bask in the anonymity. There was far too much at stake to risk carelessness.

Her assault on the city that morning had left a good portion of the spaceport in ruin. Not only was there one less dock for the lumbering intragalactic civilian transports, but the port had been shut down entirely upon the discovery of the missing officers. Those two events had left hundreds of people stranded, but she was glad; there were more crowds to blend into, and her downtrodden face didn't seem out of place at all.

She'd been loitering with a group of other confused travelers when news about the military's attack on the *Vigilance* began streaming. The thought that her entire crew was gone after all the trouble she'd gone through to keep them alive sickened her. She'd spent the past several hours silently berating herself for not considering the possibility of a gas attack. Granted, there had been a very limited amount of time to come up with a plan, and circumstances hadn't been ideal for much deliberation, but damn it, she should have thought of it. She'd pictured her soldiers putting up a grand fight, using their positions aboard the ship to their advantage and cutting down the majority of the Haphezian strike teams. The gas just seemed so...*unfair*. She wondered if the Haphezians had used it on purpose for irony's sake.

Regardless, her crew was gone, and she was positive it was her fault. She tried to remind herself that if she'd stayed behind to fight with them, she'd most likely be dead, too. While that was true, it didn't make her feel any better. A little voice in the back of her head tried to convince her that she really *had* run away to save her own skin. What made her so important? Why did she get to live when they had to die?

*I'm Commander Sadey Payne*, she told herself. *That's what makes me so important.* She was one of the Resistance's most trusted and respected leaders. Her name was on several of the Federation's most-wanted lists. She was skilled in ranged, melee, and hand-to-hand combat. Unlike the majority of those who had served under her, she was an invaluable asset. It wasn't that her crewmembers weren't important—they were all highly intelligent, skilled warriors as well—but she was the one who could make things happen. She was the one whose voice carried the most weight among the other Resistance leaders. If she remained alive, she could still play a pivotal role in winning this war. It was the reason she and her officers had been allowed to escape in the first place. She just required constant reminding, and it didn't make the loss of her crew hurt any less.

Sadey tightened the grip on the small communicator she carried as she made her way through the throngs of stranded travelers. She may have been safely anonymous in the crowd, but that didn't stop her from seeking a change of scenery every so often. Abandoned garments found their way onto her back, bags onto her shoulder. For all intents and purposes, she was just another refugee, and she needed to look the part. All she needed to do was hold out until morning, and then it would only be a matter of hours before Ronan and the rest of the fleet arrived. She wanted desperately to make contact, let them know she was still functional, but not while there were so many eyes on her. With a sigh, she reluctantly returned the communicator to her belt.

She would play the part of a stranded traveler for the rest of the night, she decided. Talk of the military curfew was all over the news, so wandering around in the city was guaranteed to draw attention. Yes, she would wait until daylight; she wasn't expecting the Haphezians to have given up their search by then, but there would be more people out and about during the day, allowing her to move around less conspicuously. The military had certainly increased the law enforcement presence in the city, and additional HSP agents were being flown in from the planet's other regions, but there were also plenty of non-natives who had gone out of their way to assist in the relief efforts. Perhaps she could play the part of a concerned visitor and join them, and maybe procure a mode of transportation in the process.

The question then was where she would go next. The longer she thought about it, the more appealing finding Payvan sounded, but she hadn't the foggiest idea where to start looking. The *Vigilance* hadn't wiped out nearly as much of HSP Headquarters as she'd originally hoped—her helmsman had almost done *too* good a job of landing the thing—so the chances that Payvan had been claimed by the crash were lower than they had been in the first place, assuming she was even in the area. Waltzing into the heart of the crash site was out of the question, but there was always the option of exploring the area immediately surrounding Headquarters and gleaning information that way. The HSP medical center might be a good place to start. Part of her dreaded going there, but the other part knew it was the last place anyone would expect her to be.

Satisfied with her plan, she pressed forward through the crowd until she came to a familiar bench. She leaned forward under the pretense of stretching her calves and ran her hand along the underside of it, brushing her fingers over her kytara where it rested securely on a lip underneath. She'd been searched and asked about her business by two different groups of security officers, as had many of the other travelers, and they'd seemed satisfied by what they'd found, or lack thereof. One of the agents had even offered her an apologetic nod upon seeing her again. She wasn't sure what he was sorry for: searching her, or the fact that she was stuck there. Either way, she had these people fooled, at least for the time being. For the first time, she didn't feel so bad about waiting patiently, though she still admired Ronan's ability to do it for over twenty years without trouble.

*Yes*, she thought, leaning back and resting her head against the wall behind her. She would wait. It would be a long night—she didn't dare risk sleep under these circumstances. But she would wait.

# · 51 ·
# TARBIC RESIDENCE
## NORO, HAPHEZ

A series of strange clicks startled Ziva out of a sleep she didn't remember falling into. Her eyes refused to open for several seconds—exhaustion had finally gotten the upper hand—and she was forced to wallow in a strange, semi-conscious state. She was sitting up as far as she could tell, although she was so disoriented that she couldn't be sure. The crick in her neck told her she certainly wasn't lying down.

The sensation of something warm and heavy in her lap reached her as she struggled through the haze. One hand rested against something prickly. Increasingly confused, she rolled her head around and finally managed to pry her eyelids open for a split second, only to be blinded by the sunlight streaming in through the window. Those clicks, louder and clearer this time, repeated again, and she realized someone was knocking on a door. The sound finally drew her out of her stupor.

Blinking against the bright light, she looked down and was startled to find that the object in her lap was Aroska's head. Her fingers were running through his hair, almost as if she'd been stroking it in her sleep. His eyes were still closed, and his face was contorted as if he'd been plagued with terrible dreams.

It was all she could do to keep from pushing him away and leaping to her feet. She vaguely remembered collapsing to the floor when the sobs had finally overtaken his body and his knees had given out. It wasn't often that she heard grown men weep in such a way, and when she did, it usually had a selfish undertone as they begged for their lives. Not so with him. She hadn't known what to do other than drop to her knees right along with him, and she hadn't had much choice considering he'd still had her wrapped in his arms as he'd fallen. She honestly had no idea how long the two of them had sat there crying together before sleep had overtaken them.

Her back was against the short wall separating the kitchen and living room, and his head and shoulders rested against her legs. It didn't seem like a particularly comfortable position for either of them, but it apparently hadn't mattered. The knocks came again, and this time it was clear that the caller was at the apartment door. Doubtful Aroska was going to wake up, Ziva slowly eased her legs out from under him, shushing him as he began to stir, and got to her feet.

Her eyes once again felt like they were full of sand, and she could see the puffiness in her peripheral vision. She couldn't remember the last time she'd legitimately cried; she'd shed more tears recently than she would have liked, but never had it been anything this substantial. She ran the heel of her hand across her face, desperately trying to wipe away the tear residue and compose herself as she staggered toward the door.

The knocking had stopped by the time she got there, and she could hear heavy footfalls moving away down the corridor outside. She opened the door and stepped out anyway, fixing her eyes on the wild orange mane belonging to the would-be visitor.

"Skeet."

He stopped and turned when he heard her voice, lowering the communicator he'd been holding to his ear. "Z, wha—" He paused, clearly shocked to see her there, and glanced between her and the apartment door. Even from a distance, she recognized the flicker that flashed across his eyes. Quizzical. Confused. Maybe even a little accusatory. *You spent the night here.*

She braced herself for another tirade about opening up to Aroska and not him, but she could see his face soften significantly as he approached and studied her swollen, tired eyes. He gave her a slight nod of understanding and respectfully remained silent.

"What do you need?" she croaked. Her hand went to her throat, attempting to massage away the lump that still felt like it was lodged there.

"There have been some developments with the GA's recon team and Emeri wants you back at Headquarters," he said. "I've been looking for you all morning. I couldn't reach anyone on comm, so I came here to see if Tarbic had seen—" He stopped and glanced over her shoulder, and Ziva could sense Aroska standing behind her in the doorway.

"What's wrong?" he asked.

"We're needed at Headquarters," she answered. She started to turn around and go back into the apartment but realized she hadn't brought anything with her. "Go grab what you need."

He nodded and retreated from the hall, leaving her to stand there in awkward silence with Skeet. She was sure he wanted to ask what she'd been doing there, and she dreaded to think of what kind of assumptions he was making, but he kept a couple of paces between them and didn't press the matter. She strained to figure out why she didn't have her communicator and concluded that she'd left it in the car, along with her weapon. Emotion had made her sloppy.

"You okay?" he asked quietly.

It was hard to believe a full day had already passed since he'd asked her the same question in Salex. She managed a nod and gave him the same answer: "I will be."

Aroska returned a moment later wearing a jacket not unlike the one he'd used to try to stop Maston's bleeding. He fell into stride with them as they headed for the elevator, still fiddling with the clasp as he secured his sidearm to his belt.

"The GA hasn't heard back from their scout ships yet," Skeet explained as they filed into the elevator car and rode it down to the parking bay.

"I heard it was a stealth mission," Ziva said, letting her hair down and raking her fingers through it before tying it back up into a fresh ponytail.

"It was. No one was supposed to make verbal contact, but we were still expecting to receive some data transmissions. Those scouts have had plenty of time to get to Forus and do a fly-by. Something's wrong."

The elevator opened into the parking area. "What are they planning on doing?" she asked, turning toward the borrowed HSP car while Skeet angled for the one he'd brought.

"Sounds like they've changed their timetable. The GA wants to mobilize as soon as possible—the fleet has been prepping to leave since the initial attack on Na. They've got a couple of reps at Headquarters on standby for a holo-conference with Emeri and Officer Ganten. They're just waiting for you."

Ziva almost asked why but realized she knew better. She was the so-called Nosti expert, the one they were all still relying on to save them. She couldn't help but roll her eyes. The last thing she wanted was to stand around a table with the politicians, trying to decide on the best course of action.

"Meet you there, then," she said, using her key to remote start the car's engine before she reached it.

She wasn't sure what she'd been expecting, but for some reason she was surprised when Aroska slid into the passenger seat beside her. Perhaps Adin had flown him home from the med center the night before and he had no vehicle. Either way, his presence triggered an odd silence, and thoughts of the night before came flooding back. They lifted off without a word and followed Skeet's car out of the bay and into traffic.

This sector of the city was still under military control, but the soldiers' presence seemed less prominent now in the daylight. Vehicles and pedestrians moved about almost like normal, though there was a certain urgency in the air that kept all the movement strict and efficient. GA officers and HSP agents alike held posts at nearly every intersection, a deterrent for the inevitable looters and a barrier through which the missing Resistance officers should not be able to pass.

"I said some awful things to you last night," Aroska said, watching as a pair of identical HSP groundcars zoomed by in the oncoming lane with their sirens blaring.

Ziva gnawed at the inside of her lip and tightened her grip on the steering controls. "Doesn't mean they weren't accurate."

He drew in a breath as if he were about to say more but shut his mouth and let the breath out in the form of a sigh. She was glad he didn't argue. The way she saw it, there was never any need to apologize for telling the truth.

They arrived at Headquarters in mere minutes, and after producing appropriate identification, they were ushered through the military blockade and directed toward the ops building. The lockdown had been lifted from Code Red to Code Orange for efficiency's sake, but Ziva wouldn't have been able to tell save for the color of the lights flashing from the security scanners they passed through. With the way everyone was moving, she was half afraid they'd be detained by one of the skittish GA soldiers roaming the halls. They acted as if this was their facility now.

Aura Stannist met them on the way to the elevator, keeping a curious but wary eye on Ziva as she approached. If they were as much alike as Ziva had guessed, the woman could no doubt read the emotion that still lingered in both her and Aroska's faces.

"We have a situation," she said, handing them each a data pad.

"So we've heard," Ziva muttered, wishing someone would just come out and give them all the details. She glanced down and skimmed over her data pad as the four of them crowded into the elevator.

"We last heard from the scouts as they passed by Uturn in the Iaonides system, the halfway mark," Aura explained. "It was their last scheduled check-in before going dark."

"When was this?" Aroska asked.

"Last night. We were supposed to receive an encrypted data package this morning after they'd performed their fly-by of Forus and cleared the area. It never came. We've given them two extra hours."

It didn't take a genius to figure out what she was alluding to. The GA believed their recon team had been taken out. The theory made sense; Ziva didn't know where, when, or how it had happened, but it was the most likely explanation for the silence. If the *Vigilance* and the *Titania* had been in the area at the time of the scouts' departure, perhaps they had managed to intercept a transmission and warn the Resistance base.

The elevator opened onto Emeri's private floor, and the group moved forward toward his office. The door already stood open, a sight Ziva wasn't sure if she'd ever witnessed. She took another look at her data pad. "But if the military is still wanting to send the fleet out—"

"We'll be going in blind!" Emeri's voice roared from inside the office, completing her thought for her.

They entered to find him standing on one of the comm pads at his conference table, flanked by the two GA reps Skeet had mentioned. Across the table stood the silvery-blue holograms of three more military men in formal uniforms, as well as a man Ziva assumed to be Royal Officer Jan Ganten, based on the insignia on his uniform. The three officers flickered unsteadily as if their transmissions were struggling to get through from Na.

"The fleet is ready to go," Ganten said in response to the director's outburst. "We can't afford to have it sitting around while we wait for another scout team."

Emeri opened his mouth to speak but clamped it shut again, wisely choosing to keep his thoughts to himself. Ziva couldn't help but stifle a snicker. His eyes did all the talking: "*With respect, sir, you're not the Royal General.*"

He looked over when he saw her and gestured wildly toward one of the vacant communication pads. "Payvan, get over here!"

And just like that, the brief moment of amusement was gone. Ziva straightened her shoulders and strode forward, though the movement felt mechanical, forced. The thought of herself offering tactical advice to the planet's military leaders seemed absurd. She didn't know the first thing about battle strategy on such a large scale. Under normal circumstances, she'd be part of that recon team, swooping in from behind and working quietly in the shadows. She stepped up onto the comm pad, taking a moment to steady her breathing before clearing her throat.

"Captain Payvan," Ganten said. "Your reputation precedes you."

His tone made it hard to tell if he was impressed or disgusted. Either way, she decided to take it as a compliment. "Thank you, sir."

"I trust everyone on your end has been apprised of your… situation."

Based on the way Emeri was watching her, she guessed he was talking about her Nostia, or at least her knowledge of the Nosti presence. She doubted the director would have given up her secret entirely, but by now, there was no point in hiding the fact that she'd been the source of the nostium intel. Still, she turned and looked back at Skeet, Aroska, and Aura, then examined the faces of the two military men beside Emeri. They both watched her in silence with looks verging on awe, and the pins on their uniforms indicated that they were of high enough rank to have been briefed on the nostium originally.

She cleared her throat again. "Yes, sir."

"Good. Payvan, I don't know how you know what you know, but I want you running point on this thing."

His words surprised her. *Running point?* Leading the attack? It would still mean having thousands of people relying on her, watching her every move, but the thought of finally getting to join the fight—to do what she was best at—was irresistible. But there was something odd about the way Emeri was looking at her, almost as if he knew something she didn't. Suddenly Ganten's offer didn't seem so generous, and she refrained from responding.

"Report to Haphor this afternoon," the Royal Officer continued. "You'll be advising our strategists from the command center here."

Ziva clenched her teeth, glad she'd caught on to Emeri's glances so her spirits weren't completely crushed. The director was still watching her, the look in his eyes warning her to tread carefully.

"Respectfully, sir," she said, doing her best to keep the volume of her voice from rising, "I do *not* feel like that would be the most efficient use of my skills."

"Director Arion predicted you'd say that. He and the other officers I've consulted all believe this is the best place for you. You're the only person even remotely qualified in the area of Nosti strategy."

*Other officers?* Ziva set her jaw and turned toward the group who waited by the door. She'd been with Aroska all night, ruling out his involvement in the decision. The possibility that Skeet had been on board with it sickened her, and she was relieved when she saw how wide his eyes were. He gave a subtle shake of his head and glanced to

Aura, who stood with that same old deadpan look on her face. For a split second, she looked almost apologetic when she realized she was under scrutiny, but Ziva looked away again before she could tell for sure.

"Ziva, believe me, I know you want to be out there," Emeri said. "But think about this. If you're overseeing things from the command center, it's like you'll be everywhere at once. Imagine if we were trying to stay in constant communication with you while you were in the field. You'd never get anything done. It would be impossible to know what was happening on all fronts."

The last thing she wanted to do was admit he had a point. "Send me in for a solo strike!" she cried, not caring that she was nearly shouting. "I can take Ronan out, cripple the Resistance at their source. You can be damn sure I'm the only person 'qualified' for *that!*"

The way everyone at the table shuffled their feet and averted their eyes told her the last thing they wanted to do was admit *she* had a point.

"The decision is final," Ganten growled. "You'll report here to Haphor by fifteen hundred hours. Agent Stannist will escort you."

Ziva drew a deep breath in through her nose and released it in the form of a sharp sigh. "And what of my team?"

"Unless I am mistaken, *Captain*, they're not 'your' team anymore. They will report to Director Arion as they normally might."

Emeri cleared his throat. "Because Officer Vax is still out of commission, Lieutenant Duvo and Sergeant Tarbic will accompany you to Haphor to provide support and oversee the HSP teams taking part in the assault. They *will* remain under your command."

Ziva heard a gasp behind her. She wasn't sure if it had been Skeet or Aroska, but whoever it was stopped when she held her hand up for silence. "I hope you realize," she began, shifting her eyes to Ganten and reveling in the way he fidgeted under her glare, "that you're throwing away the best agents HSP has to offer."

It only took him a moment to recompose himself. "I understand your concerns, Captain. Trust me, I do."

"Then let me go after Ronan."

"I told you, my decision is final. We'll see how well you perform, see how the assault is going. If we see success after a couple of days, we may send you to Forus."

Ziva couldn't help but think that it would be too late by then. Either the worst of the battle would be over by the time she got there, or Ronan would escape and disappear for another twenty years.

Her thoughts were interrupted when an alarm on the comm console began blaring. The holograms of the three military officers on Na turned red and fizzled away completely before being replaced by a different man who had been patched into the conversation. Sweat glistened on his brow and his hair and uniform were disheveled.

"Sir, we have a problem. You need to see this."

Ziva watched as a panoramic image was projected from the center of the table where everyone had a clear view of it. According to the navigational data that appeared on the small screen before her, they were looking at a sector of space just outside the Noro system, an area free of FTL lanes that should have been completely devoid of traffic. But now it wasn't. As she watched the series of images move through a time-lapse, she realized two things: the scout ships had indeed been destroyed, and nobody would have to go to Forus after all.

# · 52 ·

# HSP HEADQUARTERS

## NORO, HAPHEZ

A roska, Skeet, and Aura moved forward as a unit, eyes fixed on the projection hovering over the table. It was difficult to tell how many ships there were; Aroska estimated at least fifty, though more moved in and out of view every second. He saw fighters. He saw gunships. There were several freighter-sized ships that appeared to be the same model as the *Titania*. The majority of the larger vessels were agile frigates akin to the *Vigilance*, though several massive cruisers were beginning to appear toward the back of the procession.

"Where's this coming from?" Ganten demanded.

"Freighter pilot, sir," the soldier stammered, breathing hard. "He tried to send the live feed back to us, but his communications were being blocked. Had to turn around and get out of their jamming range before he could transmit."

"You're telling us this is a recording?" Emeri exclaimed. "From how long ago?"

The man swallowed. "Almost an hour. We just received it minutes ago. It was difficult to get a fix on the incoming ships—we're guessing they're using some of the same stealth measures that made the *Vigilance* and the *Titania* so hard to find."

"If this was an hour ago, how close are they now?" Ziva asked, leaning aside to give Aroska and Skeet a better look at the screen in front of her.

"We estimate they'll be entering Haphezian airspace in the next five hours."

The entire room fell dead silent for several long seconds. This fleet was clearly large enough that it had needed to leave FTL early to regroup. A smaller group of ships might have come out right on top of them, so in that sense, the large numbers were a blessing. Still, despite the fact that it had cost the Resistance the element of surprise—at least partially—this armada was larger than what Aroska had imagined. He'd always assumed the majority of their firepower existed on the Res-controlled worlds within the Core, and he shuddered when he realized that could very well still be the case. This might only be a fraction of their true strength.

When he looked back up, the three holograms from Na had rendered again, though now the men were a far cry from the composed soldiers he'd seen upon entering the room. All three were rigid, fidgety, pausing at intervals to turn and bark orders at other people in whatever rooms they were in.

"You have my authorization to proceed as you see fit," Ganten said. "Ensure comms are functional and mobilize the fleet."

The men saluted and all the holograms from Na faded once more, leaving Ganten the only person not physically present in the room. Aroska was beginning to wonder what this would all mean for Ziva, and he almost felt guilty for wondering what it all meant for *him*. He'd spent so much idle time the previous day formulating a plan for exacting his revenge on Ronan and the Resistance; being locked up in a control room in the capital was not what he'd had in mind.

Ziva turned around to face them, eyes wide. It was a look of desperation Aroska had never seen before, and he wasn't sure if he liked it. *Do something*, she mouthed, though he had no idea what she expected them to do. Based on her expression, she didn't, either.

"Duvo, Tarbic!" Emeri said before he had a chance to dwell too long on it. "Fetch Officer Vax from the med center. If she still needs medical attention, she can get it in Haphor. I want her to stay close to you during this mess."

They both stood there dumbfounded for a split second before

making any move to comply. "Sir," Skeet finally muttered, clearly just as unhappy with Ganten's decision as anyone. They turned and headed for the door, and Aroska was aware of Ziva's footsteps as she began to follow.

"Payvan, stop!" Ganten roared. He couldn't see her if she wasn't on one of the comm pads, but the fact that she'd left the table likely told him enough.

"I'm not allowed to go make sure my friend is okay?" she snapped. Even at a distance, her agitated voice was loud enough to carry through the comm system.

"Ziva, if I let you walk through that door, I have no way of knowing if you'll come back," Emeri said. His voice remained surprisingly calm. "Stay here and get ready to depart for Haphor."

The security detail that had been posted outside the office door stepped in, waving Skeet and Aroska out while Ziva was still focused on the director. Aroska recognized them from the med center the night he had accompanied her during her brain scans. Once upon a time, their sole purpose had been to help her. Now it appeared they were willing to do everything in their power to hinder her.

"You've got to be bloody kidding me," she said when she turned and saw them there. Her voice remained sharp, her eyebrows furrowed, but after what Aroska had seen on the hill in Salex and in his own home the previous night, it was difficult to miss the slight droop in her shoulders, the glimmer of fear in her eyes. His own confidence ebbed when he saw these things, and he vowed then and there that he would fix the situation. His plan would not change after all.

"Na is reporting that the fleet is in motion," Aroska heard Ganten saying as he and Skeet reluctantly resumed their journey to the elevator. "All troops in the city are being recalled to rendezvous with them."

And that would be his way out. He'd have a ride, plenty of firepower, people to back him up until he was able to break off and carry out his own mission. These were all things he'd wondered about as he'd sat there in the med center the day before. He'd be reprimanded for defying orders for sure, would probably even lose his job, but he wouldn't have a job to lose if the Resistance wiped everyone out.

The elevator opened onto the commons, where soldiers and agents were scrambling to react as news of the Resistance fleet's arrival trickled down through the ranks. Aroska and Skeet broke through the front doors, shielding their eyes as they both looked up to observe the ascending GA ships. A cluster of smaller gunships idled in an area that had been converted to a temporary landing zone off to their right; they too would be gone within a couple of minutes, and any chance of joining up with the fleet would be lost.

"Tarbic, let's go!" Skeet called.

Aroska realized he had stopped in the middle of the grand staircase and looked down to find Skeet still hurrying toward a bank of parked groundcars. He forced his feet forward, turning instead toward the landing area. "Go get Zinni!" he shouted back. "I'll catch up!"

He shook away the guilt wrought from lying to a friend and picked up his pace. Disregarding orders was not something he took great pleasure in, but if Ronan was going to be stopped, it was necessary. Necessary because thousands of innocent lives were being taken, not only in Noro but all over the galaxy. Necessary because fathers and brothers like Maston were being stripped from their families in the blink of an eye. Necessary because Ziva, HSP's greatest weapon, had been rendered virtually useless by the very people who regarded her as such. Emeri had said it himself: she was still in command of her team. She was the one who had told Aroska to do something, and that's exactly what he was doing.

He fished his credentials out and waved toward the gunship as soldiers loaded into it. They stopped and looked back, readily helping him climb aboard when he arrived. For a moment, he was afraid they would turn him away, but upon closer inspection, they almost looked relieved to have an extra man on their side.

"Glad to have you here, sir!" one of them shouted above the roar of the engines as the craft lifted off. "Didn't know the agency was sending anyone up yet."

Aroska nodded and displayed his badge. "Sergeant Tarbic, spec ops," he said. "I'm here on Officer Ganten's orders."

# · 53 ·
# HSP MEDICAL CENTER
## NORO, HAPHEZ

Z inni reached down, struggling to secure the straps on her boots.
Her muscles had atrophied a bit, the doctors said. Spending
five weeks lying immobile in a dark cargo hold having countless tests run tended to do that to you. She cursed her stiff fingers and
paused to flex them; they still came just shy of creating a solid fist, and
it was infuriating. No wonder she hadn't been able to successfully hold
on to the kids aboard the ship.

Even putting on her boots felt like a chore, and by the time she
sat back up, she was out of breath. She'd awakened in the middle of the
night and hadn't been able to go back to sleep. When the nurse had
come in a few minutes earlier to inform her someone from Headquarters would be by to collect her shortly, she'd been excited by the
prospect of getting out of bed and being productive. Now she wasn't so
sure.

*The Resistance.* It was still mind-boggling. Based on the few foggy
snippets of interaction she'd had with her captors, she would have
never guessed they were Res soldiers. She was glad Skeet had been
there to answer all of her questions when she'd awakened—otherwise,
she imagined she'd still have no clue about anything that had happened
or was happening now. It was hard enough to keep track of everything
as it was. Five weeks was a long time to be kept in the dark...*literally.*

The med center had already provided her with some comfortable
clothes to replace the tactical suit she'd been found in. With her boots

successfully donned, she was ready to go. She eased off the edge of the bed and stood on quivering legs, testing out her balance. Someone had left a sleek cane for her; her first instinct had been to be stubborn and refuse it, but now that she was actually on her feet, she welcomed the thing. The message from Headquarters had said she was going to Haphor. She had no idea why, but somehow, she got the feeling it meant there wouldn't be any fighting going on. For once, she was glad.

She caught a whiff of Skeet just before his head appeared in the doorway of her room. "You ready to go?" he asked. His shoulders rose and fell in a steady rhythm as he sucked in deep breaths and let them out, and she wondered if he'd run up the thirty floors to her level. The fact that he seemed to be in such a hurry prompted her to pick up her pace as best she could.

"What's going on?" she asked, falling into stride beside him and clutching his arm with one hand, the cane with the other.

They entered the hallway, and he glanced around as if to make sure nobody would overhear them. "Ronan is here," he murmured. "There's an entire Resistance armada coming into the system. They won't enter Haphezian airspace for another few hours, but they've got considerable firepower. Our fleet is moving to intercept now."

*Ronan.* It felt so odd to be able to put a face to the name—*well, sort of*—after weeks of trying to figure out what Ronan even was. It was frustrating listening to Skeet talk about it like it was old news. While it *was* for him, her tired brain was still struggling to keep up with the most mundane of tasks, let alone this barrage of new information. Even being in a well-lit room again meant figuring out how to divert some of her already-dwindling energy back to her sense of sight, something she'd learned to live without for the past five weeks.

"And what are *we* doing?" she said as her mind managed to process the fact that going to Haphor meant they wouldn't even be joining up with the fleet.

Skeet was silent for a moment, his lips pressed into a thin line. "We're accompanying Ziva to the capital to coordinate all of HSP's involvement in this."

*Ziva.* It was like hearing these names flipped some sort of power switch in Zinni's mind, both allowing her to remember old details and overwhelming her with new things to keep track of. Ziva was the only member of the team she hadn't seen yet upon her rescue. Skeet had of course spent the majority of his downtime there in the room with her, and she'd seen Aroska the day before, had mumbled a few incomprehensible words to him before falling asleep again. The last clear image she had of Ziva was in this very med center upon returning home from Argall. She thought she remembered seeing her superior and maybe even talking to her in the cargo hold aboard the freighter—the *Titania*, as Skeet kept calling it—but that didn't make any sense. It must have been a dream.

Zinni had accepted the fact that she wouldn't be seeing combat any time soon, but the rest of the team? She stopped, partially to allow the news to sink in and partially because her legs already felt like jelly after walking down a single hallway. "You aren't joining the fight?"

His face had grown grimmer by the second, but that crease had also appeared on his forehead, telling her he was both angry and concerned. He ran a hand through his hair. There was still something he wasn't sharing with her.

"Look," he began. "I wanted Z to be the one to explain this all to you someday, and maybe she still can once we get underway. The reason we knew the gas on Na was nostium, the reason we know this is the Resistance...it's because she *is* one of them."

She couldn't see the expression on her own face, but his reaction gave her a good idea of what it looked like.

He dipped his head and sighed. "Okay, that came out wrong. She's a Nosti." He was nearly whispering now. "She said she doesn't even like to call herself that, but she's got the abilities. This substance that's killing everyone else? It only made her stronger. She's even got one of those swords."

They were both silent for a moment, Skeet allowing the information to sink in and Zinni trying desperately to make space in her head for it. She wanted to laugh; she'd known Ziva since signing on with HSP's Junior Guard and had seen her plenty of times during basic training before that. There was no way her friend could have been hiding such a secret that whole time. And yet...

"That man she killed," she murmured. She hadn't intended to voice the thought out loud, but Skeet nodded as if he understood exactly who she was referring to.

"Ganten said he wanted her 'running point' on this assault, but he only meant he wants her working with the strategists to figure out the best way to combat these people."

"Why can't we just blow their asses out of the sky?" she exclaimed. The extra effort it took to raise her voice left her breathless.

He shushed her and began helping her along as they continued toward the elevator. "Maybe we can now that we don't have to go all the way to Forus. Come on—let's see if we can talk some sense into Emeri and Ganten."

Zinni put careful thought into every step she took, placing one foot in front of the other and doing her best to gain speed with each stride. Her short legs already had enough trouble keeping up with Skeet and the rest of the team under ordinary circumstances, so the fact that they needed to be hurrying now only contributed to her frustration.

They arrived at the elevator and waited a moment for the door to open. When it did, they found the car occupied by a lone human woman about Zinni's height with short brown hair and icy blue eyes. She moved to the far side of the wide car to give them space and spared them a fleeting glance before fixing her gaze once more on the elevator's control panel.

Zinni's foot caught and she faltered, clutching Skeet's arm and hoping he'd attribute the stumble to her weakened legs. In truth, the scent within the elevator had hit her like a punch to the gut and she'd had to force herself to not hesitate before entering. Her olfactory system was still working in overdrive after being her primary source of information during her captivity. Not only that, but this particular smell sent her right back to the cold floor of that pitch dark cargo space, and for a split second, that was the only fact her mind could process.

"You okay?" Skeet asked, helping her regain her footing as the elevator door slid shut behind them.

"Yes," she gasped, glancing between him and the woman, who

looked on with concerned curiosity. Their gazes locked for the briefest of moments, and in that time, Zinni saw an unmistakable flicker of recognition.

She swiveled on the cane and took up a position on Skeet's right, keeping him between herself and the mysterious woman. The only interaction she'd had with her captors had either been in the dark or while she was unconscious, so she'd never seen any faces. But this woman's scent was all too familiar. Not only did it bear the same vague qualities as the *Titania's* crew and the children after they'd been taken from the room, but there was also something distinctive about it, something unique. *She was there*, Zinni thought. *This woman was in that room with me at some point.*

She heaved a sigh, sniffed, and then squeezed Skeet's arm all in quick succession, hoping he'd catch the hint that something was awry. He sniffed in response and reached up to wipe his nose, telling her he too recognized the scent. After spending hours interrogating live Nosti and clearing out a frigate full of dead ones, she didn't blame him. He knew this was a Resistance soldier sharing their elevator, likely one of the *Vigilance's* missing officers.

What he couldn't know, however, was that this woman knew Zinni, knew she was someone who could alert the authorities to her presence.

Something had to be done, but the prospect of facing a warrior who specialized in melee combat in such close quarters was daunting. The same adrenaline rush that had heightened her senses in the cargo room gave her strength now as she tried to form a plan. She slowly released her grip on Skeet's arm, relying on the cane as her primary source of support. Using his body to block the Nosti's view of her hand, she reached for the holster strapped to his thigh and wrapped her fingers around the grip of his pistol. He shifted his weight to his other leg, preparing to lean out of the way as soon as she was ready to move.

Zinni drew the weapon and took aim at the exact moment the woman came at her, a newly revealed kytara in her grasp. She got a shot off, but the plasma bolt veered off to one side and the gun was wrenched from her stiff hand by an invisible force. It clattered to the floor in the corner, leaving her stunned and exposed.

The kytara blades sliced through the air, narrowly missing Skeet's head as he ducked out of the way. The only consolation was that the fully extended blades were long enough to make the weapon cumbersome in such an enclosed space, but it was no less deadly. The woman seemed to be aware of this and was slowly working her way out of the corner, forcing Skeet and Zinni into the opposite one.

Unsure what else to do, Zinni dropped to her knees and rolled, lifting the cane above her head. As she successfully absorbed a blow from the kytara, she couldn't help but conjure up some memory of a curtain rod from the one and only time Ziva had recounted her duel with that Nosti she'd killed all those years ago. She was now happier than ever that she'd brought the cane with her, and she couldn't help but recognize the irony of the situation. She was supposed to go to Haphor so she could avoid this. *So much for staying out of combat.*

Skeet had a knife—this was good. It and the cane could be pulled from their grasps just as easily as the gun, but when they were crossing blades with the kytara, the woman risked throwing off her own balance by stripping them of their weapons. The key would be for one of them to get the pistol back while she was busy with the other. Zinni preferred to leave the latter task to Skeet; she wasn't sure if she could handle the force of that sword in her current condition.

She kept the cane above her head, fighting away the blackness creeping inward from the edges of her vision as she ducked and dodged. This Nosti woman had skill—there was no denying it—but two opponents in such a small space were proving to be a challenge, especially with Skeet attacking from above and Zinni coming in from below. In order to face one, she had to turn her back on the other. She had no doubt been on the move since the *Vigilance* crashed and appeared to be just as tired as they were.

Zinni jammed one end of the cane into the small of the woman's back, forcing her to take a staggering step toward Skeet. He thrust the knife forward, filling the elevator car with the screech of metal on metal, and pushed upward, forcing the kytara toward the ceiling. He didn't even have to look at Zinni to tell her to go; she was already lunging for the pistol. She snatched it up, rolling onto her back and firing straight up into the woman's chest just as a kytara blade whistled down toward her head. She flinched and leaned away, but the sword clattered harmlessly to the floor.

Skeet picked it up and held it over the woman as she fell back against the elevator wall, clutching at the smoldering hole in her chest. Her blue eyes were glassy as she glanced between the two of them, and each breath she took was like a hissing cry. She lifted her eyebrows as if a sudden thought had come to mind. "Too...late," she managed, her facial expression morphing from one of fury to one of desperation. It was still like that several seconds later when she finally fell still.

Zinni closed her eyes, sucking in raspy breaths of her own. She'd grown so accustomed to lying on a gently swaying floor that this almost felt comfortable. She allowed the pistol to slip from her grasp, focusing once more on flexing her stiff fingers. Somewhere in the back of her mind, she could hear Skeet asking if she was okay, feel him reaching down to help her up. She managed a nod, but as the elevator came to a stop and the doors slid open, the only thing she could think about was the fact that she was actually making a fist.

## · 54 ·

# HSP HEADQUARTERS
### NORO, HAPHEZ

E meri and Ganten's conversation continued on a bit longer, though it was just muffled noise in Ziva's ears. She watched Skeet and Aroska until they disappeared into the elevator, then shifted her attention to the two guards blocking her exit. Both had their hands resting on their holsters, and she decided against trying to take either of them out and making a run for it. Causing a scene was the last way to win Ganten's confidence. Instead, she turned to Aura, who still stood just inside the door with her ever-present data pad. The woman held her gaze for a moment before averting her eyes and looking down at the floor. Ziva was glad, at first only because she'd finally won one of their glaring matches. Then she realized it was the first time she'd actually seen the probation officer show any shred of emotion.

"...will stay here until Tarbic and Duvo return with Officer Vax, then you'll leave for Haphor immediately." She realized Ganten had disconnected and that Emeri was addressing her. "I'm going to go release a statement to the agency. Agent Stannist, please collect Captain Payvan's weapon and communicator and ensure that your transport is ready to depart."

The request was so outrageous that it took Ziva several seconds to even muster up a protest. "I refuse to be treated like a *frouchten* prisoner." She shied away from Aura's outstretched hand.

"As soon as we leave this room, you're going to contact your team and tell them to stay away. Or worse, order them to go join up with the fleet." Emeri's turquoise eyes sparkled with regret and that same fatherly concern he'd shown upon her return from Aubin. "I don't know what else to do. We need you here. Don't make this harder than it already is."

The thought of warning her team hadn't even crossed her mind, but now that she considered it, it wasn't a bad idea. It was clear that neither Aura nor Emeri were going anywhere until she complied, so she sighed and threw her pistol and comm down into Aura's palm. Both of them turned and strode from the room, leaving the two guards posted just outside, and the door slid shut behind them.

She spun on her heel and stormed over to the large picture window, gazing out at all the GA ships rising from the city. The sudden arrival of the Resistance fleet was a game changer; at least she wouldn't miss out on the infiltration of a base on Forus or some such thing. But now she worried about the size of that armada. With their fleet combined with all their ground troops, the Grand Army of Haphez represented the strongest military force in this part of the Fringe…or so they'd thought. This Resistance force had no doubt been amassed over the past twenty-plus years, slowly contributed to by a number of Res worlds so as not to arouse suspicion. It had been difficult to tell based on the hologram alone, but those cruisers bringing up the rear appeared to match even the GA's largest dreadnoughts in size. And regardless of whether the Haphezian fleet had been ready since the attack on Na, the element of surprise was still giving the Resistance the upper hand.

Ziva thought of Tobias and the force he was contributing. She had no idea what kind of numbers he had or even where he'd gotten his ships; regardless, no one would be arriving from Niio until at least that afternoon. She'd written the Durutians off after her conversation with Mae. If she hadn't heard back from them by now, she doubted she ever would, and she had to suppress the glimmer of wishful thinking lurking in the back of her mind.

From her vantage point there at the window, she saw Skeet and Aroska emerge from the front doors directly below her and begin to descend the massive staircase in front of the building. She held her breath and pressed her face to the glass when she saw Aroska stop and look around. Even from such a great distance, it was clear he was staring toward one of the many temporary landing areas that had been set up in lieu of the demolished landing pads.

"What the hell are you doing?" she whispered, instinctively reaching for the communicator that was no longer attached to her belt.

It appeared that he and Skeet had one last brief exchange before the two of them parted ways, with Skeet continuing the trek toward the med center and Aroska angling for a gunship preparing to take off from the staging area. He climbed aboard without so much as a glance back and the ship lifted off.

"*Sheyss,*" Ziva muttered, pounding a fist against the glass. "No, damn it! What are you doing?"

She could only stand there and watch helplessly as the craft continued upward. With the blast doors open, she had a clear view of his face as it passed, and she saw that he was looking straight at her. Surely there was no way he could actually see her—all the windows in the building had a reflective coating on the outside. But he knew where the office was, knew she was inside, knew she might even be watching.

This was her fault, she realized. He was doing this because she'd told him to. Granted, she hadn't meant for him to actually take matters into his own hands, but she'd said the words, planted the seed in his head. *Do something.* Yes, this was all her fault.

As she watched the ship disappear into the sky, she thought of his demeanor in the med center the day before and of the way he'd acted when she'd first arrived at his apartment. Edgy. Distant. Pensive. It reminded her a great deal of the behavior she'd seen at the start of the Dakiti investigation, back when he still wanted her head on a platter for what she'd done to Soren. Back when he'd still been plotting his revenge. She was seeing the same man now, a man with a plan brewing inside that thick skull of his. What exactly did he expect to do? Take Ronan out himself? She could see him maybe cutting down a few Nosti, but there was no way he'd be any match for the leader of the Resistance. She had doubts about her own abilities on that front. Aside from her brief tangle with Kat, it had been years since she'd used a kytara, and even then, it had just been in training with Gamon. Aroska was going to go up there and get himself killed.

*And it's all your fault.*

The guilt and feeling of utter helplessness made the time drag. She stood there for what felt like hours watching for any sign of Skeet and Zinni's return. Skeet couldn't have known what Aroska was planning—he never would have allowed him to go. Someone had called ahead to the med center to make sure Zinni was ready to go, too, so there was no way it should be taking this long. When she saw two of the GA's smaller landing craft break away and head back down to the hospital, she was sure something was amiss. Her hand once again went to her hip, reaching for a nonexistent communicator.

Cursing under her breath, she turned and strode across the room with half a mind to use Emeri's conference table to reach out to someone, but the door opened and Aura entered before she had the chance to try. Her eyes were wide and her brows furrowed, and she held a communicator—Ziva's communicator—to her mouth. Skeet's voice crackled on the other end of the transmission.

"It was Payne," he said. "I recognized her scent from the captain's cabin."

Ziva snatched the device up, leaving the transmission open so Aura could still hear. "Skeet? What happened?"

"We ran into her in the elevator on our way out. Don't know what the hell she was doing here—maybe looking for survivors. Zinni recognized her first. Said she remembered her from sometime during her captivity. We were getting ready to take her into custody, but she pulled one of those swords out of nowhere. That was...interesting. Zinni shot her."

"Shot her," Ziva repeated.

"She didn't last long," he explained. "Said it was 'too late,' whatever that means. We found a communicator on her that could help us locate the other missing officers. And we've got her kytara—if we study the variations in the design, we might be able to find a weak point that applies to all of them."

Ziva nodded. "And how's Zinni?" she asked, kicking herself for not inquiring about her friend from the outset.

"A little shaken up, but fine, all things considered. She's still weak.

But hey, listen. You'd better get going over to Haphor. I don't know where Tarbic went, but we're still trying to get this mess cleared up."

She almost said 'okay' but decided against it for fear of giving anyone the illusion that she was fine with the circumstances. "Copy that," she said instead, a simple acknowledgement of his words.

Aura held her hand out to receive the communicator and Ziva reluctantly relinquished it. "Where did Tarbic go?" the probation officer demanded, an accusatory but intuitive glimmer in her yellow eyes. She knew exactly where Aroska had gone. "What did you tell him?"

Ziva didn't have the energy to argue, didn't feel like trying to convince the woman she'd had nothing to do with his departure, even though she feared she had. "What are you going to do, have GA forces waste time bringing him back down here when they should be fighting Ronan?"

Aura pursed her lips and didn't respond. They were each silent for a moment, staring each other down in an all-too-familiar way. The silence was broken when she turned back to the door. "Let's go," she muttered.

Ziva reluctantly followed, with Emeri's two guards falling into position behind her. Skeet and Zinni would remain relatively safe at the med center, but something had to be done about Aroska. Despite the brusqueness of her previous response, she'd been perfectly serious about sparing military manpower to bring him back planetside. She had half a mind to just let him go, to just let him tag along with the GA troops. The galaxy only knew they could use the extra gun. But considering what had happened in the past when he'd been left to his own devices, letting him go off on his own was truthfully the last thing she wanted to do. He'd been far too quiet the previous day; surely he would have told her about his plan the night before if it was actually anything good.

Trying to do something about it at this point, however, meant defying both Emeri and the Royal Officer, which would inevitably cost her her job. As she trudged along behind Aura, she found herself once again considering all the options and players, just as she had in the prison transport after Tachi's assassination. Regardless of the choice she made, there would be consequences. She could go to Haphor and potentially accomplish nothing, leaving Aroska free to do something foolhardy, or she could go after him, which would require somehow ditching her escort and then facing Emeri and Ganten.

At least the latter option gave her the opportunity to participate in the battle and possibly take Ronan out in some sort of solo strike— she'd been serious about that, too. Besides, after everything she'd put Aroska through and everything he'd done for her, it was only fair that she keep looking out for him. Nearly ten years of spec ops experience told her to just leave him behind, that he was a casualty of the mission, but this was no ordinary mission. It was almost like *she* was the one being left behind, and she needed to catch up to him to ensure his mission—whatever it was—succeeded, with success being measured by whether or not he came back alive.

Escaping this situation would be messy. It wouldn't be self-defense, not like it had been in the prison transport. Any move she made now would have to be an offensive one, and those typically didn't go well for the party on the receiving end. She was in no immediate danger—that was the whole point of this captivity, after all—and thus the idea of hurting anyone was incredibly unappealing. Still, her self-preservation instincts were flaring up and she found herself glancing at the bulge at the small of Aura's back that could only be her confiscated pistol.

Aura led their little procession down to the ops levels and toward the access corridor for the same landing pad the two of them had met on. The *Intrepid* was still docked there, unless Ziva was mistaken. It could provide an excellent means of escape and was outfitted with enough weaponry to make a decent contribution to the battle with the Resistance fleet. If she was going to take action, it would have to be soon. She studied the layout of the door and its controls as she approached. A quick step at the last second could put enough distance between her and the guards that she could shut the door and cut them off, leaving only the probation officer between her and her ship.

Coming within a few strides of the door triggered that familiar slow-motion effect. She heard the individual rhythms of each guard's footfalls behind her, heard the tones as Aura entered a code into the keypad in front of her. She drew a deep breath and prepared to sprint forward as the door hissed open, but the sight of the *Intrepid* idling alone on the landing pad made her hesitate. There was just enough time for her mind to process that something was amiss before Aura pivoted and spun around behind her. Ziva sidestepped and cleared the doorway, but instead of handcuffs on her wrists or the shock of a stun baton, all she felt was a gun being pressed into her palm, followed by a powerful shove.

"Move!" Aura ordered.

Ziva took off for the ship, heard a hiss, an angry shout, the discharge of a pistol behind her. Then came a second set of footsteps pursuing her across the landing pad. She risked a look over her shoulder and found Aura crashing up the boarding ramp, looking back over her own shoulder at the arm protruding from the door and the smoldering exterior control panel she'd just blasted. She ducked past Ziva and angled for the cockpit, and the ship began to lift off before the boarding ramp was even retracted.

For a moment, Ziva could only stand there and ponder what had just happened. Based on Aura's actions, she deduced two things: their destination was no longer Haphor, and the Royal Officer had no knowledge of this little deviation. Not yet, anyway.

She moved forward toward the cockpit on light feet, half-expecting this to still be a trap. She had yet to holster her pistol, so she maintained a tight grip on it and kept it ready at her side. Several seconds went by and no one jumped out at her; all the hatches and storage spaces in the corridor remained properly secured. Aura's scent was the only one she could smell as she drew nearer.

She hesitated in the cockpit doorway, watching through the front viewport as the Noro skyline dipped out of sight below them and was replaced by the hazy mid-morning sky. All she could see of Aura from this vantage point was the back of the woman's head as her hands flew over the ship's controls. The fact that she'd done exactly what Ziva had planned on doing to facilitate their escape was both impressive and baffling. Still, Ziva couldn't bring herself to trust the woman just yet. Those same self-preservation instincts kicked in and she raised the gun to the back of Aura's head.

"What is this?" she demanded.

Judging by the way the woman straightened in her seat, she knew she was being held at gunpoint, but she apparently didn't care enough to divert her attention away from what was in front of her. "Did you hit your head in Salex or something?" she muttered, altering the ship's course a bit before handing back the confiscated communicator. "I seem to recall telling you I was loosening my grip on your leash." Then, under her breath, "I just never planned on letting go of it entirely."

"Doesn't really answer my question."

"Well, what do you think we're doing? I'm taking you to find your man."

Was it so hard to answer one bloody question? Ziva holstered her weapon, satisfied for the moment, and moved up to sit in the co-pilot's chair. Within seconds, she had assumed control of the ship and angled them in the direction Aroska's gunship had gone. "I'll do the flying," she said. "You need to do some talking."

Aura sighed and leaned back in her seat. She was quiet for a long time and didn't clear her throat to speak until after they'd passed through the atmosphere and were moving past Na.

"I was spec ops like you," she said quietly.

Ziva risked a glance at her. Her jaw was set, and she stared straight ahead with the light from the sun reflected in her eyes.

"My team and I were behind enemy lines out on Zaganti. We completed our mission and were on our way to the exfil point when a group of insurgents came out of nowhere. My intelligence officer was killed, and my sergeant and I got separated in the chaos. I couldn't raise him on comm—figured he'd been captured or killed, too—and the pilot picking us up was tracking a group of enemy ships headed our way. The mission had been a success. I had a memory stick with the data we'd gathered, and that was the important thing. So I left."

Ziva remained silent as she guided the ship forward. She had a hunch she knew where the story was going, and if she was correct, it put some of Aura's actions from the past few days into perspective.

"We were halfway out of the system when a transmission from my sergeant came through," the probation officer continued. "He was alive and unharmed. He'd just been hunkered down and wanted to know when exfil would arrive since his comms had been down for a while. Have you ever had to tell a comrade you left him behind, Captain?"

"No," Ziva replied quietly, gripping the controls with white knuckles. She told herself this was mainly because the people she worked with were good enough to not get left behind in the first place, but she realized in a couple of cases it had been because of her unwillingness to *leave* a teammate behind. She thought back to Taran Reddic's little jab in the café on Aubin, the way he'd been surprised she was planning on rescuing someone. It seemed like she did it more often than not. Some spec ops agent she was.

"I told him I didn't know," Aura continued. "Didn't want him to know I was already gone. I checked with the pilot to see if there was time to go back, but he was still tracking those ships and said there wouldn't be time to go back planetside and get away again before they were on top of us. I reminded myself that we needed to get that data back to HSP intact, and we kept going."

Images of Dakiti's white hallways flashed through Ziva's mind as she recalled going back for Aroska despite the imminent threat posed by the GA. "Did your sergeant make it out by himself?" she asked, aware Aroska wouldn't have been capable of such a thing.

Aura hesitated. "I picked up another transmission from him about an hour later. He was looking for me, said he couldn't find me at the rendezvous point. I finally told him where I was—he begged me to come back for him, but I told him it was too late. The insurgents found him while we were talking, and I got to stand there and listen to him die." She drew in a hissing breath through her nose and let it out. "The thing is, I would have been able to save him if I'd just gone back after the first transmission. We may have ended up having to outrun a few enemy ships, but there would have been time."

She swiveled her seat around until she was facing Ziva. "If I would have gone back for him, we both could have been killed and that data would have been lost. At the very least, it would have been a breach of spec ops protocol. That's why I transferred to the Royal Offices after that, why I do what I do. My job is to make sure other agents follow protocol. I've spent the past fifteen years trying to convince myself I did the right thing."

Ziva threw her a glance. "And you're still not sure." It was a statement, not a question.

"Right now, you've got a chance to save your agent, and I'm here to make sure you take it, protocol be damned. Don't make the same mistake I did. You'll be stuck living with the knowledge that you could have done something, and in turn, you'll be constantly second-guessing yourself in the future. That's certainly not going to help you do your job."

Without even asking, Ziva understood why the woman had never made good on her threats to turn her and Emeri in for going to find Skeet and Aroska. She'd seen it as an opportunity to do what she herself had failed to do years before. They'd *both* been seeing bits of themselves in the other.

Aura continued with a sigh. "More importantly, what I told you before still goes. You *are* the only person on this planet qualified to go up against Ronan, but HSP hasn't spent the past ten years turning you into a weapon only to have you locked up in a control room talking strategy. I understand that now. You need to do what you were built for, which is covertly infiltrating that flagship and taking the Resistance out at the source. I don't know how the hell you plan on doing that, but after seeing everything else you've done this week, I have the utmost confidence in your ability to get the job done."

Ziva turned to look her in the eye. Aura had a real talent for maintaining that impassive expression, but there was something else in her eyes, that same desperation Ziva had seen in the med center the day before as Emeri explained what was expected of her. But this time, there was an element of trust mixed with it, and maybe a little uncertainty. The message was clear: *This needs to be done, and I'm letting you do it your way. Don't make me regret it.*

The truth was she had no idea how she was going to pull this off, either. The prospect of facing real Nosti—people who had spent the majority of their lives training for this—was rather intimidating. Yes, she'd spent the majority of her *own* life training in one way or another, but ranged weapons and even superior size were useless assets when the enemies were agile, skilled in melee combat, and could move objects with their minds. Despite the lack of practice, she'd at least be able to hold her own for a while, but she doubted the same could be said for the rest of the GA troops and HSP agents caught up in the fight. She found herself hoping they'd spend most of their time fighting ship-to-ship rather than hand-to-hand.

She leaned back in her seat as the ship settled into a cruising speed, comforted by the feeling of her kytara jabbing into her side where it dangled under her jacket. If she was going to be fighting Nosti, it was the one object that might afford her some success. Right now, however, her biggest concern was finding Aroska and making sure he didn't try anything foolish. She now understood how he'd felt while watching her load that Korberon rifle with the intent of finding and killing Dasaro on Chaiavis.

"Take over for a while," she instructed Aura. "I'm going to go do a quick inventory."

She switched full control back over to the pilot's console and made her way through the ship to the cargo space. The vessel had been docked at Headquarters since the team had arrived home from Aubin, so everything Skeet, Zinni, and Aroska had taken on their mission to find Ronan should have remained aboard. A quick glance around the room revealed a variety of HSP-issue ordnance, as well as a few larger weapons she didn't recognize as belonging to the agency. There were three jet suits—two large ones for the men and a smaller one for Zinni—designed for individual aerial reconnaissance but only capable of reaching an altitude of about a thousand meters. No good in space anyway. She found the comm console the Durutians had destroyed in the hotel in Zylka and wondered if there was any information that could be pulled from it. Trying would likely be pointless; if they wanted to learn about Ronan now, all they needed to do was look out the window.

Satisfied that they had more than enough supplies at their disposal, she returned to the cockpit and sat back down, monitoring the sensors as Aura continued to pilot the craft. The GA's ships had gotten enough of a head start that it was at least an hour before they appeared on the

*Intrepid's* scanners. Even then, another lengthy stretch of time passed before the two of them had a visual. From their vantage point, the Haphezian fleet was nothing but a vast cluster of silver specks in the distance, with a couple of smaller vessels in the foreground that appeared to be medical frigates. The view was breathtaking, and this wasn't even the whole fleet. At least a quarter of the military's total force had stayed behind to act as a final line of defense for the base and Haphez itself. The idea that the Resistance fleet was just as big if not bigger sent chills down Ziva's spine.

"Look here," Aura said, gesturing at the control panel.

Some of the front-line Res ships were beginning to appear on the scanners. They were meeting the enemy halfway, a move Ronan likely hadn't anticipated. Sure, coming out of FTL speed farther from Haphez had given the GA more time to react, but Ziva doubted the Resistance had planned on the Haphezian fleet already being completely assembled. Ronan's ships would be forced to engage out in the middle of nowhere, sparing all the innocent people back home the terror of having a battle raging right over their heads. Ziva only hoped the Haphezian blockade would continue to hold if any Res ships managed to break away from the action out here.

They sat still with their eyes fixed on the view ahead as they drew nearer, alternating between forming a plan and long periods of reflective silence. It was decided they would start by rendezvousing with the Haphezian command ship, the *Soroya*, where they'd see if they could locate Aroska. Then they'd follow the GA's lead from there. The last thing they needed to do was launch their own offensive and find themselves caught in the line of fire.

The group of incoming Resistance vessels grew larger and larger, rapidly closing the space that separated them from the Haphezian fleet. The first plasma bolts had already begun to fly when the *Intrepid's* comm system crackled to life.

"Unidentified *Infiltrator*-class runner, this is Rear Admiral Ostin of the *Soroya*. Be advised that we are locked on to your position. Identify yourself."

"I'll do the talking," Aura said, reaching forward to switch on the comm receiver. "*Soroya*, hold your fire. This is Agent Aura Stannist representing Royal Officer Jan Ganten aboard independent vessel *Intrepid*. Authorization code Alpha 37401. I've been tasked with recovering a wayward HSP agent who stowed away aboard one of your landing craft in Noro."

Despite the probation officer's heartfelt story and encouraging words, Ziva wondered for a split second if this was all still some sort of ruse. Her hand moved toward her pistol, but she lowered it again when Aura turned and gave a subtle shake of her head. It was a ruse, but it wasn't directed at her.

"Agent Stannist, all our ground troops from Noro have been accounted for. If there was an HSP agent aboard my ship, I'd know about it."

Ziva already had her communicator out and was in the process of entering Aroska's comm code. The transmission went through, but as she'd expected, there was no answer.

Aura ended her conversation and motioned for Ziva to plug the device into the ship's console. "Try to pinpoint his location—we should be close enough."

A new blip appeared on the scanner, a blue dot among hundreds of yellow ones. Aroska's signal was moving farther forward into the chaos, and a quick glance out the front viewport revealed a likely—and very large—destination.

"*Intrepid* to *Soroya*," Aura said, reestablishing the connection with Ostin. "You have a small craft on course to intercept a Res dreadnought. What's your play?"

"Initial scans were unable to locate exterior shield generators," the admiral replied. "There are three of them *inside* the vessel, and they appear to be regenerating shields for all the enemy fighters in the vicinity as well. I've never seen anything like it. We're not going to make any progress until those generators are dealt with, and I've sent runners in with strike teams to take them out."

"Any of those strike teams come from Noro?"

"They very well could have."

Ziva and Aura exchanged a glance.

"*Intrepid*, I'm adding you to the network," announced another voice on Ostin's comm channel. "Good luck out there."

"Thank you," Aura said. "*Intrepid* out."

"What the hell does he think he's doing?" Ziva muttered, watching Aroska's blue dot on the screen. The majority of the dots around it—including the one it was headed for—turned red as the *Intrepid's* central computer connected remotely to the GA fleet's network. The blips representing the Haphezian ships turned green.

She turned her attention back to the controls, glad to have a better idea of who was who—not that it was that hard to look outside and see the difference between the GA's sleek silver ships and Ronan's matte gray ones. They were in the thick of things now, caught up in a tangle of opposing fighters while most of the larger ships hung back and fired on each other from a distance with heavier artillery. Just as Ostin had said, streams of translucent purple energy were projected from the largest Resistance dreadnought at intervals, restoring the shields on their fighters to full strength before the agile ships could be destroyed. Even after such a quick observation, it was plain to see that the GA fighters were struggling to penetrate.

The thought struck her that after several years of studying the captured fighters on Forus, Ronan probably knew every single one of their weaknesses. Or, if not their weakness, at least how to best defend against their strengths. The Resistance had come prepared. She muttered a curse.

"Our shields are at full power," Aura announced. A sheen of sweat glistened on her forehead and her face appeared to be carved out of stone as she maneuvered the *Intrepid* through the fray, narrowly avoiding the beams of plasma coming at them from all sides.

"Weapons systems are online," Ziva replied, prompting the targeting computer to pull its data from the scanner. "Auto-targeting engaged."

They pressed forward, allowing the ship's guns to target any vessels not deemed friendly by the scanner. The runner Aroska had finagled his way aboard must have been the ship his landing craft had docked with. Ziva studied its position on the screen and strained to catch a glimpse of it outside, but it was far enough ahead that it had already been swallowed up by the dreadnought's shadow. It was impossible to see much through the chaos anyway.

Her attention was drawn back to the foreground when the proximity alarm began to screech and the targeting reticle on the viewport's heads-up display zeroed in on a downed fighter headed straight for them. "Watch out!" she exclaimed, squeezing the trigger.

Aura veered away as the guns locked on and tore the damaged fighter into hundreds of tiny pieces. The *Intrepid* shuddered upon impact, but the shields held fast and they were back on course within seconds.

"See what you can get on that dreadnought," Aura ordered.

Ziva selected the ship from the dozens of red dots crawling across the screen. A three-dimensional image was projected from the console, and she abandoned the controls long enough to manipulate the hologram.

"There's an open hangar," she said, positive that was where the GA runner had gone.

Out of the corner of her eye, she saw Aura risk a glance at her. "What do you want to do? It's your call."

For several seconds, all she could do was stare out at the sea of silver and gray and plasma and debris. Until a few days ago, she'd never imagined battling the Resistance, much less having such a personal stake in that battle. Aroska, a man she'd vowed to never care for, was aboard that ship, and more likely than not, so was Ronan, the Nosti leader she'd never expected to cross paths with. It was too late to turn back now, and the only way to stop all of this was to finish what she'd started.

She shrugged, sighed, and nodded for Aura to continue on ahead. "Here goes nothing."

# · 55 ·
## RESISTANCE BATTLECRUISER *MARAUDER*
### NORO SYSTEM, FRINGE SPACE

I f he held very still and listened, Aroska could feel the distant vibrations brought about by the raging battle outside. For the most part though, the Resistance flagship was so large and its shields so thick that he wouldn't have even known there was a battle on if he hadn't seen it himself. The runner his squad flew in on had been agile enough that he'd missed most of the excitement anyway.

He snorted to himself when he realized he'd just thought of the group of GA troops as 'his squad.' They'd gotten him this far, and that was all he needed. He wasn't even sure where they all were now. A total of two runners had been sent in, each containing two six-man strike teams commissioned with infiltrating the dreadnought and taking down its shields. The two small generators responsible for maintaining the fighters' shields wouldn't take them long to deal with, but the big one that protected the ship itself would be harder to reach. He had to give the Resistance credit for thorough architecture; if anything, it would give him more time to complete his own task.

He'd decided his main goal would be to find some sort of central computer aboard one of the Resistance ships that contained information the Federation might find useful. What better place to find such a thing than the flagship itself? He'd been ecstatic when he'd learned that was his squad's destination, though the term was relative to the situation. In truth, there was nothing whatsoever to be ecstatic about. This was huge, bigger than anything he'd ever expected to be involved in even once he'd been bumped to full-time spec ops. None of the Haphezians should have been involved in this. This wasn't their fight.

But what was it Emeri had said? *"Whether we like it or not, it is now."* Aroska reminded himself that was the very reason he needed to follow through with this little mission: it shouldn't ever *have* to be their fight. Obviously, some Nosti forces had survived the first Federation eradication. If he could get into a database and send the Feds detailed information on all the previously unknown Res activities, they'd be able to make sure nothing like this ever happened again. The Nosti would never be able to bounce back, and innocent Fringe civilizations would never have to suffer again.

He paused and listened as he came to an intersection in the corridor. So far, the majority of the crew had been focused on the threats outside the ship rather than the ones inside, and those who did focus on the ones inside only seemed to care about the GA strike teams heading for the shield generators. Aroska wasn't even sure if they were aware of his presence. He hadn't informed any of the soldiers of his intentions; he'd simply helped himself to their weapons cache under the pretense of joining them on their mission before splitting off. He wasn't using them, per se, but if the Resistance troops just so happened to be distracted by their presence—therefore allowing him to move about undetected—then that was fine with him.

The sound of approaching footsteps reached his ears and he flattened himself against one of the steel supports running up the wall of the corridor. Hushed voices. Two people. They were moving at a brisk pace, possibly responding to sightings of the strike teams. He held his breath and strained to hear their conversation.

"What do you *mean* we're not getting any support from the Core?"

"That's just what I heard. Ronan's pissed and has been briefing everyone—says we'll need to revise our strategy if we want to hold out against this fleet."

Aroska shrank farther back into the shadows as the two of them jogged by.

"Is the Core refusing to send help? Are they really disregarding a direct request from Ronan?"

"They can't get *through*," the other man said. "The Federation has blockaded all the FTL lanes that would get them out here in time, and they're hesitant to fight their way through for fear of compromising the rest of the plan."

The first man swore. "It's like the Feds already knew we would be here. The Haphezians, too."

Their voices trailed off as they rounded the corner and disappeared. Aroska held still for several more seconds and listened for anyone else who might be approaching before slipping out of his hiding place and continuing on his way. As far as he knew, they *hadn't* known the Resistance was coming until just a few hours ago, but they'd at least known who they were dealing with, and that was half the battle. Still, he was surprised to hear the Federation was cutting off Res forces coming from the Core. Yes, they typically did everything in their power to keep the Resistance contained within the Core, but if he understood correctly, the Feds were *deliberately* preventing any additional Res resources from reaching Ronan's fleet. They were protecting the Fringe. Protecting Haphez.

That didn't make any sense. Thanks to the neutrality agreement, the Federation was obligated to stay out of all Haphezian military affairs, positive or negative. On top of being unlikely to interfere, Aroska had no idea how they'd even *know* to interfere. He highly doubted anyone from Haphez had called for help; his people steered clear of the Federation just as much as the Federation steered clear of them. Besides, blocking all the relevant FTL lanes wasn't something that could be done in mere hours or even overnight. No, this undertaking had been going on behind the scenes for at least a couple of days and had required a reasonable amount of planning. It had also required someone with inside knowledge of the situation.

His communicator buzzed as he crept along and he reached down to switch it off, glancing at the screen as he did so. Ziva again. She was no doubt in Haphor by now, wondering where the hell he was. Part of him felt awful for leaving her behind, but the rest of him knew this needed to be done. He'd gone back and forth on the trip out trying to decide if he should have revealed his intentions—surely she wouldn't have actually tried to talk him out of coming here. She understood as well as anyone how high the stakes were, and if she was caught up in all of the Royal Officer's red tape and unable to make a real contribution, he'd just have to do it for her...and pray he didn't regret it.

He was deep within the heart of the ship now, and he imagined any sort of control room with a computer console would be near the bridge. That was also where he was bound to run into the highest concentration of Res soldiers. They were either there, manning the weapons systems, or gearing up to board any crippled Haphezian vessels they came across. It left all the corridors relatively clear, but it also left crowds in all the places he wanted—and needed—to go.

More voices approaching. He stopped and took a knee, bringing his finger to rest on the trigger of the rifle he'd selected from the runner's weapons cache. He and the GA troops had opted to arm themselves with plasma rifles, partially to prevent excess noise but also because everyone had heard the old stories about how a skilled Nosti could stop a bullet in mid-air and propel it back toward the shooter with enough force to kill them. In theory, they could do the same thing with a plasma bolt, but he'd donned an anti-plasma shield and wasn't too worried about what might happen if they tried.

He'd be safe as long as he managed to maintain distance and cover, the latter of which he was currently lacking. The two Res soldiers who had passed earlier had both been armed with service pistols, and he thought he recognized the generic black bars that somehow transformed into deadly kytaras secured to their belts. He had a knife, but he didn't have much faith in its ability to withstand an attack from one of those sleek blades. His best bet was to catch them by surprise and take them out from afar. They'd be perfectly capable of shooting back, but he had his shield and he'd at least been trained for such situations. Anything was better than being impaled by a sword that wasn't even supposed to exist anymore.

He emerged from the corridor and found himself in a wide circular space—with no cover to speak of—where three other hallways converged. The voices were approaching from the one on his left. The one directly across from him appeared to lead to a bank of elevators, but even if one were standing open for him to duck into, there was no possible way he'd make it across the room without being seen, and retreating would only carry him farther from his destination. Beads of sweat began to form on his forehead as it dawned on him that facing these people head-on was his only real option. If he had any intention of keeping his distance, he'd need to move now before they got any closer.

Aroska raised the rifle, keeping the stock pressed firmly into the crook of his shoulder, and moved in a wide circle around the room until the four Resistance soldiers entered his sights. Their eyes grew wide when they spotted him, but they didn't have time to stare as the plasma bolts began to fly. The man in the front of the pack went down first, his center of mass riddled with smoldering holes. The other three were impressively quick and dove to the floor, though not before one of them took a hit to the shoulder. Their compact, agile bodies rolled easily, and they were back on their feet within moments, closing the distance with the same fervor with which Aroska was trying to maintain it.

His pulse spiked. *Sheyss.*

He continued pulling the trigger as fast as he could. It was clear that they weren't wearing shields, but some unseen force was tugging on his rifle barrel, throwing off his aim. He'd made sure the weapon's strap was secured over his shoulder for exactly this reason, but if he couldn't hit anything, he might as well have the gun ripped from his grasp anyway.

Okay, maybe that was a little bit of an exaggeration. The first soldier was upon him and a pair of kytara blades engaged with a familiar metallic *shink.* It was all he could do to turn the rifle sideways and use it to block the oncoming blow before one of those blades found his shoulder. He brought his knee up with the intent of catching the shorter man in the stomach, but the Nosti danced away, kytara spinning as he adjusted his grip on it.

Aroska turned his attention to the other two men as they came at him from opposite directions. Now it was his turn to drop and roll. He rose back up and took aim, straining to keep the rifle steady in this invisible tugging war. These men all wore black reinforced suits identical to the ones worn by the crew of the *Vigilance*; it had been established just moments before that the armor wasn't plasma resistant, but it did seem to be designed to withstand superficial piercing. That was fine. Fire-arms were his weapon of choice, followed by his own two hands. He'd save his knife as a last resort, or, if need be, a stolen kytara.

*A stolen kytara.* He rushed forward, once again using the rifle as a shield as he lowered his head and rammed his shoulder into the chest of the Nosti he'd first tangled with. He spun and fired while the man was still staggering backward, sending him to the floor with a mass of charred flesh where his face had been. From the new vantage point, he had a clear view of the first man he'd shot. The black kytara hilt gleamed on his belt, free for the taking, but now Aroska had one right at his feet, already engaged.

He wasted no time in slinging the rifle around to his back and snatching the sword up. Assuming he survived all of this, he imagined he'd look back and laugh at what a ridiculous predicament he'd found himself in. At the moment, it was no laughing matter. His heart was thundering in his chest and his hands were slick with sweat as he gripped the kytara. If he was going to fight these people, it would be best to even out the playing field. He thrust one end of the weapon forward, blocking a blow from the man in front of him, then spun around, deflecting another from the man behind him. HSP put all its ops agents through basic melee combat training, but they used metal poles. The worst they could do was leave bruises or maybe fracture a bone. He simply pretended he was wielding one of those poles and tried not to think about the fact that these swords could take his head off if he wasn't careful.

The kytara was surprisingly lightweight. He recalled the few minutes he'd spent holding Ziva's; he'd expected it to somehow feel heavier with the blades extended, but the bulk of the weight seemed to be located within the hilt. He had no idea how the technology worked, and now was not the time to find out. Relying on two pieces of razor-sharp metal that felt light as air to defend him was nerve-wracking, but the blades held fast despite the continual clashing.

His height and weight were proving to be an advantage. Neither of these men stood any taller than his shoulders, but they were quick. He could block their attacks and take his own swings, relying on sheer strength to carry him through, but the two of them seemed to be everywhere at once. Feet shuffled behind him as he crossed blades with the other Nosti. He swept the kytara around, hoping the move would ward off a rear attack for at least a couple of seconds. It did—the man sidestepped and jumped away—but the one in front of him wasted no time in taking advantage of his defenselessness. The hilt of a kytara caught him under the chin the moment he turned around. His head snapped back and he took a staggering step, slashing his own weapon back around to counter what the Nosti had likely hoped to be a finishing blow. The thought occurred to him that his back was now completely exposed, and he expected to hear the sound of a blade penetrating his flesh, feel it pierce his heart. A brief echo somewhere in the back of his mind told him coming here had been a bad idea.

*This is it.*

A blade did pass through flesh, but it wasn't his. The sound of a man choking on his own blood filled Aroska's ears, followed by a familiar female voice: "You might want to duck."

He complied without question, using his forward momentum to force the remaining Nosti's kytara aside. Another blade materialized over his left shoulder, reflecting the greenish tint of the room's lights as it careened forward and embedded itself in the man's stomach. Aroska shied away as Ziva wrenched the sword to one side, throwing the smaller man to the ground; how the delicate blade didn't break was beyond him.

A moist ripping sound echoed through the room as she yanked the blade free and plunged it into his neck, putting a halt to his struggle. He lay there writhing for a moment as blood gushed from his throat. Having no desire to watch, Aroska spun and saw that the other man had been impaled in a similar fashion from behind. He too lay there in a pool of his own blood, though he'd already fallen still.

By the time he turned his attention back to what was in front of him, Ziva was kneeling down and using the loose fabric from the man's uniform to wipe the blood from her blades. Reacting to her words had felt so natural, almost like a simple reflex. It took him a moment to remember she wasn't supposed to be there.

"You come here to try to stop me?" he asked, unsure why he felt compelled to add a bit of an edge to his tone. Perhaps it was partially the embarrassment of realizing he'd bitten off more than he could chew.

She rose to her feet, breathing hard. She had stripped down to a simple tank top and also sported an anti-plasma shield; he could see it shimmering around her if he squinted a little. Based on the blood splatter on her face and neck, she'd already had another run-in with some Nosti soldiers. The fact that she was standing there relatively unscathed and they were nowhere to be found told Aroska all he needed to know.

With a flick of her wrist, the blades retracted into the kytara. "I'm not going to kiss you, if that's what you're asking."

Heat rushed through his face as he recalled what he'd done in Kat's garage. He'd been honest when he'd told her it wasn't how he should have handled the situation. It had been an impulsive move, a diversion to make her think twice about going off to face Dasaro on her own. Since then, he'd wondered on a couple of occasions if he'd subconsciously done it to express how much he truly cared for her, despite the fact that he'd still been trying *not* to care for her at the time. Either way, he'd only made the situation worse for her.

He gave her sweaty, bloody body another once-over and feigned disgust. "I'd rather you didn't, anyway," he said, though after all they'd been through, he almost wished she would. At least it would seem like a sincere gesture this time.

Then it dawned on him that coming here had been the sincerest of any gesture Ziva could ever give. He had no idea how she'd finagled her way out of going to Haphor, but he had a sneaking suspicion she hadn't done it with permission. If that were the case, she had risked not only her career but also her life to come after him, just like she'd done at Dakiti.

"How'd you get here?" he said. "I saw those guards. Emeri and Ganten were hell-bent on keeping you planetside."

"We have an unlikely ally."

She proceeded to give him a quick rundown of the situation, describing how Aura Stannist—of all people—had helped her escape Headquarters in the *Intrepid* before recounting an experience that helped explain her motives for doing so. They'd traced his comms to this vessel and Ziva had followed his scent from the docking hangar.

The look on her face told him she was glad she'd found him when she had. He was, too.

"So what's your story?" she asked, glancing down each of the corridors in turn to make sure they weren't about to have company. "Thought you'd play hero and come up here to take on Ronan by yourself and avenge Maston?"

Aroska felt his face flush again; avenging his brother had certainly been a large part of his motivation. "Not exactly," he replied, going on to explain his plan to find a computer and transmit all the Res data to the Federation.

To his surprise, Ziva actually seemed interested. "Not a bad idea," she said.

"So you didn't just come to get me out safely."

"Hell no. I came all this way—might as well do what I can to rip the Resistance a new one while I'm here."

He couldn't help but crack a smile as he beckoned for her to follow him in the direction he'd been headed. He still had no idea how the two of them could possibly fare against Ronan and a whole dreadnought full of Nosti soldiers, but her presence alone brought him indescribable comfort.

She stopped him when he began to discard his kytara and bring his rifle back around in front of him. "Keep that. It may just save your life."

He almost asked if she was serious, but the look in her eyes answered that question for him. "I don't have a clue how to use it, and I haven't had any melee training in years."

"And you think I have?" she scoffed. "It's kind of like piloting a hoverbike. No matter how long it's been since you've done it, it all starts to come back before long." She broke into a jog and threw a cynical glance back over her shoulder. "Just pretend it's one of those training shafts."

Well, at least they were on the same page. Aroska shook his head and smiled again as he rushed to catch up, no longer quite so afraid of what was to come.

# · 56 ·
# HSP Headquarters
## Noro, Haphez

"**Y**ou mind telling me where the hell you are?" Skeet hissed into his communicator, unsure why exactly he felt the need to keep his voice down. It wasn't like Zinni and Emeri couldn't hear him.

"You know good and well where I am," Ziva's hushed voice replied.

Emeri had resigned to his desk and sat there massaging his forehead. "Payvan, do you have any clue how much troub—"

"Would you believe me if I said this wasn't even my idea?"

Skeet turned toward the director and shrugged. Based on the story they'd gotten from Emeri's two guards, Agent Stannist was indeed the one who had made the first move. She'd failed to check in with the pilot who was supposed to deliver them to Haphor and had instead led Ziva to the landing pad where the *Intrepid* was docked. One of the guards had come away with a broken arm, and a control panel had been completely fried, but in both cases, the damage had been caused by Aura alone. Part of Skeet was glad she'd finally decided to see reason, and the other part was still having a hard time comprehending that she would have done such things.

"Look," Ziva continued. "Aroska rode out on one of the military transports. I couldn't leave him up here on his own."

"You found him?" Skeet said. After close to an hour of trying to figure out where Tarbic had gone, they'd traced his communicator to some point in open space, moving progressively closer to the incoming

Resistance fleet. They'd simply had to sit by and hope for the best; it was futile to waste resources bringing him back, the same reason they'd let Ziva and Aura continue on their way. "Is he okay?"

"Fine," came Aroska's voice. "Might not be if Ziva hadn't shown up when she had."

"Dare I ask where you are now?" Emeri asked, his voice tired but firm.

"Aboard Ronan's flagship," Ziva answered.

The nonchalance of her response made it sound like they were simply taking a stroll in the park. Skeet almost laughed out loud at the ludicrousness of it all, but the idea that his two friends were pressing forward into such dangerous territory suppressed his chuckle.

"I assume Agent Stannist is with you," Emeri said.

"Negative. She remained aboard the *Intrepid* and is manning the guns in order to keep the hangar clear. We're going to need a way off this bucket eventually."

"What can we do on our end?" Skeet asked, throat dry.

"You can start by making sure nobody blows this thing out of the sky while we're aboard. The GA's got strike teams in here trying to take out the shield generators so it will be a while before it *can* be blown out of the sky, but I don't know how long our little task is going to take."

Skeet began to ask what, precisely, that 'little task' was, but she continued talking before he had a chance to say anything.

"Were you able to find anything useful on Payne's comm?"

He moved over to where Zinni had been set up in a comfortable chair in front of Emeri's conference table. A dozen holographic screens rendered before her, each one depicting video feeds from corresponding HSP strike teams. A larger screen branched off from those, displaying tracking data for the teams that had seen success as well as those that had not yet found their quarries.

"Coded messages had been sent out to twenty-three individuals," Zinni explained. Her hands flew over the keypad even as she reclined. A rep from the med center had even come over to give her an IV and monitor her vitals occasionally. "We traced those transmissions and sent teams out to find the recipients. Fifteen have been neutralized so far, and we're closing in on the others."

"Hey, you," Ziva said, her voice softening significantly. "Good work. How are you holding up?"

"Not bad, all things considered."

Despite her amicable response, Skeet saw Zinni bristle a bit. She had yet to comment further on Ziva's newly revealed connection with the Resistance, but he had a hunch that was what was causing her current discomfort.

"Shall we keep you updated?" he asked.

"No," Ziva answered. "We're going dark in a few minutes—getting too close to the bridge to risk the excess noise. Coordinate with Aura in the *Intrepid* and do what you can to keep Ganten off our backs until this thing is over."

"Got it," he said with a sigh. "We're monitoring the fleet from here. Looks like everyone is holding just fine, but we can't do much until those shields are down. Based on their attack patterns, the Resistance wasn't expecting us to be ready for them, and it has thrown them out of rhythm. We're closer to matching them in numbers than I originally thought. It probably won't be pretty, but we should be able to take them out eventually."

"Yeah, about that...." Zinni murmured.

When Skeet looked back at her, she was sitting bolt upright, her gaze directed straight ahead as she manipulated the controls and minimized the screens. A holographic representation of the battle appeared in its place, with the relative positions of all the participating vessels marked by colored dots. They'd tapped into the GA's network, so all the Resistance ships appeared red while all the Haphezian ships had turned green. She zoomed out until the battle was hardly more than a tangled mess of red and green spots. A smaller cluster of yellow dots appeared on the edge of the hologram—the edge of the GA's sensor radius—and moved steadily toward the conflict. At least twenty more ships were approaching, and they were coming from the same direction as Ronan's fleet.

"What's happening?" Ziva demanded. Skeet had almost forgotten the transmission was still open.

"I'm trying..." Zinni said, eyes narrowed and brows furrowed as she brought the incoming ships into full view and sorted through the data the GA was picking up on them.

Relevant information appeared after just a few seconds, which both relieved Skeet and startled him. The ships weren't Resistance; that much was clear. They were from a world that had just as little business participating in this fight as the Haphezians. And based on the hail that was now coming through, they belonged to a person he'd never expected to see in this part of the galaxy.

"Hey, uh, Z? You wouldn't happen to know what Tobias Niio is doing here, would you?"

# · 57 ·

# DURUTIAN SCOUT SHIP *DEONIDA*
## NORO SYSTEM, FRINGE SPACE

As the ship surged forward through the FTL tunnel, Taran still couldn't believe he was on comm with the head of the Niiosian Mob. He could hardly consider himself 'on comm,' though—the gangsters were busy trying not to get themselves shot down by the Haphezians, who were quite understandably on edge. The transmission to Tobias Niio's ship was still live, but the man had probably forgotten about Taran by now, caught up as he was in conversation with some admiral aboard the Haphezian flagship.

"Stand down, *Soroya*," crackled a new voice. "New intel from home. These people are on our side—add their ships to the network."

"On whose authority?" Admiral Ostin cried.

There was muffled shouting in the background, followed by a perturbed female voice: "—st patch me through." The voice sent a chill down Taran's spine.

"*My* authority," she said, her voice clearer now. "Captain Ziva Payvan, HSP spec ops. And before you tell me I have no authority in this situation, I want you to stop and ask yourself if you really want to win this battle."

"Agent Payvan, it's wonderful to hear your voice," Tobias crooned. "Ziva did invite us to this party, Admiral, and I would tend to agree with her. You people need all the help you can get."

Taran swiveled in his chair to look at Mae, who shook her head and kept her gaze directed ahead as she piloted the ship. He'd been on comm with Tobias for the past hour, and not once had the mobster mentioned being summoned by Ziva. Then again, Taran hadn't mentioned it either, mostly because he was still considering this a matter of defending his own people, not helping the Haphezians. As far as the other party knew, each of them was responding to Ronan's presence for personal reasons, and they'd just happened to stumble across each other's fleets on the way.

Ostin sighed. "Fine, add them to the network."

"I should also inform you that there's a Durutian fleet en route in the Alpha 26 FTL lane," Tobias continued. "You'll want to extend this courtesy to them as well."

"The Durutians?" Payvan said. "About damn time!"

Mae leaned over and tilted the comm receiver toward her. "You didn't think we'd let you have all the fun, did you?"

Taran was glad to see that her face remained emotionless. Despite the joking nature of her words, she wasn't smiling. *Good.* She'd been far too cordial with the Haphezians from the beginning, in his opinion.

Payvan made some sound that might have been a cynical chuckle; it was hard to tell with all the noise on the channel. "What's your play?"

He spoke up before Mae could, hoping to reinforce the fact that both his people and the Niiosians were there of their own accord. "We're still a few minutes out, but we're planning to break out of the FTL lane at the last minute and take the Resistance by surprise. We'll be coming in from the southwest while Ronan's fleet is focused on Tobias's ships approaching from the northeast. Our force consists of sixty-three vessels sent by the Durutian army as well as five of our scout ships that have been commissioned by the Galactic Federation. Combined, we'll have more than enough firepower to overwhelm Res forces."

"Good," Ostin said. "I'll send ships to fill in the perimeter when you arrive."

In all honesty, the plan had been Tobias's; Taran had to give him credit for being a good strategist, and he wondered if that skill came from years of having an entire moon—hell, an entire sector of the galaxy—under his thumb.

"All the ships in the universe won't do us any good until we can get those shields down," Payvan said.

"What can we do?" Mae asked.

"We could use some additional manpower aboard Ronan's flag-ship. Help the strike teams take out the generators, or at least run interference and keep the Res troops occupied."

Mae shot Taran a glance. "Will do."

"Copy that. We're going dark—Payvan out."

The channel was silent for a moment before someone from the *Soroya* came back on. "Durutian scout ship, we're picking you up on our scanners now. Transmitting network codes."

Taran turned his attention to the screen on the dashboard, watching as hundreds of colored dots appeared. A smaller cluster representing Tobias's fleet moved in behind the Resistance ships, and the group representing his own ships was closing in on the battle with incredible speed.

Mae's hands flew over the controls and she opened a second comm channel for their fleet. "Leaving FTL in three, two, one…"

There was a brief jolt as the *Deonida* jumped out of the FTL lane. Space stopped swirling and the view outside came into sharp focus. Despite the distance that still remained between their ships and the battle, the combined forces of Ronan and the Haphezians completely filled the front viewport. Taran's first thought was that it wasn't what he'd been expecting to see, but if not this, he wasn't sure what he *had* been expecting. The fact that the Resistance had been building an armada of this size aside from what they already possessed within the Core was inconceivable, yet there it was, right in front of him.

Mae reached over to mute the comm system. "You didn't mention the fact that Matney is on his way out here with more Feds."

"It's irrelevant," Taran replied, watching as several of the larger frigates they'd brought surpassed their ship and headed toward the conflict. The *Deonida* was agile and was outfitted with basic weaponry, but Command had ordered them to let some of the better-equipped vessels lead the assault. Now that Taran was getting a look at the scene for himself, he had no desire to argue. "It's not like he's actually planning on taking part in the fight. All he wants to do is wait on the sidelines and take Resistance prisoners once the rest of us have done all the dirty work."

"Well," she sighed, "at least the Federation blockade is still holding." She nodded toward the mess in front of them. "This is a big enough fleet for my taste—we can't afford for Ronan to have any more reinforcements coming from the Core."

Taran drew a deep breath and readied himself to take control of their weapons systems. "So, where shall we start?"

"You heard Payvan," Mae replied with a shrug. "I'm picking up strong shield readings on that flagship, and there's no way we're taking that monster out until those shields are down. I don't know about you, but I have a hunch Ronan's aboard that ship, and in that case, I'd suggest we make it a priority."

Taran smiled. It was tempting to reach over and take her hand, but he decided against it for fear of compromising her ability to fly and his ability to control the guns. "We've established that we're ready to save the galaxy," he said. "You ready to make good on that?"

# · 58 ·
# RESISTANCE BATTLECRUISER *MARAUDER*
## NORO SYSTEM, FRINGE SPACE

They were finally on the command level. Without a schematic and without a comm connection, navigation had been difficult. The sheer vastness of the ship hadn't helped. The only time Ziva had set foot on a vessel this size, she'd simply stopped in a docking bay long enough to exchange a prisoner for payment. But based on the frequency of their run-ins with Resistance soldiers and the fact that the elevators would go no higher, they had to be headed in the right direction.

She couldn't help but recognize the familiarity of the situation. She and Aroska creeping through a hostile environment together—it reminded her all too much of Dakiti. At least they'd been able to blend in a bit there, though the reasons behind that still made her shudder. The real difference now was that neither of them was ready to shoot the other in the back. She caught herself when she realized she was glad Aroska was there. So often, she preferred to accomplish tasks alone, or if not alone, with people she trusted wholeheartedly. The fact that he now fit that description still surprised her. After everything they'd been through together in such a short time, she had to admit there was nobody she'd rather have backing her up right now.

The entire ship reeked of nostium. More accurately, the *crew* of the ship reeked of nostium. Even after spending the past couple of days in the presence of so many Nosti, it was a bit of a shock to smell it so strongly again after close to ten years. The scent made the hairs on the back of her neck stand on end as she recalled her final battle with

Gamon. Killing him had allowed her to escape both his control and his plot to take her to Forus, and the freedom had been such a relief. But this scent—this *stench* so similar to what she'd once smelled in his presence—sent her right back to that tiny apartment where she'd struggled for her life. If he'd succeeded in taking her, she wondered if she might still be here on this very ship, fighting against her own people right now. Perhaps Gamon had even been on comm with Ronan that day.

"We've got to be getting close," Aroska murmured, pulling her from her thoughts.

Ziva hummed an agreement and paused to listen where two hallways converged. *Yes, just like Dakiti.* Except now their world shuddered and trembled every so often, a stark reminder of how unstable the situation really was.

They'd had to stop and find somewhere to hide on three occasions now, watching with bated breath from tight spaces as groups of Resistance soldiers jogged by. They'd opted to engage a couple of the smaller squads, with Ziva using her Nostia to strip them of any comm devices while Aroska took advantage of the distraction and got several shots off. The routine had worked considerably well; with luck, they'd only had to take on one or two Nosti at a time with the kytaras. As much as the sword-fighting skills were coming back to her, Ziva had to agree with Aroska in his belief that nothing beat a reliable firearm.

Their tactic had also been successful in that they'd made it this far without anyone on the bridge being alerted to their presence. She was sure someone on the ship knew they were there *somewhere*—they'd left quite the trail of bodies and hadn't had time to stop and clean up—but at least they'd been able to prevent anyone from calling for reinforcements. Most of the squads they'd crossed had probably been on their way to investigate the newest corpses.

The thought prompted Ziva to glance down at the strip of cloth tied around her left bicep. She had no desire to recall all the cuts and gashes she'd sustained while learning to fight with Gamon, nor the one he'd left as a parting gift on her face. The makeshift bandage was currently the only thing keeping the fresh laceration underneath from bleeding all over the floor. The last thing they needed to do was leave a blood trail.

The corridor widened ahead, transforming into an administrative area. A variety of consoles jutted from the walls, and a quick glance told her they were for running the ship on auxiliary power. She released a sigh of relief; no crewmembers would be rushing in anytime soon to man their stations.

Out of curiosity, she tapped at one of the control panels and was disappointed to see that the console did nothing more than regulate the power distribution to the ship's systems. It appeared to only activate if the secondary systems were online, and even then, at least half of these consoles would need to be manned in order to accomplish anything. Her hopes that they might be able to recover some data or cause some damage from here were dashed.

She sighed and beckoned for Aroska to join her behind one of the workstations, crouching down in case any more Resistance troops came along. She took the opportunity to check her bandage before shutting her eyes and tilting her head back against the wall for a moment.

"You okay?" he whispered.

She nodded and cleared her throat. "If we advance any farther, there'll be no turning back. That's not to say we *won't* come back, but we'll have to finish what we've started. We could retreat now—go back to the *Intrepid*, let the GA finish dealing with the shield generators— but it would mean giving up on finding that command console. I'm willing to press on, but I need to know you're with me."

"I am," Aroska said without hesitation.

"But here's the thing. I need you to focus. Focus on the *enemy* and do whatever it takes to keep yourself alive. Do not think about me. Do not worry about me. The second you take your mind off of what's right in front of you, they'll know it, and they'll exploit it."

This time there was a short pause before he managed a nod.

"I don't even need to tell you we'll be outnumbered. I'll bet there are fifty people on that bridge. If you want to have any chance of coming out of this alive, you *have* to focus." She realized she'd been speaking through gritted teeth. Trying to make him understand was difficult when she was having a hard enough time convincing herself of what needed to be done.

"I get it," he said, and she saw in his eyes that he truly did. "But listen, if we don't make it through this, I want to say—"

"Shut the hell up."

"Just listen to me."

"No! You will not talk like that. If I ever hear those words out of your mouth again, I'll make sure you *don't* make it out alive." She stared him down until he complied and then sat back with an exasperated sigh. "*Sheyss*, Aroska. Now's not the time to be arguing."

In all honesty, she was more concerned about what he'd been trying to say than whether they'd survive. In her experience, however, thinking about the possibility of not surviving greatly increased the probability of not surviving, so she felt her anger was legitimate.

As much as she desired a rest after running through the ship and cutting down so many Resistance troops, she also didn't want to still be aboard once the shields were down and the real bombardment started. She risked a glance back and forth down the corridor before gesturing at Aroska. "Let me see your belt again."

He sat up straighter, showing off the collection of items he'd brought from the GA runner. Aside from his rifle, he was also armed with a pistol and carried spare plasma cells for each. There were the three Malesium-core thermal grenades; based on the klaxons that sounded throughout the ship, the bridge had been sealed off, so these could be used to breach it. Despite their short blast radius, using them on the bridge itself was out of the question except as a last resort, as detonating them near the viewports could take the whole ship down and them along with it. Smoke and flash grenades would be more useful—he carried two of the former and one of the latter.

She'd spent much of their journey through the ship formulating a plan, having expected to not find the central computer until they reached the bridge. If it was set up anything like the stills she'd seen from the *Vigilance*, there would be a variety of consoles along the walls, similar to the ones she and Aroska were currently hiding behind. There'd be a large control board stretching across the front for the helmsmen, as well as a podium of some sort where the commander—likely Ronan—could stand and give orders. The majority of the soldiers occupying the bridge would probably be communications techs, analysts, and operations officers working in the CIC. Many of them might not even be Nosti. Even if they were, they were likely to be sitting down at first, putting them at an immediate disadvantage.

If they both started shooting from the outset, they might be able to make a good dent in enemy numbers before any of the troops had even gotten to their feet. The smoke grenades would come into play next, concealing their movements as they advanced farther inside. The key then would be to somehow seal the bridge back off so no reinforcements could get inside until they'd done what they could to neutralize the threats within.

She had just opened her mouth to vocalize her thoughts to Aroska when her ears picked up the sound of boots headed their way. Lots of boots. More than any of the other squads they'd encountered so far. The sound was headed toward the bridge. Headed right for them.

It was ironic that she'd just been chastising Aroska for having a potentially negative outlook on the situation. Her own mind was now going places she normally never allowed it to. She pictured them being trapped between the bridge and the group of incoming soldiers with nowhere to run, stuck there behind the auxiliary consoles of all places.

"*Sheyss*," she muttered, readying her kytara. If she moved now, perhaps she'd at least be able to take a few Nosti with her when she went down.

As she rose to her feet, two things struck her: the fact that these newcomers didn't reek of nostium like all the other crew members, and the subtle whirrs, clicks, and chirps that could only be the result of cybernetic implants.

Relief took over for only a moment before she realized the Durutians were probably ready to shoot anything that moved. "Hey!" she called, listening as the footsteps slowed. "HSP, behind the consoles. We're coming out—don't shoot!"

"Payvan?" a man replied. "Show yourself!"

*Reddic.* Ziva drew her pistol and held it out where he could see it, signaling for Aroska to do the same. She stepped out from behind the terminal to find a dozen...no, *two* dozen Durutian soldiers watching her from behind the barrels of their myriad of firearms. More were appearing by the second.

They all lowered their weapons on Reddic's command, and Ziva and Aroska returned theirs to their holsters.

"I believe you called for assistance," Mae said.

"Think forty people can take the bridge?" Reddic asked. He shrugged and gestured at them. "Forty-two?"

Ziva had to fight away a smile as she surveyed the group of 'borgs amassing behind him; indeed, there appeared to be forty of them. "I think so, yeah," she replied. "How'd you get through so fast?"

"Command sent a pair of personnel carriers to come around behind Ronan's fleet with us. We found a ship—your ship from Aubin—in one of the hangars, so we knew we were moving in the right direction. We were just headed for the bridge—never expected to actually run into you. Crossed paths with a couple of Nosti squads, but we took care of them without too much trouble."

"Turns out the ability to stop bullets with your mind is vastly ineffective when there are twenty different people shooting at you," Mae quipped. It was difficult to tell thanks to those glowing implants, but there may have been a twinkle in her eye.

"We saw some of your, ah, handiwork on the way up here," Reddic said. "You two did all of that?"

Ziva nodded and held up her kytara hilt. A quick glance over the group revealed several other Durutians who had picked up discarded kytaras, so she imagined nobody would find it odd that she had one. The fact that she actually knew how to use it would be a different story entirely.

She gave them a quick rundown of her idea. The thought of executing it with only two people seemed completely ludicrous now that she was addressing such a large group. The overall structure of the plan had been sound enough, but lack of manpower had been the major issue. Incorporating the 'borgs was bound to ensure success.

"We have more smoke bombs," Reddic said, nodding his approval. He pointed to his silver eyes. "And we've got thermal imaging, so we'll be able to see through the smokescreens. If you two go in first and draw their attention, we'll hit them with the bombs and take them out before they even know what hit them."

Both he and Mae were much more enthusiastic than Ziva had expected. "Good. Once we're all through, station a few of your men near the entrance to pick off any reinforcements headed this way. We can create a choke point—use the narrow opening to our advantage."

Reddic dipped his head and turned to address his men, giving her the opportunity to turn and address Aroska. She was pleasantly surprised to find that the uncertainty in his eyes had disappeared altogether.

"You ready?" she asked.

He nodded and gave her the faintest of smiles.

They all turned as a unit and resumed their trek toward the bridge and the CIC. Aroska removed two of the thermal grenades from his belt as they came to a stop at the base of a ramp leading up to a wide, sealed door. There were likely Resistance troops lurking just on the other side, waiting for a force to try to breach it. Ziva doubted they'd be expecting a force of this size.

Aroska flipped the grenades' primer switches and tossed them up the ramp. They adhered magnetically to the door, one at the top and one at the bottom. Everyone shielded their faces as the devices went off, but there was no time to waste. Ziva was on her way up the ramp before the fireball had even faded, ducking through the opening with Aroska hot on her heels.

Her anti-plasma shield was still functional—she'd made sure of that—and the thought brought her some comfort as she dashed forward. She saw and heard everything around her as a fresh adrenaline rush kicked in. As expected, the layout of the bridge was similar to the area they'd just left but on a bigger scale. Workstations lined the walls on either side of the room, and two massive circular tables were situated on each side of the center aisle, one displaying holographic statistical data on the battle and the other displaying holograms of other fleet commanders.

The soldiers who'd been watching the door had all shied away during the explosion and were just now regaining their bearings. A quick glance at them revealed that they were armed with plasma rifles rather than projectile; Ziva ignored them and let her shield absorb their fire as she pressed on, satisfied that she'd successfully captured their attention.

The sharp cracks of metal objects hitting the floor rang out behind her, followed by angry shouts and a sudden volley of gunfire. Several loud pops preceded a low hiss, and she knew the smoke bombs had been deployed. The Durutians poured in behind her, and Nosti began to fall. She holstered her pistol in favor of her kytara and engaged the blades just in time to block a blow from a man who swung his own sword at her. Her forward momentum threw him off balance and she parried, catching him in the face with her elbow before driving one end of her kytara through his rib cage. She wrenched the blade free and continued on, barely breaking stride.

A pair of Durutian soldiers had caught up to them, detonating more smoke bombs and providing cover fire as they pushed forward. The helm itself was separated from the CIC by a narrow walkway flanked by trenches that contained several more weapons control officers. The smoke consumed them and Reddic's men began shooting, keeping them occupied while Ziva and Aroska turned their sights on the figure who watched them from the platform ahead, kytara already in hand.

Ziva slowed to a steady jog and then stopped moving altogether as she regarded the person. Full Nosti armor. Glossy black hair. Merciless black eyes. Average stature but strong, just like the rest of the Resistance troops.

Aroska pulled up short half a step behind her. His voice was hardly more than a whisper: "Oh *sheyss*."

The woman on the platform was at least a head shorter than either of them but no less menacing for it. The battle raging just outside the front viewports provided a violent backdrop for her as she took a step toward them. She kept her gaze locked with Ziva's, looking on with an unmistakable recognition in her eyes. Ziva tightened her grip on her kytara as confusion was replaced by realization; despite the fact that she'd never seen this woman in her life, she knew exactly who she was.

*Tav Ronan.*

She was roughly the same height as all the other Nosti they had encountered, built for speed and agility. She was well-muscled but maintained a certain poise that could only be the result of a long military career. Her long, dark hair had been bundled into a heavy braid that trailed all the way down her back.

Ziva took a couple of precious seconds to listen to the action behind them, not daring to remove her eyes from Ronan. The Durutians had advanced farther into the bridge and were keeping most of the officers occupied. The four chief helmsmen at the forward control panel were too busy trying to maneuver the ship through the chaos outside to pay them any mind. That left her and Aroska free to deal with the leader of the Resistance.

"You *did* say you wanted to be sent in for a solo strike," Aroska muttered, moving up to stand beside her and readying his own kytara with a surprisingly steady hand.

She couldn't argue with that, and she silently reminded herself that this interesting new development by no means altered the playing field. Ronan was Ronan, and she needed to be dealt with either way.

"Ziva Payvan," the woman murmured, shifting her kytara to her other hand. The look in her eyes told Ziva she'd been waiting for this moment, maybe even expecting it. "It's a pleasure to finally meet you. A pity you couldn't have joined us sooner."

Ziva merely shook her head, not in the mood to chat. She'd already been forced to relive all her time with Gamon over the past few days; hearing the story of her intended fate would only make matters worse. It was eerie enough that Ronan even knew who she was.

Not wishing to waste any time, she readied her kytara and sprang forward, but she only made it a couple of paces before being blinded by a brilliant flash of light that filled the entire front viewport. The bridge shuddered, throwing them all to the ground. Ziva reached for Aroska to keep him from falling down into the weapons control alcove, but his hand slipped from her grasp and he rolled over the edge of the walkway. She turned her attention back to the helm just in time to see the residual shimmering of the shields following the blast outside...and just in time to see Ronan's kytara blade barreling toward her face.

For just an instant, she was transported back to that tiny apartment and saw Gamon's sword coming at her. She jerked her head away, cringing at the sound the weapon made as it scraped across the floor beside her ear, and could almost feel Gamon's serrated blade where it had cut into the side of her face. She raised her own kytara, deflecting another blow from Ronan as she swept her legs around and caught the woman squarely in the knee with the heel of her boot. Ronan stumbled backward with a grunt and found herself in the sights of one of the Durutians, but the plasma bolts he fired veered away from her as if she'd shot them herself. Ziva ducked away instinctively despite her shield and regained her footing, closing the distance between the two of them while the Nosti still had her attention on the shooter.

The screech of metal on metal filled her ears as their kytaras clashed. Perhaps it was just something about *Ronan*—the name that had been plaguing them all for nearly three months—that made this particular battle seem so much more significant than the others. She slid her primary blade against Ronan's until it struck the hilt and the woman was forced to adjust her grip, all the while trying to convince herself that this was no different than any of the dozens of Nosti she'd already struck down on her way through the ship.

"You might want to duck," said a voice behind her.

She did, and Aroska's blade whistled over the top of her head, meeting Ronan's with a sharp *clank*. The Nosti steeled herself, parried, and spun, in perfect position to put her kytara through Aroska's chest if not for the fact that her aim was thrown off when the heel of Ziva's hand slammed into her face.

A distant explosion rumbled somewhere within the hull, and alarms began to screech at the helm. "We've lost primary shields!" one of the pilots cried.

*The generator.* Ziva could see in Ronan's eyes that she knew it, too. With the shields down at last, the GA wouldn't hesitate to give this ship their full attention. She'd be relieved if not for the fact that she was still aboard.

A wave of Nostia slammed into her from Ronan's outstretched hands, hitting her like a punch to the gut and sending Aroska flying backward into the wall. He slumped to the floor, dazed and blinking, and his kytara skidded across the bridge and disappeared under a workstation.

"He's making a valiant effort," the Resistance leader said, "but really, Payvan, your people should not be meddling in affairs which aren't theirs."

"Oh, you *made* it our affair," Ziva retorted. A tingle coursed through the back of her head, and she threw her hands forward as if shoving an invisible object. Her own wave of Nostia struck Ronan, knocking her to the ground and propelling her backward into one of the helmsmen's chairs. "You made it our affair when you sent Jak Gamon here to turn a little girl into a piece of contraband, you *vehr frouchten shouka!*"

The look on Ronan's face sent a chill down Ziva's spine. Despite the blood gushing from her nose, it wasn't a look of pain. It was a display of shock, awe, maybe even pride. "The formula worked," she murmured.

Ziva was upon her again in seconds. "It didn't work!" she shouted, taking the time to drive her kytara into the stomach of a pilot who had pulled out a pistol. She sidestepped and brought the sword back over her head, stopping Ronan's blade from slicing into her shoulder. "You killed hundreds of people!"

The Nosti came in at a low angle, slamming the hilt of her kytara into Ziva's shins. She was quick, stronger than Ziva would have expected of a human woman her size. But size was still her weak point; she could dodge and dart and slash all she wanted, but she couldn't defend against such high attacks forever.

Fueled by rage now, Ziva went at Ronan again, feinting left before sweeping her kytara around from the right and slicing downward. The Nosti jabbed upward in response, switching to a one-handed grip just long enough to deliver a hard right hook. The blow struck Ziva directly in the mouth and was followed up by another flood of Nostia that sent her careening backward.

As she regained her footing and spit out some of the blood streaming from her split lip, she saw movement in her peripherals past Ronan's left shoulder. Aroska was on his feet again. That knowledge triggered a fresh surge of adrenaline, and she rushed forward once more, determined that this would be her final attack. Her first blow was blocked effortlessly. Ronan stopped her next one as well, their blades scraping harshly together until the Nosti's caught on the edge of Ziva's hilt. Ziva pushed down, taking a moment to study the positions of the swords. If she broke off and brought the other end of hers around, she'd be vulnerable for a split second and Ronan's kytara would be buried in her neck before she knew what hit her.

"You came all the way up here," the woman spat. "Did you think you were going to just kill me?"

*More movement. An idea.*

"Nah," Ziva replied. "I figured *he* would."

She squeezed her kytara's hilt, lifted, and pulled. It separated just as easily as it had that night in Aroska's kitchen. She kept the left blade crossed with Ronan's, pressing down with all her strength. The right blade she tossed to Aroska as he came within a meter of the Nosti leader. There was a brief look of confusion on the woman's face before the short sword plunged into her spine. Ziva sidestepped to avoid the blade as it burst through a seam in her armor's chest plate. Aroska yanked it upward, then ripped it back down into her gut. She collapsed to her knees with the sword still impaling her, and her own kytara clattered to the floor. She was looking straight into Ziva's eyes when she finally fell forward onto her stomach, the pool of blood spreading quickly beneath her.

Ziva watched her until her spastic attempt at breathing ceased altogether. Another enemy dead...that's all it was, she told herself. Another Bothum. Another Saun. Another Dasaro. It didn't matter who Ronan was, didn't matter that she'd been behind the scenes of Ziva's tenuous upbringing. What mattered was that she'd been responsible for the deaths of thousands of people across the galaxy and that her plan likely involved killing thousands more.

She felt Aroska's gaze on her as she stooped down and tore the short sword free from Ronan's body, fitting the two halves back together and wiping off the blood before retracting the blades. The three remaining helmsmen all watched her with mouths agape, but she paid them no mind; they'd either die when the ship went down or have their escape pods blown away, and there was no need to kill them here.

Based on the look on Aroska's face, he wanted to say everything and nothing at all. He placed a hand on her shoulder and settled on a happy medium: "Let's find a computer."

She shrugged his hand away and turned to jog back toward the CIC, where the Durutians were picking off the last of the deck officers and tending to their wounded.

Groans from wounded 'borgs and not-quite-dead Res troops rose up throughout the residual smoke that still drifted around the room. Reddic appeared through the haze, gripping a back-up pistol in one hand while he mopped at a cut on his scalp with the other. His silver implants glowed in the shadows and reflected the red strobes flashing from the ceiling in sync with the still-wailing klaxons.

"We need to go," he said, rushing over to help someone who came staggering through the smoke. It was Mae, coughing and sputtering and clutching at a long gash that had torn her arm open from her shoulder to her elbow.

"Not until we get what we came for," Ziva said, coming to a stop at the main control panel for one of the large tables.

"You're telling me *that* wasn't it?" he exclaimed, gesturing toward Ronan's mangled body.

"Far from it. Get back to the hangar and prep for takeoff. This place is going to start falling apart around us. We'll be right behind you."

He didn't look convinced, but he turned to Mae, who hadn't removed her eyes from the Resistance leader's corpse.

"It's done," she murmured. She shook her head and scoffed. "Tav Ronan."

Unless Ziva was mistaken, there was something wistful about her tone, almost as if she'd been hoping to kill the woman herself.

They exchanged one more uneasy glance before the Durutians broke away, leaving her to sift through the data on the screen. Ship names. Crew manifests. Schematics of facilities on Forus. A list that appeared to contain the names of every known Nosti. After only a minute of searching, the stream of information seemed endless. There was no way she'd be able to choose relevant data to transmit to the Federation; it was *all* relevant.

"Find anything?" Aroska asked, helping a couple of straggling Durutians to their feet.

"There's so much here," she answered as her eyes pored over the text on the screen. "Transmission would take...." She shook her head.

"How long?"

"Longer than we have. Call Aura and make sure she's ready to go." She risked a glance back to the helm, where the three pilots were struggling to keep the massive ship steady. "We'll need to get out of here fast."

She continued reading, listening to Aroska initiate the conversation with Aura as she tried to decide what to do. There was always the option of just transmitting everything to the Federation and hoping something useful would get through before the ship was destroyed. It would be faster than standing there trying to decide what data would be most valuable. She'd at least mark the facility list and roster of names as priority and get them sent out first; with any luck, those files would transmit entirely, and the Feds could act on it even if the rest of the information never made it through.

The ship was already connected to the rest of the Resistance network within the Core, so establishing a connection to the Federation took no time at all. Ziva initiated the transmission, beginning with the data on the Forus facilities, but hesitated for a moment with her eyes fixed on the roster.

*You know your name is probably in there.*

Aura's voice echoed in the background. "—but we're holding. Between the *Intrepid*, the GA runners, and the Durutian ships, we've managed to keep any enemy fighters from landing in the bay. Squad of Res soldiers came in here with a mounted gun to take us out—took care of them, too."

*You send that out and the entire galaxy is going to know who you are.*

"We were safe while the shields were up, but now they're trying to fire on us. The ship's already going down—they don't care if it sustains more damage."

"You said the ship's going down?" Aroska said.

"It's drifting. Stabilizers are gone. The GA's been picking at it since the shields went down. They know we're in here but they're not going to wait forever. The soldiers have more of the same explosives they used to take out the generators. If we can remotely detonate a large number of them in the hangar, we can cripple this thing for good."

Ziva swallowed, unable to help but sort the list by location and search for Haphez. Gamon's name was there, struck out in red. Her stomach sank when her gaze fell upon her own name right below it. A quick glance around the screen revealed no way to remove it—the data was read-only.

*There's no more time to think about this. Just send it.*

It was true. If they didn't leave now, they'd be vaporized along with the ship. And if she didn't send this list, the Resistance would continue its expansion into the Fringe. Another Ronan would eventually rise up, and innocent people would continue to die.

She added the roster to the transmission without another thought.

"Many of the escape pods are being jettisoned already, so you should have a fairly clear escape route. Get here as soon as you can."

"Copy that," Aroska said as he ended the call. "You ready?"

Ziva nodded, ensuring the entire database was set to transmit before stepping away from the table. "I prioritized some data the Feds might find…interesting."

"Good. Let's get out of here."

After a painstaking infiltration, it was always amazing how quickly the trip out of a place went. In this case, part of that was due to the fact that they weren't tiptoeing around and weren't running into Resistance soldiers at every corner. Those they *did* run into only ever managed a few half-hearted plasma shots before continuing on their way to the escape pods. Now that their secret—their presence—was out in the open, there was no reason to continue their little suicide game. Saving themselves and preserving their way of life had become the priority.

By the time they made it back to the hangar, both were out of breath and Ziva's pulse was hammering in her ears. Aura, a GA soldier, and several of the Durutians waited in the access corridor with weapons trained on the entrance. All the explosives Aura had mentioned were wired together along the corridor wall, fitted with a remote detonation receiver. The *Intrepid* sat undamaged just ahead, though the same couldn't be said for two of the Durutian ships.

Aura gestured for them to hurry just as the first shots rang out behind them. A quick exploration of her belt told Ziva that her shield generator had been damaged in the fight with Ronan. Aroska darted forward and she ducked through the hangar entrance behind him, taking cover against the wall just inside the door. Aura took up a similar position on the opposite side, leaning away to dodge the spray of plasma that made it through the opening. She turned and fired several blind shots toward the approaching soldiers, slowing their advance and giving Ziva a chance to step away and reach the door controls.

Hurried footsteps echoed through the hallway as she hit the control panel. The door slid shut but hissed open again the moment she removed her hand. She pressed the button again, holding it this time. Blackened, melted wires jutted out beside her hand, the result of a stray plasma bolt. There certainly wasn't time to fix it before the ship was destroyed, and the moment she let go, the Resistance soldiers would be pouring through. She looked over the door itself, searching for an override, but saw nothing.

She turned back toward the hangar. "Get to the ship!" she ordered, looking Aroska in the eye as she did so. "I'm not going to tell you again!"

The Durutians complied without question, and to her surprise, so did Aroska...or maybe he'd just gotten caught up in the crowd. She watched them for a moment before returning her focus to the control panel and studying the path to the ship. She saw no form of cover; if the door were to open, they'd be picked off before they could reach the *Intrepid*, and if any of the explosives were hit, they'd all be dead in an instant.

"That goes for you, too," she muttered in Aura's direction, swallowing hard as she closed her eyes and listened to the angry shouts on the other side of the door.

"I don't think so." A hand settled over hers, maintaining pressure on the switch. "Go."

Ziva turned and once again found herself on the receiving end of the same steely look she often gave people. Aura's mouth formed a straight line as she used her free hand to pry Ziva's out from under her own. The door held fast.

"I left someone behind once. I'm not going to do it again."

Ziva took a step away, surprised by the ease with which she did. "And now you expect me to leave *you* behind?"

Aura didn't even bother arguing. "You were right—I'm not convinced I did the right thing back then. Let me do the right thing now. I'm saving your life here." She held Ziva's gaze for another beat. "Go on! Go!"

Ziva turned, but rather than head for the ship, she beckoned to the Durutians who had been waiting in the corridor. "Where's the remote detonator?"

One of them appeared in the *Intrepid's* hatch and passed a small object off to Aroska where he waited at the base of the boarding ramp. He jogged over and lobbed the detonator to her. She caught it and pressed it into Aura's empty palm.

"See if you can take a few of the bastards with you."

Aura gave her a terse nod and jerked her head toward the ship.

Ziva didn't look back as she and Aroska sprinted across the hangar and up the boarding ramp. Taran and Mae and a handful of their soldiers were crowded into the cargo area and more lined the corridor to the cockpit. Ziva slid into the pilot's seat and brought the ship up off the floor, following the remaining Durutian ship and the two GA runners out of the bay.

"*Soroya* to *Intrepid*," a voice crackled over the comm. "We're picking up your exit from the port docking hangar. Confirm."

"Affirmative," she replied. "You're all clear—fire at will."

The *Marauder* shuddered violently just as they cleared the hangar. Something large and heavy struck the rear of the *Intrepid*, and the ship listed sideways.

"No idea what that was," Aroska said in response to the look Ziva shot him as she struggled to regain control. His eyes remained fixed on all the readings displayed on the control panel. "Shields still look good."

None of the readings on her side seemed out of the ordinary, either. She risked a look down at the scanner, pleased by the dwindling number of red dots. She maneuvered the ship toward the edge of the battle as the other two vessels broke off and rejoined their respective fleets. "You got weapons handled?"

"Mmm hmm." The targeting reticle danced across the HUD, zeroing in on the Resistance fighters that were no longer protected by the *Marauder's* shield generators.

Ziva allowed herself a sigh of relief and started to open a transmission to Skeet, then opted to send it directly to Emeri's office. Maybe Ganten would be listening in, and she wanted him to be well aware of the contribution she'd just made.

Minimized holograms of Skeet, Emeri, and even Zinni appeared on the projection pad in seconds. To her delight, Ganten's rendered a moment later. None of them would be able to see her unless she got up and stood on the cockpit's comm pad, but they'd certainly be able to hear her voice.

"We're out," she said before any of them could get a word in edgewise. "The Resistance flagship is doomed. Ronan is dead. I've got a massive packet of data en route to the Federation. Agent Stannist sacrificed herself so we could get out safely. We've got a squad of Durutians on board who need medical attention. We're breaking off from the battle now—should be home within a couple of hours."

Out of the corner of her eye, she saw Emeri open his mouth to say something, but she ended the transmission and left it at that.

# · 59 ·
# HSP Headquarters
## Noro, Haphez

**N**ight had fallen in Noro by the time the *Intrepid* touched down on the landing pad, though with the number of lights illuminating the platform, Skeet hardly noticed how dark the sky was. He began to move forward with the rest of the emergency personnel who had gathered to help the incoming Durutians, but the soft hum of repulsors behind him prompted him to slow down and wait for Zinni to catch up in the hoverchair the med center had provided her with. She didn't even seem to notice she'd almost been left behind; her gaze was directed straight ahead at the figures making their way down the boarding ramp.

Despite the fact that Ziva had contacted them from the ship, he was beginning to wonder if she was even aboard. More 'borgs spilled out by the second, some unscathed, some already patched with crude bandages, and some leaking blood and fluids everywhere they walked. When Taran Reddic appeared in the hatch, Skeet felt his face flush with anger. But when Mae came up beside him with her hand clamped over a nasty wound on her arm, the anger subsided a bit. After learning the truth, he could hardly blame them for their actions on Aubin, and their presence had obviously been a huge help in the battle.

He pulled up short when Zinni stopped, unable to get her chair through the congestion at the end of the platform. They watched from a distance as Ziva and Aroska finally emerged from the ship, bloodied and bruised. Aroska moved down and began ushering some of the

Durutians toward the containment area that had been set up inside while Ziva sealed the ship and disappeared around the back of it.

Skeet waited another few moments for the crowd to clear before he and Zinni wandered over. They found Ziva standing up on the edge of the starboard engine housing, examining a severely dented area that had been blackened upon reentry.

"She took a beating," he observed, trying to keep his tone as upbeat as possible. "Damage to the heat shielding?"

Several long seconds passed before Ziva came up with an answer. She held perfectly still and stared straight ahead at nothing in particular before lowering her head. "Looks like it. A piece of debris hit us on our way out of the flagship's hangar. Whatever broke off must have burned up during reentry. One of the thrusters is exposed."

"Is it bad?" he asked.

"It'll be fine." She jumped down, wiping her greasy hands on her already-soiled pants. "How's it going on your end?"

There was something in her manner that Skeet didn't like, something about the way she changed the subject that made him uneasy, but he shrugged anyway. "Going well," he answered. "All but one of the officers from the *Vigilance* have been found, and Emeri has devoted half the ops teams to tracking him down." He gave Zinni an approving glance. "And the docs say our dear intel officer will make a full recovery after some good old-fashioned R-and-R."

"And the fleets?"

"Still going at it, but Resistance numbers are already way down. Your friends helped, and taking out that flagship was a huge morale drain." He paused, considering for a moment what must have gone down on the *Marauder*. He studied Ziva's bloodstained clothes, aware blood splatter like that certainly wouldn't have been the result of a gunfight with plasma. His eyes were drawn to the black bar attached to her belt.

"*What are you going to do with it?*"

"*I guess I'm going to stop Ronan.*"

Well, she certainly had. He made a point of fixing his gaze on the kytara before giving his head a subtle tilt toward Zinni.

Ziva picked up on the cue and looked down at the intelligence officer with the same shame in her eyes that she'd shown while explaining her secret to Skeet. "I wanted to tell you."

Zinni shook her head and struggled to stand up, ignoring Skeet's offer for help. "Don't worry about it," she said. "You did what you had to do."

He couldn't be sure, but some of Zinni's discomfort seemed to have abated. He was by no means pleased with circumstances either, but after recognizing what was at stake and what Ziva had accomplished, he couldn't help but relax a bit as well. It wasn't like she'd ever flaunted her strange abilities, and the only times she'd ever used them, it had been for good.

"I should have never even revealed myself," Ziva muttered.

The look on her face told Skeet she didn't believe the words coming out of her own mouth. "That's not true," he said. "Tarbic would have died at Dakiti and Ronan would still be here, wiping us all out. The Resistance has had this plan in motion for a while. Imagine trying to come clean about the nostium if there weren't already people willing to help you."

Zinni shifted her feet and turned to look when the door across the landing pad opened. "Speaking of...."

Skeet turned as well and found Aroska rushing toward them, eyes frantic and focused solely on Ziva. It was difficult to tell whether he was shocked, afraid, or angry. Perhaps it was some combination of the three.

He pushed past the two of them and took Ziva by the shoulders, breathing hard. "What did you do?" he demanded.

The confusion only remained on her face for a moment. She set her jaw and shrugged away, turning back to the door and watching as Emeri emerged with a pair of agents, Taran Reddic, and three of the uninjured Durutians.

While her expression morphed into one of mere disappointment, Skeet and Zinni could only stand there, bewildered. "What *did* you do?" Zinni said.

Without looking at any of them, Ziva drew her pistol and handed it stock-first to Aroska, then passed him her kytara as well. She kept her hands in plain view as she stepped away and moved toward the approaching group. "My name was in those files," she muttered.

Over the past couple of days—and throughout the past couple of hours, especially—Skeet had grown accustomed to the look of dismay on Emeri's face, but it was worse now than he'd ever seen it. "You realize there's no way I can get you out of this," the director said as he came to a stop in front of Ziva.

She nodded and glanced at the HSP officers and Durutians who had formed a perimeter around her but had yet to draw any weapons.

Reddic stepped forward, removing his finger from his earpiece. "Ziva Payvan, on the authority of Colonel Adrian Matney..." His words seemed forced, his voice strained. "I'm placing you under arrest for crimes against the Galactic Federation."

# · 60 ·

# HSP Headquarters

## Noro, Haphez

Ziva shut her eyes, which did absolutely nothing to drown out all the voices demanding answers from her. "One at a time!" she shouted, evoking a sudden silence. She opened her eyes, fixing her gaze on Reddic. "You first."

He stepped forward and released the shackles he'd insisted she wear when she'd been escorted inside to a holding room. "I contacted Matney. He has agreed to let you remain in the agency's custody until he arrives here tomorrow." There was silence as he glanced around at the room's other occupants: Emeri, Aroska, Skeet, and Zinni. "He believed your claims that no one here knew about your abilities before today. I don't for one second, but I saw what you did up on that ship so I'm not going to argue. You may have single-handedly turned the tide of this battle."

She assumed he was talking about killing Ronan, which she could hardly take the credit for. Aroska had delivered the final blow, after all. "And what about my other request?"

Reddic sighed as if he didn't believe what he was about to say. "He has decided to honor it," he answered with an incredulous wag of his head. "Your fleet's response—and the fact that the Resistance laid waste to half of your city—was enough to convince him you're not in league with them. Those files you sent from the flagship do contain plans to target Fringe worlds, including Haphez, though Matney says his people haven't had time to study them carefully yet."

"What was this request?" Skeet asked.

"That I be allowed to fly my own vessel up to meet the Federation ships when they arrive," Ziva replied.

She saw him give her a dubious look.

"The fact that you willingly gave yourself up in order to send that data was a contributing factor," Reddic continued. "Because of that and because Haphez wasn't involved in the Resistance plan, the Feds are willing to honor the neutrality agreement and stay out of Noro airspace. Word is there was even some persuasion from the former Royal General."

*Njo?* Ziva doubted it. Perhaps Jada—or maybe even her mother—had managed to get a word in for her.

"What's the plan, then?" Emeri asked.

"Matney's ships will wait in orbit and allow Payvan to take off from here with a fighter escort—likely myself and Mae so we can ensure a smooth transition. She'll rendezvous with them and be taken into custody. If she tries to run, she'll be blown away." This he said while looking her in the eye. "You'll be taken to Edean, where you'll stand trial. I'll warn you now: if someone has even minimal traces of nostium in their system, they're given a death sentence without question."

"Wouldn't be the first time I've been slated for execution," Ziva said with a scoff, fighting away the sinking feeling in the pit of her stomach.

Reddic watched her with something that might have been sympathy for a moment before offering his hand. She glanced down and saw it was the mechanical arm that had replaced the one she'd blown off. The gesture seemed sincere enough, but she couldn't help but feel like it was a subtle jab, one last act to let her know he was still unhappy with everything that had happened on Aubin and before.

"My team will be posted here until Matney arrives," he said as she finally grasped his hand and shook. "You're in Director Arion's hands now."

Reddic turned and disappeared out the door, leaving Ziva caught in the crushing collective gaze of Emeri and her team. She held up her hand for silence when they all began to talk at once and shifted her attention toward the director.

"Njo vouched for me? What's my family's status?"

"I believe it was your mother," Emeri replied. "And they're stable. Despite the fact that their symptoms manifested so quickly, the GA's countermeasure has done some good. They're still not sure about the long-term implications, though. If they do survive, they'll have some irreparable brain damage."

"But the kids from Salex—?"

"Should be fine. Initial tests showed neurological anomalies, but as far as we know, none of them showed symptoms before their rescue. They've all been treated and are being monitored now. Your scans helped save their lives."

"Good," she sighed. "Now, I want you to listen to me." She paused a moment, surprised by the severity of her tone. Her impending fate was beginning to go to her head. "*This*—" she waved her hand in a circular fashion around her team "—stays. I want Officer Vax treated to the fullest extent. You keep this team together. Understand?"

Emeri dipped his head as if he'd never even considered an alternative.

She gave him a terse nod of approval. "Now, if you don't mind, I'd like a few minutes alone to speak with my team."

He complied without question, but even with him gone, the stares of the remaining three were still enough to make her uncomfortable. She wasn't sure if she'd ever seen any of them so genuinely terrified.

"You're planning on flying your ship with that damage you showed me?" Skeet said.

"It'll get me up there," Ziva replied quickly, crossing her arms. "I checked it out, and everything will be fine. I just want one last flight in my ship."

He appeared doubtful until she sent him a look that warned him not to push the matter. "Well, you see that?" He turned and pointed at the door. "That door is going to stay open. Emeri's not going to hold you prisoner, not until we have to make it official tomorrow. You can walk out of here, save yourself. If you go with the Feds, they'll kill you."

While she was sure that was true, she didn't dare admit it. "You don't know that."

"You think they'll let you off the hook just because you killed Ronan? Even if they threw you in prison instead, the Resistance would still have people trying to get to you. They're never going to stop."

"That's not going to happen!" Ziva retorted. "*Sheyss*, Skeet. It'll be a fair trial—all the Nosti prisoners are going to get one. If I plead my case, they might see reason." The words sounded ridiculous coming out of her mouth; she knew what a long shot it was.

"If you walk out now, you won't even have to worry about it," Zinni put in, remaining a fair bit calmer than her orange-haired counterpart. "Just go. You know how to disappear."

"If I do that, the Feds will know you were all complicit." Ziva shut her eyes and massaged her forehead. "They'll be hounding you for the rest of your lives. They'll torture you for information, use you to try to get to me, flush me out. Who knows what the implications would be for the neutrality agreement? If you think there's any way in hell I'm putting you all through that, you're wrong."

"Why send that data to the Feds in the first place?" Skeet said. "Why not just exclude that file? You could have avoided all of this."

"That roster contained the names and locations of every known Nosti in this galaxy," Ziva answered. "The Feds could hunt down all the ships and hidden bases they wanted, but without that list, most of those people would disappear into the Fringe and start rebuilding all over again. You want the Resistance to come back and attack us again in a few decades?"

Zinni steadied herself against the back of the room's tiny sofa. "Why not send it back here first, then? I could have removed your name with no problem."

"There wouldn't have been time to get it back and include it in the package. We would have had to transmit directly from here. Can you imagine how that would look, sending confidential Resistance data from HSP Headquarters?"

Aroska stepped forward now. "I don't understand how the Feds found you so quickly."

Ziva hadn't either at first, but then it had dawned on her that the data had probably been sent in the order it had last been read, the order that put her name and homeworld at the top of the list. She explained this to the others and was met with melancholy silence.

"Just go," Zinni said again after several long seconds.

"I'm not going to do that," Ziva replied. At this point, she was still trying to convince herself as much as she was them. "Knowing the danger it would put you in…that's worse than any prison sentence. I can take care of myself, okay? Everything will be fine." *And if it's not, I'm the only one who will know it.*

It was quiet once again as they each reflected on the situation. The lethal operative in Ziva argued once more that she should never have bothered to save Aroska that day at Dakiti. Should never have revealed herself to anyone. Should have instead done everything she could to save her own skin. But the voice was overpowered by that of her inner leader, which reminded her of all the good she was doing for not only her home and her squad but the galaxy as a whole. She only wished it didn't have to be this complicated. The thought crossed her mind that it would have been easier to die with the press of a button in the *Marauder's* hangar.

The silence was eventually broken by Skeet's sigh. "Well, Emeri put us in charge of making sure the Durutians stay in line. Better go see to it."

Ziva nodded. If she knew Skeet, what he really meant was, *"Better go do something—anything—that will keep my mind off of what's really going on."*

He paused once more when he and Zinni reached the door and knocked on the frame. "It's open," he reminded her.

She stood there listening to their departing footsteps until the thought occurred to her that Aroska had not left with them. When she turned to face him, she found him standing less than a meter from her, watching her with an unwavering gaze eerily similar to what she'd seen on Kat's balcony on Chaiavis.

"You're really determined to go through with this, aren't you?"

Her heart rate quickened and she nodded.

Aroska sighed. "Well then," he said, closing the distance between them.

She bristled but didn't resist as he placed his hands on her waist and guided her backward until her back met the wall. He moved one hand up to cradle her face, brushing some strands of loose hair out of the way before tilting her head up and covering her mouth in a deep but tender kiss. Everything about him—his mouth, his hands, his body—was so strong, yet so gentle. He was holding back, giving her the opportunity to say no like she'd done in the past. To her surprise, saying no was the last thing she wanted to do right now.

Ziva allowed herself to relax and leaned in to meet him, closing her eyes and cherishing his warm, spicy scent for what could very possibly be the final time. She once again felt oddly at home, and in many ways, she still couldn't understand why, out of everyone in the galaxy, she'd connected so well with him. Part of her still hated herself for getting so close to him, but there was no denying that the damage had already been done. It had been done a long time ago.

A warm tingle had just begun to spread across her skin when Aroska let out a short gasp and jerked his head away. Her pulse spiked and her eyes snapped open. "What's wrong?"

"Oh," he breathed, hardly more than a whisper. Ziva was startled to see a grimace forming on his face, but after a moment, she recognized that teasing glimmer that was so often present in his eyes. "I just seem to recall you threatening to castrate me if I ever did that again."

The corners of her mouth curled upward. "I *did* say something like that, didn't I?"

"Yeah, well…it was worth the risk. I felt like I needed to do that for real, at least once."

Her stomach wrenched itself into a knot and she swallowed, struggling to maintain eye contact. "And I wish you wouldn't have," she said, attempting to fend off the sudden fear and panic she felt building inside her at the thought of what the next day would bring.

The teasing glimmer vanished instantly, replaced by something verging on pain. Aroska's hand fell away from her face. "Why?"

She hesitated. "Because it's a reminder that I'm actually leaving something behind."

His features softened and he wrapped his arms around her again. "Still trying to convince yourself you've got nothing to lose?"

She nodded and let him hold her for a moment. "I don't want to go."

"Then don't," he murmured, leaning down and bringing his forehead to rest against hers. In such close proximity, it was impossible to miss the tears welling up in his eyes.

"Oh no," she said, leaning back far enough that she could see his face clearly. "No, don't you dare start this."

"I know, I know, I'm sorry." He forced out some noise that might have been a poor excuse for a chuckle. "I shouldn't make it worse. It's just...I don't want to lose you. I've finally *found* you."

"And now you have to let me go. You understand why I need to do this, don't you? Tell me you understand."

"I do. Doesn't mean I have to like it." He brushed his thumb over a bruise on her forehead and swept the loose strands of hair away again before bringing his palm to rest on her cheek in a familiar fashion. "Listen. What I wanted to tell you back on the flagship...I'm glad I gave you a chance. There's a lot more to you than I ever imagined. You're strong, incredibly intelligent, *more* than a little crazy...."

She lifted her eyebrows and bowed her head, unable to help but crack a smile.

"But...remarkable, to say the least. All things considered, it has been an honor serving with you."

"Well," Ziva said, straightening his jacket, "you know I'm not very good at being complimentary, so..."

"Mmm, I believe you told me once that I'm—how did you put it— 'not so bad'."

"That I did." This time she had to fight to maintain a positive demeanor. He was stalling; she could feel it. It was only making things harder.

His smile was just as forced. "This isn't working, is it?" He winced.

She shook her head and placed her hand over his, giving it a quick squeeze before removing it from her face. "You have to let me go. Don't try to come after me. Don't try to fix the situation. You'll just make everything worse."

Aroska leaned in and embraced her once more. "If you say so."

His eyes glistened when he turned and took a hesitant step toward the door. Tears were forming in Ziva's eyes as well, but she blinked them away before he could notice, infuriated by the emotional response he evoked in her. *The more you get attached to something, the more painful it will be to lose it.*

"I suppose it wouldn't hurt to remind you one more time that this door is still open."

She looked up and nodded. "Acknowledged. But it's not going to happen."

"Well then." He resumed his trek out of the room. "I'll have some clean clothes brought in for you if you'd like. You look like hell. Get some rest, okay? And I'll, ah…I'll see you later."

The door slid shut behind him, but the light on the control panel remained green. Now that she was alone, the realization that she *could* just walk out sunk in. Zinni was right; she could disappear with no trouble. The *Zenith* was still docked at her house with all her relevant belongings aboard. But no, her way was better. She could kill easily enough if ordered to, but making a personal decision that would condemn those she loved to a life of misery or even death…she didn't think she could live with that.

She rubbed her clammy palms together as she moved over to the control panel. Her hand hovered over the door controls for a moment before coming to rest on the intercom button. "Hey," she said, able to hear her own voice coming through the comm at the warden's station outside. "Can I get a blank data pad in here? There's something I need to do."

# · 61 ·

# HSP Headquarters

## Noro, Haphez

**M**orning came all too soon, and Aroska wasn't sure if he'd gotten a wink of sleep. He'd found a bench in the spec ops locker room and had settled down with the intent of resting his eyes for a bit, but try as he might to relax, the thought of lying there idle was unbearable. He'd spent half the night wandering aimlessly through the building, particularly the holding block. Emeri had ordered them all to leave Ziva alone, as Reddic was watching and it needed to look like they were cooperating. As far as Aroska knew, she hadn't left her room yet, and it was confounding. He tried to put himself in her place and was sure he'd want to make a run for it if given the opportunity. With her reputation, he would have expected her to do the same, but here she was preparing to do what was quite possibly the first truly selfless thing she'd ever done.

The Federation ships had arrived in the Noro system in the middle of the night and, after ordering the GA's fleet to stand down, had destroyed what little remained of the Resistance armada. The technicalities had elicited many an eyeroll among the Haphezian higher-ups. The Feds had been called in by Reddic two days earlier to respond to Ronan's presence and were now there to pick up HSP's Nosti prisoners, not to offer assistance to Haphez in any way. Galaxy forbid they actually *help* the Haphezian or Durutian fleets win the battle. No matter though; the remaining Resistance forces had been doomed anyway. Tobias's ships had gone slinking back out into the Fringe, and the only

Durutians who remained were part of the Special Tasks Unit under Reddic's direct command. They were currently working with the agency to move the prisoners to a secure Federation transport.

A shuttle was being sent down to collect the 'borgs, as were a pair of fighters Reddic and Mae would fly up behind the *Intrepid*. Aroska had to admit he was glad they were being allowed to perform the escort. Maybe it was just because they were familiar faces, but he somehow trusted them more than he would have trusted a couple of random Feds.

He strode down the main corridor of the holding block, glad Ziva had been placed in one of these nice rooms and not in an interrogation room or detention cell with the other Resistance prisoners. Nobody had been ordered to come get her yet, but he'd volunteered himself for the job anyway. Matney's ships had arrived in Haphezian airspace, and once the prisoner transfer was complete, it would be her turn to leave.

The display on the control panel still glowed green when he stopped in front of her door. Part of him hoped he'd find the room empty, but deep down, he knew she was right. Leaving with the Federation was the only way to protect everyone. He just wished it didn't have to be her. Surely she had to see that she was going to die, yet she was still willing to go through with this. It was so tempting to try to come up with a plan, try to help her, but the fact that she'd warned him against doing that almost made him wonder if she already *had* a plan. He'd simply have to trust her to figure something out, he decided. It felt like the hardest decision he'd ever made.

His heart sank a bit when he found her still sitting on the sofa. One leg was draped over the other, her eyes were closed, and she held a deactivated data pad in her lap. She said nothing as he entered, so he said nothing in return. There was nothing he could say that she didn't already know anyway. *It's almost time. Today's the day. I don't want you to go.* All meaningless.

So he sat down beside her instead, staring straight ahead at the wall and doing his best to let his mind go blank. It wasn't the first time he'd found himself envying her cold disposition. Her ability to care or not care with the flip of a switch would come in handy right about now.

Ziva didn't move for the duration of the time he sat there. He wondered if she was somehow asleep, but he didn't dare speak to her or touch her. She was aware of his presence, though; he couldn't tell whether she'd visibly relaxed, but the air in the room seemed less tense than it had when he'd entered. The possibility that she was glad to have him there brought him some comfort as well.

The silence was broken when his communicator buzzed. "Yeah," he answered, a dry throat making his voice even quieter than he'd meant it to be.

"They're ready for her," Skeet said.

*Already?* Aroska checked the time on his comm and realized he'd been sitting there for half an hour. For a moment, he wondered how Skeet had known he was there, but then he looked up at the tiny cam mounted in the corner of the room. He hadn't been the only person hoping to keep an eye on Ziva.

"We'll be there soon."

She was already on her feet by the time he ended the transmission, headed for the door as if nothing were wrong. The only thing about her that made the situation seem any different was her face. There was genuine sadness there, maybe even fear. It was a far cry from the indifference she usually showed while preparing to do something risky.

They both remained silent as they moved out into the hall, with Ziva setting a brisk pace and Aroska struggling to keep up. He wasn't sure how she could be motivated to move so fast, given what awaited her once they reached their destination. Perhaps she saw no point in dragging things out any longer than necessary.

When they arrived on the landing pad, the prisoner transport was lifting off from the ground far below, flanked by three Federation fighters. The *Intrepid* remained docked right where they'd left it the day before, and two more Fed fighters had set down beside it. Reddic and Mae waited in full flight gear; Skeet and Zinni stood off to one side, sans the hoverchair, and Emeri approached from the front of a long line of security personnel. Aroska guessed they were mostly there for show—if Ziva hadn't gone anywhere by now, she wasn't going to.

"I can't believe you're really doing this," Emeri said, falling into stride with her.

Ziva didn't even slow her pace. "Believe it or not, Director, I was thinking of leaving anyway."

Aroska imagined his own face mirrored the shock Emeri was showing. "What?" he exclaimed, taking a few jogging steps and cutting her off.

She shot him a glare that compelled him to back off before shifting her attention back to the director. "After everything that happened with Dasaro, it's time for me to move on. This wasn't really what I had in mind, but it's the way things are. Take care of my team."

Aroska could only stand there for a moment wondering what she'd meant. Was she talking about the way the agency had turned its back on her, or the fact that her face and name had been spread all over the Fringe? Either way, it would have potentially made her job harder, but he still tried to convince himself they were lame excuses for leaving altogether.

They arrived at the end of the platform and Ziva moved over to lower the *Intrepid's* boarding ramp before returning to address the group. An ominous wind whistled by, signaling the approach of a storm. Gray clouds hovered low over the city, creating a bleak atmosphere Aroska found appropriate for the occasion.

As he stood there watching her shake Emeri's hand and exchange a few words with Skeet and Zinni, he realized how the fact that he was even out on this landing pad right now was a testament to the kind of person she truly was. He was there because of the connection, the connection that had saved his life and had allowed him to save hers in return. It was a connection that only existed because she truly cared about people, and he'd somehow ended up lucky enough to fall into that category.

He saw her give them each a warm hug—something he'd never expected to witness—before she directed her attention toward him. She stopped with about a meter between them and scrutinized him with her hands on her hips as if trying to decide what to do.

"You don't have to do this," he said. "You don't have to carry all of this on your shoulders."

"Sure I do. After all, I can't stand the thought of everything not being about me."

He bowed his head and stifled a chuckle.

"You'll be okay," she said, squinting against a ray of sunlight that broke through the clouds. "I promise."

How she could say such things was beyond him, but he nodded anyway and offered his hand. "I don't know what to say."

"I know." To his surprise, she stepped forward and threw her arms around his neck, leaning up to rest her chin on his shoulder. Never in his life had he expected her to do such a thing, but the realization that this was no ordinary embrace hit him when her whisper tickled his ear: "What time is it?"

It struck him as an odd question, but when he pulled away and saw her steely face, he knew she was serious. She still carried that data pad and was perfectly capable of checking the time on her own. The thought occurred to him that she wasn't asking for herself.

He glanced down and made a mental note. *10.03*.

She seemed satisfied by this and turned back toward the ship, signaling to Reddic and Mae that she was ready. They acknowledged her and climbed into their fighters, and she paused at the base of the boarding ramp long enough to glance back over her shoulder. Then the ship swallowed her up.

As he stood there watching the ramp retract, it was all Aroska could do to keep himself from sprinting forward and stopping her. One look at Skeet and Zinni told him they were thinking the same thing. But Ziva had a plan—he could feel it. Maybe she would figure out some way to avoid the Federation ships and make an FTL jump. There had to have been a reason for asking about the time, too. He checked again and found that only a minute had passed.

The *Intrepid's* engines roared to life and the ship sat there humming for a moment before it lifted off with the two fighters hovering on either side. As it turned to move out over the city and begin its ascent, a soft but high-pitched squeal reached his ears, followed by a subtle rattle. He caught sight of a large dent with a burnt-out area in its center and recalled feeling something hit the ship as they'd fled the *Marauder*.

"Damn it, Z," Skeet muttered, "that's not going to hold."

"What is it?" Emeri said.

"Damage we sustained yesterday," Aroska replied, searching his communicator's call logs for the last transmission he'd sent to Ziva's ship.

Skeet beat him to it and held his own comm out where they could all hear. "Thruster's exposed," he said as they waited for the transmission to connect. "It's already running hot trying to compensate for the pressure loss that hole is causing."

"I hope you're not going to try to talk me into coming back down," Ziva's voice crackled.

"You have to, Z!" Skeet cried. "The ship's not stable. You'll blow before you hit five klicks. Even if you don't, you'll never break atmo."

"*Sheyss*, Skeet. I told you everything would be fine. I've got it under control."

"Don't be stupid, Ziva!" Aroska shouted past the lump forming in his throat.

"I'm not going to debate this."

The transmission ended abruptly. For what felt like hours, all Aroska could do was stare at the ship as it continued soaring upward and listen as Skeet tried time after time to reconnect. It wasn't long before both the *Intrepid* and the Durutians' fighters disappeared behind a veil of clouds.

Zinni swore. "What the hell does she think she's doing?"

"I don't kn—"

Aroska flinched when a muffled boom echoed through the sky. The sound morphed into a series of sharp cracks, followed by one last blast that drowned out all the city noises around them. A fireball erupted from the spot where the *Intrepid* had disappeared, spitting massive chunks of smoking black material out behind it.

Skeet's shouting ceased, and Zinni's weakened legs collapsed beneath her. The lump in Aroska's throat felt like it had grown to be the size of his fist. Maybe it was actually his heart lodged there. He tried to scream, tried to yell, tried to say *something*, but no sound emerged. He fell to his knees, unable to breathe.

He already found himself wishing he could rewind time and stop her despite all the times she'd told him not to. Everything had been fine just minutes before. She'd been standing right there, displaying genuine emotion, acting like a real person, baffling him with her cryptic last words: *"What time is it?"* The thought prompted him to check again. *10.07.* The time he'd lost yet another significant person in his life. A time he swore he'd never forget.

His thoughts—pleasant compared to the harsh reality—were torn apart like the *Intrepid* itself when he became aware of Emeri shouting somewhere behind him. He turned to find the director on comm with someone aboard Matney's ship, demanding to be redirected to Reddic's fighter. There were several seconds of silence before the Durutian came on.

"What the *hell* happened?" Emeri cried.

"Don't know, sir," Reddic answered through static. "Something blew on the rear of the ship, and it caused a chain reaction. There was a bright flash…I think the FTL drive went. Everything that didn't break off in the initial explosion has been completely vaporized. The *Intrepid* is gone."

# · 62 ·
# HSP HEADQUARTERS
## NORO, HAPHEZ

The view through the window in the director's office looked different at night, in Aroska's opinion, and not just because he had a clear view of the swath of destruction the *Vigilance* had left in its wake. The portion of the city visible through the glass just seemed dead now, but maybe that was simply because he himself felt dead. He'd already come to understand Ziva's concerns about attachment after Maston's death, and the lesson wasn't any easier to learn the second time around.

He had to remind himself that he was only standing there because Ziva had given herself up. If she'd run away like he'd wanted her to, the Federation might already be there knocking down their doors, ready to tear apart their lives until they found her. He might have been fine with sacrificing his own freedom so she could escape, but Fed presence would affect all of Haphez, just like she'd said. She'd saved their whole civilization from this immediate threat, and by sending off that data, she may have even saved the whole galaxy.

Periodic sighs or faint shuffling of feet were the only ways he knew Skeet and Zinni were still present in the office. Emeri had summoned them all there but had been called away again to deal with the ongoing efforts to clean up the agency campus and get the wreck of the *Vigilance* moved. They'd been waiting in silence for at least ten minutes.

That silence was finally broken by Skeet's low voice. "She knew it was going to blow."

Aroska turned and found him sitting in one of the chairs across from Emeri's desk, hands folded in his lap, staring down at the floor. "You think so?"

"She checked that damage out—she wasn't lying about that—but I saw her face. She knew exactly how severe it was."

"It was a suicide run, then," Zinni murmured.

Skeet nodded to himself. "She knew she'd be dead if she turned herself in, but she knew we'd be dead if she made a run for it."

Aroska pondered this for a moment. Agreeing to go with Matney had successfully alleviated any hostility the Federation might hold toward Haphez, so in a sense, she'd saved them all just by getting on that ship. But piloting the doomed vessel had been her way of saving herself; she wouldn't have to endure execution, imprisonment, or spend the rest of her life looking over her shoulder after somehow escaping custody. The idea simultaneously brought him comfort and made him furious. Damn it, they could have helped her figure something out if she'd just let them. But at the same time…

Zinni summed up his thoughts perfectly. "She went out on her own terms."

"That she did."

The new voice drew their attention to the door, where Emeri was entering with three data pads in hand. "In that sense, I believe we should be happy for her. After everything she accomplished, she didn't deserve to die at the hands of the Federation, but I wasn't about to tell *them* that."

He continued across the room and handed them each one of the pads. "She drafted personal recommendations for each of you—we received them this morning. None of you are going anywhere for a while."

Aroska took the device and looked it over, recalling the one Ziva had been holding that morning. The opportunity to stay in spec ops was a bit of a silver lining in these unpleasant circumstances, though he wasn't sure how much he liked the thought of doing it without her.

"She must have transmitted them just seconds before the explosion," Emeri said. "Perhaps that's why she was so agitated when you contacted her. I believe there's a personal note for each of you as well."

The thought of Ziva sitting there composing personalized messages seemed absurd, but when Aroska flipped to the next file on the pad, sure enough, there it was. He sat down to read it.

Tarbic—

You told me you would stay in spec ops if you were given the chance, so here it is. You're a good agent, and I think you'll do fine. Just remember I won't be there to pull your ass out of the fire anymore. Skeet and Zinni have your back and will do whatever they can to help you. Listen to Skeet and learn from him—he's a good leader. Not very many people get an opportunity like this, so don't screw up. No pressure, though.

I meant it when I said I was glad you took me up to the hill the other night. I'm sorry for everything I put you through. You were right—I probably should have just told you the truth at the beginning. Might have saved us a few bruises and hard feelings, right? Sometimes I still can't believe I actually told you everything. You're one of the few people who gets under my skin, and I kind of hate you for that...but thanks.

Take care of yourself, Aroska. It's been real.

He tried to fight the smile he felt tugging at the corners of his mouth, but the effort was futile. It was fascinating how she could be so candid but still so...Ziva. He realized he wouldn't have it any other way.

His eyes were drawn back to the final line of the note as his mind conjured up two separate memories. Hadn't he said those exact words to her as he'd left the med center after she'd been shot? He was fairly certain she was just quoting him—she'd been doing that a lot lately, it seemed. But another quote came to mind, something he'd said in the café in Salex: "I guess I don't know what's real anymore."

There was hardly time to ponder what she'd meant, however, when he caught sight of the timestamp at the bottom of the screen. He hadn't really even been looking at it—he'd just been staring at that particular spot while lost in thought. But now that he saw it, he couldn't take his eyes off of it. Surely it had to be a mistake. No, all the planet's time-keeping devices and comm logs were controlled by a central computer in Haphor. All Haphezian timepieces were perfectly synchronized.

But there it was. It should have been impossible, but if it meant what Aroska thought it meant, the time for grieving was already over.

*10.08.*

He smiled.

# Epilogue
# 10 Hours Earlier...

```
Initializing...
10.01.0036
        Startup sequence
        Type: H-15 Infiltrator
        Title: Intrepid
        Primary User: 40317 Ziva Payvan


ACTIVITY LOG
    -   10.01.0571 - Security breach detected (main hatch)
    -
    -   10.01.0726 - Security override
    -              - Source: Primary User
    -
    -   10.01.1104 - Hatch status: OPEN
    -              - Ramp status: DOWN
    -
    -   POWERING UP...
    -
    -   STANDBY
    -
    -   RESUMING...
    -
    -   10.03.5327 - Primary ignition sequence initiated
    -
```

- 10.03.5698 - Engine 1 status: GREEN
- - Engine 2 status: GREEN
- - Repulsion: 85%
-
- 10.04.1603 - Hatch status: CLOSED
- - Ramp status: UP
- - Repulsion: 100%
-
- 10.04.2022 - Lift off initiated
-
- WARNING: Hull breach detected
-
- WARNING: Starboard thruster core temperature
- rising
-
- 10.04.5851 - Nav computer confirmation:
- Coordinates received
- - Destination: -3h48m7.9s, 45°42'72.1"
-
- WARNING: Starboard thruster pressure loss detected
-
- WARNING: Starboard thruster core temperature 12%
- above safe threshold
-
- 10.05.0602 - Autopilot system engaged
-
- 10.05.1319 - SYSTEM CHECK...
-
- 10.05.1624 - Power transfer: port thruster
-
- WARNING: Port thruster overloaded
-
- WARNING: Starboard thruster core temperature 28%
- above safe threshold

- STABILIZING…

-

- 10.05.5786 - Incoming transmission
-               - Origin: Registered Secondary User:
-                 40318 Skeet Duvo

-

- 10.06.0212 - Transmission reception: Comm Node 4
-                 (cargo bay)
-               - Transmission log:
  - ZP: *I hope you're not going to try to talk me into coming back down.*
  - SD: *You have to, Z! The ship's not stable. You'll blow before you hit five klicks. Even if you don't, you'll never break atmo.*
  - ZP: Sheyss, *Skeet. I told you every-thing would be fine. I've got it under control.*
  - (UNKNOWN): *Don't be stupid, Ziva!*
  - ZP: *I'm not going to debate this.*

-

- 10.06.2397 - Transmission end

-

- WARNING: Starboard thruster core temperature 43%
-          above safe threshold

-

- WARNING: Starboard engine core temperature rising

-

- 10.06.4206 - Incoming transmission
-               - Origin: Registered Secondary User:
-                 40318 Skeet Duvo

-

- 10.06.4613 - Suggested action: Initiate emergency
-               landing procedures

- Authorization from Primary User required…
- Authorization from Primary User required…
- Authorization from Primary User required…
-
- 10.06.5615 - Status of Primary User: UNKNOWN
-
- 10.06.5833 - Initiating thermal scan
-               - Searching…
-
- 10.07.0524 - Incoming transmission
-               - Origin: Registered Secondary User:
-                 40318 Skeet Duvo
-
- WARNING: Starboard thruster UNSTABLE
-
- WARNING: Starboard engine HOT
-
- WARNING: COMBUSTION IMMINENT
-
- 10.07.0872 - Thermal scan complete
-               - ANOMALY: Primary User located
-                 (port airlock)
-               - Status of Primary User: MOBILE
-
- 10.07.1389 - Initiating anomaly check
-               - Searching…
-               - Searching…
-
- 10.07.1924 - Incoming transmission
-               - Origin: Registered Secondary User:
-                 40318 Skeet Duvo
-
- 10.07.2363 - ANOMALY: Inventory check failure
-               - Jet Suit 2 status: MISSING
-

- 10.07.2705 - Initiating secondary thermal scan
-             - Status of Primary User: STATIONARY
-               (port airlock)
-             - Portable data storage device detected
-
- WARNING: Starboard thruster pressure level 0
-
- 10.07.3177 - SYSTEM CHECK...
-
- 10.07.3249 - Engine 1 status: ORANGE
-             - Engine 2 status: RED
-             - Repulsion: 35%
-
- WARNING: EXPLOSION DETECTED (starboard thruster)
-
- 10.07.3956 - ENGINE 2 FAILURE DETECTED
-
- 10.07.4003 - EXPLOSION DETECTED (Engine 2)
-
- 10.07.4121 - HEAT WARNING: Emergency action
-               Required
-
- 10.07.4224 - ANOMALY: Port airlock OPEN
-
- 10.07.4309 - Status of Primary User: UNKNOWN
-
-
-
-
- SYSTEM OFFLINE

# RONAN

# SPECIAL THANKS...

...to Tanni, once again, for sticking with me over the past couple of years and being such a wonderful critique partner. You've sacrificed a lot of your free time and I thank you for that.

...to the rest of my awesome beta readers: Lauren, Kegan, Marian, Brandy, and of course, my mom. Fresh sets of eyes and open minds are invaluable when it comes to getting the job done.

...to every single person out there who has supported me and taken the time to read these books. Hearing from you and getting to interact with you makes this whole experience worth it.

Like what you read? Tell someone about it!
Taking the time to leave an honest review is immeasurably helpful
for any author, new or established. Your opinion helps other
people make informed decisions about their reading options and
allows the book to reach its target audience.

Your ratings and reviews are greatly appreciated!

# ABOUT THE AUTHOR

EJ Fisch is a long-time action junkie and fan of the science fiction genre. She'll readily admit that she has a vivid imagination, which can be both a blessing and a curse. She has been writing as a hobby since junior high and began publishing in the
spring of 2014.

When she's not busy writing or working her day job as a data analyst in the medical field, she enjoys listening to music, working on concept art, reading, gaming, and spending time with her animals. She currently resides in southern Oregon.

Ronan is her third novel, Book 3 in the Ziva Payvan series.

Find EJ Fisch on your favorite social media site!

Keep up with news, catch sneak peeks, and more at:
**www.ejfisch.com**


Questions? Comments? Use the resources above or email at:
**ej@ejfisch.com**

Your thoughts about the characters and storylines are always welcome and appreciated!

www.ingramcontent.com/pod-product-compliance
Lightning Source LLC
Chambersburg PA
CBHW031939260626
47157CB00016B/71